BENT ON DESTRUCTION

THE HYBRID OF HIGH MOON - 3

RICK GUALTIERI

DEDICATION &
ACKNOWLEDGEMENTS

*For Falkor, Axel, and Toby, my three personal "werewolves" …
even if one of them is a cat.*

*Special thanks to my awesome team of beta readers — Jeremy,
Eric, Katie, Simon, Carla, David, Jim, Kristi, and Korionna.
You guys helped make sure this book might be bent but it was
far from broken.*

PROLOGUE
BEFORE

F lames rose from the bowl as the barest spark was added to the mixture within – orange at first but then quickly turning blue, telling the young witch she'd succeeded in this part of the incantation.

It was her first time officiating in front of an audience – her mother and the coven elders, the most unforgiving of judges. Both the pressure and scrutiny upon her were immense, so much that even her sister had skipped her usual teasing and simply wished her good luck.

However, Lissa McGillis, future Queen of the Monarchs, was far more curious than nervous as the magics of the invocation worked their mysteries. She knew the ceremony by heart, had practiced for countless hours on inert components until she could practically measure the ingredients in her sleep. If anything, she'd been tempted to steal away to the woods and perform it for real on no less than a dozen occasions. She was certainly bold enough to try but, in the end, not so reckless as to risk it.

Without a consecrated circle of sufficient strength, the spell was more likely to fizzle than succeed. Sadly, those near her home in Crescentwood Pennsylvania were warded against intrusion.

Recently, though, rumors had reached Lissa's ears of a nearby sacred glade, one where the walls between realities were especially thin, even thinner than in the circle where she now performed the ritual. In such a place, a skilled practitioner could potentially make their pleas heard to those who lay *outside*.

Pity, that was easier said than done.

As luck would have it, this *thin spot* supposedly lay deep within the lands claimed by their enemies. Even at the tender age of sixteen, Lissa didn't fear the lycanthropes. She'd been raised to trust in her own power, her own strength. Nevertheless, she was wary of crossing paths with the guardian who lay between Crescentwood and her goal. Old things such as *it* were to be treated with...

"One drop only," Lissa's mother whispered from behind her, rankling her nerves. "No more."

Lissa was tempted to turn and tell her that she knew what she was doing. However, that would not only get her scolded but could likely ruin the incantation ... or worse.

Instead, she focused on the ethereal flames. Plucking up the ceremonial athame from the spot before her, she held her free hand over the fire, although it wasn't really a normal fire anymore. Lissa knew her physics. Blue flames burned the hottest – over two-thousand degrees Fahrenheit – more than enough to char her hand to a crisp at this distance. Yet, if anything, the air around her had cooled considerably.

The ritual had opened a tiny sliver between her reality and what lay beyond – a space where mortal eyes were not meant to dwell. Beyond it lay infinite danger ... but perhaps also opportunity.

Invoking the ancient tongue, Lissa beseeched Queen Brigid and her most holy court to accept her offering then pricked her finger, letting a single drop of blood fall into the fire before pulling her hand away.

"I saw you hesitate with the blade."

The ceremony complete, the formal part of the evening was over. Half the gathering had dispersed to fire up the grills, while the rest were gathered around the coolers stacked just outside the outermost ring of the circle.

Lissa had retreated down below to change out of her robes and into attire more suited for a backyard barbecue, not realizing her mother had followed.

"I was ... nervous."

"Spare me the patronizing bullshit, Lissa," Vanessa McGillis, current Queen of the Monarchs and leader of the Crescentwood coven, replied. "Your father was a world-class shoveler, so I can smell it a mile away."

Though her words were harsh, her tone wasn't. Lissa could tell her mother was pleased with her performance, a rare good mood from an otherwise unforgiving teacher. However, she was also smart enough to hold her tongue and let the elder witch take the lead. She turned and raised an eyebrow, feigning ignorance.

"You're my daughter," Vanessa continued, stepping around her. "The McGillis women have always been bold, a proud line of coven matriarchs dating back over two centuries. You're no different. Why, I remember you melting your tricycle into slag while the other new acolytes were still trying to conjure their first sparks." She smiled as if the memory was a pleasant one. "Tell me the truth. You were tempted to up the offering, weren't you?"

Lissa realized there was no point in denying it. Her mother would likely hound her for the truth otherwise, keeping her from joining the evening's revelry. Besides, Gavin was waiting for her topside, hopefully with a few cans of purloined beer. With any luck, they could sneak away to...

Realizing a blush was beginning to spread across her face, she quickly said, "Maybe an extra drop or two, no more."

Vanessa nodded. "I thought so. I won't lie and say I haven't been tempted as well. A single drop seals the covenant of our fealty. It's a small offering, all that's asked of us, so that our strength might nourish the eternal garden of our ancestors. But more... That might attract the attention of something else, something greater. I can't pretend that communing with a member of our dear queen's court, even the lowliest of her circle, isn't something I've dreamt of."

"Then why..."

"You know as well as I do," Vanessa interrupted. "Those who dwell beyond the veil of our world are also outside its rules. Something as simple as a conversation to us could very well become an undying oath of enmity to them ... or a binding contract. You know how disastrous such things can be."

Lissa nodded. She was a student of both Draíodóir lore and their history, which was rife with tales of communings gone wrong. "But that was all in the past."

"Yes," her mother replied. "And true, the past was different, more dangerous for us. There was a time when we didn't have High Moon and its guardian to stand between us and the lycanthropes. They would raid our lands and steal our children. Even with all of our power, it was barely enough to hold them at bay, but we persevered." She began to circle the room.

Lissa recognized what she was doing, becoming lost in the lesson. Once started, she could do nothing but wait until her mother made whatever point she was trying to get across.

"But not everyone agreed with our methods. Some reached out to beyond our world, to the *outside*. True, many had nothing but good intentions, but some had motives that were less pure. It didn't matter, though. They were putting themselves at risk either way. Only the most skilled could complete the covenant and walk away unscathed. And yes, our legends speak of these heroes and their exploits. But history is fickle. It celebrates only those who were truly exceptional. Those who were not ... well, all we have to go by are rumors and whispers. People vanishing in the night, driven insane, or worse."

"Worse?" Lissa asked idly.

Vanessa shrugged. "Or so our history hints. Warlocks having their bodies twisted and deformed, witches giving birth to monstrosities, and then there are those who simply vanished into the void – their bodies and souls lost to the infinite blackness."

"The void? Isn't that..."

"The so-called space between worlds?" Her mother nodded, a haunted look upon her face. "A place both infinite and empty. A soul trapped there would be lost for all eternity with no hope of ever basking in the light of our holy queen's court. Not even all the prayers in the world could reach one unlucky enough to be cursed in such a way. It would truly be a fate worse than death."

Vanessa continued on, speaking to her daughter of the dangers of pushing the boundaries of their magic, but it was all stuff Lissa had heard before. It wasn't long before she tuned out her mother's words, focusing instead on those who'd been bold enough to try and skillful enough to succeed.

Her mother was right. Such Draíodóir were legends, remembered for eons afterward. Power, glory, fame, and respect were heaped upon their names. But it had been a long time since such heroes had walked the Earth.

Perhaps too long.

It was something to think about, or possibly discuss with Gavin ... although, maybe that could wait until after their own personal festivities were finished for the evening.

1

PRESENT DAY

"**G**et back here, whatever the fuck you are!"

Thank goodness for enhanced senses. If it weren't for this thing's decisively *off* odor, I'd have lost it by now.

Never mind that dusk was rapidly approaching as I raced through the hollows, a place I very much was not in favor of being in after dark. And go figure, I was alone, too.

Freaking wonderful.

Every single other time I'd stepped foot into these damned woods, there'd been a werewolf or ten waiting to plant their foot up my ass. Oh, but not anymore. Over the course of the few days that I'd somehow found myself in charge, everyone had suddenly changed their tune. Now, instead of hostile glares, it was, "You're our leader, Tamara, so could you kindly take care of this problem all by your fucking self?"

Pack mentality, my ass. Bunch of flea-bitten dickheads.

Still, I guess they had a point. Cass had been giving me pointers in what it meant to be the acting alpha of the

Morganberg pack, not that she had much more of a clue than I did. Regardless, I was not only the pack's current leader but its protector, too. That meant I was expected to be on the front lines, taking care of any threats that reared their ugly heads. To do less would make me appear weak and thus ripe for a coup.

It was quite the raw deal, especially considering I wasn't even a fucking werewolf. I was a half-breed, a hybrid. My dad was their reigning alpha, but my mother was a whole other ball of wax. She was a witch, a Draíodóir if you cared to mangle your tonsils trying to pronounce it. They were supposed to be enemies but had instead fallen in love and had me – all while under the auspices of living under a fake treaty marriage. Talk about a shit show.

Sadly, both were also currently missing.

That thought slowed my steps, causing me to lose focus. It was stupid to be thinking of them now, but I couldn't help it. They'd been taken by my aunt as part of an insane power play, offered up as a sacrifice to a fairy queen, and were now supposedly being held prisoner somewhere in her realm. Mind you, prisoner was a lot better than dead, although the fact they were in a completely different dimension – or so I'd been told – didn't exactly make things better.

Not helping was that, in the handful of days since their disappearance, things had gotten even stranger than usual – both here in Morganberg, home of the were-wolves, and over in Crescentwood to the west, stronghold of the Draíodóir. The only place that, so far anyway, seemed to be spared was the buffer between them: my hometown of High Moon.

A general sense of unease had descended upon the two warring supernatural factions. There'd been talks of unusual portents, a strange heaviness in the air, and then there were the sightings – of *things* that didn't belong, such as whatever the hell I was currently pursuing.

I'd gotten a frantic call a few hours earlier from one of the pack members – no idea how they all seemed to suddenly have my cell number – that a doppelganger had infiltrated Morganberg. So far, it had only targeted pets, but there was no telling when it would get bolder and start going after larger prey.

Doppelgangers were supposedly some sort of nasty, demonic shapeshifters – the kind that even werewolves feared. I only knew this because I'd once been accused of being one, almost getting strangled by my late uncle as a result.

Now, I was the one who was supposed to be doing the strangling, assuming I could catch whatever this thing was. I'd staked out some of the homes on the fringe of town, bordering the hollows, mostly wandering around being cold and bored out of my mind.

But then, out of nowhere, I'd caught a new scent – something that very much felt like it didn't belong. It was hard to explain how I knew this. I simply did the moment it hit my supersensitive nose – smelling faintly of manure soaked in vinegar, not exactly a savory aroma. Then, while my eyes were still watering from the acrid odor, something had plowed into me from behind, knocking me face first into a snowbank.

I'd pulled myself up just in time to catch the barest glimpse of scar tissue-like skin before it disappeared into the woods on four legs. From there, the chase was on.

My unique heritage afforded me plenty of perks. In addition to enhanced hearing and sense of smell, I was superhumanly strong, durable, and fast. Sadly, quick as I was, I was still confined to two legs. After a few minutes, it became painfully clear that I needed a better plan, before this ended up becoming a merry chase through half the fucking state.

I stopped in a clearing to catch my bearings, taking a sniff of the air and finding it practically saturated with the creature's reek. It had definitely come this way. With any luck, I'd...

"*I'd say that's far enough*," a gravelly voice replied from the surrounding trees, sounding as if someone had broken their jaw, gotten it wired shut, then had it broken again.

"Far enough for what?" I called back, trying to home in on the source.

"*Far enough*," it replied, the voice seeming to circle where I stood, "*so that nobody will question when you return and declare the all clear.*"

With those last few words the cadence of the voice changed, becoming familiar ... *disturbingly* so.

A figure stepped from the trees and faced me. All I could do was stare as I took in its - *her* appearance. She stood about five three, with an athletic frame, hazel eyes, shoulder-length dark brown hair, and the cutest nose imaginable.

I knew it well, considering it was mine. But my face wasn't the only thing it had copied.

It was also dressed identically to me, down to the rips and tears my winter coat had suffered as I'd run through the forest in hot pursuit.

In short, it was like looking in a mirror.

I mean, I'd known this creature was capable of imitation. Still, that hadn't prepared me to face ... *myself!*

The doppelganger looked down at its body. "Not bad. I could get used to this. Now let's see who we've got here." The other me pulled a very familiar looking Sailor Moon wallet from its back pocket.

What? It had been a gift from my friend Riva.

Even so, that was a level of mimicry I hadn't anticipated, unless...

I reached a hand toward my own pocket.

"Don't bother," it replied. "I snatched it when I knocked you down back there."

Huh. A pet-eating shapeshifter *and* a pickpocket. Some mythical monsters had no scruples whatsoever.

"Happy New Year to me." It pulled a couple of twenties from the wallet before removing my driver's license. "Let's see. Tamara Bentley. Quick question. Is that Tamerra or Tuh-mara?" it asked, changing the emphasis from the first to the second syllable.

"Second one, why?"

"Oh, no real reason. I just want to make sure I get it right after I kill you and take over your life."

"Oof!" The back of my head smacked into a tree trunk and I dropped to the ground, still tasting the sole of my own sneaker.

I had to admit, whatever doppelganger Tamara lacked in physical strength, which wasn't much, she more than made up for in raw speed and agility. I'd rushed in, looking to end this fight quickly, only for it to side-step and nail me with a kick to the face, making it look like the easiest thing in the world.

"Curious," it said, standing just out of my reach. "A blow like that should've snapped your neck."

I pushed myself back to my feet. "Maybe you should demonstrate for me."

"Back up already? Well, that's certainly not normal." It put a hand to its chin, as if thinking it over. "Let me guess. You're not human, are you?"

"Nah, they just grow us tough out here in Pensy."

It inclined its head. "Hmm, not a lycanthrope. You'd have already changed. They're terribly predictable that way."

Other Me probably had a point on that one, but I was far more interested in listening to it choke on my fist.

I stepped forward and launched another attack, but this one was a feint. Now that I knew how quick this thing was, I needed to be more strategic. I couldn't just hope for a lucky blow to end this before it could hit me with enough potshots to put me down.

The creature dodged easily enough and then spun, throwing another kick my way, but I was ready for this one. I caught its foot before it could flatten my favorite nose again.

Or at least I thought I had. Before I could see how this thing liked the taste of bark, it lifted its other leg and wrapped it around the opposite side of my head. Off balance from the extra weight, it easily flipped me over, sending me tumbling into another snowbank.

It wasn't exactly a finishing move, more embarrassing than anything. Nevertheless, lying there waiting for my bruised ego to heal wasn't going to win me any points. I kipped up to my feet and spun to face the false me.

It raised one eyebrow, causing its mockery of my face to disturbingly resemble my mother's for a second. *Is that how I actually look when I do that?*

"Not one of those annoying Draíodóir either." I couldn't help but be miffed that it was able to pronounce their name much better than me. "Most of them wouldn't know physical fitness if you strangled them with a barbell. Unless, that is, you care to prove me wrong with some silly spell or two. Go ahead, I'll wait." When I didn't, it smiled, and I saw my father's grin staring back at me.

God, this was weird, and not a tiny bit upsetting, too. However, I needed to focus on the fight, not my emotions.

"Just as I thought," it continued. "So, that begs the question of what exactly are you?"

"What can I say? I'm a mystery, wrapped in a riddle, which will soon be wrapped around your throat."

"And not afraid of me either. Ooh, I have to admit, this is making me all tingly inside. Once I'm done with you, I may have to shed these bothersome clothes and take care of business, if you catch my drift. I do so find the female form best suited to ... self-gratification."

"Seriously?"

It laughed. "How did that old song go? Something about when I'm thinking of you, I touch my..."

"I get the point. And believe me, you've painted more of a mental picture than I really care to imagine."

"A bit of a prude, too. Well, don't worry. We'll fix that."

"What?! I am not a prude..."

This time it was the doppelganger's turn to feint, but with words instead of actions. While I was busy expressing my outrage, it stepped forward – quick as lightning. One moment we were facing each other from across the clearing, the next it was in my face.

Before I could so much as let out a squeak of surprise, it drove a fist into my gut. It was a solid shot, right on the money, but I was made of sterner stuff than most. The blow would have ruptured the internal organs of a normal person. Heck, it might've been enough to plow right through their stomach and to the gooey center within. All it did to me, though, was knock the wind out of my lungs.

I'd taken far worse, and not just from monsters like it. A decade of amateur wrestling had led to a scholarship at Bailey University, not that I was likely to be returning there anytime soon. Nevertheless, I'd suffered more than one cheap shot over the course of my career, most of them from guys who had no compunction against trying to knock a woman down a peg or two.

The bottom line was, I knew how to take a hit and – more importantly – how to return the favor. I leaned back, ignoring the ache in my gut, then snapped my neck forward catching Alternate Me straight in the face with a headbutt.

It wasn't exactly a move that was allowed on the mat but, ever since discovering my powers back during the waning days of summer, I'd been working to up my repertoire, especially when it came to fighting things that went bump in the night, and I didn't just mean ex boyfriends.

The doppelganger landed in a heap, a strange muddy brown blood pouring from its shattered nose. I moved to capitalize on that, hoping to do something unsportsmanlike, like maybe stomp its head into paste.

Sadly, injured though it might be, it still had plenty of fight left in it, rolling out of the way and back to its feet before I could see how many limbs I had to rip off its body to make a difference.

The creature wiped the viscous blood away, the gunk possibly smelling even worse than the beast itself, then grabbed its nose and yanked it back into place with a disturbing *crack*. "Very curious," it said, grinning again, a few of its teeth now sitting crooked in its mouth. "In all my three centuries of life, I don't think I've met a creature like you."

It was *that* old?

A small sliver of fear wormed its way through my bruised gut, one which had nothing to do with the deepening shadows within the hollows. The prospect of facing something so ancient was daunting as hell. Age meant experience. Anything that had lived for so long in the violent world of the supernatural was no doubt a survivor

– and this was one that could choose to be quite literally anyone it wanted to be.

However, I wasn't about to let it know that. "So, what brings an old as dirt doppelganger to my neck of the woods, aside from getting its own snapped?"

Other Me spat out a hock of blood and smiled, although I noted the grin wasn't nearly as wide this time. "Such a crude name. Personally, I always preferred skin-walker. The indigenous people of these lands were always so much more eloquent with their names. It didn't stop me from slaughtering them like cattle, mind you, but I respected them for it." I made a hurry up gesture and it narrowed its eyes. "Oh, very well. If you must know, I felt the breach when it happened."

"The breach."

"Stupid little girl. The Window of Worlds. I could feel it being flung wide open. It called to me, offering promises of the chaos to come."

That wasn't good. Window of Worlds, that was a term Riva had used, or she had back when she'd been possessed by ... *something*. But I knew what it meant now. She'd been referring to the sacred glade deep within the hollows, a spot where the walls between our world and what lay beyond were paper thin. Or at least they had been. When last I'd been there, I'd ended up going through that paper like my name was Edward Scissorhands, culminating in releasing ... well, I wasn't sure, but I was certain I'd inadvertently allowed something into our world that wasn't meant to be here.

At the time, I hadn't really known what that meant, other than it was probably not good, but I'd been too busy worrying about my parents to really care. Now, though, hearing this thing's words, I began to wonder whether it might be even worse than I suspected.

Guess that old saying about no rest for the wicked

truly was apt. Regardless, that was yet another concern to file away for later. For now, I balled my fists as I faced the creature.

"You came looking for chaos but found me instead. Believe me when I say, you're going to wish you hadn't."

2

I couldn't help but think my brother Chris would've been nerding out right about then. Hadn't I once overheard him arguing with his loser friends about who would win in a fight between Superman and the Flash?

Speed versus power. It was an interesting question, one without an easy answer. The doppelganger had me beat in that first department. I could move fast, much faster than a regular human. I'd never clocked myself, but I could definitely haul ass when I needed to. Yet, this thing made me look like I was standing still as it dodged, weaved, and played hit and run.

The only upside was that this asshole hadn't copied my abilities when it assumed my face. So, when I did land a blow, it counted more – even if it was a bit weird trying to ugly myself up. From prior experience on the mat, I already knew what I looked like with a black eye and, believe me, it wasn't flattering. I could only hope that this thing would be good enough to change back to its native form once I stomped it flat. The last thing I needed were any hikers discovering *my body* and reporting it to the police.

Sadly, after several minutes of back and forth fighting, it became clear I was losing on points. We weren't quite at a TKO yet but, if this kept up, I didn't like my odds.

Other Me stepped in with a series of capoeira kicks, moving like this was an eighties breakdance contest and someone had just laid down a sick beat. Enhanced durability or not, if I hadn't been a trained athlete this thing would've roundhouse kicked my face into mush by now. As it was, I just barely managed to block the worst of it.

And that's when I realized the problem. I was playing this creature's game, letting it go all kung-fu master on me while I focused on defense. That was a losing strategy in a battle where only the winner got to live.

It was time to take one for the team, in this case the team being my face, and refocus on turning this into my kind of fight.

More kicks came my way, with a couple of punches thrown in for good measure, all of them moving lightning fast and starting to take a toll. I needed to turn the tide now or risk being bludgeoned to death.

I crouched low, hopefully looking like I was trying to shield my body from the relentless attack. But, in actuality I was taking advantage of my lower center of gravity, planting my feet, observing its moves, and waiting for the perfect...

Now!

The doppelganger spun, no doubt readying to deliver another flurry of kicks Cuisinart-style. In the split second its back was turned I launched myself forward, arms wide. This left my midsection wide open for attack, but also put me in perfect position to grapple this thing.

That was the one disadvantage of speed: it didn't mean shit once your opponent had you pinned. I collided with the creature, wrapping my arms around it as we hit the forest floor, our momentum sending us both rolling end over end. It was imperative I not let go, otherwise I'd have wasted the opportunity and put myself back at square one, with this thing warier of me than ever.

I held tight, putting ever more pressure on its limbs, enjoying the feel of it struggling against my superior strength, even allowing myself a grin of my own.

It was an ill-timed celebration on my part as the creature's face contorted, dropping the guise it held. I could only watch as my cute nose, one of my better features if you ask me, caved in on itself. The doppelganger's jaws widened and elongated, splitting down the middle into grotesque mandible-like appendages.

Far worse than how it looked – and believe me it was horrifying as fuck-all this close up – was the fact that its actual face was more than capable of taking a bite out of mine if I didn't make a move and quickly.

Fortunately, we skidded to a halt against a stand of dead brush and, through more luck than skill, I ended up on top.

The rest of the creature was rapidly giving up my form. Its clothes melted back into its disturbingly clammy flesh, covered in boney appendages which made it near impossible to hold onto. But that was okay. I had no intention of touching this thing longer than was necessary, except maybe with my fists.

I let go with one arm, holding it down with the other, and then drove an elbow smash into the side of its head with everything I could muster.

There came the snap of bone as several of its ... err ... teeth-like thingamabobs shattered. I followed through with a punch which scraped the hell out of my knuckles, but was more than worth it.

The quips and trash talk were done. All that was left

were two beings of preternatural power locked in a life or death struggle, with nothing to bear witness save the silent forest around us.

And then, just as quickly, that silence was broken ... by me.

I reared back, looking to pound an indent of this thing's head into the ground, when it freed one of its arms. I grabbed hold of it and screamed as one of the bony thorns covering its sickening flesh impaled my palm.

The pain was incredible, only overshadowed by the burst of rage I felt. There was something about the hollows which did that to me. Whenever I was here, my temper tended to fray more easily than elsewhere. I had a feeling that had to do with our proximity to the so-called Window of Worlds, but for the moment I was too busy seeing red to form coherent thought.

Bleeding badly, I still managed to force my fingers to close around its arm. With a cry of pure fury, I wrenched it back, *hard*, looking to snap the creature's vile appendage ... *off.*

I ended up tumbling backward into the snow, the doppelganger's severed forearm still in my grasp. It screeched in pain as it lurched to its feet, but seemingly had enough for one day.

Rather than continue the fight, it turned and fled, racing through the trees like a howler monkey with its tail on fire, not that I had any idea what that might actually look like.

As for me, I sat up, grabbed hold of its arm with my good hand then, bracing myself against the hurt to come, pulled the spine free from my palm.

"MOTHERFUCKING SHIT NUGGETS!!!!"

Hopefully any squirrels hibernating in the treetops above didn't have overly sensitive ears, because I lambasted the forest with every curse in my repertoire, and maybe even a few I made up on the fly, until I got myself under control.

By the time I was finished, the flow of blood from my punctured hand had slowed to a mere trickle, no doubt thanks to my werewolf-half's turbocharged healing. By tomorrow, it would be fine. For now, though, it still fucking hurt – a lot.

Rather than bemoan the fact that I hadn't thought to bring any bandages with me on my stakeout, I looked down at the severed arm in my hand. It was a clean break, snapped off at the elbow. Maybe a bit too clean.

I wasn't about to speculate on the physical characteristics of this thing, but damn if it didn't strike me as the same thing some lizards could do with their tails. If so, next time we faced each other I'd need to be mindful to grab a leg instead. I bet that would stop it from running off like a hyperactive jack rabbit.

Still, this was a pyrrhic victory at best. Not only had the damned thing gotten away, but now I'd have to worry about it taking out a mortgage in my name. I glanced down at the forest floor, hoping to see my wallet, but there was nothing but snow and frozen dirt. Guess when it dissolved its clothing it somehow managed to keep its pockets. Just great. On top of all the other shit going on in my life, now I needed to get new IDs, too.

Ralph Johnson, the sheriff of High Moon, had recently spilled the beans that he was more than simply the chief of police. He was some sort of guardian as well. However, he'd also made it more than clear that upholding the law was his top priority. It would be the height of embarrassment to have him haul my ass to jail for being stopped without a license, especially with all the big plans currently afoot in my little town.

And big they were, almost too ambitious for me to want to think about. In my heart, I was a small-town girl.

I'd been raised in High Moon and had spent the first eighteen years of my life as a resident. Making regionals in wrestling was considered hitting the big time here. Hell, packing up and going off to college in Illinois had practically been a mind-bending ordeal for me at the time.

Yet, here I was now, not only fighting off doppelgangers but trying to bring two warring races – The lycanthropes of Morganberg and the Draíodóir of Crescentwood – to the negotiating table. Talk about biting off more than I could chew.

The goal was, in actuality, twofold. A tentative peace was needed. Sure, there was already a treaty in place, but I wanted more: something to finally put the cold war between them to an end. That part was necessary if I wished to have any hope of accomplishing my second goal: an incursion into another dimension so that I could save my parents – their respective leaders.

Never let it be said that I didn't reach for the stars.

Regardless, I was so far off the map with this one I didn't even know where to begin. It was like being lost in a fogbank with nothing to guide the way. Yet somehow I found myself leading the charge, both now and probably later when the time came to step foot from this world into that other realm. I didn't fool myself into thinking otherwise.

I mean, sure, it was possible some enterprising souls from either side might decide to do the noble thing and volunteer instead. But counting on that was likely a fool's errand.

It was a cold day in the hollows, but as much as these woods might be my personal Hell, I had a feeling a whole different place would need to freeze over before I got that lucky.

3

"My fellow aberrants, though I know our respective peoples haven't often seen eye to eye, the time has come for us to put our differences aside. I stand before you as living proof that our two species can not only work together, but flourish as one. But now, a grave injustice has been wrought, one that requires us to work side by side to retrieve our leaders – my parents, your queen and your alpha – so as to bring them home safely."

I locked eyes with each member of my audience, daring them to challenge my words.

Finally, after several long seconds, Chris broke the impasse. "My money's on them kicking your ass."

I narrowed my eyes at my dweeb of a little brother, but then realized Cass wore the exact same expression. "The aberrant line was too much, wasn't it?"

She held up a hand, her thumb and index finger an inch apart. "Just a bit."

"Sorry. I figured it was better than me calling them monsters or butchering Draíodóir in front of everyone."

"Maybe just skip that line altogether," she said. "I have

a feeling you're gonna be dealing with a hostile enough room as it is, so it might be best to get right down to business rather than let anyone argue semantics."

She probably had a point. The fact that I'd managed to make it this far was a near miracle in itself, not that the werewolf side of the delegation was being given much choice in the matter.

I was currently the acting alpha, with Cass as the newly chosen female alpha – even though we were both girls. Go figure, in the space of a single evening we'd somehow managed to drag lycanthrope gender politics into the twenty-first century. Even so, I knew we were barely hanging on by a thread. The majority of the Morganberg pack was less than pleased to suddenly find themselves under the command of two *kids*, and that wasn't even counting the fact some were still looking for an excuse to gut me over what I'd done to their previous alpha, my late uncle Craig.

At least I had rank and tradition on my side with them, along with the dangled bone of retrieving their true leader – my father. Over in Crescentwood, the only pluses in my favor were the confusion and betrayal they'd suffered on Christmas day – that, and a cousin who, in her grief, had been willing to speak on my behalf to their remaining elders.

Mind you, it was still risky as all hell. I remembered Mom's warning of what her people would do if they discovered the truth of my existence. Much as I didn't like being in charge of the Morganberg pack, I had a feeling it was the only thing staying their hand. Resistant to magic I might be, but alone there wasn't much I could do if they decided to bombard High Moon with a magical meteor shower.

But with the pack in my back pocket – in theory anyway – the equation changed significantly. Between that and the bloody nose my aunt had recently given them via way of her betrayal, they'd been receptive to the proverbial olive branch my cousin Mindy offered them on my behalf. At the very least, they seemed to be taking a wait and see approach, for now anyway.

Either way, my entreaty for parlay was accepted. Somehow, I'd managed to cajole both sides to the negotiating table. That was good, because I wasn't prepared to take no for an answer. If saving my parents meant busting some heads, then so be it.

But perhaps it was best to at least try refining my carrot before reaching for the stick.

"Okay, Maybe I'll work on that opening speech a bit." I shrugged. "At least I still have homefield advantage."

"Yeah, about that..."

I cut my brother off at the pass. "We already talked about this. Not happening. You're staying home."

"C'mon, Tamara. Can't I just sit in the back and watch?"

"This isn't some pep rally. It's not open to the public."

"They're my parents, too."

His reply stopped me in my tracks, but fortunately Cass was there to pick up the dropped ball.

"I know, but if we want to help them then this is for the best. Both sides are already going to be on edge as it is. No offense, Chris, but having a human there is only going to distract them. We need everyone to stay focused on the task at hand."

I wasn't sure whether it was her logic or being a pretty blonde but, rather than protest, Chris simply nodded ... for now. I didn't doubt he'd try again, though.

Good thing I didn't plan on telling him where it was being held. Mind you, it probably didn't hurt that I didn't know yet either.

The Draíodóir elders had initially insisted we hold the

talks in Crescentwood. Big surprise there. After some back and forth, though, with Mindy arguing on my behalf, a compromise was reached. Any ceremonies, spells, or whatever was needed to retrieve my parents, would be conducted there. After all, it stood to reason they were best equipped to contact the *outside,* as they called it. However, the talks regarding our plan of action would take place in neutral territory, and that meant High Moon.

Thankfully, according to Chief Johnson anyway, my request was within the provisions set forth in the current treaty. That was good. Less good was his insistence on finding a proper venue to host our supernatural summit. Obviously, this wasn't something we could simply host down at borough hall. He wanted to find a place that was a bit more off the beaten path, a spot where any shenanigans from either side could be quickly contained and neutralized – his words, not mine.

Nevertheless, the pieces were slowly falling into place, albeit not all of them.

I took advantage of the lull in conversation to step into the kitchen and check my phone. Still no word from Riva. I'd planned on asking her to keep an eye on Chris while this all happened, to make sure he didn't try anything stupid. But I hadn't heard from her since Christmas, back when she'd accompanied my brother to the hospital.

I'd figured maybe she needed a few days to collect herself or was simply just busy, but it wasn't like her to not even acknowledge my texts. Being best friends for well over a decade meant you kind of knew what to expect from each other. This wasn't like her.

Screw it. I need a break anyway.

I walked over to the closet and grabbed my coat. "I'm heading out for a bit."

"Where to?" Cass asked.

"I'm gonna pop by Riva's. Hey, do you mind keeping an eye on..."

My voice trailed off as I saw the look on her face.

I'd informed Chief Johnson in advance that, as my fellow "alpha", I needed Cass's help to set up this meeting, thus ensuring he didn't take steps to forcibly eject her from High Moon, as he'd threatened back on Christmas. Regardless, I could tell she'd been nervous when I'd invited her over, although perhaps he wasn't the only reason why.

My house was the home of the true alpha of the Morganberg pack, which probably precluded her from making herself too comfortable. However, if thoughts of my father made her nervous by way of his rank, my mother – the so-called Queen of the Monarchs – terrified her because of her power. She held an almost boogeyman-like status among the rank and file of Morganberg, one which was well deserved.

I guess I could understand how sneaking a bag of chips in a house potentially warded to blow up werewolf intruders could be a bit daunting.

And, well, it's not like I minded her company.

"On second thought, you up for a quick ride?"

The three of us piled into my mother's car and pulled out of the driveway. Normally I wouldn't think twice about leaving Chris home by himself for a short while, but he'd been a bit squirrelly ever since Christmas, and with good reason. In the space of a day, his entire world had been upended. Not only were our parents both missing, but he'd learned that there really were monsters in the prover-bial closet. So, I wasn't about to argue when he grabbed his coat to join us.

The day was overcast and cold, but otherwise unre-markable – a typical winter day for rural Pennsylvania. For now, all was quiet and peaceful, even if nearly everything about our town and the surrounding area itself were as atypical as it got. Turning down the side streets – and making it a point to take them extra slow being that I was technically sans license – it was easy to lose myself in the fantasy that the last several days had been nothing but a bad dream and that we'd return home to find our parents waiting for us.

It was a dream that I had every intention of making a reality for me and my brother, but I didn't dare fool myself into thinking it would be smooth sailing. Hell, I wasn't even sure the rescue mission I planned to propose was even possible – locating and plucking my parents from the court of the fairy queen. Tell me that wasn't the plot of a bad teen fantasy novel.

Still, my aunt had somehow sent them there, so I had to hold onto the hope that a round trip was possible. Without that lifeline to grasp onto, I would surely be lost.

"Nice neighborhood," Cass remarked from the passenger seat of the mid-sized sedan as we turned onto Riva's cul-de-sac. She pointed out the window. "Except for that place. Bet they're a real hit with the local homeowner association."

I followed her gaze, noting the broken mailbox post at the curb of Riva's house. "When did that happen?"

An older Volvo sat in the driveway – Mr. Kale's work car, but there was something off about it. It wasn't until I parked at the curb that I realized it was sitting on four flats, the body covered in scratches and rust marks.

"What the hell?"

I'd been here only a couple of days earlier, picking Riva up for a sleepover. It had been late at the time, but not so dark that I wouldn't have been able to tell what a mess his car was. Hell, now that I took a better look around, I saw the entire property had a neglected feel to it that hadn't been evident when last I'd been here, culminating in... "Oh my god."

The picture window that looked in on her family's living room was completely shattered. Only a few jagged shards of glass around its periphery remained.

"Are you sure this is the right place, Bent?" Cass asked.

I shut off the engine and opened the driver's side door. "Wait here."

"But...," my brother started.

"Don't argue with me."

The tone of my voice must've been harsher than I realized because he zipped his lip. Oh well, I could always apologize later.

For now, I stepped out of the car and started walking up the driveway.

"Wait up," Cass cried from behind me, the sound of her door slamming shut catching my ear.

"Stay with..."

"Take a look around. It's broad daylight. Nothing's going to happen to him."

Normally, I would've concurred. Hell, everything else here seemed right as rain except for Riva's place. Still, she was probably right. Rather than protest and waste time, I shrugged and continued forward.

It was only as I approached the house that I realized the storm door was the only thing standing between us and the interior. The actual front door was missing, the foyer visible beyond.

What in the name of...?

I quickened my pace, panic starting to set in. "Riva?"

Bursting inside with Cass hot on my heels, I stopped as I stepped foot into their living room.

The place was a mess, the furniture bloated and discolored. Mold could be seen on the walls, and water stains marred the floor – a far cry from the obsessive neatness Riva's mom usually insisted on.

"Is your friend squatting in this dump or something?" Cass asked from behind me, but I paid her no heed.

My eyes were instead focused on the massive hole in the drywall next to their staircase.

I remembered it well because I'd been the one who made it.

It had happened this past summer, the night the Morganberg pack attacked High Moon.

Two werewolves had come here, under orders from my uncle, to take out Riva and her family. They'd found me waiting for them instead.

The battle played out in my mind as I surveyed the scene before me. One of the wolves had gotten a fist through the stomach, followed by a one-way ticket out the front window. The other I'd slammed through the wall, right before breaking its jaw in half.

The damage we were seeing now was the same I'd caused back then ... only appearing much older, as if the house had sat neglected ever since.

"What the fuck?"

4

"**R**iva actually lives here?"

I turned to Cass, my mind racing back and forth between panic and confusion. "No, I mean yes. But it's not supposed to be like this."

"I would kinda hope not."

"You don't understand." I took a moment to explain what happened back during the waning days of summer, just as I'd filled her in on the doppelganger when she'd arrived at my house earlier today.

"And you're certain they didn't move somewhere else?"

I nodded. "One hundred percent."

"When was the last time you were actually here?" she asked, her nose wrinkling as she took a sniff of the air. "Because it doesn't smell like this place has been lived in for a while."

I turned toward her. "Just last week, right after our meetup during the equinox. I was kinda wired after what happened, so I picked Riva up for a sleepover."

Cass inclined her head, continuing to look around. "And she was here to let you in?"

"Yeah, I..." But that wasn't true. Riva had already been waiting for me out by the driveway when I'd pulled in.

Stepping away from Cass, I thought back to the summer. After the attack by Craig, things had been hectic for everyone. Even so, Riva and I had seen each other during the short period between then and when she'd driven me back to school. But, as I was only realizing now, I hadn't actually been inside her house during any of those times.

"No," I amended. "I actually didn't come inside. But that still doesn't make sense. The car in the driveway. It wasn't all rusted. And their mailbox, it was fine when I picked her up. I'd have noticed if it wasn't, not to mention the giant honking hole where their front window should be."

I racked my brain, thinking of that night. Yeah, I'd been a bit distracted, having gotten my face nearly rearranged by Mitch, the then beta of the Morganberg pack. But there's no way I'd have missed the utter state of neglect that could plainly be seen from the curb. It had been dark out, but not *that* dark. I said as much.

After a moment, Cass put a hand – her fingers slim but powerful – on my shoulder. "I believe you."

"The problem is, I'm not sure *I* believe me. I mean this ... it makes no sense!"

She shook her head then lowered her voice, almost as if afraid of being overheard. "Maybe it's spreading."

I didn't have to reply. We both knew she was talking about what had happened Christmas night in the hollows – the fight which had ended with my aunt dead, Cass transformed into a dinosaur sized wolf beast, and the sacred glade erupting in magical flame.

"Think about it, Bent. The pack's been acting spooked ever since. And now, for a doppelganger of all things to show up..."

"I'm gonna go out on a limb and assume that's not an everyday occurrence."

She shrugged. "Not as far as I'm aware. From what I've heard, they're super rare and tend to avoid other shapeshifters, mostly because we can sniff them out. So, for one to just show up out of the blue, and now this. I'm having a hard time believing it's a coincidence."

I wanted nothing more than to dismiss her concerns but couldn't, not when my body double had basically confirmed what she'd said — that it had been drawn here because of the glade.

My silence was apparently all the answer she needed.

"You should check in with your cousin over in Crescentwood. See if anything weird is going on over there ... *weirder* anyway."

"I will," I said with a nod of my head. "But some random monster showing up doesn't even begin to explain what happened here or where Riva is now."

"I know. I'm not going to pretend there isn't some Doctor Who level shit going on."

I grinned back at her. "Don't let Chris hear you say that. He's liable to drop to his knees and propose..."

I was interrupted by a car horn blaring from outside. Speak of the horny devil and he shall appear. "Hold that thought."

I stepped to the front window and looked out. All was clear, but I could see Chris in Mom's car staring back toward the house. Guess we'd been standing in here talking longer than I realized. I waved to him to let him know I was okay and then, seeing him wave back, turned to face Cass again. "Guess we forgot to leave a window rolled down for the dweeb."

"You should be nicer to him. He's holding up like a trooper."

She was right. The doctors, with a little prodding from

Chief Johnson, had released Chris from the hospital after two days. He'd taken a pretty good bump to the head, but after a few days of rest seemed to be back to his normal annoying self. Cass had a point, though. He'd been through a lot but was still standing. Not everyone would've been so brave. "Sorry, force of habit."

She waved it off. "Hey, what about the neighbors?"

"Mine or..."

"Riva's," she clarified. "Did they know each other?"

"Mr. Kale was, *is*, sorry. Anyway, Riva's dad is one of those infectiously nice guys. The kind who even if you want to hate, you just can't because he's always so cool. But yeah. I've been to a lot of cul-de-sac parties here. You haven't lived until you've had a hot dog smothered in Mrs. Kale's curry."

She inclined her head. "Hopefully I'll get to try it one day, but that's not what I meant. We should talk to the other families here, see if they can corroborate your story. If nobody's noticed anything weird about this place before now, then at least that tells us something."

"But what?"

Cass threw up her hands in frustration. "I don't know! Maybe it was ... some kind of localized time magic."

"Is that even a thing?"

"Beats me. I have no idea how this stuff works." I opened my mouth to say something, but she was ready for me. "And don't get me started on that alpha female crap. I was in the wrong place at the wrong time. I never asked for Grandma Nelly's job."

I didn't doubt that. "Have you tried..."

"Changing since then? No. And I'm not sure I want to. What if I turn into that ... *thing* again and can't control it?"

The thing in question had been a werewolf, but not just any werewolf, an uber-wolf ... for lack of a better term. Nelly had been the pack's previous alpha female, a clunky title but essentially their chief mystic and high priestess. In turn, the powers she channeled had made her into something else. Normal werewolves, if such a term applied, were scary as all hell. Anywhere from six and a half feet tall to north of seven feet – all of it muscle, claws, and teeth. Atop them stood the roles of alpha and beta, both of whom were further empowered by some type of blessing which resulted in them being bigger and a shit-load more frightening.

But they had nothing on Nelly. When she'd changed, it had been nearly mind-boggling to behold. Think of the twelve foot tall, grey-furred werewolf monster of your nightmares, then make it about three times more terrifying and you might be in the ballpark ... *might*. We're talking daggers for claws and railroad spikes for teeth. And now all of that joy potentially belonged to my friend here. Well, that and other stuff. "Make any progress on her books?"

Cass laughed. "Yeah, all of it slow. Nearest I can tell, they're all written in ancient Vandalic which, just in case you were wondering, Google Translate isn't particularly helpful with."

"What about Marge? Has she been of any use?" I asked, speaking of Margaret Bentford, an otherwise unre-markable second grade teacher over in Morganberg who, I had since learned, was also the pack's designated beta female.

"Not much, aside from giving me side-eye whenever I open my mouth. Pretty sure she's pissed I rank-skipped her."

"Not your problem. I'll have a word with her if you want." I paused, remarking how quickly I'd seemingly fallen into the role of leader. Barely a week ago, I wanted nothing to do with the pack. Now I was in charge, even if only temporarily, as their new beta – holding down the fort in my father's absence. Much as I still wanted little to do with the whole bunch, I couldn't just let it go to voicemail whenever they called.

Speaking of which, I was about to tell Cass we should go and talk to the neighbors, when the dulcet sounds of *Feel It Still* started playing from inside my pocket. "Oh, for Christ's sake, what now?"

"Maybe Martians have touched down in the hollows and they want you to sort it out."

I shot Cass the stink eye as I dug my phone out. "Don't even joke." Then I quickly turned serious as I saw the number – Chief Johnson, not someone I considered it wise to keep waiting. "Hey, Chief. To what do I owe the pleasure?"

"*Just another beautiful day in glorious High Moon Township, Ninja Girl,*" he replied with a chuckle, using the name he'd dubbed me with last summer. "*I'm gonna need you and blondie to scoot over to Burnt Mills Lane and meet me there.*"

"Listen, I'm glad you called. I'm over at Riva's place and..."

"*That Kale girl?*"

"Yes. And something really weird is going on. I need you to..."

"*And I need you to fill me in when you meet me over on Burnt Mills.*"

"But..."

"*Ain't no buts, girl, 'cept my ample one and it's already in the car. You get yours and your hopefully not hairy friend on over here. I don't have time to mess around today. I need to be over at Swallowtail Park by two to go over the New Year's fireworks display and that's not even mentioning the DUI checkpoints I still have to sort out. In short, I got a full plate, so if you need to talk, it needs to be on my dime.*"

He hung up and I put my phone away. I could only

imagine the juggling act he needed to perform day in and day out, keeping the town safe, not only from the general populace but from the shadowy underworld surrounding it. Even so, I couldn't pretend it didn't annoy me to be blown off so quickly.

"What's the word?"

"The word," I replied, "is we need to get our asses back in the car and head over to Burnt Mills Lane to talk about fireworks … the ones they're going to shoot off on New Year's Eve and whatever will blow up in our faces if these peace talks don't go well."

Burnt Mills Lane ran through the southern edge of town, a few blocks past my house. There, the homes were spaced farther apart as the normal yards gave way to wide fields, some of which were still active farmland.

Chris had pestered us for details when we'd returned to the car. It was tempting to give him a watered-down version of what we'd seen, maybe let him think there'd been a minor accident with the window frame. But ever since our ordeal, running from my aunt on Christmas day, I'd promised to tell him the truth – at least until such time as I managed to save our parents. After that, well, if Mom wanted to erase his memories of the past week, that was probably her business. But until then, a promise was a promise, so I brought him up to speed, even though I could see by his expression in the rearview mirror the news scared the crap out of him.

Me, too, kiddo.

And apparently the day wasn't finished weirding us out yet. I turned onto Burnt Mills Lane and began scanning for the chief's patrol car, only to spot it in front of a familiar house.

"You've gotta be fucking kidding me."

"What is it?" both Chris and Cass asked simultaneously.

I pointed out the police car, sitting parked only a few feet away from a "For Sale" sign stuck into the lawn at the edge of the property upon which it sat.

"So?" Chris asked.

"So, that's the old Crendel place."

I explained to them how, after stopping the werewolves at Riva's house, her family had sought refuge there. The Crendels had a reputation as preppers, which was more lifestyle for them than reputation as it turned out. They had a bomb shelter out in their backyard, within which Riva and her family had ridden out the werewolf apocalypse in style – minus her having to spend an evening being hit on by the Crendels' son. Funny. I'd been out here only last week, the same night I'd picked Riva up for a sleepover. To say it was odd that Chief Johnson now wanted to meet us here for some reason, well, that was a bit of an understatement.

"Another weird coincidence?" Cass asked, as I remained seated behind the wheel.

I turned to face her, feeling like someone had driven a steamroller over my grave. "I hope so, because what's the alternative?"

"Probably too terrifying to think about"

"Fate," Chris said from the backseat. "Or Fates plural."

I turned his way. "What?"

"We learned about them in history class. They were the weavers of fate in Greek mythology, deciding every mortal's ultimate destiny. And then there's the Norns in Norse myth. Kinda the same deal."

I raised an eyebrow. "Who'd have ever thought you paid attention to anything that didn't have the Marvel logo stamped on it?"

He laughed. "They actually show up in *The Mighty Thor* from time to time."

"Figures. I don't suppose these Fates have any cousins in Gaelic mythology?"

"Beats the shit out of me."

"Mom wouldn't like that language," I said, the words slipping out of my mouth before I even realized I was saying it.

"I know." He averted his eyes for a moment, then quickly added, "But you can still suck my ass."

"Ewww, not even if my life depended on it." I turned around, back toward the Crendel place, seeing Chief Johnson standing on the front porch and looking our way expectantly. "Speaking of which, I have a feeling our lives are going to get a lot more difficult if we leave the good chief hanging for much longer."

Chief Johnson raised an eyebrow as the three of us, my brother included, approached, but he didn't say anything. By this point it was painfully obvious Chris was in the know. Besides, Johnson seemed far more concerned with maintaining order than in keeping tabs on who knew what.

"How are you feeling, champ?" he asked Chris as we joined him on the front stoop.

"Okay, I guess."

"No headaches or anything?"

"A few, nothing too bad."

"That's good." He clapped a meaty hand against Chris's arm, almost knocking him over. "Gotta love the resiliency of youth."

"So why are we here?" I asked, despite having a feeling I already knew the answer.

"Right to the point, eh, Ninja Girl?" Johnson replied. "I can appreciate that."

Chris turned to me and grinned. "Ninja Girl?"

Oh crap. I'd forgotten my brother didn't quite know *all* of my secrets. "Nothing you need to worry about."

"I can't wait to hear this one."

"Too bad, because you're going to be waiting a long time."

Chris eyed the chief, but he simply shook his head. "Ain't my story to tell, partner. Besides, we have more pressing matters at hand." He gestured toward me and Cass. "Neither of you strike me as stupid and believe me I've seen plenty of that in my day. So I'm thinking you've already guessed it, but this here is where I want you to hold your negotiations."

I nodded. The weirdness of his choice aside, it made a good deal of sense. "It's at the edge of town, neighbors aren't close enough to snoop, and it's been empty ever since the Crendels moved."

The chief peered at me from over his mirrored sunglasses, looking every bit the stereotypical small-town cop. "Bugged out is more like it. No forwarding address, nothing. They were here, then next thing you know, they weren't."

"I didn't know that."

"Not too many people do," he said, "and I've been making it a point to keep it that way. Considering when they up and left, I figured it might be best to not kick that particular hornet nest. Lenny over at the post office owes me a few favors, so I asked him to spread the word that Edgar got himself an unexpected promotion and needed to move his family down state."

"What do you mean *when*?" Cass asked, having been mercifully elsewhere on the night the rest of her pack had invaded High Moon.

"At the ass end of summer, right after your alpha decided to take a good long piss on the standing treaty," Johnson replied in a matter of fact tone.

"Former alpha."

"Noted," came the reply. "Either way, if I had to guess I'd say either Edgar or Bridget saw something that night which spooked them out of their minds. Wouldn't have been hard. Both of them were always a bit squirrelly. Don't know exactly when they left, but it had to have been before the Draíodóir got around to blanking this section of town."

That made sense, I guess. But either way, it was ancient history so far as I was concerned. My family hadn't been friends with the Crendels, although a part of me would always be grateful to them for offering Riva and her parents sanctuary during the siege.

Apparently sensing he'd answered the question to our satisfaction, he continued. "Had a few kids try to break in around Halloween. Seemed they were looking for a place where they could scare their girlfriends' panties off with a good ghost story." He glanced at Chris for a moment, as if remembering young ears were present. "You might want to pretend you didn't hear that part. But aside from that, this place has been untouched. Everything inside is in good condition and it should be more than big enough for whatever you need to do. I already told Charlie Walker down at the bank that there's going to be some construction work going on. The road will conveniently be closed on the day you need it to be, so no point in bringing any prospective buyers around."

"Good idea," I replied.

He fixed me with a stare. "Mind you, I expect this place to still be standing when you're finished. I've already called in enough favors without having to fudge any

43

reports about gas main explosions ... especially since this place has oil heat."

I couldn't lie and pretend that wasn't a concern. On any given day, the werewolves were walking fuses with the Draíodóir happy to be the lit match. The original peace talks were supposed to be led by my parents, both of whom were highly esteemed and feared in their respective clans, not to mention well liked, too. With me trying to lead these talks instead, that fuse and match were likely meeting in a room filled to the brim with gunpowder. Hell, had I been a betting girl, I'd have put all my money on a fight breaking out within fifteen minutes. I told them as much, watering down my own doubts just enough to not cause panic in my immediate company.

"Is there any chance you..."

Johnson held up a meaty hand. "I know what you're going to ask. My plan is to keep my distance, ensure there's no spillover into the town proper. Besides which, I doubt my presence is going to ease tensions much. That said, I'd recommend keeping my number handy. Should anything go wrong..." He slid his hand down to the butt of his gun as if for emphasis.

"I hear you."

Left unsaid was the fact that if things reached the point where I actually needed to call in the cavalry, then I'd likely already be standing at ground zero of a bloodbath.

5

The old saying about knowing when to shit or get off the pot is more apt than most people realize.

Though I desperately wanted to save my parents, I was also terrified of screwing things up worse than they already were.

That said, as much as I wanted to push this off, even I couldn't deny that New Year's Day would be the perfect time to hold these talks. Though it gave both sides a mere week to lick their wounds from what had transpired on Christmas, it was also one of the few days of the year when – even with the precautions the chief was putting into place – we had a good shot of nobody noticing that the abandoned home on Burnt Mills Lane wasn't as abandoned as it should be.

Between the late parties the night before, the town fireworks, and the fact that most non-essential personnel would have the day off, both sides agreed it was ideal. And if anyone among the participants happened to be hungover, all the better for ensuring they were less likely to start shit.

With the decision finally made, I was committed to doing my damnedest to make this work.

New Year's Eve rolled around before I even knew it. I checked in with Mindy early on. To say she sounded frazzled was an understatement. Poor girl had lost her twin sister less than a week ago. I wasn't even sure there'd been time to hold a funeral yet. But if so, I hadn't been invited – which was maybe for the best. Fortunately, though, my great aunt Fiona had stepped up to the plate to help. She'd lost a sister in the attack as well, making her more than motivated to see this through. However, she was also one of the Draíodóir elders, with far more pull and experience than my cousin.

Bottom line was, as Mindy told me, they'd be ready for the meeting.

Though I wasn't sure whether it would be appreciated or even wanted, I told her to pass on my thanks before hanging up.

That was one side accounted for – which still only left us halfway there. Go figure, organizing the Morganberg pack fell into my hands, something I'd been a bit neglectful in doing the last few days.

Thankfully, Cass was around to pick up the ball where I'd dropped it. While I'd been busy trying to be the adult in my suddenly very empty feeling home, she'd used her pull as the new alpha female to call a meeting of the pack elders and hopefuls – the hopefuls being the young werewolves with aspirations toward becoming the new alpha one day. Though I personally had doubts about meeting with a group who were training to essentially kick my father's ass at some point, or mine as was currently the case, she assured me this was simply how things were done in a werewolf pack.

Who was I to argue?

Turns out a member of Chris's nerd herd was throwing a New Year's Eve party, meaning I had a safe place to leave him while I drove over to Morganberg and played den mother. He didn't even protest too much at going, perhaps understanding he was getting one night of normalcy in a week that had been anything but.

I dropped him off and then turned east, toward Morganberg. Rather than head into the town proper, I took a left off Crossed Pine Road onto a small, easy to miss turnoff. My destination wasn't someone's home or the town library. I was heading back into the hollows.

A small part of me was terrified to be making this trip alone, as I'd never quite gotten over my fear of this place – despite now being in charge of all the scary things taking up residence there. However, an equal part was glad nobody was with me, as I pretty much jumped at every shadow or overhanging branch I passed – certain I'd see a one-armed version of myself lying in wait.

Thankfully, if the doppelganger was still in the area, it chose the better part of discretion as I parked and got out, letting the sounds and smells of the hollows fill my enhanced senses. I realized Cass was waiting there for me a moment before she spoke.

"Any trouble getting in?"

"Smooth sailing so far," I replied, locking the car despite there being no need. I mean, who was going to steal it out here? Still, it was my mother's sedan. The last thing I needed was some wandering werewolf pup to smell her lingering odor and decide to take a crap in the front seat.

Ugh. Now there was a thought I was unlikely to get out of my head anytime soon.

"Lead the way," I said, noting she was fully clothed.

Thank goodness. Werewolves had a thing about walking around the hollows bare-ass, even in the middle of winter – something to do about standing before their god with nothing but the strength of their bodies to back them up. This wasn't an official ceremony, though, so hopefully nobody felt the need for tradition, especially since it was really freaking cold out.

"No can do," she replied. "Sorry, but it's not going to help your position if the others think I'm leading you."

I glanced around, not seeing much as it was already past sundown. Sadly, while my nose and ears were super-charged as a result of my heritage, my eyes hadn't gotten the memo. All I saw with my limited range of vision was dark forest. "Did you lay out a trail of breadcrumbs or something? Because unless they glow in the dark..."

"Not too far off, but even better. Take a sniff."

Rather than waste time asking stupid questions, I did as told. My nostrils filled with the myriad scents of the forest – layer upon layer, painting a picture of the surrounding area in my head. Mind you, not a good enough picture to navigate by.

Wait a second.

I definitely sensed Cass, as well as other more distant scents – other lycanthropes, the ones no doubt waiting for us. But Cass's odor, oddly enough, seemed to be in multiple spots. She was here, but she was also further in the forest, and then again and again. No. Those scents were fainter and they didn't have her various underlying odors. It was almost like they were olfactory afterimages of a sort.

"I scented the way there for you," she explained. "That way, if we get separated you can find your way back."

"Scented?"

"Yep. That should help until you learn the route yourself."

"How did you do that?"

She raised one shoulder sheepishly. "Do you really want to know?"

I seemed to recall seeing some show on the Adventure Channel, or maybe it was Animal Planet, that mentioned how prides of lions marked their territory. *Ewww.* "No, not really."

"Probably for the best."

The meet and greet area for the Morganberg pack was underwhelming to say the least. Horror movies might have a person guessing they'd be stepping foot into some dark murder den, littered with human skeletons. The reality was more your basic clearing in the forest, lined at the edge with some picnic tables and a couple of old charcoal grills. If it weren't for the fact that we were surrounded by dark woods, you'd have thought we were hanging out in someone's backyard.

Ditto for the company waiting for us. Werewolves in their human guises simply weren't all that intimidating, especially when most of them looked bored out of their minds.

I instinctively opened my mouth to apologize for making them wait but then quickly clamped it shut, remembering something my father had told me when last we'd been here.

Being the alpha means you can arrive fashionably late.

It had been a joke, but at the same time it wasn't. His meaning had been clear. If anyone else was late, they could apologize. But when you were in charge of a wolf pack, the meeting didn't start until you got there. In short, no matter when you arrived, you were always right on time.

I was beginning to understand what he'd meant when

he'd said that the transition from a beta to alpha mindset was no small thing. All my life, I'd considered myself the tough girl, never backing down from either an argument or a fight. But the thing was, that attitude was only a small part of me. I was only realizing it now, but most of my youth had been spent taking orders from someone or other – whether it had been my parents or coaches. Scrappy or not, I was used to being a team player. But now *I* was the coach. The buck stopped with me. Yeah, behind closed doors I could ask Cass for advice, but out in the open that simply wouldn't fly.

Now wasn't the time for such thoughts, though. Now was the time for action. The side representing Morganberg in these talks wasn't something that would come together on its own. It was *my* responsibility to choose them, so I'd better choose well.

Hah. No pressure there.

I eyed the group waiting for us – about a dozen in total. The majority were senior members of the pack, ranging from middle-aged and up. I saw Marge Bentford, the beta female, among them – glaring at Cass through her glasses. Guess being a werewolf didn't make one exempt from being near-sighted. Who'd a thunk it?

Off to the side, however, stood three who didn't quite fit in with the older pack members, all of them fit males around my age – including David Hood. I'd had a run in with him about a week ago, during the equinox, a meeting in which he was a lot more naked than he was now. The image of his dark hair, six pack abs, chiseled chest, and ... *other parts* had been pretty well etched into my memory.

Perhaps noticing me staring, Cass said, "By your request, I've assembled Curtis's former advisory council as well as the top three hopefuls."

Supposedly every pack had a group of young studs ... err ... males being groomed to one day challenge the alpha for the top spot. Savage as it sounded, Dad had been pretty casual about the whole thing, dismissing it as nothing more than a tradition meant to ensure the pack's survival in the long term. Even so, I had a hard time not giving them some shade.

I mean, let's face facts, in any sport you were either the top dog or vying to knock the top dog off its perch. That was a given. But the act of making it formal kinda weirded me out a bit. It was like handing someone a dagger and telling them to make sure they trained hard so they could one day stab you in the back with it.

It was likely because, acting alpha or not, I was an outsider. All of this shit was brand new to me. If one were indoctrinated from an early age, I'm sure this all would've been the most natural thing in the world. Of course, it could also be because I was treading new ground. Not only was I not one of them, but I was a woman, too. That was two strikes against me, meaning everyone likely had twice as many daggers waiting to nail me with.

Speaking of nailing, though, David met my eyes and threw me the barest of smiles. All at once, I felt my knees go weak and it had nothing to do with any incoming challenges.

Oh boy, if I didn't head this off at the pass quickly, this meeting would do nothing to instill anything in this bunch other than I needed to be killed ASAP. It was time to put my game face on.

"Hopefuls, eh?" I remarked, doing my best to return David's grin with nothing more than indifference. "Anyone care to get lucky tonight?"

Okay, that really didn't come out how I meant it to. Fortunately, I managed to pull out of that nosedive by cracking my knuckles. "If so, now's the time to try, because come tomorrow I expect everyone to be in line."

"We don't have time for this foolishness," one of the

older men said, a guy with thinning grey hair and wearing equally threadbare overalls. I recognized his face from the past week, but not his name.

"I don't recall asking your opinion ... um." I waved him on, hoping he got the hint.

"Earl."

Of course. He looked like an Earl. "Thanks. But I think it's best we get this out of the way now. You know, be frank with one another?"

"Um, Frank's my name," one of the hopefuls, a muscular ginger-haired dude bro said.

Good to know at least one of them was an idiot.

"I meant let's be honest with each other here. I'm not one of you, nor, from what I understand, your typical idea of a pack beta."

"No, ya ain't," Earl replied.

"But," I continued, "I also defeated your former beta in fair combat, not to mention kicked the shit out of a doppelganger while the rest of you were hiding in your dog houses waiting for the all clear. So, like it or not, I've earned my rank. Cass, too."

Technically she'd been in the wrong place at the wrong time when the former alpha female, Nelly, had been bisected by killing magic, but I figured it might be best if I cast a vote of confidence in her favor.

"So, I'm putting it out here in the open. If anyone is planning to challenge *either* of us, now's the time to do it, because if I have to deal with any petty bullshit tomorrow, I am not going to be a happy camper."

I would've put money on Cass not being pleased that I included her in my ultimatum, especially since she didn't know what would happen if she tried to change into her other form. Fortunately, her only tell was the quick glance she threw my way for the barest of moments.

Good, because I knew what I was doing, or hoped I

did anyway. I was betting that werewolf challenges were most often made during moments when those in charge appeared weak. That was the time for a wannabe to step up to the plate and swing for the fences. By turning the tables and offering it up at a time of my choosing, however, I was hedging my bets that everyone present would think twice.

Sure enough, that seemed to be the case. The hopefuls looked among each other for a moment, no doubt wondering if any of their fellows had grown a set, before turning back toward me. A few from the advisory council glared my way, but none said so much as "boo". As for Marge, she quickly averted her eyes.

"Anyone?" I asked. "Going once, twice..."

Nothing but silence met my ears.

"Good. Then let's talk about tomorrow."

6

"Hey, you got a minute?"

I looked up from where I was sitting at one of the picnic tables to find David Hood approaching.

After establishing myself as the big dog in this kennel, the rest of the meeting had been long but also fairly easy, with everyone talking like rational adults. Go figure. Once we got past the pissing match, Earl and the other advisors had some good suggestions. Even Marge chimed in to help out.

It was decided that our contingent would be seven strong, apparently a lucky number no matter what god you prayed to. Cass and I were a given, nobody tried to argue against that. It was decided that three of the advisory council, including Earl who seemed the most outspoken of the bunch, would join us. That left two of the hopefuls – David and Frank – to tag along, both as a learning experience and to ensure the pack's future interests were taken into account.

Along with the rest of the elders, Marge, as the sole

other werewolf with a formal rank, would stay behind to ensure the pack wasn't without leadership on the off chance something went wrong. From the look on her face, she wasn't overly distraught by this decision.

And that was it.

The meeting broke up around eleven thirty, just a bit shy of the new year.

While the others began to wander back to their respective lives, I decided to take a few minutes to catch my composure. It was crazy. A tough fight could tire even me out, but being mentally drained was another thing entirely. And to think, I still had tomorrow to look forward to.

So, enhanced senses or not, I was caught off guard when David approached.

"Um, yeah," I sputtered, no doubt undoing hours of authority in the span of a second. "I mean, what can I help you with?"

"Nothing," he said. "I just wanted to let you know you're a natural at this." He lowered his voice, no doubt wary of being overheard. "You shut everyone down right away and took charge. Don't tell them I said this, but a few of the guys were talking shit earlier about how they'd take over if given half a chance. But then you dropped your challenge and not a peep. I tell you, I about pissed myself."

"Well ... I'm glad you didn't." *Gah! How could I be so freaking lame?* And how could he just stand there so casually? Did he not know how cute he was, with or without clothes?

He laughed at my pathetic joke, the sound musical to my ears. "They're never going to live it down, but they're not going to say shit about it either. You established yourself as firmly in charge back there. They might talk trash with each other, but I guarantee if you say jump, they'll ask how high. Me, too."

His words painted quite the vivid picture in my head. All I had to do was give the order and he'd have no choice but to tear my panties off with his teeth and take me as many times as I desired.

And why shouldn't I?

Cass had told me not too long ago that it wasn't unheard of for the male leaders to take advantage of their station with the so-called pack bitches. I saw no reason that door couldn't swing both ways.

All at once, I realized David was still talking and I had absolutely no idea what he was saying, stuck in my little dominatrix fantasy as I was.

"...but I'm not sure he even wants the position."

"Come again?" *Shit!* Talk about a poor choice of words. Hopefully he didn't realize what a massive double entendre I'd just dropped. "I mean, say that again. I have a lot on my mind."

"Oh, I don't doubt it, especially with what's happening tomorrow," he replied, seemingly oblivious. *Typical male.* "But I was just saying that Earl's probably your best choice out of the bunch. He's been an advisor since all the way back to Caleb's time. Far as I know, though, he's a behind the scenes guy. Never showed any interest in the big roles."

"Best choice for what?"

"For beta of course."

"But I'm already the beta," I pointed out.

"No, you're the alpha."

"I'm only the acting al..."

"There's no such thing," he interrupted, before holding up his hands. "Sorry. Didn't mean to be rude."

I waved him off. "Forget about that. What do you mean there's no such thing?"

"Exactly that. The position of alpha isn't a seat you keep warm for someone else. If the current alpha dies, or goes missing I mean, the beta automatically takes over unless there's a challenge. And, no offense, but I think you squashed that pretty handily tonight."

"But the whole point of this summit is to get my father back."

"I know and, believe me, I have full faith that you will. But once you do, you'll still be our alpha. It's just the way things work. Curtis will either have to accept that or fight you for it."

"Can't I just ... give it back to him?"

"I guess technically you could."

"Technically?"

"Yeah." He smiled sheepishly. "But it would make you both look weak. There would be ... how do I put this gently ... doubt."

Goddamn, I hated werewolf politics! So much macho bullshit. I could see where the phrase *peeing with the big dogs* came from. "Okay, fine. We can cross that road when we come to it. But what does any of that have to do with Earl?"

"Oh, I was just saying we got so caught up in the weeds tonight that we never discussed who would be your beta tomorrow. I just figured Earl made the most sense, even if he doesn't want the job. But if you said so, and nobody argued against it then..."

"But Cass..."

"Has her own place at the table. She needs to be there in case questions come up which challenge our faith or beliefs. It's not really her job to have your back for the rest of the negotiations, even if I don't doubt she will."

"You seem to know a lot about this stuff."

"Well, yeah. I'm one of the ... hopefuls." He held up

his fingers in quote marks for that last part. "They make us study this stuff. Although, just between you and me, I think it's going to be a long time before I'm ready to challenge anyone to..."

"Sold. You're my new beta," I said, the words just slipping out.

"What?!" he cried, his voice loud enough to draw the attention of those still in the vicinity.

"You heard me. You obviously know this stuff a hell of a lot better than me." *And Cass*, I silently added. She hadn't filled me in on any of this, but I realized it was likely because she didn't know herself, also being a bit of a black sheep.

Sure, the older folks likely knew all this, probably better than David did, but they also brought along a lifetime of baggage in the form of absolutely hating the Draíodóir. David was my age meaning, that while he'd grown up beneath their *dog*ma, pun intended, he hadn't had decades upon decades to reinforce those stereotypes. Cass, at the very least, had proven to be somewhat open minded when it came to the pack's enemies on the far side of High Moon. Hopefully David would, too.

"But..."

"Shut up," I said with a grin. "Your alpha commands it." Ooh, I could get used to this. Once again, visions of commanding him to pin me down momentarily filled my head, but I pushed them away. Maybe I could run with that idea when this was all over, save it for my victory dance if this all worked out. For now, though, I raised my voice so that those still within earshot were sure to hear me. "I'm declaring David Hood to be my beta for the upcoming talks with the Draío ... the peace talks. Does anyone challenge me?"

"They have to challenge me," he whispered, sounding a bit less than enthused.

"I mean, does anyone challenge *him* for the role?" I waited for several seconds, noting a few disgruntled noises but nobody outright saying anything, then turned back toward him. "Congratulations. You're in charge of feeling me ... I mean feeling out the room tomorrow and backing me up."

Alpha I might be, but cool I was most definitely not.

For several long seconds, David stared at me, as if unable to think of what to say. It was cute, along with just about everything else about him.

"You know, it won't do if the cat's got the tongue of a werewolf beta," I said with a smile.

"Sorry. It's just that ... wow ... I didn't expect this. I mean, I'm not even sure I'm ready for it."

"Nobody really is, trust me."

"I ... I know what this means, but how do I act around my friends? I didn't expect to find myself..."

"Outranking them?" I finished. "I wish I had better advice, David. And truth of the matter is, I probably spoke without thinking and I'm..." *Don't say you're sorry. Alphas don't apologize.* "...I'm sure, however, that I made the right choice. I..."

Rather than finish that sentence, I let out a squeak of surprise as the sound of distant explosions filled the air and the sky above the treetops lit up. And I may have sort of jumped into the arms of my new beta in the process.

Oopsie.

"Um, good reflexes," I lamely said, stepping back as more explosions filled the air. "Those must be the fireworks over in High Moon."

"You know what that means, right?"

"What?" I asked, still seriously lost in the moment.

"Happy New Year."

Quickly, before I could wimp out, I said, "You know, there's a tradition that it's good luck to share a..."

"Sorry to interrupt, but this really can't wait."

The moment absolutely ruined, I turned to see Marge, the female beta, approaching. Cass was with her, the look on her face suggesting she was absolutely mortified to be stepping in right now.

I took a deep breath, banishing all thoughts of wicked things, and faced her. "Yes, Marge, what can I do for you?"

"The blessing of Valdemar. If David is to be the new beta then it needs to be conferred to him and, considering the potentially explosive situation tomorrow, we really should attend to it ASAP." She glanced over her shoulder toward Cass. "And, no disrespect intended..."

"Spit it out."

"But it's something Ester needs to learn."

I couldn't help but notice she called Cass by her far less appreciated given name. No doubt a subtle dig. I turned toward my friend expectantly.

"She's not wrong," Cass said, sounding none too pleased. "Valdemar chose me for whatever reason. I can't merely be a figurehead."

"Valdemar is wise," Marge replied. "Though we might not understand his actions now, they will become evident ... one day."

I remembered hearing the so called will of Valdemar in my head during my fight with my aunt. Though I wasn't about to say so out loud, his so-called wisdom had amounted to little more than inarticulate snarling. Still, even if their god was little more than a rabid dog, I had faith in Cass.

Despite Mindy's best efforts, it would be stupid of me to think the Draíodóir wouldn't be sending some heavy hitters to the table. It was perhaps not the stupidest idea to ensure our deck was similarly stacked. "Agreed. Do what you can to get this moving."

Marge nodded. "I'm glad you see it that way, because from what I understand his most glorious blessing was interrupted before it could be transferred to you."

I should've seen that one coming.

At the time, I'd been willing to accept it, take whatever advantage I could get to stop my aunt. But then all hell had broken loose in the sacred glade. The thing was, while I wasn't averse to a power-up, I'd had more than enough of that clearing, especially considering what had happened right before Cass and I had hauled ass out of there.

With my aunt defeated – *dead* – Riva had appeared, but it hadn't been my friend. It had been something else wearing her guise, perhaps as a way for my mind to accept it without losing my marbles. Whatever the case, Possessed Riva had heavily implied that my actions had let something into this world that was never intended to be here. What that was, I didn't know.

A part of me didn't want to know.

I wasn't naïve enough to think that gave me a get out of jail free card. But it didn't mean I was ready to poke that hornet nest again. "Save it for another time."

"But..."

"I mean it," I said, putting some steel into my voice. From the way she flinched, I got the impression I succeeded. "It makes sense for David to have it, but I need to appeal to both sides tomorrow. I'm not just speaking for us, I'm speaking on behalf of my parents. That's going to be hard enough, but I have a feeling it'll be that much more difficult if I'm fully invested in this blessing or whatever it is."

I didn't need to explain myself to her or any of them.

An alpha's word was law. A simple no would've sufficed. But I sort of needed to hear myself say it.

I was the Morganberg pack's alpha, but I wasn't one of them. I never would be. I existed in both worlds, whether any of us liked it or not.

To pretend otherwise was pure folly, nothing more.

7

H igh Moon itself was quiet by the time I crossed the town line. A good chunk of the evening's revelry had likely died down with the last of the fireworks. I had no doubt there were still parties raging, though, and a part of me was tempted to go find one. There was little question I could gain admittance to some rager somewhere, drink my fill, and maybe even find a nice boy to take me home for a one-night stand.

But that would only be pretending. Come tomorrow I still had a duty to fulfil.

I decided to take one quick detour before heading home and seeing how much melatonin it took to knock out a supernatural hybrid for a couple hours of needed sleep.

The chief hadn't yet closed Burnt Mills Lane. It was probably because a few people were still out and about, likely heading home from whatever merriment they'd partook of. Whatever the case, it allowed me to pass by the Crendel place, the site of tomorrow's – *today's* – peace summit.

In a few short hours, this place would play host to

beings of vast supernatural potency, capable of communing with gods and harnessing the very powers of creation. Both Draíodóir and lycanthrope would be sitting down together, two destructive races who really didn't like each other. And the only thing keeping them from tearing each other's throats out would be me, a person somehow cursed to have one foot in each world.

Yeah, later today this place would be brimming with explosive potential. But for now, it sat there looking very empty and alone ... just like I felt.

Despite what some might think, there are plenty of downsides to having enhanced senses. You end up over-hearing conversations you really don't want to hear, smelling body funk that's best not dwelled upon, that sort of thing. However, as I forced my eyes open, I realized perhaps the worst part was no longer having any ability whatsoever to sleep through the shrill chime of an alarm clock.

Mind you, my powers weren't particularly kind on the clock either, especially not when I brought my fist down, shattering it and the night table upon which it sat.

"Serves you right, asshole," I groused, pushing myself up from the Olympic-size puddle of drool on my pillow.

On the upside, it made me kinda glad that Marge had cockblocked me last night. I had a feeling I was sporting morning breath that would give even a werewolf pause from partaking in a wake-up quickie.

Fortunately, that didn't stop me from bringing those thoughts into my parents' bathroom for a shower, complete with their pulsating massage head. Don't get me wrong, I would've given my life to bring them back safe, but there was no doubt it was kinda cool having the house all to myself for a bit.

Freshened up and with a bit of extra spring to my step, I headed toward my room to get dressed.

Therein lay a bit of a conundrum. Was there a dress code for unprecedented events such as the one I would soon be presiding over? The Draíodóir, from what I'd been told, loved their ceremony. Would they show up in their best wizarding cloaks and be offended at anyone who didn't? As for the werewolves, hell, there was no way of knowing if they'd even bother wearing clothes. How the fuck was I supposed to concentrate when half the table might be full commando?

Fuck it. When in doubt, go functional – boots, jeans, sweater, and a jacket, all of it over a sports bra and boy shorts. I could save the thong and minidress for afterwards if all was successful.

I got dressed and looked at myself in the mirror. Okay, that probably worked – a nice neutral place between what I assumed for each of the parties today. Not to mention, a good choice in case I needed to kick anyone's ass.

There was just one thing missing. Sure, it didn't quite go with my color scheme, but there was no way I was leaving home without it today.

Come on, where is it? Cursing my lack of anything even remotely resembling organizational skills, I rummaged through my top drawer before finally pulling out the pendant my mother had given me for Christmas. It was a jeweled monarch butterfly on a chain that was not quite platinum, as evidenced by the fact that it was instantly warm to the touch.

Mom had hinted that it was special, something I could use back at school in case I ran into any more weird-ass monsters looking to eat my face. Sadly, she hadn't given me any clue as to what it did or how it worked.

But that was okay. It wasn't the pendant's powers I was interested in so much as what it symbolized. I put it on and debated for a moment whether I should lay it under my shirt before deciding it was perfect as it was, front and center for everyone to see.

Though I might well be the only one there to get it, to me it sent a clear message. Yes, I was the alpha of the Morganberg pack, but I was also the daughter of the reigning Queen of the Monarchs – even if it was still a stupid ass title. Regardless, I was proud to wear it. And if it pissed off either side, that was their problem so long as I got what I wanted.

"The way I see it, *Ham*ara, is you've got two choices. You can either bring me along, or you can leave me here unattended and hope I don't do something destructive like dunk your pillow in the toilet tank."

I cracked my knuckles, imagining burying both fists in my shit of a little brother's face.

Chris had arrived home shortly after I'd gotten dressed, dispelling any hope that maybe he'd spend the day at his friend's place.

Thing is, he had me over a barrel. Sure, my parents had employed sitters over the years, but that had been *before* either of us knew what was really out there. Up until yesterday, I'd been counting on Riva. Everyone else, at least that I trusted, was either a part of the meeting or would be busy keeping the peace in town.

True, Chris was technically old enough to leave on his own. But he could be a grade A dipshit when he wanted to, like that time he decided to nuke some waffles, set the timer to twenty minutes instead of two, and then forgot about them. He might be more careful now, knowing what was at stake, but there was no way of telling.

There was also the truth behind his bullshit. I could see the fear in his eyes. It was there and very real. He didn't want to be left alone. And I was pretty sure there was more. Though I doubted I could've beaten it out of him, he was well aware there was a chance – however slim – that I could walk out that door and not come back. If so, that would leave him all alone in a world in which monsters indeed lurked in the shadows.

The reality was we fought like cats and dogs, and I couldn't easily count the number of times I'd had to cash in my big sister card and pummel the little shit-weasel, but he was still my brother and I loved him.

Mind you, that didn't mean we were about to get all huggy kissy with each other.

"All right, here's the deal," I said, jabbing him in the chest with my index finger, hard enough to make him back up a couple of steps. "The power's going to be on for the day, the chief said as much. You bring your phone, your Nintendo Switch, a bunch of games, and every fucking charger they need. You stay upstairs and out of sight. If I see you even trying to catch a glimpse of what's going on, I will dunk every single possession you own in the Crendels' septic tank and make you eat what's left. Are we clear?"

Despite my disturbingly over-descriptive threat, a big grin broke out on his face. "Crystal."

And with that, it was time for us to get going.

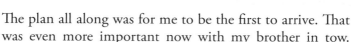

The plan all along was for me to be the first to arrive. That was even more important now with my brother in tow. With any luck, his presence upstairs would go unnoticed.

Yeah, there was the problem of the werewolves and their fucking noses. As their alpha, I would be in the right to deck any that dared open their mouths to say something, but hopefully it wouldn't come to that.

Thankfully, I'd come prepared.

I drove around the road closed signs now in place on Burnt Mills Lane – *thanks, Chief* – and parked a bit away from the Crendel place, hopefully far enough so that any passersby might assume my destination was elsewhere. Then Chris and I got out and walked toward the house.

"Hand me your backpack," I said as we approached.

"Why?"

"Just do it."

He did, at which point I pulled a small spray bottle out of my coat pocket and spritzed the pack with its contents. I gave it a quick sniff, wrinkled my nose, then turned to my brother. "Okay, your turn."

"What?"

"Turn around. We don't have much time."

"But..."

"Move it, dickhead!"

"Fine."

He did as told, and I likewise hosed him down, back and then front. When I was finished, he took a breath and grimaced. "Ugh, what is that shit?"

I smiled. "It's not shit. It's urine, wolf urine to be exact."

"You sprayed me with wolf pee?!"

"Keep your voice down, piss boy. It's not like you usually smell much better. Besides, do you want them sniffing you out upstairs or what?"

He looked like he wanted to throw a punch at me. Heh, good luck with that. However, after a moment he regained his composure, some of it anyway. "Why the fuck do you even have that crap?"

"Oh, I picked it up at Vickson's Sport Shop earlier this week. Thought it might come in handy if I ever needed to mask my scent in the hollows. But it should do the trick here, too."

I handed him his backpack and he took it with a glare. "I'm going to get you back for this. You know that, right?"

"Yeah, yeah. Just do it without touching me. Man, you really do stink."

8

I figured worst case was I'd need to break in to the Crendels' home, a minor issue for someone who could rip a car door off with her bare hands, but instead I was pleasantly surprised to find an envelope waiting for me, taped to the front door. Inside was a key and a note.

Lock up when you're finished, Ninja Girl, and drop the key at my office. Everything's been prepped inside. If you need me, I'm only a phone call away. Good luck.

It was signed with the initials RJ.

"Thanks, Chief," I said in a low voice, before turning to my brother. "Shall we?"

"Let's get Mom and Dad back."

"You bet."

I would never admit it to him, but suddenly I was glad Chris was there with me. What a crazy world we lived in. Turning away from him, I allowed myself a quick grin then put the key in the lock.

Truth be told, I didn't have high expectations. From what I'd heard, the Crendel place had sat empty for the last four months or so. While that probably wasn't long enough for it to feel like some kind of derelict haunted house, I fully expected to find myself brushing cobwebs out of my hair. The only upside being that it was winter, so hopefully the spiders themselves had long since sought out warmer places to set up shop.

But then I stepped across the threshold and flicked on the light switch. Not only had the chief been good to his word about the power being on, but he'd meant it when he'd said things had been prepped. Hell, if anything, he'd downplayed the shit out of it.

The place was spotless, as if the Crendels had simply left for the day. Outside of the foyer, there was a fairly open floor plan – a large living room and dining room combo, or what had probably once been. Now, the bulk of the space was taken up with a large wooden table surrounded by high-backed chairs. Above it all hung an ornate chandelier.

I hadn't exactly been friends with the Crendels, but that seemed sort of out of place for what I would've expected to find. Lending to this theory were the buffet tables lining the walls, all of them covered with metal platters full of meats, cheeses, and fruit. There was even a coffee station next to an array of buns and bagels.

"When the hell did he have time to set this up?"

"Who cares?" Chris replied, immediately filling up a plate with every hors d'oeuvre he could get his thieving hands on.

"Pretty sure that stuff is meant for the guests."

He turned to me and grinned. "Pretty sure you wouldn't want me sitting upstairs starving and having to sneak down for food."

"Pretty sure that would lead to me pummeling you in front of company."

He shrugged as if that were my problem then stepped into the kitchen.

"You realize nobody actually lives here, right? It's probably empty."

"Holy shit! They have Mountain Dew Throwback."

I glanced past him. Sure enough, the refrigerator was stocked to the gills with refreshments, several of which my brother was helping himself to.

It was like being the first to arrive at a feast.

Fuck it.

"Grab me one while you're there," I said, picking up a plate.

"What happened to it being for the guests?"

"A good host always samples the food first, to make sure it meets her expectations."

"You almost sound like you believe that bullshit."

"Hey," I replied, popping a cheese cube into my mouth, "someone's gotta make sure this stuff isn't poisoned."

I almost felt bad for spraying my brother down with wolf piss as I helped him carry a small mountain of food upstairs, hopefully enough to keep him from dying of hunger for a few hours – always a dicey proposition where preteen boys were concerned. The smell of the spread downstairs, including fresh coffee, would almost certainly be enough to distract even the werewolves from any human scent in the house. But oh well. What was done was done.

We'd been hoping to find maybe a bedroom in decent enough shape for him to hole up in, but again the chief was one step ahead of me. Whatever furniture was missing from downstairs seemed to have been relocated up here. A comfy couch sat in the middle of what had once probably been the master bedroom. On the wall in front of it was a flat screen TV, complete with remote and all the cables Chris would need to connect to it, including a wired set of headphones.

It wasn't quite a man cave, but it was damned close.

"Think you can survive in here?" I asked numbly, setting several cans of soda down onto the coffee table in front of the couch.

My brother chuckled, a big ass grin on his face. "I don't know. It's kind of rough, but I'll do my best."

"Uh huh. Thoughts and prayers headed your way. Now, use the bathroom if you need to, then I expect this door to stay shut and those headphones to stay on. Are we clear?"

Once I was certain my brother was settled in for the long haul – almost envying him, set up like royalty as he was – I headed back downstairs. I had no real idea what supernatural decorum called for when it came to seating arrangements, so I fell back on what I knew – placing a can of Coke at one end of the table, signifying that I'd called dibs on that chair. If the Draíodóir didn't like it, that was their problem.

I made another quick circuit of the first floor, amazed at how much the chief had done for me. Hell, the master bathroom was even stocked with fresh towels and rolls of toilet paper. I wasn't sure if it was hard work, calling in favors, or simply having domestic trolls at his disposal, but he was definitely getting a thank you card when this was finished.

Everything was perfect. There was nary a finger for me to lift, other than maybe grabbing a couple of last-minute melon slices.

And then I realized why. Everything else was left to me. The ball was in my court. He'd done what he could, lowering my stress levels as much as was humanly – or otherwise – possible. Now it was my turn.

That realization alone almost made me want to puke up what I'd eaten. One moment I was simply marveling at what had been done, the next I felt the weight of the world upon my shoulders.

I stepped into the bathroom and splashed some cold water on my face, feeling goosebumps break out on my arms that had nothing to do with the temperature.

And then my supercharged ears picked up the sound of car engines outside, followed by multiple doors opening and closing.

Perhaps that had been the chief's goal all along, to distract me with everything he'd done so I didn't have time to make myself sick with worry.

If so, he'd succeeded in spades because, like it or not, it was showtime.

I stepped to the front door and opened it, not having any clue what I'd see. For all I knew, I'd find witches and werewolves slaughtering each other on the frozen lawn. If so, that would definitely take the pressure off any speeches I might've prepared this past week and subsequently forgotten in the last five minutes.

However, no such luck. It seemed the lycanthropes were the first to arrive. Cass and David led the way, the contingent we'd decided on last night falling into step behind them. On the upside, everyone was dressed casually, as if this were any other day. That at least made me feel better about my choice of attire. It was bad enough being in charge without also standing out like a sore thumb.

I held the door open as they approached. "Um ... happy New Year."

God, what a loser I am.

Cass chuckled as she stepped in, mouthing, "Are you okay?" I gave her a quick nod, not that I had much choice. The moment she arrived with the others, I had to become their alpha again. The time for curling up in a corner and crying had passed.

David was next.

"My alpha," he said with a smile.

"Welcome, my beta," I replied, putting way more flirt into my tone than the situation warranted. Fuck it. Let the others say something. It would give me an excuse to let off some steam by busting a jaw or two.

Earl was next. He gave me a respectful nod, but then his expression soured when his eyes fell upon my pendant.

"Any problems?" I asked, my tone even but stern.

"Not at all. Just admiring your jewelry. Quite the piece."

"Thanks. It was a gift from my mother."

And that was apparently all that needed to be said, thank goodness.

The others filed in after him, all of them greeting me in ways that ranged from formal to cool. However, their attitudes soon changed when they saw the spread waiting for them.

"Holy shit," Cass cried, sipping from a Styrofoam cup. "Is this French roast?"

"Um, maybe. Enjoy!"

And just like that, the ice was broken. Another point in the chief's favor. The tension went out of the room as everyone helped themselves and then made their way over to find seats.

I couldn't help but notice the wolf side of things went heavy on the cold cuts. I sure hoped there were no roast beef fans among the Draíodóir because they were going to be shit outta luck.

Cass and David took seats on either side of me, and

the rest filled in the chairs next to them, clearly signifying which side of the table this was. I was about to ask if everyone was ready, when Earl produced a pen and pad of paper.

At my questioning glance, he shrugged. "Never done anything like this before. Figured, y'know, maybe someone should take notes."

That was actually ... surprisingly thoughtful. It was yet another reminder that I was out of my league here. I hadn't even considered that there might be stuff we wished to remember later, or points of contention that might need clarification. "Thank you. I appreciate the foresight."

Earl took the compliment stoically. As the most vocal of my father's advisors, I could tell the others looked up to him. I probably wasn't quite on his Christmas Card list yet, but I at least got the sense he was here to take this seriously.

That settled, Cass and David both turned to face me. They made eye contact with each other, apparently deciding she should be the one to speak first. "There is ... one little thing we should probably go over before the Draíodóir arrive."

"What?"

"Last night in the glade..."

Speaking of the devils, though, just as she was getting started, the doorbell chimed. Oh well, it could probably wait.

"Let's table it for now."

Cass shared a not-insignificant glance with my new beta, raising my curiosity a few notches, but then she nodded and moved to stand. However, I put a hand on her shoulder.

"I've got this."

"Are you sure?" David asked. "Usual decorum dictates..."

I cut him off. "We're in uncharted territory now. I don't know what past alphas have done, but I want to put my best foot forward and welcome them personally."

I waited a beat to see if anyone was going to call me out on the obvious bullshit I was making up as I went, but no one did.

"Wait here, make yourselves comfortable, and try not to chew with your mouths open."

That last one was meant as a joke and, thankfully, a few chuckles met it. How bad would that've been to let their enemies in while they were all busy glaring holes in my back?

Reaching for the front door, I realized the easy part was already over and done with – letting in the people who pretty much had to do what I said. From here on in, things could get tricky.

Hah! Get it, I was letting in witches ... tricky?

Yeah, my sense of humor sucked when I was nervous.

Bracing myself, I opened the front door ... and found no one except my cousin Mindy waiting, her green eyes staring at me from beneath a bun of red hair.

She was my height, about five three, but slender where I was more muscular. A former gymnast, she and I had shared a friendly sports rivalry growing up, helped by the fact that she and her late sister were barely a year older than me. But that also meant we'd been fairly close, too – default hangout buddies at family get togethers. Sadly, that had all changed a mere week ago.

Her sister, Melody, was struck down just as Christmas dinner had begun, while Mindy herself had been enslaved by our aunt in an insane bid for power. I'd managed to free her and, in turn, she'd been instrumental in helping me reestablish the aborted peace conference my parents had first proposed. However, all of that had been over the phone. In her voice I'd heard sorrow mixed with anger, but there was also more ... an undercurrent of fear. I had a sneaking suspicion that was due to her learning that I was far more than a human orphan adopted into the family.

My mixed heritage was a blessing when it came to dealing with murderous werewolves or crazed sorceresses, but it carried with it a curse. Those I'd known and loved all my life were all seemingly revolted upon learning the true nature of my parentage. It was good old-fashioned racism at its finest.

At the same time, though, my powers made me a threat to both races, so I could kind of understand the feeling.

My cousin and I continued to stare at each other for several seconds, neither saying a word.

Realizing that someone needed to end this standoff, I asked, "So, is anyone else coming?"

She raised an eyebrow at that. Oh great. I'd no doubt made my first faux pas of the day. Then she said, "By her majesty, Queen Brigid, I..."

"I what?"

"Oh, the hell with this," Mindy said, right before grabbing hold of me and dragging me out of the house.

9

Generally speaking, my first reaction to someone grabbing me like that, especially these days, was to knock them into next week.

Fortunately, I resisted those instincts, because Mindy pulled me in for a big hug instead.

I stiffened for a moment, caught by surprise, but then returned it full force.

"I never said thank you," she sobbed into my ear.

"I'm so sorry," I replied, tearing up.

We stood that way for several long seconds, until Mindy finally pulled away. She took a moment to wipe her eyes, then smiled. "We should probably stop before anyone comes looking."

She was right, although it took longer to compose myself than I would've liked. The simple act of kindness she'd just done had touched me far deeper than I'd expected. To date, I'd had both my aunt and uncle turn on me when I'd needed most. I guess I'd started to assume that would be the same with my extended family on both sides. To learn that wasn't the case, even from just one person, well, it sort of cracked the wall I'd been building inside myself.

"So," I said, after another minute, still trying to keep from bawling like a baby, "are we cool?"

Mindy actually laughed. "You've never been as cool as me, Tamara. Never will be." But then she leaned in and lowered her voice. "But you're pretty darned cool in my book."

We chuckled, probably not low enough for the folks at the table to miss, but whatever. They knew who I was and what my agenda was for these talks. Nevertheless, it was probably time to put our game faces back on.

"So, where were we?"

Mindy nodded then backed up a step. I took a moment to take in that she was dressed much more formally than me and my wolf buddies. It wasn't quite Yule Ball at Hogwarts, but it was certainly Sunday best. When next she spoke, her tone became much more businesslike.

"By the glory of her majesty Queen Brigid, I present the Summer Council of Crescentwood."

I lowered my voice to the barest of whispers, noting the frozen grass behind her. "They're a bit out of season."

She in turn offered me a half grin. "You're lucky. They wanted me to say all that in Gaelic."

Then, as if knowing she might be caught, she bowed and stepped aside ... revealing, once again, the empty front lawn.

Before I could make another dumbass comment, though, half a dozen columns of flame simultaneously erupted from the ground in front of me. Had I not seen this before, I'd have been tempted to think I was under attack ... right after shitting a brick. But fortunately, I was well versed with the spectacle that was Draíodóir teleportation.

The flames all shot up to a height of six or seven feet, before coalescing into human shapes and solidifying. When it was finished, I found the Draíodóir contingent standing before me, making me eternally grateful that Chief Johnson had the foresight to shut down this stretch of road. I don't care how bad someone's hangover was, there was simply no way of explaining shit like that.

My great aunt Fiona was at the head of the procession. Her grey hair was up in a tight bun and her dress, though formal, was considerably more dated in appearance than my cousin's. If anything, she looked as if she'd just stepped out of a time machine from Victorian era England.

My memories of her typically involved she and her two sisters, Theresa and Jezebel, chain smoking and gossiping with each other, usually sharing opinions on who was a bastard and who was a son of a bitch. Sadly, Auntie Theresa had been another victim of the Christmas attack. Bad as I felt for her, though, I hoped it steeled Fiona enough to overcome whatever prejudices she might have, so we could make these talks a success.

I recognized nearly everyone behind her, most of them being related to me in some form. However, I couldn't help being surprised at the sight of one of them – my mother's uncle, Clay Byrne, more commonly known to me while I was growing up as simply Doctor Byrne. More recently, however, another, far more interesting tidbit had come into my knowledge.

He was a skilled alchemist and one of the few Draíodóir outside my mother to know my true heritage – before now anyway. He was also the man who'd created the pills which, until recently, had caused everyone to believe I was a normal human.

There was no doubt he noticed my gaze falling upon him. Where the other Draíodóir displayed about as much emotion as marble statues, his eyes opened wide and he quickly averted his gaze.

It wasn't hard to figure out why.

My powers were such that offensive magic, the primary weapon of the Draíodóir, didn't do much to me. I had what was apparently an unprecedented resistance to it, on the outside anyway. If something was able to get past my external defenses, though, like, say for instance in pill form, then that was a different story altogether. While in the grip of said *medicine*, as I'd been a week ago on Christmas, my scent resembled that of a normal human as did the rest of my physical abilities. Strength, endurance, supercharged senses, they all went kaput while I was hopped up on his creation. Oh, and as a bonus they were also addictive, meaning the trip back down came with some nasty side effects, not the least of which was puking my guts up.

I knew why my parents had given those damnable pills to me, telling me they were medication for an illness I didn't have. Hell, I'd even made some peace with it. But here now, it was hard not to imagine wringing his neck for helping to perpetuate the bullshit that failure to take my pills like clockwork meant I was likely to die.

It would be so easy.

No. Tempting as it was, that was a reckoning for another day. And, truth be told, that reckoning might never come if Byrne played ball and helped me rescue my parents. If not...

I narrowed my eyes at him one last time, then turned my attention back to the rest of the Draíodóir – still standing where they'd appeared and all looking at me.

Call me crazy, but I had a feeling they were waiting for more than a simple New Year's greeting.

Oh well, when in Rome...

I adopted my best formal tone, hoping I didn't crack

up laughing in the middle of whatever came out of my mouth next.

Just don't try to say Draíodóir, nobody needs to hear you butcher that.

Fortunately, my cousin had given me an out, saving me from calling them something like a bunch of magic flinging motherfuckers – which would've likely garnered me few points with this crowd, humorless as they appeared.

"I bid welcome to the Summer Council of Crescentwood. Dark times have recently fallen upon us all, but today signifies the New Year and, with it, I hope we might have a chance to celebrate a new start. I invite you to these talks in the spirit of friendship and cooperation." I trailed off, then remembered something Chief Johnson had said to me and Cass last week. "May the council of the elder fae bless and watch over you all."

That last part seemed to do the trick. Auntie Fiona raised an eyebrow and nodded so slightly it would've been easy to miss. Guess I didn't completely fuck that up.

If things ever got back to normal again, I'd need to consider taking a semester or two with Bailey U's dramatic society.

I stepped aside and gestured to the door, glad to see none of the werewolves had decided to do anything stupid. "Right this way. Please feel free to help yourself to the refreshments."

Ugh, so lame. One second I was all formal and proper, the next I sounded like the hostess at the local Denny's. Oh well, one had to pick their battles.

Fiona stepped forward then turned to my cousin. "Mindy dear, would you be so good as to hold the door while Tamara leads the way inside?"

I almost asked why, since I was standing right there, but then it hit me. As the leader – reluctant or otherwise –

of the lycanthropes, they weren't about to turn their backs on me. Though I doubted my father would've pulled a cowardly double cross in such a situation, it was easy to believe Uncle Craig might've thought otherwise. And before him there was my grandfather Caleb. I hadn't known him, but the few tidbits I'd heard suggested he would've sooner gutted a Draíodóir than talk to one.

The burden of trust thus fell upon me. It was a risk I was more than willing to take for my parents – albeit, knowing I was resistant to magic didn't really hurt either.

"I'd be happy to lead the way."

That got them moving. Fiona approached and the others fell in line behind her, Dr. Byrne conveniently taking up the rear as if wishing to be as far from me as possible.

I realized there likely wouldn't be another opportunity like this once we were all inside, so I took a moment to ask Fiona, "How are you holding up?"

She actually smiled, although there was a sadness behind it. "It's very kind of you to ask, my dear," she replied. "As well as can be expected."

"Auntie Jezebel?"

"I'll send her your regards when we return. For now, I think it might be best if we got down to business." Before I could turn away, though, she added, "But if the opportunity presents itself later, I would very much like to … catch up."

A big smile threatened to overtake my face. It was probably premature, but I guess I'd gotten used to being dismissed as nothing more than an abomination.

"Don't act so surprised, girl," she said a moment later, falling back into her normal tone. "I'm far too old to jump to conclusions without at least hearing someone out first." And with that she made a shooing motion, telling me it was time to move my ass and get this party started.

The Draíodóir were far less trusting than the other side, probably because I wasn't in charge of jack shit as far as they were concerned. They only stopped glaring at the werewolves and helped themselves to some snacks once Mindy and I walked over to grab some, giving me an excuse to pop a few more cheese cubes before getting things started. *Ah, cheddar, is there anything you can't make better?*

As the others were filling their plates, I sauntered over to my former family physician. "Dr. Byrne."

"Hello," he replied nervously. The good doctor wasn't what one might call an intimidating man - only a few inches taller than me, with grey thinning hair, glasses, and a plump middle that suggested physical fitness wasn't at the top of his priority list. "It's ... been a while since your last checkup, Tamara."

"What can I say? My gastroparesis seems to have cleared right up. Quite the miracle for an incurable genetic disorder."

He lowered his voice as much as he dared. "I know you're probably a bit testy about that."

"Testy is a word for it."

"And I also know that an apology will only get me so far. But for what it's worth, I truly am sorry."

I narrowed my eyes, but the frightened look on his face went a long way toward defusing the situation. Besides, there was business to attend to. I started to turn away, but he caught my arm first.

"One more moment, please," he whispered, so low even I could barely hear him. "Assuming these talks go well, and I have no reason to doubt they will, perhaps we can sit down and talk at some point."

"Talk?"

"Yes. I may be the only person alive with some insight into your ... condition. It might not be much, but I would be happy to tell you all I know, both out of loyalty to your mother as well as my way of trying to make amends."

I wasn't really interested in any half-assed apologies, but that caught my attention. And it made sense, too. Sure, Byrne had acted as my doctor growing up, but he actually was a physician. He'd run blood tests, examined me, all of it. The very fact that he'd formulated my pills attested to that fact. I wasn't sure what he could possibly tell me that I didn't already know, but I wasn't foolish enough to throw that away. There was also one point in his favor. Whether through fear, loyalty, or something else, he'd kept my secret for twenty years.

"Okay. I'd like that."

"Me, too."

I disengaged from him before anything could ruin the moment and made my way over to the meeting table, where both parties were now settling down into their respective seats – Auntie Fiona claiming the spot opposite me, no doubt taking the lead for the Draíodóir contingent.

As the others took their seats – those in the middle visibly bristling to be in such close quarters to their ancient enemies – Fiona and I remained standing, facing each other, until finally she said, "Do offer the chief my regards for providing lunch."

I raised an eyebrow and smiled. "How do you know this wasn't all me?"

"You inherited a great many gifts from your mother, Tamara, but I know full well the ability to organize a soiree is not among them."

"Are you insulting our alpha, Fiona?" Earl asked, turning toward her.

"Why, Earl, you son of a bitch. How is an old coon-hound like you still alive?"

He let out a sound that was either a choked growl or a laugh, it was hard to tell which. "I'm like the commercial says. I take a lickin' but I keep on tickin'."

"So I see," Fiona replied. "Nevertheless, no. I was not insulting your alpha, merely passing on an observation about my niece."

An uncomfortable beat passed as all eyes on the table turned my way.

"Fine, you got me," I said, the smile never leaving my face. "I didn't even remember to bring the paper plates."

A few chuckles burst forth and almost immediately the tension ratcheted down in the room.

The ice broken and the first hurdle crossed, we all settled in, knowing there were likely several battles of far greater importance ahead of us.

10

"We'll invoke the wrath of Valdemar and force them to accept our demands."

"You be sure to have fun with that, Earl. After you're done being flayed alive, the rest of us can step in and offer our great queen a proper tithe."

"That's your plan, you want to buy Curtis's freedom?"

"We want to secure Lissa's release, not end up as fertilizer in Queen Brigid's garden. But if you're so intent on killing yourselves, be my guest."

"All right, enough!" I cried, tired of the bickering. We'd made progress over the last several hours, moving from one point to the next, but it was slow going as seemingly every detail had to be argued over.

I glanced over at the magic ... err ... chalkboard, for lack of a better term, to see where we stood.

Upon the start of the meeting, at Fiona's beckoning, one of her people, my second uncle Ronald, had conjured it. Much to Earl's consternation, it took over his note-taking duties — automatically inscribing compromises that were agreed upon and allowing us to tweak the language until both sides were happy.

Made me wish I had one of those back at school.

Already we'd agreed on several points, albeit far more of them were aimed at my parents' rescue than a lasting peace. That was fine by me. Let them take over that part once we got them back. I was no diplomat, nor did I have any plans to change my major anytime soon.

As expected, Crescentwood was chosen as the place where we'd conduct the ceremony to breach the walls of reality. Thankfully, Cass didn't try to counter by offering up the sacred glade in the hollows. Hell, if anything, she'd remained silent throughout that entire discussion. Thank goodness, too. Though ostensibly it might have been a better choice, being a thin spot between worlds, I had no real interest in stepping foot inside it again anytime soon.

Considering what that one-armed shape-shifting asshole had told me the other day, it was probably safer to do it in Draíodóir territory anyway.

Seven in total, a number of power according to my great aunt, would be permitted to cross over into the land of the fae queen – enough to act as emissaries, but not so large as to be mistaken for a war party. Three from each side and me.

A few on the other end of the table argued against that, claiming it would unfairly tip the delegation in the lycanthropes' favor, a sticking point they didn't seem keen to drop as it took us a fucking hour to get past it. However, Mindy and I were able to argue that I'd be there less as the werewolf alpha and more representing both sides – as a hybrid between the races. Eventually, enough of the Draíodóir conceded, silencing the dissent and allowing us to move on.

From there, the discussion turned to how many werewolves would be allowed in Crescentwood, what kind of protection would be afforded them, that sort of thing. That ate up another good hour until both parties were satisfied, the wording on the board changing perhaps a dozen times until no more objections were raised.

All things considered, it gave me a new appreciation for diplomats. I couldn't imagine trying to do this for a living and not going insane – or inadvertently causing a war.

Now, the question on the table was how to go about securing my parents' safe release. Earl and his buddies seemed in favor of strong-arm tactics, which didn't strike me as the smartest of solutions. Sure, I'd never met this Brigid chick, but the Draíodóir pretty much worshipped her as a god. And, as was already pointed out, we weren't going in there with enough manpower to act as a strike team. That was the whole point, to look non-threatening.

Their idea of invoking Valdemar struck me as some mix of pure fantasy and batshit madness. At worst, we'd be standing there hoping a bunch of pissed off fairy lords didn't call our bluff. Best case scenario wasn't much better, though. What if Valdemar actually showed up and decided to start shit, with us caught in the middle?

And yes, the fact that I actually considered that a possibility said a lot about how far down this rabbit hole I'd gone.

Needless to say, this was one area where I found myself siding with the opposing team.

"What kind of tithe?" I asked.

"Surely you can't be serious," Earl replied. "You wish for us, a proud warrior race, to prostrate ourselves and offer up a reward for the wicked deed done to one of our own?"

I was just about to tell him to not call me Shirley, when another voice answered from behind me ... a skeevy little preteen voice that was supposed to fucking stay upstairs.

"If it'll get my parents back, why not?"

All eyes in the room turned toward the top of the staircase, where Chris could be seen peeking down at us.

Oh boy.

After a beat, I felt some of those eyes – Cass's included – turn toward me.

I shrugged at her. "I couldn't find a sitter."

"Christopher," Fiona admonished, standing up. "What did your parents teach you about interrupting your elders?"

"Sorry, Auntie Fi," he replied.

"I thought you were going to stay upstairs," I said through gritted teeth, envisioning beating him over the head with one of his game systems, "where nobody could see you."

"I'm out of soda."

I was sorely tempted to drag him upstairs and give him a good long drink out of the toilet, but then David spoke up.

"Why do you smell like..."

"Don't start," I warned, cutting him off.

"But anyway," Chris continued, now that the cat was most definitely out of the bag, "ransoming prisoners was a pretty common thing throughout history, especially for anyone holding rank. There was no shame to it. It was just considered business – a fair trade of something you wanted for something they wanted. So why don't we give them something they want rather than argue about it?"

"Get your soda and go back upstairs," I snapped, before turning to the rest of the table, my face redder than I would've liked. Even so, the little history nerd had possibly helped a bit. "He has a point. This isn't about shame or honor. If anything, the dishonor was in the way my parents – Curtis and Lissa – were captured."

"And since that party has been ... dealt with," Fiona added, "honor is satisfied, and we should instead work on rescuing our fellows in the most expeditious manner possible."

"Exactly," I replied, glad she didn't ask for details as to how my aunt had been *dealt with*. Despite the fact that she'd betrayed us in the worst possible way, the memory of quite literally beating my Aunt Carly to death was not something I cared to relive. "So how about it? Can we focus on that?"

Earl narrowed his eyes for a moment, but then asked, "Is there anyone else you're hiding upstairs?"

It was all I could do to keep my eyes from rolling out of my head. "No. That's it. And, may I add, apologies ... to our honored guests for not disclosing this sooner."

That was close. I almost apologized to the pack, a big no no.

Earl let out a sigh then turned to Fiona. "Very well. As our esteemed alpha has so declared, what tithe do you think would..."

"And what makes you think you have anything they want?" a disturbingly familiar voice called from the direction of the staircase.

What the?!

"Um, Tamara," Chris stammered.

I turned to find him at the foot of the stairs, looking up. As footsteps sounded from above, he began to back away.

Once again, all eyes turned in that direction.

Everyone had been caught off guard to learn Chris was here, but I sincerely doubted any of them were more surprised than me when my best friend in this world walked down from the second floor and turned to face us.

"Riva?" The word was little more than a whisper on my lips. Quickly turning to my brother, I asked, "How did she get up there?"

It was perhaps the stupidest thing I could've said, outside of incoherent babbling, but I was desperately hoping to hear a tale of her showing up with a ladder and him opening a window.

Sadly, Chris was far too pale for me to think this was some dumbass surprise on his part. "She wasn't up there. I – I swear it."

"For Christ's sake, Tamara," Fiona said, a huff of annoyance in her voice, "this isn't Who Wants to be a Millionaire. This is a sacred gathering. You can't just stuff as many damned lifelines as you want upstairs."

"I didn't, I..." I took a deep breath, gathering what few wits I had left, which wasn't much at the moment. Around me, the werewolves were starting to get agitated. I could see fangs descending among some of their number, David included. First and foremost, I needed to reestablish control. "That's enough. Stand down, all of you. I mean it!"

"You would be wise to heed your ... alpha."

I turned back toward Riva. "Same goes for you. Zip it for now." Then I addressed the rest. "This meeting is in recess until I can figure this out. Any objections?"

Thankfully, there were none.

I stood and nodded toward both David and Cass. "Keep the peace."

Then, before either of them could object, I walked over to Riva, grabbed her by the arm, and dragged her past the kitchen and into the back parlor. On the way, I threw my brother a quick, "Go back upstairs ... and make sure nobody else is up there."

"Where the hell have you been the last week and how did you get up there?" I asked, a second before my higher brain functions registered just how not right this all was.

Guess the stress of the day had made me a little slow on the uptake. Not only had my friend, someone who usually didn't like standing on a chair to change a light-bulb, somehow scaled the second story of a house in order to make a dramatic entrance, but she wasn't dressed for the adventure either.

It was January in northern Pennsylvania. That meant it was cold as a witch's – err, a well digger's shovel anyway. We're talking well below freezing. Yet Riva stood before me as if she were on spring break in Cancun. Her black hair hung freely around her shoulders and she wore a simple white sundress. It was a good look for her. Too bad it was horseshit insane for this time of year. Even crazier was the fact that she was barefoot.

Fuck all that. My friend was the type to start pulling sweaters out of storage once late August gave way to September.

A part of me wanted to believe it was that doppel-ganger again, here to fuck with me. Problem with that theory was I'd seen this look on Riva before. The memory of it sent a chill down my spine.

Back in the sacred glade, after I'd spilled my aunt's blood upon the eternally hungry ground of that damnable place, things had gotten even weirder. Riva had appeared, dressed as she was now, but it hadn't been my friend. It had been something else, something which had appeared to me twice before, during times of great stress – mostly to berate me for being a disappointment.

The first time it had happened I'd been sure I was hallucinating, but the second time had solidified that I was seeing something strange and unworldly, likely taking on a form my mind could understand without cracking like an egg.

"Only partially correct," she said, seeming to pull the question straight out of my head. "Your mind is capable of withstanding a great deal more, as you shall come to learn."

I had no idea what that meant, nor did I really care. The fact of how she looked, along with her annoying ability to read my mind, told me the Riva before me was no mere shapeshifter, although a part of me considered decking her just to be certain.

"That would be ... ill advised."

So much for that theory. "Can you please stop doing that?"

She shrugged, a gesture that suggested she'd do as I asked but only so long as it amused her.

"You're not Riva."

"What I am is not your concern ... at least not for the moment."

"It is as long as you're wearing her face."

"Would you prefer I wear another?" she, or *it* asked with a lopsided grin that was so much my friend it almost hurt. "One of the others in this domicile perhaps?"

"Is that a threat?"

"Merely an offer for your benefit."

"Hold on," I said. "My benefit?"

"You are the one who freed us. Thus, we are happy to cater to your desires, within reason of course." Creepy Possessed Riva stepped past me and looked out the back window toward the empty field beyond. Well, not completely empty. I could just barely make out a set of angled barn doors a ways out that led down to the Crendels' bomb shelter.

That was far less my concern, though, than was the fact I had a clear head. Both times before when she'd appeared to me, I'd been a bit short of possessing my full faculties. Yet here I was, and here she was, too, in broad daylight and with nary a knock upside my noggin to convince me I'd gone loopy.

I stepped behind her and reached out, my hand pausing mere inches from her shoulder.

"It is okay. You may, if you so wish," Possessed Riva said without turning to face me.

I didn't really wish, but I kind of had to. I placed a hand on her shoulder, fully expecting it to go through and for her to dissolve into nothing more than mist. But what was there was solid, real, *alive*.

"Life and death are merely labels given by species who do not understand the intricacies of the multiverse."

"The multiverse?"

"Oh, yes. An infinite cosmos of realities. Some are but a tiny decision away from this one – little more than the difference between choosing which path to follow in the forest. Others are more alien than you could hope to comprehend. Yet I see them all – a brother reunited with a sister he thought long dead, an unsuspecting man purchasing a cursed item from a shop that wasn't there yesterday, a lowly vampire unaware that he is about to come into conflict with a god."

"Okay, and all of that means what to me?"

"Nothing. Those are other worlds, other possibilities, realities you cannot hope to touch, save perhaps in your dreams when your consciousness is allowed to roam free of its mortal coil."

"But you can?"

She glanced over her shoulder at me, one eyebrow raised. "No ... and yes."

"Well, that clears things up."

"For longer than your species, either of them, could possibly fathom, we have existed *outside*, able to peer through the windows of worlds but forbidden to step through."

Please don't say until I mucked things up.

Sadly, my cerebral cortex was apparently nothing more than an open book to the thing wearing my friend's face. She turned toward me with a knowing grin, answering my question without saying a word.

"Technically that was Jerry's fault," I said, mentioning my late unlamented fiancé, who had first shown me that damned glade ... and subsequently been devoured by it after I'd been forced to kill him.

"Destiny does not force. It merely nudges, offers possibilities."

God, this was getting creepy.

"And I am much more than simply your friend's visage."

"What do you mean by that?"

Sadly, Possessed Riva seemed inclined to pick which questions she answered and which she merely raised a bemused eyebrow at. Unsurprisingly, the mental connection we seemed to share only worked in one direction, putting me at a major disadvantage.

Creepy Riva continued to stare at me, her head inclined slightly as if waiting for me to figure something out. Grrr! I fucking hated riddles. I barely had the patience for knock-knock jokes and here Riva was ... wait, Riva!

"I haven't seen her since..."

The grin on this thing's face widened. All at once, I got a sinking sensation that my nickname for her – Creepy Possessed Riva – was way more on point than I would've ever hoped.

"I see you begin to understand."

No! It can't be. Why her?

"I believe you mortals have an apt response for such a question. Why not?"

Okay, that was kinda dickish. That aside, though, the implications were not good. Even worse, this was way out of my wheelhouse. Punching someone in the face was something I could handle, but an exorcism? But maybe it didn't need to be my thing, especially when right in the next room were a bunch of...

No! I quickly switched mental radios, not wanting the thing wearing my friend's body to pick up on my thoughts.

Riva's expression finally changed to something other than bemused. "I do not understand."

Now it was my turn to grin as I backed up, continuing to focus on things other than what I had planned.

I was only a few steps away when the door was opened from the kitchen side.

"Sorry to interrupt," David said from behind me, "but the natives are starting to get restless."

Riva glanced between me and my beta. "Ah, I believe I understand now. This is the young lycanthrope you are envisioning so vigorously mating with."

Oh crap! I knew I should've gone with a Lady Gaga album.

"Is your plan to see whether this body is interested in joining your coupling?"

My face instantly turned beet red. "Um, no."

"Because if so," Possessed Riva said, taking a step forward, "I sense this vessel's spirit would be inclined to acquiesce to such a novel experience."

"Is ... um ... everything okay?" David asked.

"Yeah," Cass replied, sounding as if she were directly behind him. "Because this sounds more like something that should be saved for the victory celebration."

I spun, narrowing my eyes, to see not only them but my cousin Mindy as well. Oh great. Just what I needed, an audience as my pervy fantasies were broadcast to the room.

My back turned to the thing inquiring about a werewolf threesome, I looked at Cass and mouthed the words that I hoped would spur her to action.

"*That's not Riva.*"

11

ass looked confused for a moment, but then the desperation in my eyes must've finally hit home.

Now to hope that Possessed Riva was only attuned to my wavelength. That seemed a rather thin hope, especially since I had no idea who or what was inside of her. So, I hedged my bets by turning up the volume on my mental radio, much as I would probably regret it.

"What is a reverse cowgirl?" she asked a few seconds later.

Oh yeah, definitely going to regret that.

I locked eyes with David, practically daring him to say shit in front of his alpha. Damn. I really needed to think of something – *anything* – else.

"Such an interesting concern for a time such as this," Possessed Riva remarked. "Worrying whether your recent obsession with procreation is a side-effect of your unique biology or due to your current dry spell. I'm curious. Why would the weather of this world play into these matters?"

"Um, it's just a saying."

"I see. And is wondering if you're turning into little more than a bitch in heat a similar such colloquialism?"

"Not a word," I snapped at David while, behind him, Cass grabbed my cousin's arm and dragged her away – hopefully not starting a war in the process, as they were technically sworn enemies. I wasn't really worried about Mindy so much as the rest of the Draíodóir taking it the wrong way, but there wasn't much else I could do about it. Not with...

"Mortals and their scheming. So ... pedestrian."

Shit! Maybe I should've stuck with the x-rated thoughts.

"Saving my parents is the only scheme I'm interested in," I said, glancing over my shoulder at the thing wearing my friend's face. "And it's a scheme that you're currently interrupting."

Oh, that's smart, mouthing off to an eternal being from beyond our world.

On the flipside, when in doubt, work with what you know.

I nodded at David and, to his credit, he merely nodded back once then turned and walked out of the room.

"You're welcome to watch the proceedings if you wish." I followed him, curious to see if Possessed Riva would fall in step as I continued to blast out mental x-rated white noise at full volume.

If she didn't, then I wasn't sure what we'd be left with – maybe ordering the lycanthropes to bum rush her while keeping our fingers crossed.

And then what?

That was a good question. This ... whatever it was, had heavily implied that it was possessing my friend, but what if that was nothing but a lie? The way Possessed Riva had, in the past, played word games told me that I should take everything she said with a grain of salt.

"I am curious as to the phrase hung like a horse," Creepy Riva said from right behind me, apparently following my lead. "One would think a lycanthrope's genitals would be more synonymous with a..."

"Care for any refreshments?" I asked over my shoulder, loudly. "There's plenty."

I expected for this creature, whatever it was, to tell me that she required no sustenance other than whatever the universe gave her, or some such fantasy bullshit. So, I was surprised to turn and find her picking up a cranberry croissant.

"I believe this body enjoys this particular confectionary."

She was right. Riva was partial to them. I mean, sure, she could've plucked that knowledge from my subconscious, although that seemed an oddly specific memory to dredge up in the space of the three seconds it took for us to step out of the parlor.

It didn't really matter either way as I turned to find Auntie Fiona and the Draíodóir mobilized in front of the meeting table.

Yes!

The lycanthropes were likewise spread out – fangs and claws on display, although none had fully transformed yet. Probably a good thing because I had a feeling the rest of the day might be a tad awkward if they were all seated at the table bare-assed.

Even so, it brought a lump to my throat. Sure, it would probably only last for minutes at most, but for the moment the Draíodóir and werewolves were standing together side by side against a mutual unknown.

"I thought you said the only scheme you were interested in was saving your parents," Possessed Riva casually said, continuing to butter her croissant as if nothing out of the ordinary were going on.

I stepped out of the line of fire and finally dropped the litany of salacious thoughts I'd been feeding her. Good thing, too, because it was starting to get hot in here. "Mostly. But don't think I wouldn't do anything to save my friend as well."

Possessed Riva took a bite out of her pastry and raised one eyebrow in an unalarmed fashion – a decisively non-Rivalike expression in the face of so much supernatural mojo.

"I command you to identify yourself in the name of Queen Brigid and her most holy court," Fiona barked.

In return, our *guest* continued to nonchalantly eat her croissant. Needless to say, I was feeling the tension in the room rise ever so slightly.

I wasn't alone either. There came the sound of fabric tearing. The werewolves were getting into the act. Though Cass herself was keeping it strictly to fangs, the others were already in the act of transforming. Next to her, David burst forth from his clothes, but in far less of a Chippendales way. His whole body expanded, brown fur covering him as he changed.

Wait, brown fur?

When David was finished, he was big – no more than a hair away from seven feet, if that. But he wasn't huge. The blessing of Valdemar somehow empowered normal lycanthropes into what I'd come to call mega-wolves, giving them jet black fur and adding at least another foot to their height. Everything about them became more exaggerated, more terrifying. In short, they were hard to miss. David, in his wolf form, was impressive, but he wasn't mega-impressive.

Despite the fact that we'd ratcheted up to DEFCON 2, I turned to Cass, a questioning look on my face. It was neither the time nor place for explanations and I guess she understood that better than me, because she gave me a single shake of her head.

Or at least that's all she was able to do before Fiona spoke again.

"I am Fiona McGillis of the Draíodóir, elder of the Summer Council of Crescentwood. You will not ignore me. *Fàinne Dé!*"

She screamed that last part in that strange triple voice her people liked to use. It was pretty damned intimidating, but there was a lot more to it than that. It was how they tapped into their magic, or so I assumed. Either way, when you heard that you knew something nasty was about to happen.

The floor beneath Riva lit up in a series of concentric circles with what appeared to be glowing sigils within. The circles flashed brilliant white then winked out, although a shimmer remained in the air around my possessed friend.

Though I'd never heard that spell before, I'd seen enough episodes of Supernatural to guess this was their version of a devil's trap.

"I have no quarrel with you, scion of the Seelie court," Possessed Riva said. "However, you are rapidly testing my patience."

"As you test mine," Fiona replied. "Brother, if you will."

Dr. Byrne stepped forward. He threw one quick glance at me, as if afraid I might use this as an excuse to kick his ass. But he didn't have anything to worry about there. He wasn't off the hook in my book, and he'd certainly be eating fist if whatever he did next hurt a single hair on my friend's hair. But thankfully, he seemed more inclined to follow through on my aunt's command.

"*Bòid làidir,*" he cried in that triple voice. "You are compelled to answer, whether you be fae or demon!"

And just like that we'd graduated from Supernatural to The Exorcist.

To either side of the Draíodóir, werewolves were looking like they were up in arms, something the remaining mages were definitely noticing, splitting their attention between their ancient enemies and my possessed friend. Fortunately, the wolves seemed focused on the newcomer in our midst. If that changed, I'd be forced to step in. For now, though...

"What the hell's going on?"

I glanced up to find my brother once again on the stairs. Talk about bad timing. Guess we were reaching the point where I'd need to set him up with a laptop full of porn, as video games apparently weren't as engrossing as they once were. Ah, little pervs. They grow up so fast. Nevertheless, I didn't need that shit at this moment.

"Not now," I barked at him. "Get back upstairs and stay there. I mean it!"

I put some extra menace into my voice, for one fleeting moment sounding disturbingly like our mother. Freaky as that was, it was necessary. The last thing I wanted was him getting curious and coming back down here again. The two warring parties were already on edge. Though they'd already seen Chris, I didn't want to risk one of them getting startled and taking a potshot at him. If so, this whole thing would end really badly.

Thankfully, that didn't appear to be on the docket. My brother might be a dumbass when it suited him, but he'd been indoctrinated into this world via trial by fire. He knew how real and dangerous it could be.

It was the space of barely a second for him to hightail it back up to his room, the door slamming shut a moment later.

In that time, apparently nothing much changed.

"I compel you to speak!" Dr. Byrne again commanded. "You cannot disobey. You must..."

The words abruptly died on his tongue as Riva made the barest of motions with the hand not holding the croissant.

For a moment, I thought she might've done some kind of counter spell to silence him ... and then the top half of his head slid off, landing on the floor with a hollow *thok*.

There was no blood, at first anyway, no slash of a blade, no tearing of flesh. It was as if she'd merely unglued his head right above the bottom jaw.

The rest of him stood there for a few seconds, his tongue continuing to flap freely now that it had no mouth to contain it. And then he simply collapsed to the floor, staining the hardwood red as his life's blood proceeded to pour out of him.

To David and Earl's credit, they reacted far faster than anyone else. The rest of us, myself included, were still processing what had happened – the murder done so casually that it was almost surreal. But the two lycanthropes – my beta and the elder wolf – both charged forward without hesitation ... or at least tried to.

They both made it about two steps, when Possessed Riva made another gesture.

It was barely anything, a mere clench of her fist, but their momentum was halted and reversed in the space of an instant. Fast as they'd reacted, they were sent flying back at twice that speed, to crash into the wallboards of the living room. Both wolves crumbled to the floor amidst a shower of wood and plaster.

It was a hard hit, but thankfully both appeared to have fared better than the poor doctor.

"A warning," Possessed Riva said. "That one presumed to hold authority over me. He has since been corrected. I would caution any of you against trying again, lest you test my patience as well."

She moved as if to take a step forward, at which point my aunt, still holding an air of authority despite everything, said, "You will come no further. The spirit ring binds you in place. It..."

Riva stepped through the shimmer as if it weren't there, the slightest smirk upon her face. "We are no mere imps, summoned for your amusement. Your wards hold no power over us now that we are free. But again, I shall offer this boon of advice. I have no quarrel here, with either Draíodóir or lycanthrope. Give me no cause to act and I shall do so in kind ... for now."

Possessed Riva seemed to have some serious pronoun issues, but that was probably the least of our problems.

The tension in the room was thick enough that one could have carved it up and served it for dinner. To the credit of all present, no one was screaming, even if I'm pretty sure most of us wanted to after seeing what she'd done to Dr. Byrne. Either they were all used to the violence of this strange supernatural underworld or were all in shock.

As for me, it was a little bit from the first column, and a lot from the second.

Whatever the case, I saw in all of their eyes that this wasn't a stalemate that would last. Fear, terror, confusion, all of that and more could be seen on the faces of those present. I had a feeling we were seconds away at most from half the beings in the room running for the door, while the rest attacked – whether it be with claws or killing magic.

Normally, I wouldn't have given odds to anything standing in the way of a combined werewolf and Draíodóir offensive, me included. However, Riva had just shrugged off two spells as if they were nothing and counterattacked with less effort than she'd put into buttering a roll.

If more bloodshed was to be avoided here, someone would need to do something, and I had a feeling fate was waiting for me to raise my hand.

"You're right," I said, taking a cautious step toward the entity wearing my friend's face. "You have no quarrel with them. Your quarrel's entirely with me, isn't it? After all, why show up here otherwise?"

"Quarrel?" Riva asked, sounding genuinely surprised. "If anything, you have our gratitude, fleeting though it might be."

Oh great. That's just what the rest of the room needed to hear: that whatever was happening was somehow my fault. A small portion of me found myself thinking that having my head unzipped like Dr. Byrne's might be the kinder fate compared to whatever happened next.

"What an odd thing to wish for," Possessed Riva said, plucking the thought from my mind as if it were a grape on the vine. "Is that what you truly desire?"

Oh, shit! I figured I'd best answer quickly and with no snark. This creature seemed to have no sense of subtext when it came to these things. "No. That's just what we call ... um, idle brain chatter."

"So, your desire remains the same, to save your parents?"

"And my friend," I added.

Possessed Riva appeared to consider this for a moment before giving me a single nod. "So be it."

In the same instant she spoke, the kitchen, the house, everything in my reality, it all vaporized around me – leaving nothing but an infinite void of emptiness.

12

For what seemed like an eternity, I was surrounded by an infinite expanse of nothing. No sight, no sound, nothing except an endless haze of grey. It was as if the world around me had been erased, condemning me to float forever in the endless void.

Then, all at once, reality started to reform around me. I could hear sounds again, could take a breath, could see shapes starting to take form where the nothingness had been.

Then, a moment later, I found myself wishing for the nothingness to take me back.

What appeared around me was like nothing I'd ever seen before or wanted to see. It was like waking up in an Escher painting, spawned from a night of drinking Drāno and shoe polish.

The ground was an undulating mass of contrasting colors that made my stomach lurch. Misshapen trees seemed to grow from it, combining with others both near and far, though it was impossible to tell distance in this hellscape. The putridly shaded sky both seemed infinitely above me yet, at the same time, felt as if I could reach out and grab a passing cloud – not that I wanted to, as they squirmed in the air like they were alive.

It was a nightmare of bizarre colors, shapes, and non-Euclidian geometry ... and I wasn't alone in it.

Possessed Riva stood there with me, somehow only a few feet away, yet also at the very edge of the horizon – her body contorted and stretched as if she'd been yanked through Satan's taffy puller. She had to be in a world of pain, her mind shattering piece by piece, as mine surely was, but the look on her grossly elongated, yet somehow still symmetrical face was one of nothing more than confusion.

"Bent? Are you okay?"

I opened my mouth, uncertain how to answer, or if I even could. It was as if the bottom half of my jaw fell away, melding into the ground at my feet.

Perhaps it was a good thing that I couldn't speak, because what wanted to escape from my vocal cords was more inarticulate shriek than anything, especially at what I saw approaching us from beyond where my friend stood. The creature, a writhing mass of endless tentacles and malevolent eyes, yet with no body to speak of, appeared to be miles away. Yet when it reached one of its nightmare appendages toward me, I was horrified to find it right in front of my face.

I hadn't read much Lovecraft in my life. That trippy ass horror shit wasn't normally my cup of tea, but a few years back – in a bid to finish out my summer reading assignments – I'd skimmed through a few of his short stories. Now, I wasn't sure whether to be grateful or horrified that I had. It was as if the creature had stepped foot, or tentacle, from one of those tales, an undulating mass with no rhyme nor reason save to strip my sanity away like the last bit of meat on a rack of ribs.

This was it. I could feel myself losing my grip as it

approached. Werewolves, Draíodóir, magic, all of that had been strange and terrifying when I'd first learned of it, but at least it made sense in a twisted sort of way. This, all of it, was *wrong!*

The creature's tentacle, short, yet also a thousand miles long, grazed my arm. Its revolting flesh rippled and deformed as it brushed against me, somehow colder than anything I had ever felt before. And in that moment I understood true madness, finally letting loose with the scream that I desperately wanted to make.

"Holy shit! Are you all right?"

In the space of an instant, the nightmare receded, replaced by ... paradise? Wrong became right as I blinked and realized the cyclopean nightmare I'd appeared in was nothing of the sort. Instead, I was standing in what could probably have passed for the Garden of Eden in some big budget remake of the Old Testament.

Grass, so green it was as if they were made of emeralds, covered the ground. Trees surrounded us, all of them perfectly formed and full of life. Flowers bloomed all around, a myriad of colors and varieties that would've put my mother's rose bushes to shame on their best day.

Gone was Squidward's nightmare cousin and in its place stood a small humanoid creature, roughly thigh high to me. It was thin with sharp features. Delicate wings protruded from its back, giving it a pixie-like quality, or it would have had the creature not been dressed so bizarrely. Despite its fairy tale visage, its wardrobe appeared to be comprised of things picked at random from the local Goodwill box, topping it all off with an oversized turban, of all things, lying crookedly upon its head which...

"Earth to Bent."

I took my eyes off the pixie thing for a moment to find Possessed Riva was somehow still here. I had no clue what she'd done to me, but right at that moment I was still too dazed for silly things like tact, common sense, or remembering how she'd killed Dr. Byrne with a simple wave of her fingers.

Before she could so much as twitch, I grabbed her by the throat and shoved her against the nearest tree – a sapling that seemed to be some bizarre hybrid between a cherry blossom and a douglas fir. "What did you do?"

"B ... buh...," she sputtered.

"Answer me! Where am I? Where are my parents? And what did you do to my friend?!"

"B ... buh... Bent..."

"What?"

"Y... y-you're ... c-choking..."

Oh, yeah. First rule of interrogation. It was hard to get answers when you were crushing someone's windpipe. I let up ever so slightly, allowing her to draw a breath. "Now, if you so much as look at me wrong, I'm going to see what cracks first, this tree or your skull."

"It's ... m-me, Bent."

"I know. You're that thing that came through the, what did you call it, the Window of Worlds."

"No," she replied, reaching up and grabbing hold of my wrist, as if to try and free herself. Yeah, good luck with that. "I'm your ... friend ... Riva."

I was about to slam her head into the bark again for good measure, when I remembered that she'd sent two werewolves flying with the barest of gestures. Forcing me to back off should've been short work at most. Sure, I was resistant to magic, so maybe that played into it, but before, back at the Crendel place, she hadn't shown even the barest hint that she was afraid of me ... unlike now.

Was it possible?

I flooded my thoughts with misdirection ... imagining a moonlit beach, a blanket spread out on the sand, and a naked Zac Efron. "How did I lose my virginity?"

"What?!"

I tightened my grip again. "Answer the question."

Possessed Riva nodded frantically, fear etched onto her face. "Junior Prom. It was in the backseat of Jeff Schlesinger's Camry."

I continued to focus on Zac and all the screaming orgasms he was giving me. Goddamn, I really was like a bitch in heat lately. "And what did I say about it?"

"You called it the most anticlimaxic two minutes of your life, which is still not a word by the way."

That was ... actually right on the money. Of course, it was possible Possessed Riva also had access to regular Riva's memories. "Tell me what I'm thinking right now."

"What?"

"Tell me!"

"I have no fucking idea. I'm not a goddamned mind reader. I don't even know how I got here or even where here is."

I was debating what to do next. A part of me wanted to believe her, but another part insisted that all I was doing was duping myself with wishful thinking. However, before I could do anything more, movement registered in my periphery. That weird pixie guy was walking toward us.

He got to within ten feet then opened his mouth. What came out was an ear-shattering screech like nothing I'd ever heard before.

All at once, strangling the creature possessing my best friend was a minor issue compared to covering my ears and keeping my brains from leaking out.

The screech not only set my teeth rattling, but upended my equilibrium as well, dropping me to one knee. It was made ten times worse thanks to my overcharged sense of hearing. The Draíodóir could've learned a thing or two from this creature. In the space of a second, it had done what most of their magic would've failed to accomplish, leave me utterly helpless.

The screech continued until, the next thing I knew, I was screaming too, but this was no battle cry of defiance. It was pure unadulterated pain and...

And then it passed as the creature stopped its insane warbling. I wasn't sure whether it thought me out of the fight and easy prey – not far from the truth – or something else. Either way it ceased, leaving my ears ringing and me with a headache that would probably require half a bottle of aspirin to quell.

"Holy shit. Are you all right, Bent?"

Despite me nearly embedding her skull into a tree trunk, Riva was by my side trying to help me up. Although, the fact that she wasn't down on her knees in pain, too, wasn't lost upon me.

"I knew you were lying," I gasped, the world still spinning around me.

"Lying about what?" she asked.

"H-how did you not feel that?"

"Feel what?"

"That ... sonic attack."

"What sonic attack?"

"From ... that thing!" Growing more frustrated by the second, I balled my fist, preparing to let fly with my rage, when the pixie creature stepped forward again.

"You gleefing stupid or something?" it asked in gruff but understandable English. "I just asked if there was a problem, being that you two looked like you were trying to kill each other? Don't get me wrong, none of my business, but if so, I hope you don't mind if I scavenge your corpses."

"What?" I asked, pushing myself to my feet. Riva tried to help me, but I waved her off. "B-but you screeched at us."

"No, he didn't," Riva said. "I heard him just fine ... um ... whatever he is."

Riva's voice cracked a bit on that last part, sounding disturbingly like my friend. Despite myself, I hesitated before pummeling her again.

She must've seen the indecision in my face because she backed up a step. "No offense, Bent, but I'm seriously starting to freak out here. So, if you can maybe ... not kick my ass, I'd really appreciate it."

Somehow ignoring the fact that I was on an alien world, mere feet from an alien being who'd just asked if he could loot my corpse, I turned to face Riva, wanting to believe her but not daring to. "How do I know you're you and not that thing?"

She shook her head. "I have no idea. Maybe ask me some marry, fuck, kill questions? I don't know. I mean, I don't think that, whatever it was, could talk like me if it tried."

She did sort of have a point. Possessed Riva was both formal yet infuriatingly naïve at the same time. Wait ... hold on. "You remember that?" The pixie guy opened his mouth again, but I held up a hand. "Just give us a minute here, okay?"

"Whatever the gleef."

"I don't know," Riva replied. "Sort of. I mean, it's kind of like being asleep and dreaming about someone else. All I know is I've been dreaming about her a lot lately. Talks in third person, acts like her shit doesn't stink and..." She looked down at herself. "And dresses like this!" She leaned in and lowered her voice. "I'm not checking in front of present company, but I'm pretty sure things are commando beneath this skirt."

She sure as hell sounded like my Riva. I realized at some point during the last few minutes I'd dropped the possessed part from my thinking of her. "You're really you, aren't you?"

"Yeah, I'm me. At least I think I am, anyway."

All at once, my vision became blurry, but it had nothing to do with magic or teleportation. I stepped in and grabbed my best friend in the biggest hug I could give her, short of crushing her to pulp. "You have no idea how much I missed you."

"I missed you, too. Sorry I haven't been around much lately. This is going to sound seriously lame, but ... I don't think I've been myself."

"It's ... understandable, strangely enough." I pulled back and wiped my eyes. "Although, just for the record, if you're lying to me and still possessed, I'm going to crush your head like a tube of toothpaste."

Riva blinked at me for a few seconds before answering.

"All things considered, sounds ... fair, I guess."

13

"So, I take it you two aren't going to kill each other?"

I spun back toward the strangely dressed creature, suddenly remembering it was there, its delicate wings fluttering in what I could only call an annoyed manner. "Sorry. Um, Mr. or Ms..."

"Ain't no mister," it replied. "Titles and things like that are for the gleefing sidhe, of which I ain't one."

"That made absolutely no sense."

"Really?" it asked. "That's strange. Her high and mightiness put a spell on this place centuries ago, for anything coming or going. All sights, sounds, and speech are supposed to instantly conform to a visitor's expectations. But if it's on the fritz than you have no gleefing idea what I'm saying anyway, so..."

"Not that. I can understand you just fine."

"Same here," Riva said.

"It's just that I didn't quite understand *what* you said."

The creature raised one hairless brow at me. "And yet you say I'm the one who makes no sense."

I held up my hands. "Okay, let's back up a second. You

said this place was enchanted so that things appear how we want them to?"

"Exactly. Makes things easier all around. Before that, from what I hear, you daoine types would visit every so often, only for your brains to instantly explode out your eye holes. Made a real mess. So her highness cast an enchantment across the entirety of the Garden to keep your fragile minds from blowing out. Thankfully, it works both ways, otherwise I'd probably upchuck my breakfast looking at whatever your true forms are."

I remembered back to the strange nightmare of bizarre shapes and angles I'd seen upon appearing here ... or that I thought I'd seen. It was weird, but the memory was already fading, becoming fuzzy, making me wonder if I'd merely hallucinated it.

"Just out of curiosity," I asked Riva, "did you see anything strange when you first, I dunno, woke up here?"

"Are you kidding? This whole place is strange. I mean, we're talking to a freaking fairy right now."

"I meant stranger than that."

"Like you going nuts and trying to pulp my skull?"

"Never mind." I turned back to our new acquaintance. "Go on."

"Yeah, I was just saying we don't get a lot of daoine around here these days, but those who do show up at least don't go instantly insane and choke to death on their own tongues."

"Daoine?"

"Yeah. That's what you fleshbags are."

"So, a girl?"

"Whatever. If that's what you want to call yourself, that's fine by me."

"I'm one, too, by the way," Riva added, giving me a look that said she was just barely holding it together.

"As if that won't get confusing fast," the pixie said. "Anyway, you two can call me Grunge."

"Did you just say Grunge?"

"Yep," he replied proudly. "They used to call me Gullysnipe, but then a couple years back some drunken Draíodóir summoned me to your world. Place was a dump, but he had the most gleefing awesome music playing from this metal box thing."

"You mean a stereo?"

"No, I think it was some kind of crazy prison. The Draíodóir said its name was Alice and he kept it in chains for some reason. I was, of course, concerned as to what this Alice did to tolph him off, but damn the music it made was so good that I didn't care. He kept calling it grunge, so when I got back I decided that's who I was gonna be. Gotta say, it also got me interested in you daoine and your world. Before that, I couldn't have given a tragnok's dunghole about you lot. But since that day I've been collecting bits and pieces of daoine culture ever since."

"Like what?" Riva asked.

Grunge – we were dealing with a pixie named Grunge – gestured down at his hodgepodge outfit. He pointed to a paperclip piercing his nose. "This one I bartered from that Draíodóir drunk who summoned me. Hah! Idiot just handed it right over. Then this one," he held up an arm clad in a ripped Lays potato chip wrapper, "I found about five seasons ago when two daoine opened a window from your world, then left it unattended while they pressed their faces against each other."

Hadn't my mother told me something similar the week before, about how it was common for young witches and wizards to play around with summoning rituals in an attempt to impress each other? Guess not all ended up being failures.

Grunge next lovingly caressed the turban atop his head. "And this here is my prized possession, I got this from some daoine who somehow ended up in the Outerwoods. Poor sap had crossed paths with something nasty before I found him because there wasn't much left ... aside from this. The dumb trufflepup must've been new to magic or something. Anyway, fortunately I know a ritual or two for getting blood out of fabric."

Riva and I did a doubletake, then she asked, "Was he a Sikh?"

Grunge shrugged. "No idea. Like I said, he was a bit too dead to give me a name."

"That's terrible. But what was he even doing here?"

Riva shared a glance with me then shrugged. "I mean, I guess it makes as much sense as anything." When I raised an eyebrow, she added, "Be real, Bent. It's kind of silly to think the only people with access to magic are lilywhite Anglo Saxons from Pennsylvania."

"Fair point."

"Uh huh," Grunge said. "Whatever the gleef that means. Anyway, his loss was my gain." He again touched the headdress. "Good thing for me he died where he did. If he'd kept going the way he was," he pointed off into the forest, "he'd have come across the flame pits of Brix. And let me tell you, those gleefers rarely leave anything but ash." He appeared to relish the memory, smiling to himself, then added, "Listen, I don't know if you two are lost or not, but offhand I'd say you probably don't want to go that way."

"Duly noted," Riva replied.

"So what are you doing here, Grunge? Do you live here?"

"In this gleefing dump?" he asked. "Nah. I got standards. Got me a burrow a couple of steps that way up the ridge."

Riva took a look around, no doubt noting how idyllic this place seemed to be. "Yeah, it's a real cesspool."

But then I remembered what he'd told us about the enchantment upon this place. Once again, that horrible nightmare land flashed through my mind, the memory continuing to fade yet still potent enough to make me wince.

"You okay, Bent?"

"I'm fine. Just noting what a shithole this place is." Riva chuckled as I turned once more to Grunge. "So, you're just passing through?"

"Nope. I sensed a window opening. Came to check it out. Was hoping to find another sleeve maybe." He again gestured to the potato chip wrapper on his arm.

"You sensed it?"

"Of course, everyone here can. It's like a ... what's that fancy word? Oh yeah, an innate ability. You don't have to be a gleefing sidhe or anything, although they can sense it from a lot further away. And word on the beaten path is her highness can sense it anywhere in the Garden."

"The Garden?"

"This land, this world. You know, the Garden."

At least it was easy to remember. I said as much.

"Okay, so now that the pleasantries are out of the way..." Grunge stepped forward and stared intently at Riva.

After a moment, she began to look decisively uncomfortable. "Are you ... trying to peer through my clothes or something?"

Grunge grimaced in response. "No. Why would I want to? Listen, no offense, I'm sure you're considered very attractive to whatever might want to mate with you back in your world, but here, well, let's just say I'd sooner gleef a tarling."

"Is that good?"

He shook his head. "No, not really." Before I could laugh, he turned his quizzical gaze upon me. "Same goes for you. I'd sooner find a knothole full of stinger beetles to shove my..."

"I get the picture," I snapped. "So then what's with the creepy staring?"

"Oh, that? Just checking to see if you maybe have anything worth bartering for. As I said, I'm a collector. Your fellow girl there doesn't seem to have anything on her of worth, unless maybe she wants to trade the shiny things covering those skinny appendages of hers."

"Shiny things?"

He gestured at Riva's hand.

"You want my fingernails?!"

"Not if it's such a gleefing big deal," Grunge replied, sounding offended. He then gestured toward my neck. "Now that there looks like an interesting trinket."

I quickly put a hand over the butterfly pendant. "Not for sale."

"Not even for some directions guaranteed to avoid Brix's flame pits?"

"I think we'll manage on our own."

"You drive a hard bargain, girl. What if I throw in some taintnuts to sweeten the deal?"

Taintnuts?

I was about to tell the weird little pixie that he'd done the exact opposite of sweetening the deal, when my ears picked up the sound of heavy footsteps. As Grunge turned to Riva, probably to once again barter for her fingernails, I continued to listen. After a few seconds, it became clear they were headed this way, and quickly.

"Um, guys. I don't think we're alone here."

A moment later, I was proven right in the worst way possible, as an entire freaking tree came flying out of the woods at us.

14

"**D**own, now!"

I turned and dived at Riva, tackling her to the ground as the massive log flew through the space where our heads had been a moment earlier.

Thankfully the soft grass cushioned our fall. "You okay?"

"Aside from nearly peeing myself?" Riva asked wide eyed from beneath me.

"You'll live."

However, that statement was put into question as I rose and turned back in the direction the makeshift missile had come from.

Having fought witches, werewolves, and even an uber-wolf once, I thought I was prepared for just about anything.

Turns out I was wrong.

Three creatures, each of them ten feet tall if they were an inch, pushed their way into the clearing, splintering any saplings that got in their way. Each was misshapen in their own grotesque way, essentially a living pile of malformed multi-colored rocks somehow glued together and given the ability to walk. They were humanoid only in the most basic sense, having two arms and legs but, where they should have had faces, only a pair of molten slits peered out of their *heads*. Far worse were their mouths, though, gaping maws full of stalactite teeth in the middle of their torsos, each wide enough to bite a person my size in half.

"Oh, gleef!" Grunge squeaked. "Rock trolls."

The one in the lead focused on him, its molten eyes lighting up in a way that didn't exactly convey comradery.

"Grunge!" it roared, its voice sounding like a rock crusher given sentience. "You pile of thieving dung. We've got a bone to pick with you. Or, better yet, we're going to pick our teeth with your bones."

It looked like Riva and I had accidentally stumbled upon some sort of grudge match. A part of me was tempted to stick up for the little guy with the turban, but truth of the matter was we didn't know him from a hole in the wall. That, and he kind of gave off a sleazeball vibe. To be perfectly honest, I wasn't too surprised to find he had enemies.

"Bent?" Riva asked from behind me. "What should we do?"

Having been an underdog most of my life, competing in a sport dominated by men, I felt some pity for Grunge. Unless he had powers that he was keeping in check – unlikely if the raw fear showing on his face was any indication – I had a feeling he was ridiculously outclassed in this throwdown. At the same time, I had bigger fish to fry. I'd planned to come here with an entourage, preferably including a few from my mother's side who presumably had a clue about which way to go. But I was here now, and my mission hadn't changed. I was in this place to save my parents, not get caught up in a local squabble.

"Back away slowly," I said. "This isn't our fight."

"Skull Cruncher, my old friend," Grunge said, putting on an obviously fake smile. "What brings you and your brothers here?"

Skull Cruncher, eh? Not exactly someone it sounded wise to go randomly picking fights with.

"Sensed a window opening nearby. Figured it might draw you out like the gafferknob you are."

"F-funny you should mention that," Grunge sputtered. "Because I was just telling these two daoine how tasty they both looked."

"Hold on. Tasty?" Riva replied.

I glanced at her. "Well, you do look really cute in that dress."

"Thanks."

Sadly, though, that wasn't what Grunge meant.

"Really?" Skull Cruncher said. "We ain't ever eaten anything that came from beyond the Garden before."

"Well," Grunge continued, breaking into a wide, if nervous looking grin, "I was just claiming these two as my dinner, but I'd be happy to barter them in exchange for, say, my life?"

What?! "Listen up, you little fruit bat..."

Whatever I had to say, though, was drowned out by Skull Cruncher's gravelly retort. "I have a better idea. How about we eat them first, then snap off those spindly little arms of yours and use them to pick the pieces out of our teeth?"

So much for this not being our fight.

"Stay back," I whispered to Riva.

"No shit."

"And if they kill me ... run."

"That's a great plan, Bent. One of your best."

I glanced back at her. "I'm more an improviser than a strategist."

"Blockhead, you grab Grunge. If he tries to escape, crush him. Thwack, you're with me. Let's round up these daoine and break 'em apart a bit so they stop squirming."

Skull Cruncher, Blockhead, and Thwack. There's gotta be a buddy movie in there somewhere.

I turned to Grunge. "We're going to have a few words when this is over."

"Happy to," he replied nervously, "assuming we're not busy being digested."

Despite the alien nature of this place, Grunge very much reminded me of a street hustler – the type of low-level conman who was always looking for an angle, while staying out of the way of the bigger fish – except when he got sloppy, like now. And somehow it had become my job to pay whatever dues he owed.

The one called Blockhead stepped away from the others, moving faster than I'd have given a pile of sentient rocks credit for. Grunge turned, presumably to run, but the rock troll pulled a chunk of stone off his thigh and tossed it, aiming so that it landed right in front of the frightened pixie with a heavy *thud*.

"Don't move or the next one won't miss."

I had a feeling it wasn't an idle threat. Hopefully the little imp wouldn't do anything stupid because I couldn't afford to focus on him, not with that monster's two buddies tromping toward where Riva and I stood.

The one in the lead turned its molten gaze our way then inclined its head at the other. "What do you want to try first, Thwack, white meat or dark?"

"Racist rock trolls," Riva commented from behind my back. "That's new."

"Gives me a reason to punch them that much harder," I replied.

"Thwack likes this one," the third rock troll said, pointing my way. It was the smallest of the three, meaning he was still easily more than twice my size. "Can I keep its skin when we're finished?"

Apparently, he was also the dimmest bulb of the bunch. Potentially useful to know.

"Nuh uh," Skull Cruncher said. "What did I tell you about playing with your food?"

Oh, this was getting downright sad.

Skull Cruncher lumbered toward where I stood until it loomed over me, raising both club like arms over its head. "Heh. They don't raise them smart outside the Garden. This thing is too scared to even run."

It was right, I *was* scared, but running didn't seem a sound strategy, not when we had no idea where we were. For all I knew, we'd turn tail, only to find ourselves somewhere worse.

No, standing my ground was the right move – at least until these things proved I was outmatched, something I wasn't quite ready to presume.

How hard can this be? They're just made of rocks.

Uh huh.

Suddenly running didn't sound so bad. Sadly, it was too late for that option. Skull Cruncher brought both of its arms down, no doubt looking to smash me into paste.

Now!

I dove to the side at the last second, leaving the troll with nothing but ground to pound. And pound it the beast did. The very forest around me seemed to shudder from the impact, but when I glanced back, I saw it had been a little too thorough in its attack. Both of its *fists* were imbedded deep in the earth.

Or they would've been if we were on Earth, which we weren't. Either way, the troll was stuck for the moment, allowing me to sidestep around him.

I am so going to regret this.

Before I could talk myself out of punching solid rock, I threw a blow at the collection of stones that seemed to make up the creature's kneecap. It was like hitting an immoveable object. Fortunately, though, I had a bit of irresistible force in me.

Stone shattered to pebbles and Skull Cruncher cried out, although whether in anger or pain I didn't know. Whatever the cause, the creature went down to its one remaining knee, its other leg sprawled out uselessly behind it.

As for me, my hand was covered in blood from where I'd scraped the shit out of my knuckles, but I gave it a quick flex. Bruised but not broken. It wasn't perfect, but I'd take it, especially since Skull Cruncher was down but not out.

"I'll smash you like a gutter worm!"

"Bent! Look out!"

I'd allowed myself a moment of victory to celebrate the fact that my hand wasn't a bloody pulp of broken bones. It was stupid of me since our foes numbered two, three if you counted the one still menacing Grunge.

However, Blockhead wasn't my issue so much as Thwack. My enhanced senses picked up the whoosh of air a split second after Riva's warning. I dropped flat just as a monstrous club of rock passed over me, right where my head had been a moment earlier.

Sadly, Thwack wasn't as dumb as its speech might imply because it brought its other fist down onto my back, not so much to crush me as pin me in place.

"I got it, Skull Cruncher! Thwack did good."

"Don't just stand there gloating," Skull Cruncher admonished. "Hobble the little gnarb-wargler."

At least that was better than being called a knob gobbler. That might've actually annoyed me. I pushed up against Thwack's fist, managing to roll over before it pressed me back down again.

"She's a squirmy one."

I grabbed hold of the stony club pinning me in place, digging my fingers in as I debated how best to rip it off and feed it to him. Before I could do much of anything, though, there came a sound not entirely unlike that of a small avalanche.

Several of the smaller stones on Thwack's body dislodged themselves and rolled up onto his free arm. There, they worked their way to the end, rearranging themselves until they formed what appeared to be crude fingers.

Neat trick.

The arm holding me in place lifted off, allowing me to rise to my feet, but I was still a hair too slow. Thwack's newly functional left hand snagged me around the waist and lifted me off the ground.

"Good job, Thwack," Skull Cruncher said, finally pulling its arms free. It shook its body, and a bunch of small rocks on it began to shift, rolling down its torso and then its leg, before reassembling themselves as a new knee to replace the one I'd shattered.

So much for my victory dance.

"Can Thwack have a taste?"

"Sure. You done good. You can take a bite ... just a small one, you hear, while I retrieve the other daoine."

Fortunately, I didn't need to tell Riva to run. She was more than capable on that front, dodging among the trees in an attempt to keep out of Skull Cruncher's reach.

Sadly, with the rock troll's size, I had a feeling it was only a matter of time before it cornered her. Too bad I was otherwise occupied as Thwack pulled me in. I turned my head in time to see the mouthlike maw in the center of its body open wide.

Oh crap.

And then it tried to stuff me inside, headfirst.

You wouldn't think a creature made of rocks would have bad breath. You'd be wrong. A scent not dissimilar to rotting vegetation assaulted my nostrils, nearly overwhelming me. I somehow doubted there were enough Tic Tacs on all of Earth to make this more palatable, not that I cared to be eaten either way.

Half in and half out, I sensed more than saw its jaws begin to close, no doubt looking to bite me in two. Thankfully, Thwack had left my arms free when it grabbed hold of my waist. I reached out and caught its jaws right before its stalactite teeth, disturbingly sharp looking from this angle, could close upon me.

It tried to force its strange stomach mouth shut, but I refused to budge – hoping it had reached the extent of its bite force, because I was nearing the limits of my arms. Much more and there wouldn't be anything I could do, except hope that it maybe choked to death on my upper half.

"Ey, Skull Cuncher!" its voice boomed all around me, distorted because it was trying to talk with its jaws wedged open. "I an't ite it!"

I couldn't see Skull Cruncher from my vantage point, but I heard him clearly enough.

"Stop talking with your mouth full. If that thing won't go down, then try tenderizing it first. Now, where was I? Get back here, you little squirmling."

"Bent!"

Hold on, Riva. I'm...

Okay, I had no idea what I was doing but, fortunately, Thwack finally eased up on the pressure and pulled me out of its mouth.

Too bad it decided to take its friend's advice literally.

Thwack reared back its arm, and the next thing I knew I was free ... to go flying through the air.

I slammed into two saplings, shattering them both and doing a job on my upper body. For several seconds, I could do nothing except lie there stunned. Unfortunately, the vibrations coming from the ground beneath me said a nap was a luxury I couldn't afford.

"Thwack thwacked you good!"

Oh, he did not just say that.

On the upside, Thwack was about as subtle as it was eloquent, and half as bright. I felt more than saw the blow coming, managing to roll out of the way just as it slammed its club arm into the ground. Any slower and it would've thwacked me all right.

Sadly, in my daze at being *tenderized*, I'd rolled closer to the creature rather than farther away as planned, but maybe that wasn't such a bad thing.

I clambered to my feet to find myself face to face with Thwack's grinning stomach maw.

"That's right," it said, its foul breath washing over me like a mouth fart. "Be a good squirmy wormy and climb right in."

"Sure. Just as soon as you get those broken teeth looked at."

"Huh? What broken teeth?"

A part of me was amazed that this idiot had let me set him up like that. Fortunately, the rest was too busy hauling off with a haymaker so as to make good on my threat.

Again, the sensation of punching stone was far from a pleasant one, erasing even more skin from my knuckles. But I managed to put my back into it, turning my fist into a horizontal pile driver that ensured Thwack would be gumming its food from here on out.

Stoney teeth shattered one after the other, leaving Thwack with nothing but a mouthful of pebbles.

The rock troll stumbled away screaming and flailing its arms, forcing me to duck before I caught a fist to the back of the head.

"She boke my teef, Skull Cuncher," it cried. "She boke my teef!"

Thwack turned and ran, wailing at the top of its ... um, lungs, I guess, knocking saplings aside as it fled.

I almost felt bad, that is until my ears caught wind of something rapidly approaching from behind me. Spinning as fast as I could, I simultaneously backpedaled as Skull Cruncher charged my way, seemingly intent on trampling me into paste.

"What did you do to my baby brother?"

"Taught him not to play with his food."

That was probably not the answer the massive troll was looking for because it swung a big club fist at me, which I just barely ducked. It tried to follow up by going low with its other arm, but I was ready for it – best as I could be – leaping up over the rocky appendage.

It wasn't the most graceful move I'd ever made, but I managed to plant one foot on its arm and kick off, giving me an extra boost right toward its stupid bolder-shaped face.

Locking both my hands together in an axe-handle, I swung for the fences. The heavy stone block of its head was harder and thicker than anything I'd ever tried to pulverize before, and I felt the impact reverberate all the way up my arms.

The thing was, while Skull Cruncher's jaw was most certainly not made of glass, apparently the same couldn't be said of the loose pile of stones that functioned as its neck.

Crunch!

I landed off balance, falling on my ass — my ribs bruised and both my hands feeling like they'd been run over by a truck with cleats. A moment later, Skull Cruncher's head landed right in front of me, carving a big divot out of the ground.

The rest of its body stood there for a few seconds longer, as if waiting for an engraved invitation that it was no longer in possession of a noggin. A small part of me began to worry that maybe I'd grossly underestimated rock troll anatomy. If so, I'd be in some serious...

And then Skull Cruncher's body collapsed into pieces where it stood, heavy rocks thudding onto the ground as if remembering that gravity was a thing.

"Well, that wasn't so hard," I gasped, ready for a nap.

Sadly, it wasn't over yet.

Beyond Skull Cruncher's remains, I could see the third rock troll, Blockhead. Its back was to me, seemingly oblivious to what had happened to its buddies. It appeared to be busy tormenting Grunge — picking the little pixie imp up, tossing him in the air, then catching him as if he were a Nerf ball.

"You okay, Bent?"

I turned to see Riva emerge from the trees. She had a few twigs stuck in her hair and her white dress was a bit scuffed up, but she otherwise looked fine.

"Nothing a tube of Neosporin and some ice packs won't fix."

She pointed to where Blockhead continued to cluelessly harass Grunge, unaware of the pile of dead Skull Cruncher only a few dozen yards away. "What about that one?"

"Blockhead? I'm thinking he lives up to his name."

"I meant Grunge."

"I suppose we could just leave him. After all, he was about to barter us away as food."

She nodded. "Yeah, and there's something kind of skeevy about him. It's like he's Tinkerbell after a weekend meth binge."

"True. The sugarplum fairy he is not."

"Nope."

I pushed myself to my feet. "Come on. I suppose we should save the little dirtbag."

"Can we kick his ass afterward?"

I turned to her and smiled. "Of course. Screw that being the better person crap."

15

Though I doubted physicists from my world had any reason to fear it splitting the atom anytime soon, Blockhead was at least a little brighter than Thwack.

Credit where credit is due. After we got its attention, it didn't take long for the troll to put two and two together – noticing the pile of rocks behind me along with my bloody knuckles.

Though it was difficult to judge emotions from a gaping rock maw, the way it ground its teeth together told me it was at least contemplating revenge – something I put a quick stop to.

"If two against one resulted in that," I said, hooking a thumb over my shoulder, "how do you think you'll fare with worse odds?"

"What are you?" the rocky abomination grumbled, taking a step backward. Though its tone was defiant, the beast's posture said its course of action had already been decided.

Now it was up to me to ice this surrender cake.

"Nothing you've ever seen before. I'm a whole lot of badass in a pretty little package."

"Humility thy name is Bent."

I glanced back at my friend, "Hey, the rules are pretty clear about these things. To the victor goes the bragging rights."

"If this were fifth grade maybe."

The rock troll was apparently more interested in saving its granite hide than in listening to our banter. It took another step away from us then reared back and threw Grunge in our direction, before turning and beating feet off into the enchanted woods.

It was the old ploy of making sure your enemies were more occupied with saving their ally than in running you down. Had I been in a vengeful mood, I'd have simply noted that Grunge had wings before taking off in pursuit. Fortunately, though, this place didn't seem to have the same effect on me that being in the hollows did. There were no voices whispering in my ear goading me to violence. Nevertheless, that didn't change the fact that the little pixie was capable of saving himself.

"Gleef my life!"

Or maybe not.

Grunge sailed over our heads to land in a heap on the ground, tumbling end over end until skidding to a halt.

Much as I kind of enjoyed the karmic justice, a part of me felt bad for the creepy little shit.

"Come on," I told Riva, leading the way.

Fortunately, depending on one's definition of the word, the little imp was apparently tougher than he looked. He was already pulling himself up as we approached, albeit gingerly.

"Gleefing rock trolls," he grumbled, massaging one of his wings. "Gonna hurt all over for a week."

"Are you okay?" I asked somewhat less than enthusiastically.

He turned toward us, a look of panic replacing whatever else had been on his angular face. "Um, if I say no will that keep you from pounding me into glif-snot?"

"Relax. I'm not going to pound you into … whatever that is. I'm not happy with you, don't get me wrong, but I figure whatever that thing did is payback enough."

"What she said," Riva added after a pronounced pause. "Unless you're planning on screwing us over again."

"Couldn't even if I wanted to," he replied, before quickly adding, "Not that I want to. I mean, you two are okay in my book for a couple of daoine, I mean girls that is."

"I liked you better when you weren't trying to suck up."

"Hold on," Riva said. "What do you mean you couldn't even if you wanted to?"

"Sidhe honor," Grunge replied, sounding none too happy. "I owe you a life for saving me. So, I have to serve you until it's been repaid."

I glanced at Riva. Wasn't this the plot of a Brady Bunch episode? "That's okay, Grunge. You don't need to…"

The sleazy little pixie stepped in front of me, his face at about crotch level. Needless to say, I backed up a step.

"No can do, Girl. It's not optional."

"Trust me, we won't tell anyone."

"You're not listening. This comes from her royal badassness herself. When I say it's not optional, I mean it. Even if you tied me to a tree, I'd have to gnaw my way free and follow you. You can if you want, but I'm just telling you so we can save each other the trouble."

"Sidhe honor," Riva said. "But you said earlier you weren't a…"

"And I gleefing meant it. If I was a sidhe, do you think I'd be living in a dump like this?"

I glanced around, noting the scenery. The weather was pleasant. The sky was clear. All in all, it was near idyllic, minus maybe the rock troll corpse littering the ground.

"I'm a sylph," Grunge continued. "The sidhe are at the top of the food chain here, the lords and ladies of the land. They call the shots. They're the cream of the Garden's crop, with her royal highness being the..."

"The cherry on top?" I offered.

"What's a cherry? I was going to say fizzlenut."

"Same general idea, I imagine."

"Whatever. So how about it, Girl? Make sense now?"

I turned toward Riva. "I suppose we could tie him to a tree and see how that works out."

"I'm half-tempted to try that myself."

Both of us laughed, then I looked back down at Grunge. "Relax. We're joking. I suppose we're stuck with you. But no more selling us out to anything to save your own skin. Otherwise I'll do a lot more than tie you to a tree. We clear?"

"As a phase gem," he replied, looking wide eyed. "You got yourself a deal, Girl."

"You can call me Tamara."

"I'm Riva."

Grunge looked confused. "Huh? You told me not a few minutes ago that your name was Girl and her name was Girl, too. How in the abyss does that make any sense?"

I shook my head. "No. We're both girls."

"Not making it any clearer."

"I mean that's what we are."

"You mean two daoine?"

"No. We're both female. You do know what a female is, right?"

He nodded. "Of course I do. It's one of those stupid things you lesser species are into, dividing yourselves up between those who have twigs and those with knotholes, as if that means anything. But that still doesn't tell me if your name is Girl or..."

"Just forget about the girl thing," Riva snapped. "I'm Riva, she's Bent."

"Bent ... but you said..."

"Tamara, or Bent. That last one's a nickname."

"Ah, I get it," he said. "Like there was this dryad I used to be friends with. Their name was ... well, unpronounce-able to anyone with tongues like yours, but I used to call them Twigshit, because..."

I held up a hand. "No need to elaborate. Anyway, if we're stuck with you, we might as well make the best of it."

"We could use him as a guide to get us to..." Riva's voice trailed off into silence without finishing.

"You okay?"

She nodded. "Yeah. Fine as a matter of fact. But I just realized I have no idea why either of us is here. I mean, are we dead?"

"Dead daoine don't beat the gleef out of rock trolls," Grunge offered.

Ignoring our diminutive acquaintance, I replied, "Wait. You really don't know?"

Riva shook her head. "The last thing I remember is sitting in Chris's hospital room with him. Oh crap! Is he...?"

"He's fine. The little turd muncher is tougher than he looks."

"Turd muncher? Don't think I've tasted any of those."

I glanced down at Grunge. "Do you mind?" Then it was back to my friend. "What about after?"

"Just bits and pieces. It's like I fell asleep there and woke up here."

I considered this. After sending her and Chris to the hospital, Cass and I had ventured to the hollows. There, we'd faced my aunt, defeating her but perhaps letting something even worse into our world. If what Riva was telling me was correct, there was no way the timing could be a coincidence. I explained as much to her, keeping it as short as I could.

"Your parents are here? Really?" she asked when I was finished.

I nodded. "At least according to Carly. She said she bartered them with the fairy queen, a sacrifice for when she claimed the sacred glade ... the Window of Worlds as she called it."

Before I could say more, Riva practically leapt into my arms, grabbing me in a hug. "Oh my god, Bent! I'm so sorry."

I meant to gently push her away, tell her that I was fine, but instead it was like a dam somewhere deep inside of me picked that moment to burst. I found myself clinging to her as if she were my last life preserver in the sea of insanity that was slowly drowning me.

I'd been on the go nonstop since that day in the hollows, doing everything I could to prepare the rescue mission to save my parents. I only realized now that the constant pressure I put on myself wasn't entirely for their benefit. No. At least some of it had been for my own, forcing myself to keep busy so as to not let the despair grab hold of me like some kind of many tentacled beast.

The thing was, I might not be entirely human, but some parts of me were – mainly my heart. Yet, I hadn't allowed myself to let any of it out, bottling up the sorrow and fear I felt, lest it consume me wholly.

Except, here now with Riva, I realized that such a

thing was foolish to fear. My grief, my sadness, it was a part of me, a part that needed to be expressed every bit as much as the rage I'd unleashed upon my aunt.

Alone, such a thing might very well overwhelm me, but with someone I loved dearly it was cleansing – her strength bolstering my own and making me understand I didn't need to fight every battle alone.

So it was that I finally allowed myself the release I didn't realize until that moment I so desperately needed, burying my head in Riva's shoulder and letting it all out – allowing her to momentarily bear the burdens I thought were mine and mine alone to carry.

We held each other for several long minutes, the tears falling freely.

At least until Grunge had to add his two cents.

"Um, are you two back to killing each other? Because if so, I have to decide which of you I owe more."

"And the moment's over," I said, pulling away with a laugh and wiping my eyes. "Thanks, Grunge. I don't know what we'd do without you."

"Probably wander into the flame pits of Brix."

"Yeah, we already figured that."

"All right," Riva said, likewise drying her tears. "What are we waiting here for? Grunge, take us to Queen Brigid."

Instead, Grunge burst into laughter, the sound far lower pitched and more disturbing than his size would suggest. Ugh, it was like listening to a serial killer chuckle right before telling you to put lotion on your skin.

After a few irritating seconds of this, he finally stopped and looked up to find both of us staring at him. "That was a joke, right?"

"Do you see us laughing?"

He shrugged uncomfortably. "Hard to tell with you daoine sometimes."

"We're not," Riva said, stone-faced. "Trust me."

"Okay, then let's back up a gleefing moment here so I can explain how things work. Her high and mercilessness is not someone you just go and meet. She is power incarnate, we're talking a gleefing volcano given form here. So long as you follow the rules, she's a benevolent power. But cross her and ... well, I've had some friends reduced to molten puddles of goo simply for criticizing her too loudly. You catching my splink here?"

I won't lie and say a part of me didn't want to catch his ... um, splink. In the back of my mind I'd known what we were up against by coming here, but only now was it starting to sink in. Werewolves, Draíodóir, even doppelgangers, these things I had a handle on. They were all tough, probably scary as all hell to anyone normal, but I could handle them ... mostly.

Here, though, I was on a mission to hunt down a freaking goddess and demand she release my parents. If the legends were to be believed, Brigid was the fount from which all Draíodóir power flowed. Just a few short days ago I'd barely survived a battle with one of her minions. Yeah, my aunt had been jacked up at the time, but I still had to think the power she was channeling was barely a blip for a being who – if Grunge was to be believed – controlled both this place and its inhabitants.

Riva must have sensed the fact that my nerves were rapidly buckling, because she stepped up and put a hand on my shoulder. "I believe in you, Bent." I gave her a doubtful look back to which she added, "We'll think of something ... together."

"Yeah," Grunge replied, backing up a step. "You two have fun with that. As for me, I prefer to live."

"What about your honor?" Riva asked.

"Gleef that. I can live without honor. Done okay without it so far." With that, Grunge turned and ran.

Or he tried to.

He made it about five steps before dropping to his knees wheezing.

"Is he okay?"

Riva shrugged as we both made our way over to the downed sylph. "Hey, are you o... Holy shit!"

I couldn't even remotely disagree. We both jumped back at the sight of him, his eyes bulging out of his head as if they were about to explode. The last thing I think either of us needed, especially Riva with her virginal white dress, was being showered with fairy brain goo.

Fortunately, though, that didn't happen. After a few seconds of pained wheezing, Grunge got his breathing under control. His eyes likewise retracted back into his skull. A couple more moments passed, then he simply pushed himself back to his feet, a look of annoyance on his face.

"Okay. I guess I *can't* live without honor. Gleefing sidhe and their twig sucking rules!"

"Um, are you all right?" I asked.

"No," he snapped. "I'm about to gleefing die, stuck with you two daoine. Maybe I should've taken one more step and been done with it."

"What would have happened if..."

"Figure it out, you gleefing shaved monkey," he spat at my friend. "Like I said, I'm stuck with you two, whether I like it or not ... and, just for the record, I do not."

I can't say I was big on the concept of indentured servitude, especially with a creature who'd already tried to barter our lives for his own. In a way it reminded me of Frodo and Gollum. I remembered sitting down with my brother one bored day and watching those *Lord of the Rings* movies with him. Can't say they did much for me, outside of Orlando Bloom maybe. Anyway, it struck me as making a deal with the devil, one you needed but knew you couldn't trust.

Although, in all fairness, Gollum hadn't had a compulsion hanging over him that would've blown his eyes out of his head if he screwed over Frodo. So maybe the advantage was a bit on our side for this one.

"Looks like we're stuck with each other again," I said.

"You gleefing think so?" Grunge replied before taking a deep breath – his body swelling a disturbing amount as he did so – and then composing himself. "I don't suppose you'd prefer I led you to the..."

"Flame pits of Brix, instead? Sorry, but unless they have my parents, the answer is no."

"I guess that's settled then," Riva said. "We've got our munchkin guide, so what say we set off to see the wizard?" No doubt noticing the downtrodden look plastered onto Grunge's face, she added, "Oh, relax. If this works, maybe I'll let you have the tip of a fingernail."

That seemed to cheer the little fairy up a bit. After a moment, he shrugged, as if finally accepting his fate, then pointed off in another direction.

"Good boy."

Riva turned and started that way with me close behind.

After a few steps, though, I realized Grunge wasn't following. I stopped and glanced at him from over my shoulder. "What's the problem now?"

His eyes, in the meantime, had opened up wide again, but not in an explodey sort of way. "I don't know who the gleef this wizard is, but I have a feeling her high and mightiness isn't in the mood to wait for us. Look!"

"Um ... Bent? What the hell is that?"

Riva's tone caught my attention more than Grunge's

fear, but when I turned back I saw that both were more than justified.

We'd been surrounded by thick primeval forest up until this point. That was still the case, but now only on three sides. In front of us, the impossible was happening. The very trees themselves were pulling away from each other, moving in a way that trees weren't supposed to move, and they weren't alone. Bushes, flowers, even the grass was doing the same, opening up a clear path before us.

"What the fuck?"

16

It was like something out of a big budget movie. Before us, trees, grass, and more continued to part, forming a clear path of packed dirt.

At first, I thought that this trick, neat as it was, would be limited in scope ... maybe clearing a couple dozen feet for us to walk down. But it didn't stop there.

Ten yards, fifty, a hundred and still going, creating a path – no, more like a road, roughly thirty feet wide, much more than the three of us needed to pass comfortably. Heck, we could have walked with our arms outstretched, fingertips barely touching, and still not reached the edges.

"I bet the PA Department of Transportation wishes they could do this," Riva remarked, her voice low as if in awe. "It sure as hell beats half the state being perpetually under construction."

"Can't argue there," I replied. "But why do all of this for us? Don't get me wrong, I don't mind the red-carpet treatment, but it's not like we need a freaking super-highway."

"That's because it's not for you," Grunge said from a few steps behind us.

"It isn't?"

"You daoine have a reputation for thinking the multiverse revolves around you. Sorry to burst your gleefing bubble, but here there's only one gleefer the world revolves around. And now you've just put us in the one place I never wanted to be: dead center in her sights."

"If it helps, that wasn't our intention," Riva said.

"It doesn't."

Jeez. Some fairies could be so touchy. Ahead, the roadway continued to form, closing in on a mile long and showing no signs of stopping. I took a glance behind us, just to satisfy my curiosity. No such phenomenon was occurring back there. Wherever this road led to, we were at the beginning of it.

Or maybe the end.

On and on the magic played out, until the pathway before us stretched to the very horizon ... telling me that if this hadn't happened, we would've likely been traipsing through forest for days to come.

Say what you will about the ominous feeling in the pit of my gut, but at least we'd make much better time now.

"What's that?" Riva cried.

"Oh gleef, not them."

"Not who?" I asked, before catching sight of what Riva had spotted. It was still far away, a few miles at least, but I spied what appeared to be a ball of flame. No, make that balls. They stretched across the entirety of the fairy superhighway and – yep, no doubt about it – were barreling in our direction.

"Is anyone else wondering why they're sending freaking fireballs toward us?" Riva asked, sounding ever so slightly stressed out."

"Um, because we're dropping it like it's hot?"

She glared at me, eyes narrowed, to which I merely shrugged in apology.

"Not fireballs," Grunge said. "Much gleefing worse. Salamanders."

"We have salamanders back where we come from. I don't recall any of them being on fire."

"Different type of salamanders, Bent," Riva replied. "In fantasy lore, they tend to be more like pissed off mini dragons. Think Charmander, but with a worse attitude."

"Oh. Too bad I left all my pokéballs back home. You?"

She gestured down at her dress. "Just my luck. No pockets."

"From the look of things, they're going to be here in less than five minutes." I turned to Grunge. "Let me guess. No speed limits in the Garden?"

His strange eyes were wide with something very familiar, despite their alien nature – fear. "More like no *us* in the Garden."

"What are they going to do, eat us?"

"Probably not. Well, hopefully not. A lot depends on what orders the Queenshield were given."

"Queen shield?"

"Yeah, who else do you think is riding them?"

"So, they're like what – Brigid's personal bodyguards?"

He let out a sigh. "Bodyguards, executioners, whatever the gleef she wants them to be! I knew I should've stayed in my rag pile this morning."

I looked away to see that the fireballs were now even closer – moving at a clip that could best be summed up as: holy shit that's fast.

"Anyone else up for hiding?" Riva asked.

"No objections here."

"Won't work," Grunge replied, sounding like he'd already been tried, found guilty of murder, and had his last plea turned down by the governor. "They've got us."

"You only say that because you haven't tried. Come on."

The little pixie remained rooted to the spot, even as Riva started toward the woods behind us. Leaving him would be wrong, not to mention the little vulture had already shown he wasn't above ratting us out, so I scooped him up and ran after her.

"Come on, Bent!"

"Don't wait for me."

I could've sworn I already felt the clomp of heavy footsteps from the ground below, maybe my imagination, but probably best to not tempt fate.

"Put me down!"

"Shut up, this is for your own good." Although it was mostly for Riva's and my own good, as I trusted Grunge about as far as I could've tossed one of those rock trolls.

"Over here!"

I followed the sound of her voice, pushing my way through the foliage and trying to use rocks and stumps for footing where I could, so as to minimize my footprints. Hopefully these salamander things weren't part bloodhound, too.

Riva had found a small hollow, maybe thirty yards into the woods, nestled deeply enough in a thicket of rainbow-colored brambles to hopefully mask our presence. I settled down next to her and turned back toward the strange road, keeping my eyes peeled for movement.

Slowly, I became aware of the sensation of tiny little hands roaming over my body.

The fuck?!

"You daoine are seriously weird," Grunge said, still in my grasp and touching my bicep. "All hard here, yet soft over here." His hands suddenly shifted *elsewhere.* "How the gleef does that work anyway?"

"Riva?"

"Yes?"

"Could you do me a favor and tell me if this little shitbag is feeling me up? Because if I look down and see him groping me, I'm going to smash his head against a tree."

"Um, Bent? That might be a problem."

Before I could ask why that was, it became painfully apparent. The trees and bushes around us began to pull away, as if we were in a crowded elevator and had just let one rip.

The path that had formed around us a few minutes earlier was reasserting itself. Worse, those vibrations upon the ground were definitely not my imagination.

"Told ya," Grunge replied, sounding both terrified and self-satisfied in the same breath.

"You don't have to be obnoxious about it," Riva said before standing up. "Come on, let's try over here."

But even as she began to make another dash for cover, I saw it was pointless. Somehow the forest was wise to our moves, the trees and everything else pulling away as if this were a game of tag.

"This is seriously not fair."

"You don't get it," Grunge replied, pulling free of my grasp thanks in part to his spindly and somewhat greasy little body. "Fair doesn't matter here. This whole place, the entirety of the Garden, it belongs to her royal divineness. She's the one who determines what is and isn't fair. No other opinions matter, not that I've heard many stories about her asking."

Well, if that wasn't a kick in the ass, I didn't know what was.

Still, there might be an upside. Our original plan had been to let Grunge lead us to the Queen's ... um, palace, I assumed. But after seeing the path laid out before us, it became painfully obvious that this was no mere day trip down the Yellow Brick Road. The reality was, Grunge kept calling this place the Garden, but we had no idea how big it was. It could've been a couple miles or it could be the same size as the freaking Earth, with her domain being at the exact opposite end of the planet for all we knew. If so, we'd be shit out of luck, as none of us were prepared for a several thousand mile hike.

The flipside, though, was now we had these guys coming for us. If the queen was having us arrested for trespassing or whatever, it would give us a fast track to get where we were going, allowing us to figure out the rest once we were there.

Of course, there was always the possibility these Queenshield, whoever they were, had been dispatched to kill us. That would definitely throw a monkey wrench into my plans, but that simply assumed we didn't kill them first – a big assumption, yes. Either way, though, it seemed like hiding was out of the question.

I stepped to the center of the newly formed clearing. "Come on."

"What are you doing, Bent?"

"Welcoming our guests, of course. Doesn't look like we have much choice in the matter."

Riva could be an obstinate friend when she wanted to be. Hell, she could be downright obnoxious when she so chose. But she wasn't stupid and, though her bravery didn't run to things like spiders, snakes, or even squirrels, she'd never once abandoned me when I needed her – even now that my life had turned extra freaky.

After a moment, she shrugged and joined me. "I guess if I'm going to be eaten by giant fire lizards, I could pick worse company to do it in."

"Speak for yourself," Grunge said. "My day was going just fine before I had the misfortune of running into you two gleefing girls ... and I mean that as an insult."

Riva turned to me and grinned. "Oh, the horror of not having a twig."

I returned her smile. "Tell me about it. Whatever shall I do without one?"

That caused us both to break out in laughter. I wasn't sure what was going to happen next, but Riva had a point. There was no one else I'd sooner meet my fate standing alongside.

Mind you, if meeting my fate wasn't in the cards that'd be okay, too. Regardless, it seemed we'd find out soon enough.

"Oh, gleef! They're coming."

Grunge must've still been under that honor thingamabob because he didn't go far, but that didn't stop him from ducking down behind some bushes. It seemed whatever was causing the forest to treat Riva and I like redheaded stepchildren didn't apply to him. The little prick was probably hoping we got killed. That way he'd be freed from his duty to tag along like the world's worst tour guide.

I turned my attention away from him, though, as he currently seemed like the least of our worries. Up ahead, I spied a row of fireballs five wide rapidly bearing down on us. They had to be doing at least a hundred, meaning that even though they were probably still a good half mile away, they'd be upon us within seconds.

"It feels like a train's coming."

I nodded. "One that's seriously overheating."

That wasn't exactly right, though. Despite each of the fireballs looking like a miniature sun, the temperature didn't seem to rise as they approached. Nor were they setting the forest ablaze as they passed, the trees at the very edge of the Neverland Throughway just as pristine as the rest.

Good for me, I suppose, since Riva was the only one of us dressed for a warm summer day. Even better, since I didn't care to be roasted alive where I stood.

The fireballs finally began to slow as they neared us, telling me their plan wasn't to simply run us down and get it over with. As they decelerated, the glow around them began to dissipate.

Where, from a distance, they'd looked to be miniature shooting stars, as they got ever closer I began to make out physical forms behind the fire. Mind you, those forms didn't exactly give me cause to whoop for joy. I mean, give me a break. We were in the land of the fairies. You'd think they could maybe throw a unicorn or Pegasus at us, something to make us weep at the mundanity of our own sad little world. But no. I was getting ready to weep all right, but it was more the piss my pants variety.

"Bent?"

"I see them."

The creatures – salamanders I presumed – were more like something Chris and his dork friends would have dreamt up for some stupid horror comic. Their resemblance to actual salamanders was superficial at best, being they sort of looked reptilian. However, each was the size of a freaking Clydesdale. Their skin was blackened and charred, like something you'd expect to crawl out of the reactors at Chernobyl. Bifurcated jaws full of needle-sharp teeth sat below glowing red eyes, and that wasn't even mentioning that each had six long legs upon which they galloped.

"Okay, so giant, burning cockroach dragons it is then."

"Not making me feel better, Bent ... oh wow."

As the creatures slowed to a trot to cover the final fifty

yards between us, the flames upon their bodies were extinguished, revealing their riders in full.

And what riders they were.

It was as if an artist had been hired to sculp the ideal fantasy men for a photo op.

Though their skin tones varied from pale to dark brown, they all shared gleaming golden armor, covering tall muscular bodies topped by chiseled faces, flowing blonde hair, and gleaming eyes of obsidian. Each was more perfect than the last, culminating in the one who sat in the middle of the group, a veritable god among men ... or fairies anyway.

Riva glanced my way as they came to a halt mere yards from where we stood.

"Do you think it's too much to hope they frisk us first?"

17

"Down, girl," I whispered to my friend, although I'm fairly certain the words came with a fair bit of drool attached to them.

I mean, I'd been recently entertaining fantasies of David and his rock-hard beta body, but these guys were like something out of those too good to be true reverse harem novels the girls back at school seemed to be into these days.

I could sort of understand the appeal.

That said, this wasn't some paranormal romance story. I mean, yeah, we technically were in another world, surrounded by what seemed to be actual fae warriors, but the expressions on these guys' faces didn't suggest they were merely on the lookout for an orgy with any errant Earth girls they came across.

Grunge had been acting like these guys, sidhe he called them, were at the top of the fairy food chain and I could see why. The fivesome dismounted from their steeds, each of them a good six foot two or taller, but not a beer gut among them. Oh yeah, Toto, we definitely weren't in Pennsylvania anymore.

"Two words," Riva whispered. "Strip search."

I turned to her. "Will you knock it off, this is serious."

Either fairy ears were extra sensitive or I'd admonished my friend a bit louder than I'd meant to. Whatever the case, the one in the lead picked that moment to speak up.

"Indeed. I'd say your trespass upon our fair queen's lands is quite serious, Earth woman."

At least he didn't call us a pair of daoine like Grunge kept doing.

The leader had golden brown skin, beneath a mane of stark white hair. Though his stature suggested either a deep romantic lead type voice or perhaps one with singsong melodic quality, what came out instead was more a growling whisper. My god, it was like some scientist had mated Idris Elba with Legolas from Lord of the Rings, and then thrown in Jason Statham's voice as a bonus. Oddly enough, this did nothing to diminish his appeal.

"Earth girls are..."

"Don't finish that sentence," I warned my friend before turning back toward our guests.

Rather than tell us to shut our yaps, the leader turned his head to the side ever so slightly. "Show yourself, sylph. I know you're there. I can smell the stench of your cowardice from here."

Riva and I followed his gaze to see Grunge step out from behind a tree, trying to look innocent and doing a piss poor job of it.

"Well well, Queenshield near my burrow. What a surprise."

"Save the flattery, Gullysnipe," a soldier at the far end of the lineup said, his voice every bit the husky whisper of their leader.

"I actually don't go by that anymore," Grunge replied, visibly sweating now. "They call me..."

"I don't care what you call yourself, sylph. I only care

about the name our illustrious queen deemed to bestow upon you at the moment you soiled the Garden with your birth."

The leader turned to the soldier, raising an eyebrow on his flawless face. "You know this one?"

"There's a complaint list on him that's as long as a trea-clehorn's snout."

"Anything serious?"

"Minor nuisances at best."

"That's me," Grunge replied, "a minor nuisance. Nothing more."

The leader stepped forward, his obsidian eyes locked on Grunge with enough intensity to burn a hole through the pixie. "And yet here you are with these two." He glanced our way. "Barely in our world long enough for the dew to dry beneath their heels, yet already murderers."

"Murderers?"

"Yes," the leader replied to me. "Or do you deny killing a rock troll shortly after your arrival?"

He kinda had us there, or at least he had one of us. "That was me ... and it was in self-defense. My friend here didn't have anything to do with that."

"I see," the leader replied. He held out a hand and the soldier to his immediate right placed a scroll in it. "Did not your fellow Earth woman say, and I quote, 'Can we kick his ass afterward?'"

His pitch rose as he said that last part, taking on a disturbing semblance to Riva's voice.

"I was talking about him." Riva pointed a finger toward Grunge but then, a moment later, she turned to me. "That didn't make it better, did it?"

"I'm thinking no."

"Threatening another citizen of the Garden in addition to the one you so callously murdered?" the leader replied, his gruff voice sounding annoyingly self-satisfied. I was beginning to get the impression that he was one of those pricks who enjoyed handing out shovels so as to watch people dig their own graves.

"Wait. How did you even know she said that?"

"The trees, of course. They told our most holy queen of your arrival and subsequent crimes."

Guess Grunge hadn't been kidding when he'd said Brigid had full control of this place and everything in it. Nevertheless, as chilling as that was, I found myself turning to the surrounding foliage. "Snitches get stitches."

Much to my amusement, I could've sworn I saw a few bushes shake in response.

Sentient vegetation. I bet that made gardening a real hoot.

The leader inclined his head toward one of his minions. "Fetch the shackles."

"Yes, Captain Uriel."

He then turned back our way and raised an eyebrow. "Unless, that is, you plan on resisting arrest."

Tempting as it was to throw him some shade, I shared a quick glance with Riva before shaking my head. Much as I didn't care to be marched before Queen Brigid in chains, this guy was likely our quickest route there. I could suck up my pride if it meant being put in a position where I could rescue my parents.

"Wise," Uriel replied. "Unusual for an Earth female. Typically, you daoine cattle prefer bluster to sense ... at least until such time as you're duly humbled."

Cattle? There was no doubt in my mind that this jerkface was probably hoping we'd do something to give them cause to sic their lizard monsters on us. I'd been on the receiving end of worse, though, some of it from my fellow teammates on the Bailey U. wrestling squad. Same with Riva. Growing up a bi Hindi girl in rural Pennsylvania, she'd had to ensure more than her fair share of grief from those who thought themselves better than her.

If anything, this guy was little more than an amateur in the game of trash talk.

"Check it out," Riva whispered. "At least we're getting chained in style."

The minion guardsman had retrieved multiple pairs of shackles from the side of his trusty lizard thing, including one that was decisively smaller than the rest – sorry, Grunge. What caught my eye, though, was the way they gleamed, looking less like handcuffs and more like a fashion accessory Miley Cyrus might wear.

Uriel nodded and two more of his lieutenants reached behind their backs and produced short sticks, which instantly lengthened in their hands into six foot spears with blades at both ends – seemingly made of the same gleaming metal as the shackles. Neat trick.

However, cool as it all was, it belied the fact that this was deadly serious business, the blades on the weapons appearing razor sharp.

"Step forward with the rest of the prisoners, Gullysnipe."

"Me?" the little dirtbag said with a gulp. "But I barely know these daoine."

Uriel grinned a predatory smile. "Barely still implies you know them. Hence, you'll come with us, too. Unless, that is, you'd prefer to resist."

Grunge was apparently a lot of things, but brave enough to pick a fight with the Legolas squad here was not one of them. He double-timed it to where Riva and I stood.

"You sure about this?" Riva asked as the guard with the manacles approached.

"Making it up as I go along."

"I guess that works, too."

"No talking," the guard growled, stepping up to us. In response, the goons with the weapons pointed them our way. That seemed to be our cue to zip it.

The only thing left to do was be trussed up like good prisoners and then hope those fire monsters were a lot less hot than they looked, because otherwise that was going to make for a seriously uncomfortable ride back.

Interestingly enough, the guard started with Grunge, as if he were the biggest threat here. He shackled the sylph's arms, legs, and then stepped around back and tied what appeared to be a silken cord around Grunge's wings. Guess these guys weren't taking any chances.

I was next in line, holding out my arms so he could chain them up. I half expected the metal to be scalding, considering where they'd been stored, but it was cool to the touch. They weren't the most comfortable things I'd ever worn, but I can't say I hadn't ever experimented with handcuffs before.

With my arms and legs shackled, the guard then moved on to Riva – cuffing her arms before bending down to one knee to secure her bare legs.

"Watch the hands, pal," she warned when he brushed against the hem of her dress.

"As if I would dirty myself," he replied, before going about his business like the asshole he was. Fairy dickheads. Just our luck.

While this was going on, I gave my manacles an experimental tug – fully expecting it to be a pointless endeavor. To my surprise, though, I felt some give with the links of chain connecting my wrists. Sure enough, I glanced down to find they'd actually deformed a bit. And I hadn't even put all that much into it.

I examined them a little more closely, noting their shine.

No way.

"Are these ... silver?"

"Indeed," Uriel replied, grinning. "Only the finest for prisoners of her majesty."

But that made no sense. I wasn't exactly a chem major, but I remembered some basic facts. Silver wasn't even half the strength of most alloys. That's why jewelers loved it. It was both shiny and easy to work with. But, while they might've been strong enough to hold a normal person like Riva, silver cuffs would be next to useless against someone like me.

That seemed ... kinda dumb. The whole point of handcuffs was to keep someone tied up. But if these clowns knew I killed that rock troll, they had to know this would be the equivalent of shackling me with a couple of twist ties.

That seemed a somewhat arrogantly stupid thing to do for guys who claimed to be the queen's elite guard.

But that was a debate for another day as I'd already made up my mind to go with them. So, technically they could've tied me up with nothing more than thin air and a promise to be good, and it wouldn't have made much difference.

"The prisoners are secured, Captain," the minion said, once he was finished.

I turned to my friend once he stepped away. "Are you okay?"

"Remind me to ask if I can keep a pair of these for my dorm room."

"I'll take that as a yes."

"Don't get me wrong, I'm freaking terrified."

"Right back at'cha."

That seemed to mollify the leader, who apparently didn't need to get his hearing tested. He grinned briefly at us, then turned to his fellows. "Karzan, Alten, secure them to your steeds for the journey back, emerald formation."

I had no idea what emerald formation was, minus the fact that I doubted it involved giving us jewelry. But the hotties apparently understood as they gave a quick salute back before...

My supercharged hearing picked up a brief whistling sound in that moment, as if a mosquito had just flown past my ears and...

One of the minions, Karzan or Alten – it's not like they were wearing nametags – clapped a hand to his cheek. A scant moment later, smoke started billowing out from between his fingers and he let out a high-pitched scream that was pretty much the opposite of the throaty growls they spoke in.

It was as if time paused for several seconds, save for the screaming, then there came the sound of a lot more "mosquitos".

"Shields!" Uriel commanded. He flicked his wrist and a metallic tower shield appeared, again from seemingly nowhere. What the hell? Were these guys keeping all their supplies shoved up their asses or something?

That was perhaps a question for later, though, as his comrades followed suit almost immediately ... just in time for the sound of tiny projectiles bouncing off metal to ring out.

Whatever was happening, it was clear we were under attack, which meant me and my friend were standing there out in the open like a couple of human bullseyes. Not the brightest strategy we could've adopted.

I yanked my arms apart, easily breaking the chains binding my wrists, and then launched myself at Riva. "Get down!"

Yeah, my warning was perhaps a bit unnecessary once I plowed into her, sending us both to the ground with a hearty whoof of breath.

"Ow!"

"You'll thank me later," I told her, before reaching down and snapping the cuffs holding my legs in place.

As I worked to free myself, something small and shiny caught my eye in the nearby grass. It looked like ... a carpet tack? *The hell?*

Now was a poor time to contemplate whether they had Home Depots in Fairyland, especially once one of the Queenshield shouted, "The prisoners! They're attempting to escape!"

Fuck me.

I turned my head, preparing to tell them that I was simply covering my own ass, when Uriel followed up with, "Cut them down!"

So much for this being easy.

All at once, it seemed like I didn't have much choice but to fight our way out of this, but perhaps doing so while a rain of tiny nails pelted the area wasn't the best time to take a stand.

"Sorry," I told Riva, before clambering back to my feet. There was no time to free her and, even if there was, she was a lot slower than me in a foot race – but not if I was carrying her. "Come on, we need to ... URK!"

Something pierced my side, lighting up my nerve endings like a fucking Christmas tree. No way was that a thumbtack.

I staggered away from Riva, unable to quite keep my footing, and managed to look down. The business end of a wicked sharp blade was sticking out of me – the few bits not drenched in blood gleaming in the light.

There was no question what had happened. One of the Queenshield had nailed me in the back with their pig sticker.

This was bad.

Nevertheless, I had to hope my healing abilities... I staggered again, feeling lightheaded just as a memory flashed through my head. It had been right before the siege of High Moon. My mother was on the phone explaining where I could find her secret stash of weapons — all of them silver due to the fact that creatures of supernatural blood were vulnerable to it.

Creatures like me.

"Oh, s-shit," I stammered, my words slurred thanks to the bubble of blood I coughed out.

In the next instant, I slammed face first onto the ground as my limbs decided to go on strike. Red hot pain flared from my side, but at least the grass felt cool and soft against my cheek in the few moments before darkness consumed me.

18

Consciousness returned slowly, in fits and starts. One moment there would be blissful silence, a peaceful cocoon of grey numbness, the next I would hear an unearthly screech that was like a boat hook to my brain – grabbing hold and dragging me ever closer to wakefulness.

That didn't make sense, though. I was dead, or dying anyway. Though Mom and I had never actually gotten the chance to sit down and discuss the finer points of silver and supernaturals, I'd seen enough to know she'd been telling the truth. Creatures like werewolves, of which I was half, were physically very tough. The extra catch was that they healed ridiculously fast – good for me, but not so good when I had an army of them on my proverbial tail. Taking one down required either another creature of para-normal blood or using a weapon made of silver. Yeah, doing a cataclysmic amount of damage would also do the trick, but that was a dicey endeavor unless one happened to have a small arsenal handy.

All of that mental exposition served to do nothing more than prolong the inevitable – letting me stay a little longer in that safe grey space, while the bizarre sounds around me continued to yank and pull me back toward the waking world.

After a while, it became too much to ignore. Oh well, with any luck I'd wake up only to immediately die again, allowing me to return to this peaceful place for all eternity.

As if things could ever be that easy.

Pain returned, along with other sensations, harsh enough for me to know there was no longer any choice in the matter of my waking. A moment later, something pressed down against my side and it was like being touched with a lit cigarette, after being doused in kerosene.

I screamed out, consciousness returning in an instant, and opened my eyes ... then immediately wished I hadn't.

As before, when I'd first appeared in this land, it was like awakening into a nightmare. I was met by a diseased landscape of contorting alien trees and undulating colors, but that wasn't the worst of it. Whereas the first time I'd been confronted with a tentacled nightmare straight out of HP Lovecraft's wet dream, now I was surrounded by much worse. Strange bulbous creatures, with odd stalk-like eyes and appendages, stood all around me. Bizarre pustules, like cancerous tumors, pulsed upon their bodies, their pitted flesh an unpleasant mix of orange and purple, like they were living bruises.

I glanced down, horrified to find one of them right next to me, as if I could actually determine distance in this crazed landscape. The alien monster pressed something to my side, causing every nerve in my body to scream out as surely as my vocal cords did.

Squeezing my eyes shut against the pain, I gritted my teeth, waiting for the torment to pass and then, when it finally did, I opened them again ... only to find I was once more in the place the denizens of this land called the Garden, an idyllic paradise of nature.

Mind you, that wasn't really what I'd call an improvement.

I was still flanked, but the creatures which had replaced the bulbous horrors were, in reality, not much better.

Garden gnomes. I was surrounded by fucking garden gnomes, except these weren't the concrete abominations my mother seemed to enjoy placing around her rose bushes. They were flesh – living and breathing and every bit as fucking creepy as their stone effigies.

"I bid thee well, Princess of Monarchs," one of them said, stepping forward.

Okay, make that even creepier than I thought. These fucking things could talk.

The one who'd spoken removed his red conical hat, revealing a perfectly smooth bald head beneath, and then bowed deeply.

A moment later, his fellows – all of them nearly identical, save for the colors of their clothes and hats – followed his lead.

"Psst. Hey, Girl."

I turned my head at the sound of the familiar voice and saw Grunge, still trussed in his silver shackles, lying nearby.

"Now would probably be a good time to escape," he whispered, looking about as freaked out as I felt.

Pity for him I was still trying to get a handle on rational thought. Forget the hollows, being surrounded by living gnomes was my new nightmare, one I was likely going to wake up screaming from for months to come. Yay for new trauma.

I tried to sit up further, wincing at the sharp ache in my side that told me escape was likely not in the cards.

That said, it wasn't nearly as bad as it should've been. I mean, I'd been impaled for Christ's sake and with silver. The fact that I wasn't pushing up daisies was miracle enough, but I'd suffered enough sports injuries during my wrestling career to know I should've been hurting a lot worse than I was.

"Wait. W-where's Riva?"

"Riva?" the gnome asked.

"My friend ... the other Earth woman or daoine. Whatever you want to call her."

"Ah. Captured by the Queenshield she was. Taken away by them."

"Shit! I need to go and save... Ow!" The pain flared up as I tried to move.

"Be at ease, Princess, please," the redcap gnome said, placing his hat back on his head. "Powerful is the unguent but needs a bit more time to work."

It was all I could do to keep from freaking out. Imagine the quintessential image of Santa Claus, but shrunk to about two feet in height, except not proportionally. An oversized head with a beard that nearly reached the ground compensated for stubby arms and legs that didn't look like they should keep this thing upright, much less afford it locomotion. Now magnify that by over a dozen of his fellows and you can maybe guess why I was a wee bit bug-eyed.

"Um ... unguent?" I asked weakly, still trying to take in the fact that I'd somehow gone from being the prisoner of studly fairy soldiers to waking up in some kind of fucked up Smurf village.

"Yes, our healer Arugula has been working hard to mend your wounds. Strong magic she possesses, but time it does take."

Not helping was his Yoda-speak but, rather than scream – as I really wanted to do – I followed his outstretched hand to find another gnome standing next to me, this one wearing a yellow hat and holding a bowl that was stained with some thick purplish ooze.

"Need to apply more, I do," she, I guess, said.

"Arugula?" I asked, to which the gnome – which looked identical to the leader, beard and all – bowed. "Uh, okay, I guess."

I went to lift up my sweater, only to find that a section had already been torn away to give them access to my injuries. As for the wound on my front side, I couldn't see it, covered as it was by what appeared to be drying purplish gunk.

As I watched, Arugula opened up a small pouch at her side, pulling a handful of fat wiggling grubs from it.

Oh no. She did not rub that all over me.

It was far worse than that, though. The healer gnome popped the squirming bugs into her mouth. She chewed them up then spat the contents into the bowl, filling the bottom with more of that purple stuff.

That's it, I'm going to hurl.

She dipped a finger into the bug guts and approached, prompting me to quickly look away while I could still pretend she wasn't going to do what I knew she was.

I turned my attention back to the leader. "Thanks, I guess."

"Our pleasure it is, Princess."

I could feel Arugula smearing my front and sides with grub gunk. *Think of something else, anything else!* "W-why do you keep calling me that?"

The lead gnome stepped forward.

"Watch out," Grunge cried from where he still lay. "They're dangerous."

"Gag that one," the gnome said, a hint of annoyance crossing his comically oversized face before turning toward me again. "Call you Princess because that is who you are."

He pointed one stubby little finger toward ... my chest?! Great. Just what I needed. Pervert gnomes. "Wear the symbol of her Majesty, Lissa of the Monarchs, you do."

Symbol? My boobs?

I looked down and finally realized what he was talking about – the pendent my mother had given me. *Duh*! At least that was a magnitude less creepy than the alternative.

Hold on ... Mom!

"You know my mother?" I asked, ignoring the now muffled protests Grunge was making. "Who or what are you guys?"

The little gnome stepped back, looking embarrassed. "Apologies for our rudeness. I am Cabbage, leader of the Nibelung."

Cabbage, leader of the... I tried to process that sentence, but my brain instead threw a rod. Cabbage. I was dealing with someone named Cabbage. This was apparently my world now.

"Um, nice to meet you ... Cabbage."

That seemed to please the little gnome with the stupid name, so he continued. "Friend to the Monarch Queen are we. Always she has treated us well and so we are pledged to look after her and her brood."

I remembered back to last summer, certain I'd seen the garden gnomes in our front yard turn their heads toward me. But then Mom had told me she'd gotten them all at Target, of all places, and...

Okay, let's be realistic here. It wouldn't exactly be the first time Mom lied to me. Probably wouldn't be the last either. I...

Grunge's muffled protests interrupted my train of thought, which was already in danger of veering heavily off the tracks. Oh, enough of this. "Can you untie him please?" I inclined my head toward the annoying little pixie.

"Oh?" Cabbage replied. "You are hungry and wish to eat?"

"Eat *him*?!" *Eww.* "No! He's my ... friend, sorta."

Yeah, it was a stretch. But the winged creep had pledged his fealty to me. Didn't seem right to leave him to whatever fate these gnomes had in mind, especially if it included frying him up for a snack. *Yuck!*

"Friend with a sylph? Untrustworthy they are."

"I know, believe me. But he's promised to serve me until his sidhe honor, or whatever it's called, is satisfied."

Cabbage stroked his beard, looking almost contemplative for a moment. "Sidhe honor powerful magic. Very well. If the Princess says so, it shall be."

He instructed the others to untie Grunge. In the meantime, Arugula had finished applying her layer of spittle goo to my injuries. Much as it still grossed me out, I was forced to admit I already felt a lot better. The angry pain in my side had subsided to a dull ache, not much worse than a bad bruise, allowing me to fully sit up while they freed my former tour guide to the Garden.

Once they were finished, Grunge stepped over and grabbed hold of my hand, but this wasn't some gesture of good friendship or anything. He was actively trying to pull me to my feet. Though I didn't weigh *that* much, I was still pretty much a giant where he was concerned, so his progress was mostly nil.

"Hey. What gives?"

"Come on," he pleaded. "We need to get out of here before these gleefing brindlespurs change their minds."

"Hold on a second. First off, I'm not going anywhere. Secondly, what the hell is a brindlespur?"

"Are you gleefing kidding me? Have you been living in a treehouse all your life or something? A brindlespur ... you know, large, mostly lives in the water, and will trample anything they set their eyes on."

"Sounds kind of like a hippopotamus."

Grunge stopped yanking my arm long enough to stare at me. "You daoine sure have stupid names for things. It doesn't matter, though, let's go!"

I couldn't believe I was saying this, but I replied, "I'm staying here, at least until I hear these guys out."

"Fine," Grunge said, backing away. "You stay and let them club you upside the head like a baby kelfling. I'm doing the sensible thing and saving myself."

The pixie turned and made a run for it ... or tried to.

He made it less than a dozen steps before he fell to his knees, making that wheezing sound again. When he turned back, his eyes once more looked like they were about to shoot right out of his head.

"Uh huh. Nice try." With that, I turned back toward Cabbage. "You were saying?"

19

I t took a while for my brain to get used to the odd way Cabbage and his friends talked, but eventually I began to get the gist of what was going on.

Seems him and his people were considered the fairy equivalent of outlaws, or maybe a terrorist cell, minus the part about strapping explosives to themselves. If anything, it seemed their big crime was simply being disliked by the queen.

Cabbage filled me in a bit on their history as I sat and mended, my enhanced healing finally beginning to take over from whatever the bug guts had managed to fix. The gnomes – or Nibelung as they called themselves – were not originally from the Garden. They came here as refugees from another world, after some kind of cataclysm – the details of which he didn't go into.

They'd hoped to be granted asylum, but instead Brigid had labeled them as outlaws and forbade them from settling in her lands. I tried to ask why, but Grunge ever so helpfully butted in instead.

"Are you gleefing for real? Everyone knows you can't trust a nieb. They're sneaky little gleefers. Nobody can see them coming, not even her royal highness. You'll be lying there, crunching on some taintnuts and minding your own business, and then bam. Next thing you know, you've been cut into pieces and are simmering in a Nibelung stew."

"You keep your taintnuts to yourself," I told him before turning back toward Cabbage, hoping for some clarification that didn't involve either taint or nuts.

"Not entirely wrong is he," Cabbage admitted. "Her highness's power extends to all these lands and those within them."

"I sense a but coming."

The gnome leader smiled up at me, his rosy cheeks shining bright red. "Indeed, Princess. The queen of these lands labels us enemies, she does, but no crimes have we committed. We are guilty of one thing and one thing only – we cannot be seen."

I blinked a few times, trying to process this. "But I can see you just fine."

"With your eyes, yes, but only with them. I know not how it works or why, but the Nibelung and those around us cannot be seen from afar. Where we walk, the plants and trees fall silent. Her highness does not trust that which she cannot control."

"Huh. Sounds like she'd fit in just fine with most of the leaders on Earth." I turned to Grunge. "I figured you'd like this, being out of earshot of those in charge."

He grimaced uncomfortably. "I might if I wasn't worried about ending up in someone's stomach."

I let out a laugh as I turned back to the gnome leader. "Can you please tell my friend you're not going to eat him."

Cabbage was quiet for a moment before asking, "He is truly the Princess's friend, yes?"

Kind of an odd question. Tempting as it was to say

something snarky, I instead replied, "Yes, Grunge is my friend."

"Then eat him we shall not."

That was about the exact opposite of the comforting answer I was expecting. Carnivorous gnomes – talk about nightmare fuel for years to come.

Hoping to change the subject to something less ominous, I asked, "So, how do you guys know my mother?"

"Ah yes, Lissa the Monarch Queen. To tell that, you must know our great secret, our great shame."

Shame? "Okay. Go on."

"Long ago, soon after we first arrived here, her majesty tried to banish us from this realm. Strong magic she gathered, many souls sacrificed to empower her spell. She sent it out as a serpent in the night, crawling throughout the land, so that even we could not hope to hide from it. Her might was such that she succeeded in driving us out, but also failed did she."

"I'm not even remotely following."

"She banished a portion of our souls from this place, but powerful as her magic was, it was still not enough to fully cast us out. We exist here and also there, in your world."

"Wait. So you're here and on Earth at the same time?" That made absolutely no fucking sense.

"Tell her," the one called Arugula said, her mouth free of bug guts. "Tell her how we are cursed to never be whole."

"Getting to that I was," Cabbage admonished. "Be not pushy." He turned back toward me and resumed his solemn tone. "We are both here and there. Close my eyes and I can reach out to your world, see it as clearly as I see you. But for all but one hour a day there we are nothing but stone – able to see and hear, but unable to do more. For one hour a day only are we free."

"Please tell me I'm not the only one gleefing creeped out by this," Grunge said, sidling up next to me.

"Not by a long shot," I replied. "So, what you're telling me, Cabbage, is that for twenty-three hours out of the day, you guys are stuck as statues over on my world, but you can still see what's going on."

"Yes," Arugula said. "Quite annoying is it. An itch on my nose I got last week, could not scratch it for half a day."

"I can see how that would suck."

"Indeed," Cabbage continued. "But far worse is being vulnerable. For, if the part of our soul there dies, the half of us here perishes as well. And though stone is strong, invulnerable it is not."

Holy crap. I guess that *really* would suck.

"Stumbled upon us for centuries, the daoine have, during our times as stone. The lucky ones have been carried home to be used as decorations or ornaments. The unlucky have been thrown off cliffs or left in the middle of your roads."

"Ooh. That's not cool." But I guess I could see where the fascination with lawn gnomes came from. People finding them in the woods, bringing them home as curios, and then eventually mass producing them. I bet that's one bit of history you won't find in the commerce textbooks. "But what does that have to do with my mother?"

"In ages past, the followers of her majesty were those we have always feared most, because her edicts they lived to carry out. It is only recently, as the incantations between worlds have dwindled, have we grown to fear them less. But fear them still we do ... except your mother."

"Why?"

"Years ago, when she was but a girl, younger than even you, we were careless in our hour of freedom. Did not realize she was nearby practicing her magic. She spied us in our true forms, watched hidden as we turned back to stone. Could have destroyed us all, but she did not. Kept our secret she did. Waited until we were free again then treated us with kindness, befriended us despite her teachings. Eventually, she offered us succor, a place some of us could be safe – a home where food and offerings she brought to us. In return, we swore an oath to watch over her, an oath we pass down to her honored heirs."

I sat back and considered this. Holy shit! So I hadn't been crazy when I'd seen those fucking things move last summer. Mind you, somehow that didn't make it better, knowing that these things were free to run around doing god-knows-what, even if only for an hour.

That was it. Once I got back home, I was painting all the windows in my bedroom black and nailing them shut.

On the flip side, that was actually cool to hear about Mom. I mean, I already knew she kind of played fast and loose with the Draíodóir rules – after all, she married my dad – but apparently she had an altruistic side I wasn't aware of. Yes, I still wished I wasn't aware of it, because that made me want to smash the shit out of the garden gnomes in front of my house even more now, but it was still awesome to know.

"When we learned your mother was brought here as a prisoner, we knew we had to act, so gathered weapons we have."

"Weapons?"

Cabbage reached into his belt pouch and produced ... a box of carpet tacks, with the price tag still attached.

I took it from him and gave it a look over. "Call me crazy, but this doesn't look like it was made locally."

Cabbage smiled, but there was a conspiratorial quality

to it. "Being of two worlds all bad is not. That which we touch there, we can bring here."

Cool trick. I was tempted to ask if they could do that with a living being as well, preferably in reverse, when Grunge peeked over my shoulder.

"What have you got ... oh gleef!" he cried, recoiling in horror. "Keep that the gleef away from me."

I'm gonna go out on a limb and assume gleef was their version of fuck, or something close to it – meaning Grunge was a bit of a potty mouth. Go figure. "They're just tacks. They..."

But then I remembered what I'd seen before being stabbed. One of Uriel's guards had been hit in the face with something which had reacted with his skin like a water balloon filled with acid. Turning to Cabbage, I held up the box. "What exactly do these do?"

The little gnome's grin instantly turned predatory. "Iron is the queen's bane, as it is for all her kin."

Hot damn. That explained the silver chains. They weren't just for show. Yes, silver was also toxic to those like me, but only on the inside. I could pick up a fork and eat with it just fine, or wear jewelry without dying for that matter. Apparently, iron was kind of the same for creatures from the Garden, only a lot more so.

I remembered briefly reading about that somewhere, probably in some novel. Come to think of it, I seemed to recall there being lots of rules when it came to dealing with fairies. Too bad I'd never been into that particular genre, otherwise I might've had clue one as to what they were. Oh well, no point in crying over that puddle of spilled milk.

Besides, I knew at least this much. The fairies had weapons that could hurt me, but now I knew what could hurt them back. Not only that, but an iron sword beat a silver one any day of the week. Sure, I didn't have an iron sword, or any sword for that matter, but it was the thought that counted.

Glancing back down at Cabbage, I asked, "So what were you planning on doing with all this stuff?"

He shook his head. "Armed we might be, but forming a plan we still are."

"Until we learned that you, the Princess, had journeyed here," Arugula said, stepping next to Cabbage and taking hold of his tiny hand.

They sort of made a cute couple, despite being identical twins.

"Special you are," Cabbage said. "Powerful, brave, different ... enough so that her highness immediately sent her Queenshield to deal with you."

I opened my mouth to reply, but then a question popped into my head. "Wait a second. You don't follow the queen, do you?"

"No queen of ours is she," Cabbage said, hocking a tiny multicolored loogie. *Gross.*

"So then why do you call her highness and your majesty instead of Brig..."

Both Cabbage and Arugula leapt at me, surprisingly fast for creatures with such lopsided bodies, and placed their tiny hands over my mouth.

My first instinct was to bat them away, but I managed to hold myself in check, hoping they had a good explanation.

"Names have power," Cabbage whispered. "Great power. Even hidden as we are from her, we dare not speak her name aloud for fear she shall hear us. And if she hears us..."

He let the threat hang in the air.

"But me and my friend have both said her name since we got here and..." And almost immediately ended up being arrested by her elite hotties. "Never mind. Point taken."

I glanced over at Grunge and he nodded. "She's capable of seeing all that transpires in the Garden, but seeing isn't the same as noticing. And let's face gleefing facts, a lot goes on here. If you're stupid enough to speak her name, though, you risk calling undue attention to yourself, if you catch my drift."

Undue attention, which a sleezebag such as Grunge would obviously not want. That explained his own lack of using her name whenever talking about her. But it also told me to be extra mindful of my tongue going forward – something I wasn't exactly renowned for.

"All right," I said, leaning forward, "now that I'm here, what's the plan for dealing with her royal cuntiness?"

"That's it?" I asked three minutes later. "The entirety of your plan is to storm her fortress, rescue my mother, and then demand equality for gnomekind?"

"A work in progress it still is."

More and more, I was beginning to think my original plan of letting Brigid's guards capture me had been the right option. I didn't ask to be rescued by creepy ass gnomes, and I sure as shit hadn't volunteered to be an insurgent. All I wanted were my parents and Riva back. The rest of this place, freaky gnomes and dirtbag fairies included, could go hang itself.

"I don't mean to interrupt and risk being made into your lunch or anything," Grunge said from my side, where he'd mostly plastered himself. Ugh. He smelled like old potato chips. "But I agree with Girl here. This plan is kind of ... not gleefing good."

Cabbage glared at him, causing Grunge to hide behind

me. I reached an arm around my back and dragged him out, not really wanting him where I couldn't see him.

"Work in progress it might be, but stupid we are not," Cabbage growled at him, before softening his tone and facing me again. "Learned things we have. Small and unseen we might be, but good ears we possess as well as allies here, others who are not fond of the queen."

"See?" I told Grunge. "You two have something in common."

"I'll keep that in mind when they're gnawing the last of the meat off my bones."

"Nobody likes a pessimist." I indicated for Cabbage to go on.

"Distracted soon the queen will be. Others journey here from far away, not of this land. To the queen's banquet hall they go for feasting and much talk."

"Others? Like her subjects?"

"No," Arugula replied. "Not subjects, not all. Some vassals, yes, but lords in their own right. Others, though, equal to her in both status and power."

"Equal to her in status and power?" Why did that not sound promising?

"Gods," Cabbage confirmed.

Oh. Well, if that didn't make this plan better, I didn't know what did. I mean, storming the castle of one freaking goddess was a clusterfuck in its own right, but now the entire place would be crawling with them. That's all I needed, to be sneaking around a corner, only to run into Zeus being all, "Hey, baby, you like swans?" I didn't consider myself a coward by any stretch, but it seemed a less than wonderful idea to conduct a hostile incursion into a castle filled with walking nuclear bombs just looking for an excuse to go off.

Cabbage and Arugula — what a pair of names — didn't

seem entirely without empathy. Arugula stepped forward and put a comforting hand atop mine.

"Know it may not seem like it, but best time it is. Her highness will be distracted. Very busy keeping guests happy, no time for other issues. The Queenshield will be, too. All the best will be in attendance..."

"Leaving the worst to work behind the scenes actually guarding the place. Because who would be dumb enough to storm a fortress full of ancient deities, right?"

"Exactly!"

"Just to clarify," Grunge asked me, "you're saying we're dumb enough, aren't you?"

"Um ... I'm not quite committing yet." Back to Cabbage, I replied, "So what's the occasion? I mean, it's New Year's Day on Earth. Do they have something similar here?"

Cabbage and Arugula merely shrugged, so I glanced at Grunge.

"How can you fit an entire year into a day?" he asked, apparently having no more of a clue.

"You know, holidays? Special days that happen at the same time every year or ... I dunno ... season?"

"Like the queen's Day of Ascension festival?" Grunge asked.

"Sure."

"Which, just for the record, I make it a point to avoid."

"Not surprising at all. So is that happening now?"

"It usually takes place at Sunsummit."

"Sunsummit? Is that a location?"

"No, it's a time ... and no, it's not now."

"Fine, but you get the idea. Is there anything like that going on now?"

"Besides this gathering of gods these gleefers just mentioned? No idea."

"Okay then. You're useless." I turned back toward the gnomes. "Let's forget about the holiday stuff and move on. There's going to be a big gathering during which Bri ... the chick with the crown will be busy. And that's our chance to sneak in and rescue my parents and Riva."

"Yes. We shall free the Monarch Queen."

"And then demand to be treated as citizens of the realm," Arugula added.

"Not to throw a spanner into that, but doesn't marching in and demanding her attention sort of defeat the purpose of sneaking in while she's distracted?"

The two gnome leaders turned to one another, leaned in, and began to whisper in each other's ears, holding a mini conversation of sorts. My supercharged hearing picked up the words easily enough, but not their meaning as they switched to some high-pitched language I couldn't even remotely understand. So much for Brigid's translation spell. Guess that was another bit of her magic the gnomes were resistant to.

After a few moments, they pulled away and turned to face me again.

"Yes," Arugula said. "Ruin our stealth it will, but necessary it is for our people."

I hated to be a dick about something like freedom, but that seemed like a good way to get us all killed, especially right when we were so close to victory. "I don't suppose we can save my parents, then maybe petition the queen another day?"

"Yeah," Grunge added. "Like maybe in another century or three."

This caused the gnomes to lean in and converse amongst themselves again. After a bit more back and forth, Cabbage stepped forward this time.

"Put it this way I shall. Your mother, the Monarch Queen, we care deeply for. Your father less so and your friend we know not. If our help you wish in rescuing them, then our terms you will meet. Fair?"

Blackmailed by gnomes. So this was how my year was starting. Wonderful. Sadly, the little fucks had me over a barrel, which I'm sure they knew. Even so, that didn't mean I couldn't maybe, I dunno, slip away once I had my parents. Who's to say we wouldn't get separated along the way, maybe accidentally turn down the wrong hallway while Cabbage and his buddies marched toward the banquet hall and certain death at the hand of multiple gods.

Yeah, it was kind of crummy of me, but it was helped by the fact that everything I'd managed to *befriend* in this place so far creeped me the fuck out.

"Before you say anything," Cabbage added, almost as if reading my mind, "I must warn that deals and promises are bonds in this place ... much like honor. To break one's bond is to invite..." he pointed toward Grunge and made a gesture to indicate his eyeballs exploding.

"Wait, that applies to me, too?"

"Afraid so," Grunge said. "Not the first time I've seen it happen to a daoine who came here and assumed the rules didn't apply to them."

Shit! More fairy rules. Guess I should've paid more attention to these things last time I had a book in my hands. Sadly, I had a feeling there was no such thing as a local library here I could use to bone up on my lore.

Either way, Cabbage still had me over a barrel, but now it was filled with hungry piranha. Just great. Guess I'd have to improvise once the time came ... or at least take comfort in the fact that my parents and I would be vaporized as a family unit.

"Deal," I said, grudgingly. "We rescue my parents and friend, then I'll make sure you at least make it far enough to get an audience with the queen."

"Accepted," Cabbage and Arugula said simultaneously, their cherub cheeks shining bright red as they smiled. *Ugh.* "Then prepare we shall to storm Dùn nan Dé."

"Dùn nan..."

"Queenie's castle," Grunge clarified. "There's just one small catch. I'm small grubroots to these guys. They'll put an alert out with my old name but then forget about it soon enough."

"You sound like you've been through this before."

Grunge grinned to let me know I'd hit the nail on the head then continued. "Not to toot my own zizzleph-weet, but I've been here for a while and plan to be here for a while longer. But you, they came after us specifically because of you. Why? I don't know, and no, I doubt it was because you killed a gleefing troll. That tells me, distracted or not, they're going to be keeping their eyes open for you. One wrong move, one slip of the tongue, and they'll be all over you like a troternaut on rotweed."

"No, they will not," Cabbage replied, his words surprisingly coherent.

"Trust me," the dirtbag pixie replied. "I've dealt with these guys before. Once the queen shoves a burr up their backsides, they won't quit."

"Yes, they will."

Grunge crossed his spindly arms across his chest as if daring the gnome to prove it. "And you know this how?"

"Simple it is." Cabbage turned toward his fellow gnomes, most of them milling about engrossed in various ... um ... gnome-like activities, and then he clapped his hands.

A few moments later, there came the sound of tiny feet marching in unison. From between a pair of neon-colored bushes came a mini-procession of gnomes.

My breath caught in my throat at the sight of them,

but it wasn't due to their appearance. It was because of what they were carrying, or should I say *who*.

I could only watch in mute horror as they carried out ... my corpse?

"They will not be looking for her," Cabbage continued, "because dead she already is."

20

I scooted away from the body as the gnomes placed it on the ground before me. I couldn't help myself. Suddenly, what had been a waking nightmare, had somehow turned into a freaking episode of *Lost.*

"Well, that's kinda gleefed up," Grunge said, looking over my corpse as if it were nothing more than an interesting paperweight.

"You think?!" I practically screamed at him before taking several deep breaths to get myself under control.

It took a couple of minutes, but eventually I felt the need to lose my mind recede a bit, so I shuffled forward again. Whoever this was, they truly did look like me, down to the tiny mole at the base of my neck.

The only difference was that she, I ... whatever, was dressed different than I was now. That said, the outfit was immediately recognizable. I'd been wearing it only a few days earlier.

The body itself was covered in tiny pinprick wounds, evidence of some sort of battle. More telling, however, was the fact that it was missing its right arm at the elbow. That alone was enough traumatic damage to...

Hold on a second. The break was clean, the wound healed over. Either this hadn't happened recently or she...

Wait just a fucking moment. Missing arm, same clothes as I'd worn just days earlier...

No way. How could this be the same fucking creature I'd fought?

There was only one way to be certain. I rolled the body over onto its side and reached into the back pocket of its jeans.

"Whoa. Looting your own corpse?" Grunge remarked. "Now that's hardcore."

"Shut up." Sure enough, I pulled out a Sailor Moon wallet – *my wallet.* I quickly checked the contents. Some cash was missing, but all my IDs and credit cards were still there. *Yes!* "Try getting a mortgage in my name now, bitch!"

"I'm missing something here, aren't I?"

"That's not me," I told Grunge, pocketing my wallet. "It's a doppelganger."

"A doppel..."

"You probably call them something else, but they're shapeshifters, nasty ones. I tangled with this asshole a few days back. Just barely fought it off, but not before it managed to mug me."

"Indeed," Cabbage replied, seemingly pleased that I'd figured it out on my own. "Caught this beast trying to sneak into your home we did. Did not expect the Monarch Queen's defenses upon your threshold. Stunned it was. We fell upon it as it lay there, brought it here."

Guess that answered the question about whether they could transport living creatures. I could only imagine the horror my evil twin here experienced in its last moments as tiny little hands reached down to ... wait a second. "How did you grab hold of it if you were all statues?"

"An hour a day we are free," Arugula said, repeating

what I'd already been told. "But we are also free to choose which hour that shall be."

And we were right back to creepy again. Oh well, it couldn't happen to a nicer asshole. "So, you killed it and brought it here?"

"No," Arugula replied. "It still lives."

"What?!"

"Poisoned it is. One of my unguents, this one designed to make a creature seem as if death has claimed it, yet it still lives on."

"Just for the record, I would've been okay with dead. No offense, but this thing is kind of dangerous."

"How dangerous?" Grunge asked.

"Remember those rock trolls?"

"Yeah."

"Well, this thing gave me a lot more trouble. I just barely beat it."

"I see. Then dead is fine with me, too. Feel free to gleef it up."

"No!" Cabbage stepped in front of us, his stubby arms held out wide. "It must live."

Seemed a rather strange place to plant his flag when he was offering Grunge up as a snack just a short while ago. "Listen. I understand sanctity of life and all but..."

"Has nothing to do with that, this does," he said. "This beast, others of its kind, feared by many."

"I get that."

"But you do not understand why. Feared because not understood are they. Hard to understand a beast that is difficult to kill. Even harder to understand when killed and no body remains."

No body?

I began to see his reasoning. "So you're saying that if we kill this thing it'll, what, turn to ash or dissolve?"

Cabbage nodded. "No body for Queenshield to find. So Queenshield will continue to search for the Princess."

All at once, I was glad he'd stepped in. Had I followed through and snapped this thing's neck like I wanted to, it would've been one step forward and half a mile back with regards to our plan – which wasn't all that great to begin with. "Okay, fine. But how do we know the Queenshield won't just stab the shit out of it instead?"

"Not how they work," Grunge said. "The queen wants you, so they'll find the body, shackle it up because that's part of their process, and dump it at her feet for judgement. She'll congratulate them on a gleefing job well done, pontificate about her own greatness, then order it tossed into the fire for disposal."

"That's a disturbing amount of detail."

He shrugged or did the pixie equivalent of it. "When you've worked as hard as I have to stay out of their way, you learn a thing or two."

I guess that made sense. I pushed myself to my feet, stretching so as to test my injuries. Not bad. Only a few twinges of pain left. Between the bug gunk and my own accelerated healing, the worst seemed to be behind me. At the very least, I was strong enough to walk – which, considering how long the Queenshield road had stretched, seemed like something I'd be doing a lot of in the near future.

There was no time like the present to get started.

I smiled as I remembered a movie quote that seemed apt. "All right, boys. Let's have fun storming the castle."

A contingent of gnomes made off with the doppelganger. The plan was to rough it up a bit then leave it in a place where the Queenshield or their agents would easily find it.

As for me, I was happy to see it gone and more then okay with the fate in store for it.

Probably coldblooded of me, but my pity didn't extend to creatures that tried to murder me and take over my life for no other reason than shits and giggles. Not that the deception would've worked for long. The werewolves would've probably sniffed it out pretty quickly, but who's to say what damage it could've done before that happened? The fact that the gnomes had caught it trying to break into my home was bad enough. What if Chris had been there when...?

Chris... *Shit!*

It was only now I realized I had no idea what happened after Possessed Riva sent me here. All I knew was that she'd been more than a match for both witch and werewolf alike. With any luck, my brother had realized that and made a run for it.

Sadly, so long as I was stuck here, I had no way of knowing either way.

Goddamnit! I grabbed hold of a nearby tree branch, splintering it in my frustration. It seemed that no matter what I did, some member of my family ended up in danger and there was nothing I could do about it. It was as if all my powers served to do nothing more than mock my inability to keep my loved ones safe.

It was a sobering thought. I remembered seeing something similar in a movie once ... *Superman*, but the old one from the seventies. Yeah, that was it. Despite all his power, he couldn't save his father from something as common as a heart attack. But it hadn't been old age which threatened my family. First had been my bitch aunt making a play for power. Now it was something else, something wearing the skin of my best friend.

I felt a tear slip down my cheek as a series of unpleasant what-ifs played out in my head. Yeah, Chris and I gave each other as much grief as two siblings could. It was just the way we were. Most of the time, there was no more rancor behind it than seeing if we could get a rise out of the other. But he was my family and I loved him ... even if I'd have sooner chewed on some of Arugula's bug gunk than admit it aloud to the little turd.

Then there was Cass. I hadn't known her for long, but in the space of a few days it was like she'd become, much like Riva, a sister from another mister.

Unfortunately, I couldn't do much for any of them standing there feeling sorry for myself. And there was no way of knowing what had transpired after I'd been cast out of my reality. Maybe Possessed Riva had backed off, satisfied that she'd proven her point to both lycanthropes and Draíodóir. Or maybe she hadn't.

A part of me was tempted to approach the gnomes and demand to see if the doorway swung both ways. If they could drag fake me here, maybe they could send the real me back home. Once there, I could figure out a way to fix things.

Or I could die, knowing I'd been given a chance to save my parents but had blown that, too.

Even if I succeeded and the Draíodóir were able to send me back here again, might I only be stepping into an even worse situation? There'd be no fooling the Queenshield twice with the ploy we had planned. It was either now or never.

I gave my head a shake to clear it. Flip-flopping back and forth wasn't helping me at all. What was that my father had told me? He'd said becoming the alpha meant adopting an alpha mindset. You didn't pretend to be in charge, you *were* in charge. There was no decision by committee, any of that. You picked a direction and then you led the pack that way. Anything less was unacceptable.

There might not be any werewolves around now, but

that didn't mean I wasn't still their alpha. Same with the Draíodóir. Though I doubted that side of the family would acknowledge it if push came to shove, the gnomes at least seemed to regard me as the Princess of Monarchs, heir to my mother.

I reached up to caress the pendant still hanging around my neck. With neither side around to either give advice or judge me, I needed to step up and embrace both roles. I had to pick a course of action, stay with it, and then own the consequences.

It was either that or do nothing, and that simply wasn't acceptable. At least by taking action there was a chance. And a chance was better than none.

"Ready are you, Princess?"

I looked down and saw Arugula standing there, staring up at me from beneath her yellow cap. "As I'll ever be."

"Excellent." She gestured and a nearby group of gnomes came marching over, carrying something between them. Thankfully, it wasn't another body. "Your weapon, Princess."

Weapon? I bent and took the object from the gnomes, studying it for a moment. "Um, isn't this a wrought iron fence post?"

"Perhaps in the other world, from which we plucked it, but here it is a spear worthy of royalty."

I doubt whoever you stole this from agrees. Somewhere back in my world, there was someone likely screaming to the police about vandals. Oh, well. Their loss. And remembering what had happened with the carpet tacks, she was likely right. Here, this simple iron rod was the equivalent of Excalibur itself.

Fuck it. Might as well play along.

"I shall be honored to wield it."

Arugula grinned, obviously pleased with my answer. "Shall we be off then?"

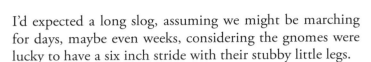

I'd expected a long slog, assuming we might be marching for days, maybe even weeks, considering the gnomes were lucky to have a six inch stride with their stubby little legs.

What I didn't expect was that they knew a shortcut that lay deep underground.

"Miners and explorers in our own world we were," Cabbage explained, maintaining a brisk pace for a guy with legs the size of a teddy bear. "Only natural it is that we would learn the ways of the below here."

I can't say I was keen on being a cave explorer. Hell, there was this one time, back in fifth grade, when my parents took me on one of those cavern tours. Snooze Ville. Yay, a big dumb fucking rock. Oh, look, another big dumb fucking rock.

That said, if I was slightly nonplussed as Cabbage led the way through the sloping tunnel we now took, Grunge seemed positively terrified in the meager torchlight.

"Oh, this is not gleefing good."

"I thought you said you lived in a burrow."

"Yeah," he replied, eying the spear now strapped to my back. "A burrow. There's a big difference between that and this gleefing hell hole."

"Oh?"

"For starters, there's nothing in my burrow that might eat me."

I hadn't considered that. Back home, the worst you might run into would be bugs, bats, worms, and maybe the occasional snake. No. That wasn't true. The worst a normal person might *expect* to run into would be that stuff. But who was to say what might be lurking in the shadows, unknown to the general populace but no less hungry? More than one movie had been made on that premise alone.

Seeing nothing but darkness past the light provided by the gnomes' torches, I found myself subconsciously taking a step closer to Grunge, despite the absolute lack of comfort he offered.

"Worry not, sylph," Cabbage called back derisively. "The way is well known to us. Before setting out, sent warriors ahead I did to clear the way." He glanced back over his shoulder and threw me a smile that made my skin crawl. "Eat well the Nibelung shall in the days ahead."

Um, yeah. I looked down at Grunge. "At least it sounds like you're off the menu for now."

After an hour or so, the cramped tunnel finally opened up into a cavern, but one unlike anything my parents had forced me to tour. Here, the gnomes put away their torches. They were no longer necessary. Multi-colored lichen glowed along the walls, the illumination amplified by what appeared to be massive gemstones sticking out of the walls here and there. Diamonds might be a girl's best friend, but they weren't lit up like a sixty-watt bulb, pulsing softly from within as if powered by some unseen energy source.

"Holy shit."

There was no doubt about it. This place was fabulous. Had my parents brought me here instead for that vacation all those years ago, I might not have groused as much.

While on the one hand the illumination served to make me feel a bit better – the light more than enough to see anything that might decide our ragtag invasion force would make a tasty treat – my ears were a different story. Every step we took, every pebble we dislodged, all of it echoed around us, creating a constant cacophony of spooky sounds. This was augmented by the occasional noise that I was certain wasn't born of our troop, making me wonder exactly what Cabbage's warriors had cleared out down here and whether they'd truly been thorough.

As we continued our long trek beneath the Garden, I found myself wishing I had a real weapon on me and not something meant to keep someone's rat dog from escaping their yard.

Hours passed, or at least it felt like it. Damn my lack of owning a decent watch, not that I could be certain time passed the same here anyway. Aside from the occasional rest break, in which I snacked on a few berries but declined the grubs the gnomes kept offering me, we marched in relative silence. Jeez. So much for stereotypes. Weren't these guys supposed to sing happy mining songs as they went about their business? I can't say I was ever a big *Snow White* fan, but I'd have gladly welcomed a few "Hi's" and the occasional "Ho".

I was just beginning to scope out stalagmites behind which I might disappear for a pee break, when the cavern around us began to change. The ceiling became lower, and the walls began to close in again. I wasn't what one might call a tall girl, but soon enough I had to crouch to continue onward.

So much for good posture.

It wasn't long before I realized we were past the cave and into a purposely dug shaft, the walls way too smooth to be naturally occurring even in this weird-ass place. It was wide enough, but as for the height, duh. It had been made by gnomes. To them, this was practically a vaulted ceiling.

And then we hit a wall, literally. The mineshaft came to an abrupt dead end, a barrier of solid stone before us.

The gnomes spread out to both sides of the tunnel, drawing tiny slings and loading them with carpet tacks.

"Um, Girl, I have a bad feeling about this," Grunge

said, pulling close to me despite the iron post still strapped to my back.

As a couple dozen cherub faces turned our way, all of them grinning the same creepy smile, I began to wonder whether we'd really been led toward the queen's castle or had willingly marched into our own tomb.

21

The standoff continued for several long seconds, with way too many eyes staring at me as I tried to gauge just how effective of a defense I could mount while bent nearly double.

Finally, Cabbage stepped from the crowd and looked up at me. "Waiting for something, are you?"

"Huh?" Was he talking to me or his minions?

"Arrived we have. Action is needed or here we will stay."

"I ... don't understand."

Cabbage narrowed his eyes. "Not understand. How can you not..."

At that, Arugula stepped up and smacked him in the head, almost dislodging his cap. "Forget to explain the plan again did you?"

"Um, thought I did." He glanced upward, as if recalling his memories, talking silently to himself for a few moments before once again turning toward me. "Oh. Maybe not. Apologies I must give. Forgetful I have become in my old age."

He let out a chuckle, to which Arugula raised a hand again, causing him to quickly point toward the dead end. "My people dug without risk of detection as far as they could. Right behind this wall lies the rest of the way but..." He trailed off expectantly, allowing me to put two and two together.

"I see. And you figure the fastest way through this wall is me?"

Cabbage nodded. "If fight rock trolls you can, minor obstacle this should be."

I guess I couldn't argue with that logic.

Breathing a heavier sigh of relief than I really meant to, I stepped forward and got down on my knees before the wall of rock.

I reached out and touched it. Strange. Much like the pendant I wore, the stone felt warm, almost alive. Wouldn't that be my luck, for this to be nothing more than another rock troll, sleeping unawares and about to get the rudest awakening of its life.

Still, it seemed we had a choice: either forge ahead or stay here until we died of old age. Pretty easy decision if you asked me.

I sized up the wall, picked a spot that seemed to be at about the middle of things, then reared back with my fist...

And paused to adjust the spear on my back so it didn't dig into the ground. So much for this so-called princess looking cool. However, it also gave me pause to think this through. Turning my fist to mush against solid rock wouldn't be a great start to this invasion.

I grabbed hold of my sweater, near where it was already torn, and ripped off another strip, revealing even more of my midriff. If this kept up, I'd have to keep an eye out for any gnomes scoping me out for underboob. For now, though, I wrapped the fabric around my knuckles, giving me a bit of cushion, kind of like a boxer preparing for a fight.

Then it was time to try again. I reared back and let out a deep breath, focusing myself. Fortunately, I knew a thing or two about throwing a punch. I waited until I felt ready, then let fly.

My fist struck the wall with a hollow thud, loud in the cramped confines, and hard enough to rattle the cave around us. I was rewarded with a throb of pain and a sound not unlike that of concrete crumbling.

Sure enough, when I pulled my fist back, I saw a healthy divot taken out of the wall and multiple cracks extending from that spot. Okay, this had potential.

I centered myself once more and struck out again. This time, the *crack* of stone crumbling became more pronounced, the divot deeper. A third time was all it took to break through, revealing the wall of stone in front of us was only a few inches thick. Good thing, too, as I was starting to feel it in my knuckles.

With a small opening before me, I was able to take advantage of the weakened structure. Within minutes, I'd managed to pull enough of it down for me to fit through. I waved some of the dust away and took a good look inside.

What the fuck?

The mineshaft gave way to a more formally constructed tunnel, arched and made of worked masonry. Good thing I'd punched through where I had, because another foot or so to my right was a drop into what seemed to be an underground river. But it was like no river I'd ever seen. The water was viscous, sludge-like. Perhaps more importantly, it was also bright pink.

Had we gone from the cave of glowing gems only to find ourselves in the tunnel of bubble gum demons?

"Good, good," Cabbage said, stepping up beside me. "In the sewers beneath Dùn nan Dé are we."

I was suddenly glad I hadn't been tempted to sample the *bubble gum*. "Did you say sewers?"

"Yes. All that is here comes from above."

I decided not to question him further, knowing how sewers generally worked. At the same time, I couldn't help the grin that crept onto my face as I imagined Queen Brigid sitting on her porcelain throne, pinching out a spool of cotton candy. Despite myself, I took a quick sniff of the air, knowing I was likely asking for trouble with my overly sensitive nostrils. Oddly enough, it wasn't even remotely as bad as I thought it might be. Earthy, maybe a bit nutty. Kinda like sniffing a jar of Nutella.

And now there was yet another thing I'd never be able to eat again.

I had to give a hand to the queen and her people. They'd accomplished what continued to elude so many of Earth's rich and powerful: their shit didn't stink.

Or did it?

As our party pushed forward along the edge, keeping well back from the pink runoff flowing to our right, I considered this. A lot of the stuff here in the Garden had creeped me out, but maybe that was just me and my own personal hang-ups. Anyone else would have likely found this place idyllic: lush technicolor vegetation, cute — sorta — pixies, handsome beyond belief elven warriors, and living gnomes. Hell, even the freaking sewer was about as inoffensive as a shit hole could get.

It was almost too good to be true. But what if there was no almost to it?

Unpleasant memories played in the back of my head, the barely remembered images almost enough to mess up my equilibrium. Twice now when I'd opened my eyes in this place I'd seen, not a paradise, but a nightmare. The first time I'd chalked it up to the stress of being shunted to another world. Tell me that wouldn't mess someone up. The second time, well, I'd been impaled by a spear. Who knows what kind of fever dreams something like that could produce in an already overstressed mind?

But what if those hadn't been hallucinations? And then there was what Grunge had said, about how this world conformed to its visitors' expectations. What did that mean for a place such as this?

I had no idea, so I pushed it away for now. It really wasn't the time for such idle speculation. I needed to be on my guard. Yes, the queen and her people – already distracted by visiting dignitaries – might think me dead, but that didn't mean she'd left the doors unlocked and the windows wide open. Even at its most relaxed, a fortress was still a fortress.

Besides, it was easier to think of such things – tangible threats like armed guards and barred doors – than it was to consider the nightmare landscape and creatures I'd momentarily beheld.

There was a good reason I wasn't a philosophy major, and now seemed a particularly poor time to consider a change in curriculum.

22

We encountered a couple of barred gateways in our trek through the sewers of Fairyland. Even down here, guarding nothing but neon pink shit water, they were made of silver, meaning I was able to make short work of them.

Someone really ought to tell these guys about platinum. Every bit as pretty as silver, yet considerably more durable. Oh well, it wouldn't be me. I had more pressing concerns than lecturing a goddess on metallurgy.

Thankfully, a few unmanned gates were all the resistance we met down in the land of strawberry squirts. There were a few moments that worried me – most of them involving air bubbles rising unexpectedly from the pink sludge. Fortunately, though, we weren't given an opportunity to find out what fae sewer gators might look like. With any luck, I'd die of old age with that still being a mystery.

Cabbage's scouts seemed to know what they were doing down here. There was no hemming or hawing on their part, resulting in us getting hopelessly lost. Instead, they led the way, until finally we stopped beneath a grate in the ceiling above us, thankfully not dripping any runoff, pink or otherwise.

"That way," Cabbage said, pointing up.

Sadly, the tunnel here wasn't gnome-sized, the ceiling rising a good ten feet above my head and with no sign of a ladder.

So instead I turned to Grunge. "I don't suppose you want to fly up there and check things out?"

He looked up at me and grinned sheepishly. "Heh. These wings are more for show. Y'know, attracting mates, that sort of thing."

"How's that working out for you?" I asked, one eyebrow raised. "Seriously, you're telling me you can't fly?"

He backed up a step. "Well, technically I could. But..."

"But what?"

"I get airsick real easy."

Great. God forbid he actually be useful. I mean, it's not like he owed me his life or anything. On the other hand, did I really want to send him up only to risk him ralphing onto my face? That was definitely not one of my kinks.

"Fine. Guess I'll do it then."

That elicited a small cheer from the gnomes.

"Take this," Cabbage said, motioning to one of his minions — a scout gnome who stepped forward holding a coil of rope.

"It's okay. I don't need it."

"Need it you do not, but we do," he stated, looking slightly embarrassed.

Oh yeah. Guess they did at that.

One could kinda understand why these guys had been on the run for so long, since it seemed the entirety of their invasion plan relied on me doing the work.

I gave them my spear and looped the rope over my shoulder, as I'd need both hands free to do this, especially if the way upstairs happened to be guarded. There was a thought. My first castle storming could come to a very premature end if I popped up, only to get my head lopped off by any guards standing ready.

"Who wants to live forever anyway?" I said to myself, stepping beneath the grate and crouching down.

I was tempted to scream out "Kobe!" as I leapt, my legs easily propelling me high enough to cover the distance and then some. But that would've defeated the concept of subtle, not to mention my present audience probably had no idea what that meant.

It didn't matter anyway. Subtle went out the window the moment I hit the grate full force with my outstretched fist. It flew off its hinges then landed with a loud clang, all while I pinwheeled my arms so as to catch myself on the edge before falling back down again.

"Be more quiet you should," Cabbage whispered up to me.

"Thanks for the tip."

Once my grip was secure, I tentatively popped my head up, hoping the last thing I saw wouldn't be a silver blade swinging my way. Thankfully, the room appeared empty, at least what I could see of it. The only light was coming from a single torch sconce set in one wall. As for the room itself, it was damp, dank, and not exactly what one might call luxury accommodations.

A dungeon cell if I had to guess by the heavy door set in one end of the approximately eight by ten room.

I hoisted myself up and waited to see if anything happened.

Something did, but it was far more infuriating than life-threatening.

Grunge popped his head out of the grate opening about three seconds after I'd given the room the once over.

"All clear, Girl?"

I turned toward him, eyes narrowed. "What was that bullshit about getting air sick?"

"I do ... if I fly high enough. But come on, who's going to be bothered by a short hop like that?" I cracked my knuckles menacingly, to which he added, "Did I also mention I have an extreme aversion to death?"

"You do realize that at this rate you're going to die of old age before satisfying your honor, right?"

"Or you will," he replied, backing up a step. "Not that I expect you to make it that long. No offense, Girl, but you're a bit on the reckless side. But whatever works."

"What do you mean by that?"

"Punching through walls, picking fights with rock trolls, ticking off Queenshield..."

"No, I meant the whatever works part."

"Oh? Didn't I mention that?"

"No, you did not."

"Yeah, it's a bit of a compromise from her royal snootiness. If whoever we're honor bound to kicks the chamber pot, then all bets are off." He must've seen the grim look on my face even in the dim light, because he quickly held up his hands in a placating manner. "Not that I hope anything happens to you. In fact, I fully plan on making good on my end of the bargain."

"You'll excuse me for not holding my breath." I uncoiled the rope and fed it down the opening. There wasn't really a good place to brace it, so I acted as the brace, holding it steady as Cabbage ordered his people to climb.

On the upside, at least they didn't do a bad job for stubby little Smurfs. Within a few minutes, Cabbage and Arugula were the only ones left down below. They tied my *spear* to the end of the rope then scooted up, allowing me to reel it in and retrieve my weapon.

"Everyone present and accounted for?" I asked, once it was done.

The gnomes sounded off one by one, revealing their leaders weren't alone in their spice garden monikers. Dandelion, Fennel, Rutabaga, et cetera – I swear, it was like marching into battle with a salad bar. When they were finished, Cabbage gave me a tiny thumbs up.

"Awesome. Where to next?"

At this, the gnome leader turned away and stared intently at the wall.

"What is it?" I asked. "A secret door?"

"No. Just admiring the craftsmanship, I am. Fine masons this world has. Should take the time to question one someday I should."

This kept up for another minute or so, until I finally glanced at Arugula. "He has no idea, does he?"

She shook her oversized head. "Made it past here our scouts never have."

'Wonderful." I turned Grunge's way. "If you have any words of wisdom, now would be the time. Who knows, you might even be saving my life in doing so."

Sadly, my offer of a carrot was for naught as he shook his weaselly head. "Sorry, Girl. Remember what I said about making it a point to never get high on the Queen-shield's hit list? Well, there's a good reason. Those who are *lucky* enough to be invited for a stay this far down in Dùn nan Dé are usually not seen again. So, if I did know, chances are I'd already be too gleefing dead to tell you."

"And god forbid I get that lucky, right?" I muttered.

"What was that?"

"Nothing, just had some bullshit stuck in my throat."

My original plan of letting the guards capture me was sounding better by the second. But no. Instead I was stuck with a group of creepy ass gnomes whose idea of a plan basically came down to searching the entire fucking castle until we found my family.

I swear, these idiots would've been better off poisoning me and befriending that doppelganger. At least it could've disguised itself as one of the guards here, giving their moronic plan a marginal chance for success. Comparatively speaking, leading a werewolf pack was a walk in the park next to this crew.

Oh well, we weren't going to get anywhere hoping my parents randomly appeared out of thin air. I stepped to the door to give it a quick once over. It looked solid enough and the metal was both dull and pitted. Guess they were a bit smarter when it came to their dungeons. But then I placed my hands upon it so as to give it an experimental push, wiping away what seemed to be centuries of grime in the process and revealing gleaming silver beneath. How much of this shit did these guys have? I swear, I needed to grab some before it was time to get out of here. A few pocketfuls and I'd have enough to put a down payment on a car.

There was neither a handle nor hinges on this side, telling me exactly what this room was for, even had it not been obvious before.

Guess we were getting out the noisy way.

"Back up and be ready," I told the others before throwing myself shoulder-first into the door. Whatever was holding it closed couldn't have been too heavy duty – for me anyway – because there came a *clank* from the other side and the door swung wide open.

Cool! That wasn't so bad...

And then it kept on swinging, until it slammed into the wall with a booming *clang* that echoed throughout the narrow corridor I now found myself facing.

Moments later there came the sound of footsteps heading our way.

So much for the stealth approach.

"Go get them, Princess!" Cabbage shouted from still inside the cell.

"Yeah, what he said," Grunge added.

Yep. Next time I was definitely letting myself get captured.

Stepping out into the hallway proper, I saw it resembled a pretty stereotypical dungeon. It was lined in carved stone, top to bottom, the roof maybe about 7 feet high. The place was lit up with more torches, maybe one every fifteen feet or so. It was more than enough to see three shapes turn the corner down at one end and come racing my way.

"Who the gleef are you?" one shouted.

"Halt in the name of her Majesty," the other cried.

I'd been expecting more of the Queenshield. I mean, sure, they might've killed me but at least I'd have died with a good view. The two guards racing my way, however, were smaller and far closer in appearance to Grunge – albeit dressed much better.

They wore helmets, gleaming shirts of chainmail, and each was carrying a crossbow tipped with what appeared to be a silver arrowhead.

That wasn't exactly ideal, but it was the third member of their party that gave me pause. It was like some kind of monstrous slug sitting atop four stubby legs. Its body was bulbous, with glowing blue translucent skin, giving me a disturbing glimpse of the organs inside its alien body.

Gross! Being stabbed with silver was bad for me, but somehow I found the concept of being snail-trailed to death by a mutant murder blob far worse.

I had to worry about the silver first, though. Both

pixie guards raised their crossbows and took aim as the slug creature charged forward, revealing it had a mouthful of fucking teeth, too, because why not?

At this point, it seemed that a peaceful solution was not in the cards. So, the first thing I did was grab the cell door I'd just kicked open and pull it halfway shut again, effectively giving me a shield.

Good timing on my part, as my ears picked up the *thwip* of their weapons being loosed, followed by two hollow *clangs* as the projectiles hit the door.

There was no time to lose.

Hoping they didn't have semi-automatic crossbows here in the land of fae, I stepped around the door and launched myself toward the pixie guards.

The blue monstrosity was gross but, fortunately, only large compared to a regular garden slug. In reality, it was about the size of a corgi, meaning it was little effort for me to vault over it as it charged forward.

"Cabbage, incoming!" I cried, just as an unpleasant tingling shot up both my legs mid-leap over the creature.

What the hell?

I landed and stumbled as my feet didn't seem to want to work right anymore. Too bad I didn't have time to stand there dicking around, not unless I wanted to be a sitting duck for the two guards busy reloading.

"Not today, assholes!" I yanked the spear off my back and held it out in front of me horizontally as I lurched forward.

While I couldn't match the speed of a fully changed werewolf, especially with my feet feeling like two lumps of meat welded to my ankles, my leg muscles had benefited greatly from my mixed parentage. I slammed clumsily into the pair, focusing my damnedest on staying upright, and pinned them both to the wall with my fence post.

Correction. Make that *splattered* them against the wall.

There came the sound of bones breaking as both pixies slumped over, their skin bubbling where it touched my spear.

Crap! I'd meant to incapacitate them, not kill them – hoping that maybe they were a bit tougher than they looked. Alas, no such luck.

Yeah, there was little doubt both had taken a shoot first ask questions later approach where I was concerned. On the flipside, I *was* an intruder in the castle they were tasked with guarding ... just doing their jobs.

Fuck me! I couldn't even call this a morally grey area. I'd unthinkingly put nearly my full force to work against foes for whom a fraction would've sufficed. I couldn't undo this, but I'd need to be better going forward.

Goddamn it all! No matter what I did, no matter who I tried to save, I ended up with more blood on my hands. And the worst part was, I was the only one who seemed to care. Even my parents had been blasé about casual murder, especially where others like us were concerned – those stuck in this merciless world of freaks and monsters. What the fuck was wrong with us that we...

"That's okay, Girl," Grunge called out. "You just stand there staring at those two plik-heads. We'll deal with this gleefing frostcrawler all on our own. No big deal."

Shit!

I'd forgotten all about the blue slug-thing. Glancing over my shoulder, I saw Cabbage's people engaging it, their tiny arms working their slings while Grunge cowered behind them.

I stepped back, letting the bodies of the two broken pixies fall to the floor, the skin on their hands little more than bubbling goo where they'd touched the iron bar. Turning around, I raced up behind the creature, sensation finally returning to my feet.

It was a standoff. The gnome's carpet tacks were

keeping slugzilla at bay, but weren't having nearly the same effect as they'd had against fairy flesh. Time to change that. This thing might be more resistant to iron than its masters, but maybe that was simply a matter of scale.

God forgive me.

Raising the fence post above my head, I drove it down – pointy end first – through the creature, impaling it.

The slug thing let out a burbling warble as it arched its back in agony. Then it collapsed unmoving onto the floor … but not before it felt like someone stabbed a fork through each of my palms where they grasped hold of the iron spear.

I tried to let go and realized I couldn't. My hands were stuck … no. They were *frozen* to the weapon. Grunge had called this thing a frostcrawler. Earlier, when I'd leapt over it, my feet had gone numb inside my boots. I'd been too preoccupied at the time to wonder why, but now it hit me. Whatever this creature was, it was capable of radiating intense cold. And, genius that I am, I'd just stabbed it with a conductive metal rod that was now frozen to my hands.

Perhaps the most awesome thing I'd inherited from Dad's side of the family was my fast healing, capable of turning ragged wounds into little more than scabs in hours or less. That said, I had no idea how far that ability extended, nor was I interested in finding out. Letting my fingers turn black from frostbite-related gangrene and then hoping they grew back later seemed a stupid gamble.

I yanked the spear out of the creature or tried to. The pointy end, now frozen solid, shattered, leaving me to stumble back holding the equivalent of a crowbar.

Still effective as a weapon, but maybe something to worry about later. I started breathing on my hands in hopes of warming them up enough to free them without resorting to force – something that would almost certainly hurt like hell.

And no, I wasn't asking Grunge or any of the gnomes to pee on my fingers.

As for the snow slug, its blood turned the floor around it into a sheet of black ice. The frostcrawler's body wasn't immune either, freezing solid before shattering into a pile of broken bits.

Safe to say this was one Pokémon I didn't particularly care to catch.

The only upside to this clusterfuck was that no alarm appeared to be sounded, no reinforcements called for – as evidenced by the fact that we stood there unchallenged for several minutes, on opposite sides of the mini glacier that had been the slug beast.

Almost as if sensing my thoughts, Cabbage called out, "Told you busy the queen was. Left nothing but a skeleton crew of her least capable she did."

I was too busy trying to warm up my hands to reply, but if that beast had been her least capable defense then I really didn't want to see the sliding scale it represented.

Finally, after what seemed like forever, I managed to pry my hands off the still frigid bar, my palms bright red as if I'd just fought a snowball fight sans gloves. Still, I'd gotten off lucky. I didn't care to speculate how I might've fared had I been fully human.

Freed, I managed to strap the weapon to my back again – *ooh, that's cold*. As I settled it into its sling, Cabbage called out from the other side of the icy floor.

"Go that way, you should. Explore this passage we will." He hooked a tiny thumb over his shoulder, pointing toward the opposite end of the hallway. "Meet up again when we are able."

"Um, you do realize that's maybe 6 feet wide at most, right? I can jump that easily."

"Yes, but cover more ground we can this way," Arugula replied logically enough, proving she was most definitely the brains behind the gnome throne. "Find your parents faster we can."

I couldn't really argue with that, even if I was considerably less than enamored with the thought of splitting up in enemy territory.

"Worry not about us," she added, perhaps sensing my unease. "Survived for a long time here we have. Survive for a long time to come we shall."

"Okay. If you're sure. But be safe."

"They might be sure, but I'm not." Grunge spread his membranous wings and then fluttered over both the gnomes and the icy patch before landing next to me. "Or have you forgotten what happens when I get too far away from you?"

"Let me guess," I said, "Also not high enough for you to get airsick."

"Gleefing right," he replied stepping past me. "Now, let's... Oh gleef! What in the name of the nine chaos gods did you do to those sylphs?"

Oh crap. I'd almost forgotten about the pair I'd so casually murdered.

Grunge bolted toward where the bodies lay. As I stood there wide-eyed, unsure what his reaction might be, he stared down at their corpses for a long moment, then dropped to his knees next to them, his head bowed.

Were they friends, family? Or was he simply paying them homage as a fellow sylph? Either way, I felt awful as he knelt there in respectful silence.

"Ooh, nice."

Or maybe a bit less than respectful.

I stepped up and peered over his shoulder, seeing the true reason he was on his knees. "What the hell are you doing?"

"Going through their pockets," he replied blithely, his

hands full of what appeared to be triangular coins. "It's not like these gleefers need it anymore."

I couldn't believe the little thief, but at the same time I could, quite easily as a matter of fact. "How can you do that? It's so ... disrespectful. They're your own people!"

"My people?" he asked incredulously. "Nah. I make it a point to not keep friends with anyone who sucks off her majesty's royal teat. Gleefing snarb kissers like these, they get swelled heads, think they're better than the rest of us, all because her highness lets them patrol the levels of her keep that the sidhe are too good for. They can all go eat a bag of..."

"Taintnuts?"

"Not the word I was going for, but if the boot fits... Speaking of which..."

23

"Halt and identify yourself!"

"The name's Gullysnipe, sir. I'm ... bringing this prisoner down to join the rest of the trash."

"Gullysnipe?" the sylph guard replied. "Don't think I've seen you on the rotation before."

"That's ... because I was just promoted. Was outside working the spice fields when I caught this daoine here squatting in her royal highness's favorite stand of sun wisps. Dragged her out to the spice chief and he handed me my armor right there on the spot."

The guard on duty turned toward me, a look of disgust on his face as he spat on the ground. "The nerve. You and your kind, coming here to the Garden and dirtying it with your filth."

I lowered my head respectfully. "My apologies."

In what had probably been Grunge's sole useful contribution to our cause, he'd disguised himself as a guard using the stolen armor of the pixies I'd killed. Mind you, that hadn't been his first inclination. No, he'd just planned on stealing their boots to replace the mold-ridden potato sacks he'd been wearing up to that point.

Since he was already in the process of desecrating their corpses, I figured going the extra mile wouldn't damage my karma any more than I already had.

Yeah, we'd adopted the oldest cliché in the book, pretending to be a guard and his prisoner. However, as painfully obvious it might be on Earth, apparently the sylph guards here hadn't seen much human television, letting us pass without a second glance. Hell, one had even given us directions to general holding, where we hoped to have better luck finding my parents, as the lower levels had all proven to be dead ends so far.

The guard in front of us now, apparently the lone fairy tasked with manning this section of the dungeon, stepped up and jabbed me in the stomach with the butt of his crossbow. "You'll be sorry all right," he growled, giving me the bad cop routine. "The queen is quite fond of her sun wisps. You'll be lucky to keep your tongue for soiling them, assuming she even lets you keep your head."

I averted my eyes and did my best to look scared, loosely shackled with silver manacles as I was.

"Fine," he said to Grunge after a moment, pulling an oversized keychain off his belt, no doubt for the heavy silver door standing behind him. "Toss the daoine in with the rest and maybe give it an extra boot to the face for me."

"Happy to do so, sir."

"Name's Pidgeflicker. Pleasure to meet you."

"The pleasure is all mine," Grunge replied grinning.

"All right. Just give me a second. Can never remember which is the right gleefing one." He began to shuffle through the multitude of keys, all of them silver and seemingly the same shape. "No. Not that one. That's for the guard lounge. Nope. That's the Queenshield's private chamber pot. Ah, here we go."

The sylph looked up, glanced toward me, then frowned. "Hold on. What's that hanging off its back?"

Uh oh. I was still carrying the broken fence post, knowing I'd likely need it.

"That?" The smile disappeared from Grunge's face as quickly as it had appeared. "It's nothing. Just a walking stick. This one is as lame as a one-legged rock troll. How do you think I caught it so easily?"

"Walking stick?" Pidgeflicker remarked, stepping to my side. Doesn't look like any walking stick I've ever seen." He leaned in and his eyes opened wide. "In fact, that looks like it's made of... AIEEEEEEEE!!!"

Unseen by the guard, Grunge had slipped behind him to give him a shove, pushing Pidgeflicker's face directly into the iron shaft.

He grabbed hold of the other sylph's neck and held him there even as Pidgeflicker began to shriek. I couldn't see everything happening behind my back, but I could hear the awful sound of the guard's skin bubbling as it made contact with the caustic metal.

"What are you doing?!"

"Getting this gleefer out of the way," Grunge replied, as Pidgeflicker's screams became nothing more than a pained gurgle.

I pulled my arms apart, easily snapping the silver holding them in place, but I was too late. Grunge stepped back, letting Pidgeflicker's lifeless – and now faceless – corpse fall to the floor.

"You killed him!"

"And then some," Grunge replied, appearing to admire his handiwork. "What do you think? Does that count as saving your life?"

"What?! No. My life was never in danger. I could've broken free and knocked him out at any time and you know it."

"Oh well."

"Don't give me *oh well*, mister. You murdered him in cold blood."

"I'm pretty sure his blood is still..."

"It's a saying, you little psycho."

"Ah, I see." He bent down and plucked the keychain out of Pidgeflicker's fingers. "Here in the Garden we have a saying, too. You can't make an omelet without breaking a few vregnets."

Grunge opened the heavy door, while I grabbed Pidgeflicker's body and dragged him inside. His death had been needless, but now that the deed was done there was no point in leaving him where any passing guard could find him.

The door opened up into another hallway, this one lined with what appeared to be more traditional jail cells, save for the silver bars of course. The opulence of the metal aside, the place had a dirty feel to it, with the floors of the cells closest to us splashed with pink. Safe to say, I had a feeling we hadn't inadvertently invaded Brigid's fortress on the day when they treated prisoners to cotton candy and unicorn rides.

The first populated cell we passed seemed to confirm this. Three inmates – a sylph, a tall creature covered in green skin and leaves, and a burly fae about three feet tall and with a long beard – were inside, all of them looking as if they'd lost hope a long time ago. We passed them by, only to see more, equally as downtrodden.

"We should let them out."

"No, we shouldn't," Grunge replied.

"How can you say that?"

"Easily. For starters, some of these Seelie definitely belong here. We're talking hardened criminals."

"Takes one to know one?"

"Something like that," he replied with a touch of pride, "except some of us are smart enough to not get caught."

"Not exactly a convincing argument so far."

"Secondly, do you really want dozens of these gleefing sad sacks running out of here at once, alerting every Queenshield between here and the Shimmering Sea?"

Sadly, he had a point. Actually, he probably had two. Sure, there were probably fairies in here who'd done little more than be in the wrong place at the wrong time, but there were likely actual criminals, too. I didn't have time to sit down and interrogate each and every one, so as to get an idea of who really belonged here. And even if I did, there was no way a breakout from general population would go unnoticed. No, much as it pained me, we had to...

"Gullysnipe?"

Behind one set of bars stood a translucent humanoid made entirely of what appeared to be sentient water. *The hell?*

"Hocking farzblargs, it is you," it gurgled at Grunge.

"Hey, Bloatreef," Grunge replied amicably enough. "How are you doing, you old bubblecrotch you?"

"The usual," the water fairy replied. "But forget about that. Look at you. You finally go legit?"

"Me? Nah. I'm just visiting. Don't mind the new clothes."

"Is that a fact?" The water creature pushed up against the bars, but somehow seemed unable to flow through them. "Say, I don't suppose you want to put in a good word for me on the way out?"

"That depends," Grunge said, putting a hand on his wispy chin. "You got the coin you owe me from our last game of traitor's dice?"

Bloatreef held his hands up. "Sorry, buddy. I seem to have misplaced my pouch. But you know I'm good for it. That's me, a trustworthy..."

Grunge started walking again. "See you later, Bloatreef."

"Eat a twig, you little plik-sucker," the water fairy spat as we kept on going.

"Are you done?" I asked, louder than I should have. "Or is there anyone else here you'd like to purposely tick off?"

"Bent? Is that you?"

I immediately turned toward the sound of the voice coming from up ahead. "Riva?"

"Yeah. Down here!"

All thoughts of pity for those we passed fled from my mind as I quickly made my way forward. Four cells down I saw a hand – hers – reach through the bars and wave us on.

I raced up to the cell to find her standing in it alone, or at least someone who looked like her.

Riva was dressed much different from when last I'd seen her. Gone was the white summer dress. Now, she was wearing a form-fitting golden tunic, matching leggings, knee-high boots, and a cape of all things.

"Thank goodness you're all right," she said. "They told me you were dead, but I didn't believe them for a second. Bunch of fucking liars."

"Actually, they weren't." At her confused look, I added, "Long story. I..." I trailed off as her starkly different appearance set off warning bells in my head. Maybe paranoid of me, but in a world where doppelgangers existed it was best to be safe before spilling the beans of our plan ... not that there was much of one. "No offense, but hey, Grunge, quick question."

"Oh, him again?" Riva said with an eye roll.

"Hey, other Girl," the sylph replied with a wave.

"Listen, Grunge. Is there any way to tell if she's herself and not something else?"

"Like what?"

"Like, you know, that shapeshifter the gnomes captured."

"What gnomes?" Riva asked.

"Like I said. Long story. Just give me a second here, okay?"

"Sure. It's not like I have anywhere to be."

I turned back toward Grunge. "Well? I just want to make sure she's her and not something else pretending to look like her."

"Why would anyone want to shapeshift into a daoine? I mean, seriously, if I could look like anyone I wanted to, I certainly wouldn't pick her." He inclined his head toward Riva. "No offense, Girl. I'm sure you're considered ... um ... passable where you're from. But you're about as attractive to me as a pile of swamp maggots."

Riva narrowed her eyes at him. "Trust me, you little shit, the feeling is mutual."

"She sure as gleef sounds like your friend."

"Maybe..."

"Fine," Riva said, sounding annoyed. "A week after you and Jeff did it at the Junior Prom, you tried it again, only for him to squirt all over your new leather jacket before you could..."

"And I'm convinced. Open the door, Grunge."

"Sure thing. Now, which key was it again?"

"Oh, the hell with this!" I grabbed hold of the cell door and yanked it open with a quick squeal of metal.

Riva stepped out and glared at me. "Fool! You think you have released your friend when all you have released is your doom!"

"What?!"

She let out a bark of laughter. "Just fucking with you."

"You might want to consider knocking off the jokes around the stressed-out girl with superpowers."

"Point taken," she said, stepping in and giving me a big hug.

"You daoine sure do like to touch each other."

"It's a girl thing," I snapped, a wave of relief cascading through me at having found my best friend again. After several seconds, I pulled away and gave her the once over. "So what's with the princess of Themyscira look?"

She let out a deep breath, a look of disgust on her face. "After the attack, they fanned out and searched for you, leaving one of those warrior elves to guard me. Anyway, the guy kept giving me side eye, which was starting to seriously creep me out."

I found myself clenching my fists. "He didn't try to..."

She shook her head. "No. His buddies came back soon enough. They tossed me over the saddle of one of those dragon things, and we rode back here."

"Good to hear. That's a fairy who just saved himself a world of hurt."

"Oh, believe me, it gets better. The ride back was uncomfortable as hell but thankfully the flames on those things seemed to be more for show. But that didn't matter much because I started to notice the other soldiers glaring at me. I'd turn their way and they'd pretend to look away, but it kept happening."

"And then what?" I asked, my voice barely a whisper.

"Then things got a little ... intense once we arrived back here."

I narrowed my eyes. All joking aside about the hot fairies, this wasn't some romance story. There was nothing even remotely amusing about the concept of gang rape. "What happened?"

"They dragged me into a room, and this time they weren't even bothering to hide it. Each one, even the captain, was glaring at me like I was nothing more than a piece of meat. By that point I was close to tears. All I could think to do was beg them not to hurt me."

"Did they..."

She shook her head. "The captain called me daoine trash, spat at my feet, and then he and his men walked out."

"Thank god."

"That's what I thought, but then a bunch of lady elves walked in, looking all haughty like their shit didn't stink..."

Remembering the sewer, I was tempted to comment, but held my tongue.

"They tossed these clothes at me and told me to get dressed, all while complaining that my wanton lack of modesty had greatly upset Uriel and his men."

And suddenly this tale took a turn I wasn't expecting. "Wanton lack of modesty?"

"Yeah. Apparently, we're dealing with a bunch of stuck-up fairy prudes here."

"Still better than the alternative."

"True," Riva said, "but kinda insulting nevertheless."

"Well, if it helps, I thought you looked super cute in your possession dress."

"Thanks."

"I didn't," Grunge remarked.

"Nobody asked you."

"I know, but it probably needed to be said." He turned to me, eying the bare midriff I was now sporting thanks to my ripped clothing. "Same with you, Girl. No offense, and by that, I mean yes I'm going to be offensive, but you're showing off far too much squishy flesh for my personal edification. Makes me glad I haven't eaten lately, otherwise I'd probably lose my..."

"Any chance of maybe leaving him in one of these cells, Bent?"

"I'm not ruling it out."

Sadly, Riva hadn't gotten much chance to gather any useful information, either on the ride back or after being tossed into her cell. According to her, every attempt at asking a question was met with them telling her to shut her Earth tramp mouth.

Unfortunately, we seemed to have also reached the limits of Grunge's disguise. The guards we met, as we went up another level and began our search anew, were different fairies than him – taller and fairer – albeit not quite the Legolas squad who'd brought Riva in. They also didn't buy for a second that a squirt like Grunge was capable of guarding not one, but two daoine trash as they kept calling us. I began to get the impression that there was either some fairy racism or caste politics at play as there seemed to be a pecking order, with those like Grunge being only slightly higher on the totem pole than Riva and me.

This place might look idyllic but that was no more than window dressing. In some ways it wasn't all that much different from home.

The only point in our favor was that the guard posts continued to be sparsely manned. The most we met were bored pairs, with the occasional frostcrawler acting as guard dog. However, I'd learned my lesson with those things the first time, making it a point to take them out from a distance – the stone of the castle walls itself becoming useful projectile weapons, after a few hits to loosen it up.

I suffered a few bruises along the way, but nothing worth writing home about. Helping matters was that both Grunge and Riva scavenged weapons as we went – the dirtbag sylph actually proving almost useful when it came to providing cover fire, albeit apparently not enough to satisfy his sidhe honor.

All of that served to keep me from losing focus as we continued to search, which was good because so far we'd found no trace of my parents. For every cell, holding room, or storage closet we checked to no avail, I was starting to realize we were searching for needles in a haystack.

Finding Riva had been dumb luck, nothing more. To hope I got that lucky again, in a place this size... Hell, I didn't even know how big it was. For all I knew, we were searching the fairy equivalent of King's Landing.

If that were the case, then it wouldn't matter how much pomp and circumstance was going on above in the queen's banquet hall. Eventually, we were going to run into a sizeable force, one big enough to stop us.

Needless to say, my hope was rapidly beginning to crumble.

Even if we somehow managed to find my parents, what then? Was I to assume that the gnomes would somehow be able to convince Maleficent to grant them voting rights and then all would be well?

It was almost ridiculous to think we could...

"Bent."

My keen ears warned me of the commotion coming from the end of the hall a moment before Riva did.

There came a cry of surprise from somewhere beyond the next intersection, about thirty feet away, followed by multiple shouts, the sound of things ricocheting off the walls, and then a heavy thud followed by muted cheers.

What the...

"I think we have incoming," Riva said, raising the crossbow she'd liberated from the last pair of guards we'd taken down.

She took aim as multiple shadows appeared along the wall directly opposite the corner ... their size shrinking as their owners neared the intersection.

"Hold on," I cautioned, just as a couple of gnomes rounded the corner.

"Princess!" one of them shouted.

"Holy shit!" Riva cried at the sight of them.

Realizing what was about to happen, I slapped the end of her crossbow toward the ground just as she pulled the release, sending the bolt clattering harmlessly across the stone floor.

Okay, that was a bit too close for comfort. I didn't relish trying to explain the concept of friendly fire to Cabbage and Arugula.

As for the gnomes, they seemed unfazed by what had almost just happened, running toward us gleefully.

"Bent?"

"I did say there were gnomes, didn't I?"

"Yeah, but I thought you were being metaphorical."

The procession of tiny warriors stopped short of us then stepped to the side to allow their leader to come forward.

"Riva, this is Cabbage, the ... um ... gnomelord, I guess."

"Nice ... to meet you," she said hesitantly, giving me some serious side eye.

"Time for pleasantries later there must be," Cabbage replied, stepping forward and sounding a bit out of breath.

"Why? What's wrong?"

"Wrong or right, we do not know."

"I'm not following."

"You will," he stated. "Because found your father we have."

24

Glancing around the corner, I beheld a pair of Queenshield standing before the heavy silver door. Between them stood two beasts – another frostcrawler, larger than the ones I'd seen below and something else, kind of resembling a honey badger, except on fire. Hah. The only thing missing from their collection was a Pikachu, although that was probably for the best.

Either way, it was obvious playtime was over.

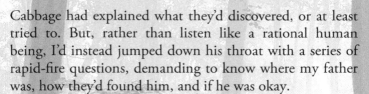

Cabbage had explained what they'd discovered, or at least tried to. But, rather than listen like a rational human being, I'd instead jumped down his throat with a series of rapid-fire questions, demanding to know where my father was, how they'd found him, and if he was okay.

"All that we know is now yours, Princess."

"That's not good enough," I snapped. "How can you be sure of anything when all you have is hearsay and a door, which you only saw from a distance?"

"The door yes," he replied. "But those we questioned, I

believe true they spoke. My people can be quite ... persuasive when arises the need."

There was something predatory about his grin as he spoke, something that gave me the willies deep down in my spine. At any other time, I'd have made a mental note to replace all the windows in my bedroom back home with sheet metal. But right then, I'd been way too frazzled to do anything but lay into him some more."

"This is my father we're talking about," I cried, my brain finally on overload. "You can't just be ... can't just ... you need to be..."

"Enough, Bent," Riva said, stepping in as the voice of reason, despite the look on her face saying she would have gladly put a mile or two between her and the gnomes. "You need to calm down, take a deep breath."

"How can I?!" By then, the tears were freely falling from my eyes, a mix of frustration, anger, and fear ... so much fear. "What if there's nothing behind that door? What if he's already..."

Riva didn't hesitate, even though I was in a state of near panic – pulling me in, wrapping her arms around me, and forcing my head to her shoulder.

Despite wanting nothing more than to lash out at someone, *anyone*, I let her.

"Shhh. He's not. He's fine, and he's there waiting for you."

"But how can any of us know that?"

"Because we have to believe it."

She was right. It was one thing to hope. But I realized in that moment that, deep down, I hadn't expected this mission to actually succeed. It had simply been something to do to stave off the despair that I was stuck on an alien world with no clue what to do.

What an absolute horrible person that must've made me, not to mention a terrible daughter. Yes, I wanted to find my parents, would have given almost anything to make that happen. But I think some part of me felt I didn't *deserve* to find them, especially once I started leaving an ever-growing trail of bodies in my wake. And, little by little, I'd been giving that part of my conscience more floor time to fill my head with its poison.

So, to hear Cabbage's words, it was like I almost wanted to disprove him, show he was wrong – because of course he was wrong, by sheer virtue of me being the murderous wretch I was. It was only now, hearing Riva speak and feeling her warmth, that I was able to step back and recognize that bullshit in my head for what it was.

At last, her words got through to me, though, and I was able to focus on reality – crazy as it was – and not the dark fantasy my subconscious kept trying to sell me. I dried my eyes and pushed my emotions down long enough to ask Cabbage to start again, this time forcing myself to listen as calmly as I could.

He once again explained their success in interrogating the guards they'd captured, something Grunge, at least, was happy to proclaim as "pretty gleefing likely," based on the gnomes' reputation alone.

Back home, I was the unknown, a thing to be feared. But here, Cabbage and his followers were the proverbial boogeymen – having been on the run long enough that fairy mothers now told their children to be good, lest the gnomes carry them off into the night.

Considering their attitude when they'd first captured Grunge, I didn't venture to guess how much of that fear was myth and how much was earned. Regardless, being overcome by an invading force of angry gnomes had been enough to loosen tongues along the way.

In doing so, Cabbage and his people had learned that a few levels above us, and just one below where her majesty was currently taking tea with extradimensional dignitaries, were cells designated for special prisoners, those the queen herself had taken an interest in. The guards they'd interrogated – and hopefully not eaten afterwards – didn't give them any names, but had spoken of a shapeshifter from Earth, a disciple of Valdemar.

Though a part of me still didn't want to get my hopes up, lest they be dashed, I couldn't help it. True, Cabbage couldn't confirm if the shapeshifter was actually my father, but at least now we knew where to hit next so as to find out for certain.

Thankfully, he and his gnomes had done a good job clearing out the lower levels. Combined with what my group had accomplished, that left little resistance between us and the V.I.P. section of the prison.

Now, standing there and observing things, I realized that even a little resistance might prove difficult to overcome.

Still, there was likely a good chance we were looking at the proverbial skeleton crew. On any other day, this section of the prison would likely be crawling with lethal refugees from *Lord of the Rings*.

This really was our best opportunity, as also evidenced by the fact that the ceiling thrummed with sound from above. Whatever was going on up there, it seemed like a raucous affair. But that was good for us, as the constant cacophony served to mask our approach.

Sadly, where most of the hallways we'd encountered up until now had been cramped and well suited as chokepoints, the passageways up here were much wider. I had a feeling this level operated not only as holding for special prisoners, but also as the headquarters for the Queenshield. After all, who was better suited to guard such high-profile criminals? Not to mention, it put them close by in case Brigid needed to summon them.

The rich tapestries which adorned the walls in places seemed to confirm this level's somewhat higher status.

None of that really helped us, though. There was a good forty feet of open space between us and where the guards were stationed. Though they didn't appear armed, that didn't mean anything. Uriel and his cronies had apparently been walking around with spears shoved up their asses. Arugula tried to correct me and explain how the guards were supplied with special fanny packs – of all things – that were larger on the inside, but I liked my version better. It made these guys seem a wee bit less imposing, not to mention the idea of fairy hipsters was a bit too much for even me.

Yeah, I'm weird that way.

I popped back around the corner and turned to my allies, specifically Cabbage and his mate. "What's the plan?"

They, in turn, stared back at me wide-eyed and silent.

"I think they're waiting for you to come up with one," Riva whispered in my ear.

"Thank you, I kinda got that. Fine. What do we know about these Queenshield?"

"You don't gleef with them," Grunge offered.

"Not helpful. Anything else to add?"

The skeevy pixie shrugged then started to turn away. However, a moment later, he met my eyes again. "Actually, maybe I do have something. That other creature that's with them, that's a sparkwomp."

"I was going with fire badger, but good to know."

"Stupid Earth name aside, you're not listening, Girl. Sparkwomps and frostcrawlers usually hate each other. Frostcrawlers will eat sparkwomp pups, and in turn spark-womp packs will hunt down frostcrawlers."

"So they're natural enemies?"

"Goes a bit beyond natural if you ask me. You talk to either of them and you'll get an earful about why the other should be wiped off the face of the Garden."

"Hold on," Riva said. "Talk to them? You mean they're intelligent?"

"Well, they ain't the brightest gleefers to blight the queen's lands, but if you catch them in the right mood they'll stop and chat with a fellow, yeah."

I glanced her way. "What are you thinking?"

"Dogs and cats," she replied. "Cartoon logic tells us they don't get along, but if you raise them together they're fine."

"Okay, and?"

"And the same for any animals really. Natural enemies can be raised to tolerate each other in captivity, especially if their needs are met. But they're just animals working on instinct. People, on the other hand, have all sorts of hang-ups, grudges, and stereotypes weighing them down. I mean, no offense, but look at your parents. They love each other..."

"But still can't stand the other side, for the most part," I replied, getting where she was going with this. Hell, the day after I'd first learned werewolves were real, Mom had flash-fried a quartet of them with no hesitation, acting as if she'd done the world a favor.

"So you think..."

She nodded. "Those two, they're not simply pets. They're employees, guards, maybe a bit lower on the rung than the hotties, but guards nevertheless. And just because they're forced to work together doesn't necessarily mean they have to like it."

"And maybe we can use that," I surmised.

It wasn't much to go on, but it was better than nothing.

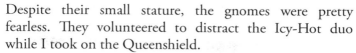

Despite their small stature, the gnomes were pretty fearless. They volunteered to distract the Icy-Hot duo while I took on the Queenshield.

Riva was a good friend, but she wasn't dumb by any stretch. When I suggested she hang back, only using her crossbow as a last resort, she didn't argue. And Grunge, unsurprisingly, was quick to volunteer to protect her flank.

The gnomes were first to act. They stepped around the corner and launched a volley with their slings.

Sure enough, a moment later, I heard one of the sidhe snarl in anger in that hot Jason Statham growl of theirs and then command, "Take them".

The sound of running feet caught my ears as I waited, pressed against the wall just around the corner. The gnomes meanwhile backed up a bit to give me the space I needed.

Closer, closer... I could now see a reddish glow approaching, no doubt from the sparkwomp.

And then they appeared. The sparkwomp was slightly in front of the frostcrawler, but both seemed focused on their prey, enough that they didn't notice me until it was too late.

I swung my iron bar like a golf club, catching the sparkwomp in the side and sending it careening into the frostcrawler, knocking both ass over tea kettle into the far wall and sending up a smokescreen of steam in the process.

Thankfully, my contact with the creature had been brief enough to not heat up my weapon because now it was my turn.

I raced around the corner, hoping I wasn't about to be cut down by crossbow fire. However, whether through arrogance or training, the Queenshield had apparently eschewed ranged weaponry. Both sported shields and those double-sided spears, neither of which they'd had a few moments earlier – giving credence to my theory that these guys had serious sticks up their asses.

Trusting the gnomes to keep up their end of the bargain, I let loose with a battle cry and charged ahead.

I couldn't tell if these two clowns had been part of the group that had tried to arrest me. Even if not, it was a fair bet they talked among themselves as evidenced by the briefest flicker of surprise in their eyes, no doubt at seeing a ghost closing in on them.

It was brief, though, as both of them instantly adopted a defensive stance – shield high with their spears pointed out ahead of them.

I was an amateur wrestler, a good one at that, but I wasn't a moron. I didn't think for one second I was qualified to go toe to toe with two trained and experienced warriors, both of whom likely had skills the Bailey U. fencing team would've gladly killed for.

That said, I'd always tried to listen when my coaches talked – and not just because I walked into pretty much every match with a target on my back. I'd gotten a ton of advice over the years, but the one that seemed most apt at that moment came from my grade school days with Coach Jenkins – always play to my strengths.

These guys were waiting as if they expected me to stop and parry with them, which was exactly the opposite of what I planned. Mind you, hopefully that didn't involve charging full speed into their spears. But thankfully I wasn't exactly unarmed.

Accelerating far past what a normal sprinter could manage, I raced forward, hoping I timed this right. With any luck, these guys hadn't been fully briefed on what I was capable of, especially since all I'd done for their captain was surrender and then promptly collapse with a spear in my back.

In the split second before I impaled myself, I swung my iron rod in an arc, but I wasn't aiming at them. The rod hit the leftmost spearpoint with a heavy *clang*, forcing it to the side and likewise deflecting the other guard's weapon as well.

It was all the opening I needed.

The guard on the left, a pale-skinned fellow who looked like he could've used a few days at the beach, raised his shield to deflect the impact. Too bad he likely wasn't expecting someone with my level of strength.

A normal human would've bounced right off, bruised or worse, leaving themselves easy pickings for these two.

Sadly for them, normal and me had parted ways some time ago.

I slammed into the guard's shield, driving the elf behind it into the wall as if he'd been struck by a speeding car. Metal and bone crunched as a splash of strange purplish blood stained the stones behind the sidhe guard.

I quickly leapt back out of range of the second guardsman, a fairy with the same hairdo and armor but much darker skin. Guess this one hadn't skimped on the tanning booth.

The first guard stood where he was a moment longer, then he dropped both his weapon and shield before crumpling to the ground in an unmoving heap. That was one.

Sadly, in evening the odds, I'd also shot my proverbial load. That attack had been my best bet to end this quickly. But now I was left with another soldier, one armed, aware, and now fully versed in what I could do. It was safe to say there was little chance of him letting me back away so as to try this again.

That said, the earlier arrogance was gone from his face,

having just seen his buddy crushed like a bug against a windshield.

"Daoine filth," he growled. "I will avenge my brother with your life."

"You're welcome to try," I replied, lacking any pithy response. I swear, if I somehow managed to get back home, I was going to devote an entire day to sitting down and watching action movies with Chris to improve my trash talk game.

Well, maybe half an afternoon.

First things, first, though. I had to prove my mettle in armed combat.

Alas that was easier said than done if our first exchange was any indication. The sidhe stepped forward, jabbing his spear at me. I countered, blocking it easily enough, but it had been nothing more than a feint on his part.

He spun it expertly in his hands, bringing the other blade up in an arc aimed at my face. The only thing I could do was step in enough so that the shaft clonked me in the side of the head instead.

Ouch!

Sadly, that also put me close enough for him to shove his shield forward, slamming it into my nose and sending blood flying.

Double ouch!

I staggered back dazed, swinging my rod wildly in an attempt to fend off any follow-up attacks.

For all of my strength, I might as well have been a clumsy three-year-old trying to hit a wiffle ball. The elven warrior stepped forward, confidence oozing out of every pore, which was a lot better than the blood dripping out of my nose. Maybe I'd get lucky and he'd slip in the small puddle forming in front of me.

"My captain reported your death, daoine, but I see

you've been blessed with two lives. Let us now see if you have three."

Damn. His lines were much better than mine. It was almost a pity I was likely going to be far too dead in another second or two to compliment him on his snark.

"Now die, filth ... eeeeeeee!"

The guard dropped his spear to grab hold of the side of his face, squealing like a stuck pig.

What the...?

But then I saw the wisps of smoke escaping from between his fingers.

I dared a quick glance back to find Arugula standing there with her sling, flashing me a thumbs up.

Saved by a gnome. Grunge was going to be so jealous, but only if I took advantage of the distraction. Thankfully, I wasn't above a cheap shot against those holding my parents hostage.

I stepped in and swung for the fences. I may not have made the intermural softball team back in second grade, but I more than made up for it now – slamming the iron rod into the side of the fairy's head with enough force to...

Gross! There came a crunch as bone shattered, followed by a spray of purple goo as the fairy's skull caved in. I wasn't sure if it was the force of the swing or the fact that these guys and iron were pretty much the opposite of peanut butter and chocolate – perhaps a bit from both columns.

Either way, this guy was getting a closed casket funeral. Not a pretty sight to behold.

I hadn't come to this place to leave a trail of death and destruction behind me, but it was rapidly starting to turn into that. Soon enough, it was going to look like I'd decided to wage full on war against the queen of the fairies, not really a position I wanted to be in.

Still, what was done was done. I turned to see how my

friends were faring, only to find them all headed my way. Further down the hall, steam billowed as the sparkwomp and frostcrawler brawled with one another, snarls and angry slurping noises coming from them.

Grunge in particular looked pleased with himself.

"Your friend was right," he said. "Didn't take much to set those two against each other. With any luck, they'll gleef each other up real good." He stopped and looked down at the corpses in front of us. "Whoa! Speaking of gleefed up. Did these guys insult your ancestors or something?"

"Um, something like that."

"Works for me. A dropped taintnut is still ripe for the picking I always say."

He got to work looting the bodies, like the slimy little thief he was. Leaving me to check on Riva and the gnomes. "Are you guys okay?"

"Right as rain," Riva said.

"Good we are, too," Cabbage replied.

After a few moments, the silence only broken by Grunge's sounds of glee as he desecrated the dead, Riva gestured to the door behind me. "Do you want to do the honors?"

I turned around and found my throat had completely dried up. Facing monsters, guards, and fairies, that was easy. Going through this door, not knowing what condition I'd find my father in, if he was there at all, that was ... a lot harder.

"W-what if he's..."

Riva's hand entwined with mine. "I'm here for you. No matter what."

I turned toward her, tears falling from my eyes and mixing with the fresh blood still on my face. Then, before I was even aware I was going to do it, I grabbed hold of her.

"Um ... B-Bent. I'm here for you, but not if you crush me."

"S-sorry. Don't know my own strength sometimes."

"Neither did these plik-heads," Grunge replied with a chuckle. "Ooh, is that a coin purse?"

"Much ground we have left to cover," Arugula said after another moment. "Do this you must."

"I know."

I turned once again toward the door, thicker and heavier looking than the others I'd seen – almost as if it were meant to hold someone stronger than the other prisoners here. Well, it wasn't going to be strong enough.

"You all might want to stand back."

"And you might not want to make a racket this close to her high and haughtiness," Grunge replied, holding up another keychain, no doubt purloined from the corpses he was busy defiling for fun and profit.

"You're probably right. Thanks."

"Don't mention it."

I took the keychain from him, the keys thankfully far less numerous than down in general holding. It only took three tries to find the right one, although I was so nervous I almost broke the first two off in the lock.

Finally, there came a *click*, followed by a meatier *clonk* as if heavy bolts were retracting back into the wall. Definitely a door meant to hold someone the fairies considered a threat. And who could be a bigger threat than the leader of the werewolves who served their queen's greatest enemy?

I held my breath as I pulled the heavy door open, revealing the dimly lit confines of the cell within.

My eyes fell upon the single prisoner – shackled to the floor – but, rather than joy or despair, a shocked numbness crept over me as I could only think one thing.

Where's the rest of him?

25

"Dad?"

A snarl escaped my father's lips as he looked toward the door of the cell, his eyes yellow and his teeth elongated as if preparing to transform. But then his gaze fell upon me and the ferocity was replaced with confusion.

"Tam Tam?"

"W-what have they done to you?"

My father was nude, probably not surprising as he'd been fully transformed at the time of his capture. But it wasn't his lack of dress that caused the words to get caught in my throat.

It was the fact that both of his legs were missing below the knee.

Rather than ragged exposed wounds, however, his legs ended in gleaming metal. It was as if the stumps had been dipped in molten silver and then allowed to harden.

"No," he said, looking away, sounding both defeated and exhausted. "Not real. You're not real."

"Oh my god, Mr. Bentley!" Riva cried stepping to my side.

"Go away. Tell your queen I won't fall for her tricks."

Tears, just barely dried from moments earlier, sprung anew from my eyes, and I stepped forward toward him. "It's not a trick, Dad. It's me."

"I said ... *go away!*" In the space of a second, his voice changed to a snarl.

The transformation was nearly as quick as thought itself. One moment, he was my father, the next – even as he swung an arm at me – he was a monster werewolf, a beast that would've towered eight feet in height had he been able to stand.

I knew all too well the capabilities he possessed in that form.

Sadly, in that moment I was vulnerable, my heart going out to him and the obvious torture he'd suffered. I raised my hands to block the attack but was a hair too slow. In the next instant, I was launched off my feet and sent flying into the far wall of the cell.

"Bent!"

I slid to the floor, the wind knocked out of my lungs, as Riva raced toward me.

Sadly, she wasn't the only one.

The heavy chains which bound my father to the floor were long enough to allow him some freedom of movement, enough to reach us anyway.

The monstrous mega-wolf clawed its way across the cell floor, using its massive forelimbs to propel it forward, easily fast enough to overtake my friend.

Dad raised one claw above his head, as if to cut down Riva where she stood.

That snapped me out of my daze.

I pushed off the floor, throwing myself at my father, and sending us both tumbling away before he could bisect my best friend. We landed with me on top, but that wasn't any real advantage considering his size and reach.

Unfortunately, there was only one option that came to mind.

"Sorry, Dad."

I decked him in the jaw with a right hook powerful enough to dump our minivan onto its side.

Dad's eyes rolled into the back of his head, stunned, allowing me to scramble away.

Riva was by my side again in the next second.

"Are you okay?" I asked her.

"Thanks to you."

"I need you to get out of here."

"No chance. I said I was here for you."

Oh, for the love of... I wasn't sure whether to hug her or deck her. Maybe both once this was over. "Okay, fine. But get behind me in case he..."

"*Tam Tam* ... it *is* you."

Dad's transformation back to his human form was a bit slower, no doubt thanks to being knocked for a loop. When it was finished, he looked up at me, an ugly bruise already forming on the side of his jaw.

"Are ... are you okay?" I asked, tentatively taking a step closer.

"I am now." He spat out a tooth but smiled anyway. "Nobody here can hit that hard. So, it's either you, or someone glamoured a mountain ogre."

"It's me, Dad."

"Me, too," Riva said from behind me.

"But how?" he asked. "We're in..."

"I know," I replied. "We were coming for you, all of us. I mean, I'd convinced the Morganberg pack and the Draíodóir to mount a rescue mission and..."

"Hold on. Are you okay? Did I hit you too hard? If so I'm..."

Remembering the blood still drying on my face, I held up my hands. "Oh, no. The welcoming party gave me this.

And no worries. It's not like my nose was super straight to begin with."

"You're sure you're okay?"

"Yep. Nothing a few wet wipes won't fix."

He chuckled then nodded. "Okay, if you say so. But seriously, you actually got the Draíodóir to listen to you?"

"Well, I was in the process of doing that, but then some things happened and I sort of ended up here prematurely."

"Same here," Riva added.

"Good to see you, Riva," Dad said to her, before raising an eyebrow at me.

"It's okay. Mom never mindwiped her. She managed to talk her way out of it."

"No, I didn't," she said, her voice sounding strangely robotic.

"You didn't? But you told me..."

Riva shook her head, looking both confused and embarrassed. "I know what I told you back then, but ... I don't think that was the truth."

"What do you mean?"

"I ... I'm not sure. But that memory, it's all ... fuzzy for some reason."

Fuzzy? That was strange. On the other hand, considering what she'd been through, it probably wasn't surprising that she was a bit confused about some...

It was only then it hit me. There I was, worrying about something that happened half a year ago, when my father was right here waiting for me now.

Goddamn, I could be such a fool.

Riva seemed to realize this, too. She shrugged then stepped back, inclining her head toward my father as if telling me, "go on".

Not that I needed the incentive.

Without further ado, I threw my arms around his

neck. "Thank goodness you're alive," I said, the tears flowing freely now that the rush of battle was subsiding. He hugged me back, and I let him for a few moments, before pulling away in horror.

"What's wrong, Tam Tam?"

"What's wrong?! Look at what they did to you. How they have you tied up like some..."

"Wild animal?" he offered.

"Not anymore."

I grabbed hold of the chain where it was bolted to the floor. Silver or not, it was a lot thicker than the manacles the Queenshield had tried to tie me up with. They meant business with this stuff.

But it wasn't thick enough, not for me.

"Don't bother, honey. I tried. It's too..."

His protests were abruptly cut off as the metal began to groan and deform.

"Come on, you motherfucker!" I glanced sideways at Dad. "Sorry."

"It's fine. Your mother isn't here."

Mom... I knew he'd meant it as a joke, a way to cut the tension a bit, but it only strengthened my resolve to free him.

I put my back into it, feeling the bolt on the floor starting to give, bit by bit...

"As impressive as that looks, Girl, might I suggest you do it in a way that gets us the gleef out of here a bit faster?"

I turned and saw Grunge leaning against the cell's entrance, twirling the keychain I'd used to unlock the door to begin with.

He tossed it my way and I caught it. A few seconds later, my father was free.

"Riva, could you..." She was way ahead of me, though. She unclasped her fairy cape and handed it to my dad.

While he was securing it around his waist, I bent down to examine his legs.

"What did they do to you?"

He let out a long sigh. "Let's just say I was a bit less cooperative than I could've been when I got here."

"So, they cut your legs off?"

Dad nodded. "Yeah. He said I needed to be hobbled after what I'd done."

"He? Who did this to you?"

"The captain of the queen's guard."

"Uriel?"

"I didn't catch his name."

"But why?"

"Guess he was a little touchy after I mauled half a dozen of his men." Then, no doubt noticing the mix of rage, sadness, and grief on my face, he added, "I'm fine, honey. At least now I am."

"You're not fine." I felt around the edge of where the silver met his skin. It almost appeared to be fused together. Unfortunately, there was little chance this wasn't going to hurt. "But you will be."

"What are you doing?" he asked.

"Getting this crap off of you."

"Don't..."

"But your healing ... maybe you can..."

He grabbed hold of my hands and gently pushed them away. "It's too late."

"What do you mean, too late?"

"It's too late," he repeated. "If I'd been given a chance to heal naturally, maybe I could have grown them back. I don't know. I mean, I saw my grandfather grow a new hand once. Took months, but he did it. But this..." He took a deep breath. "They knew what they were doing, cauterizing the wounds with silver and letting it harden in place. There's nothing that can be done."

"You don't know that."

He put a hand on my shoulder. "*Yes*, I do. When we heal from grievous wounds, there's a ... it's hard to explain, a tingle. I don't know if it's purposeful or a result of our heightened senses, but it's there nevertheless. Tells us that things are working the way they're supposed to. But there's nothing down there anymore. They're not going to get any better."

"But..."

"But they're not going to get worse either," he said, as if trying to sound reassuring, because that's what dads did. "And it'll be okay. It'll take some adjusting, but I'll survive."

I could feel more tears slipping from my eyes, but I wiped them away. He was alive, that was the important part. And he was right, too. This wasn't anything that couldn't be overcome. Maybe there was some incantation in the old tomes Cass had inherited from Grandma Nelly. If not, modern prosthetics were a near miracle. Yeah, that was the ticket. I needed to focus on the positive. I couldn't lose it, not now, not when we'd come so far.

"Okay," I said after several long seconds. "We'll figure something out. You'll be back up and running with the pack in no time."

"Maybe," he replied, sounding hesitant. "But ... I won't be running the pack."

"Sure you will. You..."

"No. I won't. And I think you know it. I told you all about this. A pack leader cannot, under any circumstances, show weakness. And besides, I think my little girl is smart enough to have already figured out that I'm no longer the alpha."

I was well aware that our window for this reunion was rapidly running out. We had many more miles to cover before the day was done. Nevertheless, I couldn't just leave it at that. "I don't want it."

"You may not want it, but you've earned it ... even if you weren't supposed to. Besides," he replied, brightening up, "you managed to actually do what your mother and I only talked about. You got the pack to sit down with the Draíodóir. Don't sell yourself short, Tam Tam. Even if you've only been the alpha for a few months, you've already accomplished more than most do in their entire lives."

"I guess. I..."

"Wait. What do you mean months?" Riva asked, catching a little detail I'd apparently let slip right by. "I'll admit, things have been a bit wonky for me. But wasn't Christmas just a week ago?"

"A week?" Dad asked. "I've been here a lot longer than that." He paused as if thinking it over. "Time. It must flow differently here. Either that or your aunt blasted me a lot harder than I... Hold on. Your aunt..."

I held up a hand. "Not an issue anymore."

Thankfully he didn't ask me to elaborate. Instead, he quickly changed gears. "What about your brother? Chris, is he...?"

"He got banged up a bit, but he's okay." *At least I hope he is.*

"I guess the time weirdness means I don't need to ask if he's doing okay in school."

"Nope. It's still winter break, or was when I left anyway."

"Princess." I turned at the sound of the voice to find Cabbage waiting by the cell door. "Time grows short. Go we must."

He was right. It was time to go, which meant it was time for me to ask the question I'd been putting off for fear of learning the answer.

"Mom?"

"I don't know," Dad replied, no doubt sensing where this was going. "But I think she's okay. They separated us early on. That's part of the reason why I had such a ... disagreement with the guards."

"What do you mean separated? How can you know she's okay, if...?"

"Partially by what I saw, but also what I've heard. They may have cut off my legs, but they didn't touch my ears, if you catch my drift."

"Not really."

"Let me put it this way. As a follower of Valdemar I'm less than nothing to these people. The only reason I'm probably still alive is because I was an alpha, a person of note, an influencer as you kids call it. And even then, I only rate being tossed in a cell and having the key thrown away. I'm garbage as far as they're concerned. But your mother is a loyal devotee of ... her highness." Seems Dad had already been versed on the finer points of not mentioning certain names.

"Doesn't seem to have stopped them from screwing her over."

"No," he admitted. "But, at the same time, the Draíodóir love their ceremony, absolutely love it. And you know where they got that from, right?"

"Queen..."

"B," Riva finished for me.

"Thanks."

"Anytime."

"Exactly," Dad replied. "When two covens have a disagreement, even when it comes to blows, the Draíodóir treat each other with a certain respect they don't reserve for others."

"And you know this how?" I asked. "I thought you and Mom didn't discuss business around each other."

Dad smiled. "Just because we don't doesn't mean I haven't eavesdropped on occasion."

We had a brief powwow with Cabbage and Arugula. There'd been no sign of Mom down here. And, so far as I could tell, Dad's accommodations were top of the line, for below ground anyway. So that meant, assuming she was okay – and I dared not think of any other way she might be – my mother had to be elsewhere.

Dad tried not to show it, but I could tell he was a bit weirded out by Cabbage and his buddies. That at least made me feel a bit better about it. Guess I wasn't the only one not overly fond of Mom's army of garden gnomes. Speaking of which...

"Unknown to us where she might be," Cabbage finally conceded. "Had hoped to rescue the Monarch Queen here, then go above and make our demands. But now..."

"Now what?" I prodded.

"Be not angry," Arugula said. "But change our plans we must. Only opportunity for this we may ever have. Rescued your father, but now must we go and confront the queen."

I held up my hands. "Hold on. We had a deal. Rescue my parents then I'd tag along as you handed the queenie your manifesto or whatever. We need each other. You know that. You can't just go changing the deal like some kind of miniature Darth Vader. I mean, he's a character in..."

"Know who he is," Arugula replied. "Watched movies in your brother's room we have while he slept."

Well, if that wasn't infinitely creepy, I didn't know what was. Of course, that wasn't going to stop me from telling him once we got back. Good luck ever getting to sleep again, bro.

"What I'm trying to say is, you need me. But if you think I'm going to hold up my end of things while you go and change the terms, think again."

"Maybe negotiate for your mother we can at the time," Cabbage said, no doubt trying to salvage a plan that was rapidly turning to shit. "Cannot hurt to try."

"Sure it can," Riva replied. "There's this concept on our world called leverage."

"She's right," Dad added. "If the queen senses she has something you or the rest of us want, we'll be as good as dead in her throne room."

"Maybe not," Grunge said, standing off in the corner well away from the rest of us.

"Maybe not what?"

"I know a thing or two about leverage," he admitted, rather unsurprisingly. "And I know that right now we have gleefing zero."

"Pretty much what I was getting at," Riva replied. "And no, that actually doesn't help at all."

"I wasn't done yet, Girl. Her high and mightiness has it all right now, and let's face facts, she'll still have most even if we do save this Draíodóir. But she won't have it all. And, I don't know about you gleefers, but I'm hoping maybe we can get just enough so some of us can continue breathing past today."

"Your point?"

"My point is, I hear things. In this world if a lone sylph wants to get by, they either gotta latch their lips onto someone else's dust hole or they have to learn to play the game. I, for one, prefer to keep my lips unattached. So, I mostly stay away from the Queenshield's watchful eyes, while keeping my own open for anything that might give me an advantage one day."

I stepped toward him. "Okay, so have you seen anything that will help us?"

"Seen? No. But I've heard of a certain fable that I think you'll find interesting."

"We don't have time for fairy tales, or whatever you guys call them here."

"You might want to hear this one. It involves her highness and one of her daughters. The daughter did something to displease her. I don't remember what. Probably something stupid like forgetting to bow at the right time. Either way, the queen was angry, so she plucked her daughter from her home and imprisoned her for a hundred years in the fortress's northern tower."

Arugula nodded. "Have heard a similar tale, but it was a son, and failed to offer up proper tribute he did."

"Exactly," Grunge said. "There's multiple tellings of this story. The details change, but the end result doesn't. It always ends with her stuffing one of her children in the northernmost tower and letting them rot."

"And we care about this, why?" I asked.

Grunge lifted one half of his face in a lopsided grin. "Because her royal mercilessness doesn't have any children."

"Definitely not following you."

"It's a ... you daoine have a word for it. What is it? Metaform? Megatro..."

"Metaphor?" Riva offered.

"Yeah, that sounds right. It's a metaphor. From what I understand, the queen considers her subjects her children – her sons and daughters, if you will. And that little rule extends both to your world and those who worship her there."

26

"Just so we're clear, we're basing our next move on a fable, right?"

"More than a fable, perhaps," Arugula replied, looking up at Riva. "But if any prisoners would be so honored as to be considered a daughter of her majesty, it would be the Monarch Queen."

I was certain Mom would be flattered by that assertion, kinda anyway. But it made sense in an arrogant sort of way. And there was precedent for it, too, at least on Earth. The rabble got thrown into the dungeons, but the special prisoners – those of royal blood – got first class treatment, right up until the point where they were poisoned, bludgeoned to death, or sent to the guillotine.

A part of me was split. What had started as an already insane rescue scheme had just gotten a million percent crazier, as we now had to venture above ground where the resistance was likely to be a lot heavier. It was, in essence, adding a ticking time bomb to what was already a suicide mission. At the same time, I also knew I'd have to check out this lead, however slim it might be. Dying while trying to save my mother was not ideal, but I was oddly okay with it. Leaving now, knowing I hadn't done everything I could ... I simply wasn't sure I could live with that.

No. I was certain I couldn't. I raised a hand to the pendant around my neck, taking comfort in the strangely warm metal. I took after my father in some respects, but in others I was fully my mother's daughter. Mom could be ... well, a conceited pain in the ass when she wanted to be. But I also knew for a fact that she'd take this castle apart brick by brick if it meant rescuing either me or Chris. There was no force outside of death itself – and truth be told, I had to even wonder about that some days – that would keep her from saving her family.

Could I do any less? Not bloody likely.

So, rather than prolong this discussion, I simply stated, "I'm sold. Where to?"

"The northernmost tower," Arugula said. "In all tales, it is always that one."

"Why?" my father asked. "And how do you know it's not just a random direction someone picked for the story?"

The gnomes looked at a loss for that one, until Grunge stepped in again.

"I can answer that." At the look of surprise on my face, he grinned. "Like I said. I hear things. These so-called honored prisoners might get a tower, true. But it's not all fizzbeans and sun wisps, no. Being stuck in the northern tower is considered a grave insult, basically the queen spitting in your face without having to actually waste her royal phlegm on the effort."

"You're sure?"

"Positive. Because to the north lies the lands controlled by her sister Queen Maeve. And, in case it's not gleefing obvious, those two can't stand each other."

I raised an eyebrow at this new information. "Queen Maeve? I thought Bri... B was absolute ruler here."

"Yeah, absolute ruler of the Garden and everything in it. But Maeve rules over the Wastes, or at least that's what we call it here in the south. I'm sure the folks who have to live there have a less ominous name for it ... unless they're all a bunch of stupid gleef-heads. I don't know. Never been there and have no plans to change that."

I considered this. Back at school I'd done some research into the lore behind both Mom and Dad's beliefs, not really getting too far, being that I had a social life and all. However, one fairly common theme was that the world of the fae was split between the seasons – a summer and winter court in most stories, with occasional mention of fall and spring as lesser lordships.

Mom had made mention of a summer court before but never a winter, leading me to assume that the tales of opposing fairy queens was nothing more than bullshit.

Guess the old saying about assuming was true.

I turned to my father. "Any of this ring a bell?"

He shrugged. "Sorry, Tam Tam, but..."

"Yeah, I've been meaning to ask," Grunge interrupted. "What the gleef is a Tam Tam? Kind of sounds like tlam tlam, which, for the record, is a species of dung maggot here."

I turned toward my father and inclined my head.

"Gotcha," he replied a moment later. "Tamara it is. Anyway, I may have snooped on occasion, but this is all news to me. Never heard your mother mention a Maeve."

"Speaking of which," Riva said, "if mentioning Queen B's name is likely to get us killed, doesn't it go without saying that her sister, who is presumably just as scary powerful, is a no no, too – despite the fact that you all just said it?"

Grunge shook his head. "Doesn't work that way, Girl. Maeve's power is blocked here and vice versa. So you can say it all you want. Heck, draw it in the dirt and take a

squat over it if it pleases you. The Queenshield will probably give you a gleefing medal for it."

"Pass."

"Probably a smart idea. So, anyway, symbolic though
it might be, being tossed into the northern tower is
adding extra insult on top of already being a prisoner.
Because what fun is it to rule the entirety of the gleefing
Garden if you can't be petty as a mud wasp while
doing it?"

"I actually understood that one," Riva replied. "We
have mud wasps on Earth, too."

"Really? Nasty things. Grow as big as salamanders and
twice as ugly."

"Okay, maybe we don't have mud wasps back home
after all."

"Who cares?" I interrupted. "The main thing is we
have a direction and someplace to check. So let's do this."

"Exactly, Tam ... Tamara," my dad replied.

Grunge in turn held up a hand. "Not so fast. You
haven't heard the best part yet."

I raised an eyebrow his way. "Is that *best part* as in
actually good, or are you being sarcastic and about to tell
us we're all going to die?"

"More the former, in this case anyway. Now, I don't
know for certain if this is true or not. Like I told you, I've
tried my best to stay off the Queenshield's watch list. But I
have friends who've enjoyed the accommodations from
time to time, as you met earlier."

"The point?"

"The point is our beloved queenie is so big on perpetu-
ating her perceived insult that rumor has it she sealed all
the upper entrances to the northern tower."

"How is that good?"

"Because the tower supposedly extends down to this
level. It's so the Queenshield can feed and torture the pris-

oners there, without her high snootiness having to dirty her eyes to see them coming and going."

I felt a grin as predatory as his spread across my face in response. "So, in theory, if we find this tower entrance, we could rescue Mom without anyone upstairs being the wiser?"

"Exactly, Girl."

My smile widened. "If this works out, Grunge, you will have officially earned your honor back."

"That's what I want to hear." He paused for a moment, then asked, "And if it doesn't?"

"Then we'll all probably be too dead to care."

Dad wanted me to leave him behind, to come back and grab him on the way out. Said he would slow us down too much. Typical male bravado for some, but I knew him. He'd have gladly given his life for either me or Mom. I suspected part of his wanting to be left behind was so he could create a distraction to allow us to escape. Legs or not, he was a terrifying beast in his wolf form, and I didn't doubt he would've taken several of the Queenshield along with him.

Too bad I had no intention of giving him the chance. Having found him, there was absolutely no way I was going to simply walk away and leave him to his own devices. I'd seen this movie before and wasn't about to sit back and let that tragic plot point play itself out.

"Hop on," I told him as we prepared to move out.

We'd dallied long enough. Cabbage's gnomes were already scouting the hallways to the north, trying to determine if Grunge's intel had any basis in reality.

"Excuse me?"

I knelt down in front of my father. "Hop on. I'll carry you piggyback."

"I already told you, Tamara. I'll only slow you down."

I was ready for his obstinance, though. "The first thing I did upon arriving here was smack around a couple of rock trolls. Trust me, I'll barely notice you're there."

"What if I have to change?"

"Same deal, Dad. This is me we're talking about. Unless you've got an extra three tons of lead in your pockets I don't know about, this isn't up for debate."

"I disagree."

He was going to make me do it, wasn't he? I could already sense the change in his tone, beginning to go all parent-voice on me. Sorry, but not this time. I spun back toward him, poking a finger into his chest. "Feel free, but don't expect me to care."

"Excuse me, young lady?"

"I may be your daughter but, in case you've forgotten, I'm also your alpha now. That means *I'm* calling the shots. Now, you're free to challenge that position, but you saw what happened when Mitch decided to tangle with me. I can guarantee it won't end like it did the first time."

We locked eyes for a few seconds until, much to my relief, Dad looked away.

Rather than appear like a beaten dog, though, he actually smiled. "Please tell me that's the attitude you used to get the rest of the pack in line."

I held up my thumb and forefinger about an inch apart. "I may have reminded them just a tiny bit why they should be afraid of the big bad hybrid."

"Very well. As you command, alpha Tam Tam."

I turned around and helped him up on my back. "Perhaps we should consider a slightly different title."

"No promises. I'm still your dad after all."

"I wouldn't have it any other way."

We finally stepped foot outside the cell he'd been kept in, the bodies of the guards having been dragged off by Cabbage's people at some point ... hopefully not to a stew pot.

"Oh, by the way," Dad said from his place on my back, "before I forget. Did Mitch manage to make it out of Crescentwood?"

"Maybe best to not ask about that."

The music from upstairs continued to seep down to our level, or at least the bass-like parts of it did. Either that or there was the mother of all throwdowns going on just above our heads. Considering the prospective guest list, I didn't care to consider what that might entail.

Thankfully, the gnomes seemed to have some sense of which way north was, even underground as we were.

They were also apparently getting better in their surprise attacks. As me, Riva, and my dad followed the two gnome leaders, we passed by several downed fairies. These weren't sidhe, but they were still bigger than Grunge – who, I might add, was a pig in shit with regards to shameless corpse looting. All of the bodies bore the telltale signs of being attacked from afar by tiny iron nails – singed, partially melted skin, and looking seriously gross.

All joking aside, it was a bad way to go. If anything, I began to understand why Brigid had labeled the gnomes terrorists. They were good at this, as well as apparently merciless.

The only question was whether they'd come here like that or been forced to adopt these extreme methods due to the way they'd been treated. I had a feeling the answer wasn't quite black and white. Hell, I might not even want to know the full truth. It was quite possible I was, ethically anyway, on the wrong side in this assault.

The thing was, I didn't care. So long as I got my parents back, none of it mattered. Yes, it was a slippery slope to take a means to an end approach, one I'd have to ponder long and hard on. But the fact remained, I wouldn't be doing so until we were back home.

Besides, the fairies who'd been taken out might not be culpable themselves, but their boss had purposely crippled my father. It made me fearful for what kind of state I'd find my mother in, and likewise what I might do if the worst came to pass.

I wasn't about to tell Cabbage, but he might very well end up trying to serve Brigid a list of demands with a blood-lusted hybrid to back him up.

Mind you, I wasn't sure what good that would do against a goddess made flesh. But who knows? If she had a jaw, maybe it could be broken.

I'm sure stranger things had happened.

For now, though, it appeared our time below ground was over. The warren of hallways terminated at an intersection. A doorway had been cut in the stone wall, and a winding set of spiral stairs could be seen beyond it. If that wasn't the way up to a tower, I didn't know what was.

Lending credence to the fact that we'd found our mark, was one of the Queenshield lying dead in front of it – smoke pouring out of the bloody holes where his eyes had once been. *Ouch.* Talk about a double tap.

However, before we could ascend, one of the gnomes already there pulled Cabbage to the side for a word in private.

My ears easily picked up the words, but they'd maddeningly switched over to their gnome language again – perhaps aware that I had supercharged ears, or maybe just being extra cautious.

"Any idea what they're talking about?" Dad whispered in my ear.

"Nope. I don't speak creepy garden gnome, do you?"

"No," he replied, "but why do I have a sneaking suspicion your mother does?"

I shrugged, just as Cabbage turned back toward us. "Is there a problem?"

"Problem we have, yes." He turned and pointed toward the dead guard. "One killed, which is good, but always in pairs do the Queenshield work. Escaped one did, so my men say. Hunting him now are they."

"Shit. Do you need my help catching him?"

Cabbage shook his head, telling me the race was likely already lost. "Long legs they have and know this place they do."

"So what now?"

"Up we must go. No other option. But I fear that the easy way it will be. Back down, we will have to fight our way."

27

A few of Cabbage's people were chosen to stay behind to guard the entranceway to the tower. I didn't fool myself that it was anything but a suicide mission, which didn't make me feel better about things.

What a freaking disaster. Yes, the Draíodóir and the werewolves hated each other, and yes the wolves were more than okay with things getting bloody if it came down to it, but they'd at least been open to the possibility of a diplomatic mission. It might've failed spectacularly in the end, but at least the option had been there for us to come here as a people united – sorta anyway – and see if the queen was willing to negotiate for the release of her prisoners. Hell, I'd have been happy to trade myself for them if the option had been on the table.

Instead, here I was, at the center of an insurrection, melting fairy faces and sending off squads of kamikaze gnomes.

The interior of the tower itself seemed to be about forty feet wide, the stone stairs themselves more than enough to allow guards to go up or down two or three abreast in full armor. Mind you, there were no bannisters at the far edge, so I'd have hated to be that guy. Even so, coming down was potentially going to be an issue as this place was large enough to not provide a good choke point.

Fortunately, as we started up the staircase, the sounds from above soon became so loud as to drown my darkening thoughts out.

After about twenty feet of climbing, the stairs ended at a large open space the entire width of the tower. Across the way, another set of stairs began, these leading up along the edge of the tower again.

Considering the volume of the noise here, I guessed we were on the same level as the queen's diplomatic soiree, yet I spied no exit other than the stairs opposite us.

A few moments later, Grunge tapped me on the shoulder and pointed. Turns out he was right. There apparently had once been an exit from this floor of the tower. The outline was still faintly visible, but it had been walled off at some point in the past.

Guess the queen really did have a mad-on regarding her sister.

That was her problem, though. Ours was the long climb ahead and, looking up, it was painfully obvious we'd just begun. This seemed to be the only floor the stairs made a stop at, other than the very top, as I could see the spiral staircase continue to wind around above us, more times than I cared to count. Go figure, a conceited fairy godmother had a castle big enough to suit her enormous ego.

And here I'd been happy with our house in High Moon, with its two floors and a basement.

After another sixty or seventy feet up, the journey started to take its toll on a few of our party. Amazingly enough, though, it wasn't the gnomes. Despite each stair requiring them to literally hoist each other up onto it, they continued onward, neither slowing nor complaining. Sadly, the same couldn't be said of the rest.

"Have I mentioned how much I always hated my dad's StairMaster?" Riva remarked, breathing hard.

"Oh, come on. A little cardio never hurt anyone."

"Says the girl with werewolf blood running through her veins."

"I did plenty of training like this before I even knew I had powers and you know it."

"Yeah," she wheezed, "which is why I kind of hate you right now."

I laughed. "You might want to save your breath. We're not even halfway there."

"Fuck you."

"Gleefing double that," Grunge added, likewise panting.

Riva turned and glared at him. "You do realize you have wings, right?"

"Of course, Girl, but I also realize I have no gleefing idea what's waiting for us up there and I'm not planning on finding out by myself."

"Misery loves company," I replied, chugging along just fine, despite Dad still hanging off my back. Speaking of which...

"You let me know if you get tired, Tamara."

"So I can what, let someone else take a turn? No offense, Dad, but I don't think the others are in any shape to help out."

"I can still change you know. I'm pretty sure I could make short work of these stairs, legs or not."

Truth of the matter was I didn't doubt him. Still...

"Save it for the trip back down. I have a feeling we'll need it."

"At least I'll have the high ground, Anakin," he replied.

"What?"

"Seriously? *Revenge of the Sith*? You remember that, we..."

"You saw it with Chris. I went with Mom to get a pedicure."

"Oh. Well, it was still a cool scene."

"Did the guy who said that win?"

"Kinda ... in the short term anyway."

"Then that's all that matters to me."

It shouldn't have been a surprise, not with the racket we made on the way up, but there were two Queenshield waiting up above, and they were ready for us as we approached.

"Halt and surrender!" one called down to us, a moment before a silver tipped spear broke against the wall only about a foot away – the curve of the staircase likely the only thing that had saved me from being properly ventilated.

"I so need to bring a gun next time," I muttered to myself, backing out of range of where they could hit me, at least without coming down to meet us head on.

Grunge and Riva were still about thirty feet below the rest of us, having stopped to take a rest break, so at least that was one less thing to worry about.

Unfortunately, the architecture that saved me also prevented the gnomes from getting a clear shot up above, and the Queenshield guards were annoyingly smart enough to not stick their heads out where we could fill them full of iron.

"You shall not be asked again," one of the guards called down.

"And you're outnumbered," I shouted back, not having much else to throw at them.

"Keep them busy," Dad whispered in my ear.

"Huh, what ... whoa!" I almost lost my balance and fell backward as the weight on my shoulders suddenly more than tripled.

A moment later, the massive snout of a mega-wolf peeked out from behind me.

There was no point in bending to put Dad down. Even without the lower half of his legs, his wolf form still towered over me. Talk about making a girl feel short.

The silver covering the stumps of his legs scraped against the stone as he pulled his way over to the edge ... and then dropped off!

I almost cried out in panic, but then I spied the very tips of his claws grasping hold of the edge of the steps, making me understand what he'd meant about keeping the guards busy.

"Surrender now!" I called out, as Dad started to quietly climb past us, doing a hell of a King Kong impersonation. "Drop your weapons and we'll let you walk away with your lives. We're not here for you. We only want the prisoner."

"The prisoner we've sworn to keep watch over?" one of the guards replied with a haughty laugh. "Fool, our lives would be worth nothing if we were to do so, our honor destroyed. So, you see, our path is set and our dedication to our duty is as unfailing as our loyalty to our queen."

Good. They were willing to monologue. Always helpful. Also useful was the fact that they were content to do so while staying out of sight, no doubt readying themselves for our inevitable charge up the stairs.

"I'm warning you again..." *Come on, Dad. Move faster.*

"I have no interest in adding your lives to all the others I've taken today. I'm willing to be merciful, but my patience has limits."

"While ours has none, foolish child of Earth."

Goddamn, these guys were full of themselves. Guess I couldn't blame them. If I were a tall, muscular, kung-fu supermodel, I'd probably have a bit of an ego, too.

I looked up and saw Dad was almost there. I just needed to give him a few more seconds.

"I'm going to give you until the count of..." No, not three. Everyone always expects a charge on two in that case. I needed a bit more time. "...ten. And then we're coming up to finish this. One... Two..."

"Count as long as you wish. The Queenshield do not heed the orders of lowly Daoiiiieeeeeeeeeeee!"

Dad launched himself over the edge of the landing right in the middle of the fairy's speech. A moment later, one of the guards came falling past us, taking the express elevator down.

As for the other, his screams quieted a few moments later, replaced with the sound of wet meat being torn asunder, a sound I really wished I wasn't so familiar with.

"*All clear,*" a gravelly voice called down to us soon after, my father likely in mid-transformation. "Watch your step. It's a bit slippery up here."

By then, Grunge and Riva had caught up to us, both of them looking as if they wished for nothing more than to join the sidhe who'd plummeted to his death only moments earlier.

"Shall I assume it's not pretty up there?" she asked.

"Probably a safe assumption."

"Are you guys waiting for an invitation?" Dad called from above.

I grimaced at Riva. "I hope those new fairy boots of yours are stain resistant."

Dad was right, it *was* slippery up on the landing. He'd apparently popped that Queenshield asshole like a water balloon. Can't say I blamed him for wanting a bit of payback. At the same time, subtle it was not.

Oh well, according to Cabbage we were fucked in that regards anyway. So what were a few more bodies to add to our already growing list of crimes?

Sadly, it seemed at least one of those bodies would've been of use to us. A quick search of the dead guard turned up no trace of a key. That likely meant it was with the one Dad had sent on a one-way trip downstairs. Alas, I doubted there was time to run down, search him, and then come back up. As for the door, it was the same heavy-duty model as had barred Dad's cell, making me wonder exactly how much freaking silver was in this damned castle.

More and more, the idea of filling my pockets for the return trip home was sounding good, but not as awesome as the idea that my mother was right behind this door.

But not for long.

There was a handle, but it didn't look sturdy enough to withstand a full-on assault. The door itself was flush with the wall, no room to slide in so much as a fingernail for purchase.

Guess it was going to be the hard way.

"Everyone stand back."

"Everyone *else* stand back," my father corrected, still in his human guise. "This will go faster if we work together."

Turns out his words of caution were more necessary than mine as, a moment later, his body swelled to mega-wolf size, leaving things a bit cramped for us up on the partial landing.

Cramped was fine, though, if it got the job done. And

he was right, two super-powered jailbreakers were more effective than one as we began to hammer the rock wall around the door – chipping away at it, blow after blow, so as to create a decent handhold.

We made a hell of a racket doing so, not to mention bloodied our knuckles in the process.

"Hurry, Princess," Cabbage warned after a few minutes. "Time we do not have."

"Doing our best here."

Dad growled something, too, probably an affirmation of what I'd just said.

Eventually, we managed to chip out enough divots for him to get a handhold with his claws. That sped things up considerably. Him pulling while I continued to hammer away at the locking mechanism ... which was far thicker than I would've preferred. Guess they took their VIP security far more seriously than the mooks down in general holding.

Finally, there came a groan of metal giving way.

I stepped in and helped Dad, planting a foot on the wall for extra leverage.

"Come on. Just a little more..."

The bolts finally gave way with a tortured screech, and the door flew open revealing the interior beyond, and the woman wreathed in flame standing within.

"*Dorn an bháis!*"

And then my view of both the room and my mother was obscured as a black bolt of killing magic was unleashed in my direction.

Shit!

The magic itself wasn't the problem. I'd gotten hit with this spell before and, unlike most others, had lived to tell the tale.

The problem was the force behind it. It was more than enough to knock me off my feet and send me tumbling ass over teakettle, something of note with a two hundred foot drop only a few yards behind me.

I just barely had time to shove Dad to the side and plant my feet ... on the blood-slicked floor. Yeah, I was screwed.

But then, just as the spell reached the threshold, it flashed bright white and fizzled out. I didn't feel so much as a gust of wind from it.

As I stood there waiting for my heart to restart, the spots from my eyes began to fade and I could once again make out the figure within, the flames around her still burning bright.

"Tamara?"

"It-it's me, Mom." I made to step in, but then hesitated, noting her guard was still raised. Probably smart of her, but bad for me if I went inside. Resistant to magic or not, I didn't care to get blasted. I held up a hand toward my dad, still off to the side. "And I can prove it. When I was six, you grounded me for a week for hand-painting Tamara Rocks on the side of your car. Then when I was eight, I did it again, but with Dad's spray paint because I was angry you didn't get me a PlayStation for my birthday..."

I rattled off half a dozen embarrassing things that only I'd know, and hopefully she remembered.

"Don't forget that time we both got busted for ditching class to hang out at Swallowtail lake," Riva called from a few steps down, staying well out of the line of fire. "Hi, Mrs. Bentley, I'm here, too."

"You brought Riva here?" Mom asked incredulously,

the flames around her body still illuminating her as if she were a goddess herself.

"Brought is a rather strong word."

"She's not the only one, Lissa," Dad said, popping his head around the doorway. Guess I couldn't blame him for being cautious. Mom's magic might not do much to me, but it was downright lethal to him. "Are you okay? Did they hurt you?"

"Hah! You almost had me," she replied after a moment, her eyes flashing with power. "But you had to push it, didn't you? I suppose Chris is there with you, too, isn't he?"

"No, Mom. I'm not fucking insane."

"My daughter would never use that language..."

"Oh yes I would! You'd just yell at me and I'd ignore it."

"Remember how we met, Lissa?" Dad offered. "That night out in the glade. We tried to kill each other, then things got a bit heated and..."

"Seriously?" I cried at him. "Could we maybe keep this PG13?"

I turned back to find indecision in Mom's eyes, but she still had her defenses up. I guess it was going to be the hard way again. "Okay, so if I'm someone else, then it shouldn't be an issue to blast me. If I'm who I say I am, I'll survive. If not, then that's one less fairy asshole to deal with."

Mom smirked but held her ground.

I was tempted to ask what the hell she needed to prove we were real, but then remembered the spell she'd thrown my way. With her current mood, I doubted she'd purposely stopped it. Warning shots weren't really Mom's style. But it hadn't just stopped. It had flared up and disappeared ... right about when it hit the threshold of the cell. She wasn't holding back out of indecision. It was because she couldn't hit me, not where I was. There was likely some sort of anti-magic field around the cell. Smart. It explained how they were able to keep her locked up without needing to mop up the guards every five minutes.

Guess I had no choice. "Fine then. Let's do this."

"Tamara?" Dad asked, but I was already outside his reach, stepping in and heading toward the center where Mom stood.

It gave me a moment to take in the surroundings. Swank. Grunge hadn't been lying when he'd said only special prisoners were given these accommodations. Yeah, she was still a prisoner, but there was a massive four poster bed in the room, a changing station, a vanity desk, a full bookshelf and more. Hell, the only thing missing was a big screen TV.

Note to self, if you're going to piss off a fairy queen, go big.

All was not wine and roses, though. Despite Mom's fiery appearance, I saw a thin chain running from her leg to a spot on the wall. Whatever it was, it was apparently able to resist her power, otherwise she'd have likely melted it off and been done with it.

But that could wait. For now, we apparently had to do the song and dance routine.

"All right, I'm here," I said, approaching her. "What's it going to be, a black bolt of death or maybe those magic laser ropes? Oh, I know. That gravity crush spell is always a hit at parties."

Mom narrowed her eyes, making me wonder if it was wise to offer up suggestions for ways to kill me. But then, rather than trying to blast me to kingdom come, the flames and light around her subsided, revealing her to be wearing a dress that seemed fit for royalty. Guess Brigid had standards to maintain while she was busy spitting in someone's face.

"Getting ready for the prince's ball?" I asked.

Rather than reply, Mom approached me quietly. She stood there in front of me for a moment, then smiled and threw her arms around me in a big hug.

She caught me totally by surprise, albeit it was a surprise more wonderful than I could ever hope to express. "M-mom?"

"Hush, Tamara. The queen of the summer court can do a lot of things, like pluck images and memories out of someone's mind and use it against them. But there are always tells."

"Tells?"

"The sidhe can, in no way, convincingly replicate that snotty attitude of yours."

I wasn't sure whether to laugh or yell at her, so I did the sensible thing – I threw my arms around her and buried my head in her shoulder, the tears already starting to fall.

"I missed you, Mom."

"I missed you too, Tamara. *lann a mharbhadh!*"

Wait, what?

Mom pulled away just as a scythe of pure black energy slammed into my side, carrying me off my feet and crushing me against the stone walls of the opulent cell.

"Lissa, stop!" I vaguely heard Dad cry out as I slumped to the floor bruised to all hell.

Bruised was not out of it, though.

"S-seriously, Mom?" I growled, forcing myself back to my feet. "What the fuck was that?!"

She, however, was smiling broadly, looking oddly delighted, despite doing her best to make me a permanent wall fixture. "It really is you."

"I told you it was!"

"I'm sorry, honey. Really, I am, but you have to understand..." She stopped about halfway to me, her head turned toward the door and a look of horror dawning on her face. "Oh my god, Curtis! What did they do to you?"

Mom tried to race toward the open cell door, falling about five feet short as the tether around her snapped taut, stopping her forward motion as surely as if she'd run into a wall.

Dad, in the meantime, had changed to a state halfway between man and wolf. From past experience, I knew it gave him access to a good chunk of his powers while still allowing him to speak semi-articulately. In this case, though, he seemed less interested in a soliloquy than in movement. His strength now far in excess of a normal human, he was able to pull himself across the floor at a pace that brought him to my mother in seconds.

He changed back to his human form just as they both collapsed into each other's arms.

"I'm so sorry, Curtis. I didn't know."

"It's okay, honey," Dad said, tears in his eyes but a smile on his face. "Probably nothing I didn't deserve."

"Don't say that," Mom snapped. "Don't *ever* say that. None of them, not the Draíodóir not your people, not even the gods. None of them know how much you've sacrificed, the good you've done for us." Those flames from earlier began to reappear around her. Fortunately, it didn't seem to be real fire as evidenced by my father not instantly combusting. "And to do this to you? No. I don't care. They will not get away with it. I swear on my mother's name and her mother's thrice removed that they will pay for..."

So much for happy reunions. Mom was nothing if not pragmatic.

Before she could finish her oath, though, I stepped in and grabbed hold of them both, interrupting her tirade. She was right to be angry, but it could wait. We were a family again, and I wanted them to understand that.

Mom's flames died down as I pulled them both in, and for that brief moment in time all was right with our world.

However, I wasn't naïve enough to think it would stay that way.

We were still in danger and a long way from being home free.

28

W e might have stayed that way for longer than was prudent, taking strength from nothing more than each other's presence. Fortunately, we had a resident dirtbag sylph to remind us that we still had a long way to go before we could truly enjoy our reunion.

"Don't mind me. Just checking to see if there's anything here that won't be missed by her highness."

Mom pulled away from us, wiped her eyes, then glanced over at Grunge. "Making new friends, Tamara?"

"You know me. A ray of sunshine no matter where I go."

"What about old friends?" Riva asked, popping her head around the corner.

Mom raised an eyebrow my way, to which I held up a hand.

"Long story. Cliff's notes is she remembers everything, and no I didn't purposely put her life in danger by asking her to come here with me. Save the rest for the post game wrap-up, okay."

Mom looked like she wanted to say something to that,

but instead she merely stood and smoothed her regal dress. "It's good to see you, Riva."

"You, too, Mrs. Bentley. You have no idea." She turned to me. "Cabbage is keeping an eye on the stairs, but he said to tell you things are starting to sound kind of rowdy down below."

"Cabbage is here?" Mom asked. "I knew I could count on him and his noble people."

"Yeah," I replied, likewise rising. "Noble people ... who live in our front yard and watch our every move."

"Don't be melodramatic. It pays to have allies."

"Not arguing against that." I bent down and began to examine the tether running from her ankle to the wall. "Just know that it'll be a discussion item once we get home."

Hmm. Looked like some flimsy silver wire, nothing more. Maybe it was enchanted to resist magic or something. Oh well, I doubted it was enchanted enough for me. I grabbed hold of it, noting how warm it felt in my hands.

"Don't bother, Tamara, that won't work."

"We'll see." I gave it a good yank and ... nothing happened. "Hold on. That was just a warm-up." This time I put some effort into it, wrapping a length around both hands before trying again...

And almost wrenching my back in the process as the pathetic little cable continued to mock me.

"The fuck?"

"Language, young lady."

"Ground me when we're back home," I snapped, preparing to try again. Weird. Maybe the climb up had taken more out of me than I'd assumed. That was fine. I still had plenty more left to give.

"You can't snap it," Mom said, sounding exasperated.

"Watch me. I'll be damned if I'm going to let some silver fishing line kick my ass."

"That's not silver."

"It's not?" Dad and I replied simultaneously.

"No way," Grunge cried, abandoning Mom's dresser drawers with a look of naked avarice in his eyes." Is that..."

"Brighdril," Mom said.

I glanced at her. "Brigh-what?"

"Brighdril," she repeated.

"I thought that stuff was a myth," Dad said.

Mom put a hand on his shoulder. "I know, dear. Believe me, that's purposeful." She turned back toward me. "It looks like normal metal, but it's not. Feel it, notice how it's warm to the touch?"

She was right. I let go, then pulled the pendant out of my sweater. "Just like my..."

"You wore it!" Mom cried, sounding pleased. "I was so hoping you'd like it."

"Well, yeah, I love it. You gave it to me."

That caused her to smile even more. "And you're correct. The frame is comprised of brighdril as well. Took me months to scrounge up enough to make it. It's exceptionally rare, extremely strong, and..."

"Let me guess," I interrupted. "Super resistant to magic."

"Quite the opposite really. It's an excellent magical conductor. But, if used the right way, it can also work as the equivalent of an eldritch lightning rod, effectively grounding itself against mystical power."

"I'm going to go out on a limb and assume this setup here is the so-called right way."

"So, it's kind of like mithril," Dad opined, catching our attention. "You know, Lord of the Rings ... Frodo and his chain shirt?"

"Yes, dear," Mom replied, obviously humoring him. "Except this is the real world."

I stepped over to the wall, opting for a change in strategy now that I had better information. "Real world or not, I'm not letting some stupid necklace chain stop us from freeing you."

When in doubt, keep it simple. The chain might be unbreakable, but that didn't mean whatever it was anchored to was.

"I don't suppose anyone would mind if I held onto that once you're done with it," Grunge said from behind me.

"Knock yourself out. Make it into a fucking jump rope for all I..." I paused in my effort as a thought hit me, causing me to glance back toward Mom. "Brighdril? Please tell me that royal asshole didn't name this shit after herself." She was silent on the matter. "Of course she did. Why wouldn't she?"

That made what I was about to do all the sweeter.

I braced myself and pulled.

"I told you, that won't work."

"The hell it won't." Holy shit this stuff was tough. It dug into my hands, but still refused to give. Well, fuck that noise. I redoubled my efforts, ignoring the pain. *Come on.*

"Tamara..."

"Shut..." *Crack!* "Up!"

There came the sound of crumbling masonry and then a section of the wall itself gave way, pulling free in a shower of dust and debris and sending me falling back on my ass.

Mom was freed ... in a sense anyway, if you considered dragging a two foot cube of solid stone down the stairs to be free. Still, it was a marked improvement.

"I admit it," she said. "I'm impressed."

I couldn't help but grin. "All right. Let me carry this part, so we can..."

"No need, dear. I can take care of the rest."

"But how...?"

"*Dòrn an ùird!*"

What the? A pulse of dark purplish energy flared past me, shattering the block of masonry into a million pieces and revealing the foot long spear of brighdril that had been used to anchor it in place.

I turned to see Mom blow an imaginary puff of smoke from her hand, as if she'd just fired a gun.

"And the reason you didn't do that before?"

She shrugged. "Pay attention, Tamara. It's exactly like I said. It was acting as a grounding wire for my power, dissipating it harmlessly throughout the entire tower's super structure. One block of it, though, is a piece of cake."

"You've still got it, honey," Dad said.

She winked at him. "Flattery will get you everywhere."

I began to coil up the magical metal, so that it wouldn't hamper Mom's ability to walk. "Speaking of getting us anywhere but here, what are the chances of you zapping us out of this place?"

She shook her head. "Zero, unfortunately. Dùn nan Dé is heavily warded against such things. The only ones who go in or out are those who Queen Brigid allows."

"Yeah, but we got in," I pointed out.

"True but, as you've no doubt realized by now, you're a ... special case. The normal rules do not apply to..."

"Are you gleefing nuts?!" Grunge cried, interrupting us. "Don't say her name!"

Crap! I'd almost forgotten about that.

"Oh, little sylph. Do you honestly think she's not aware of our presence by now?"

That was probably a good point considering the trail

of bodies we'd left below, not to mention the one who'd escaped. To think this was still a stealth mission was probably foolish.

"Fine," I said. "Hard way it is, then. Doesn't matter. I'm still getting you all out of here." I handed Mom the coil of metal – snapping the anklet around her leg would have to wait – then turned to Dad. "Ready to hop on again?"

He gave me a half smile, then turned to my mother. "I don't suppose you have anything that might temporarily ... help matters here?"

"This will have to do for now." Mom bent down and planted a big wet kiss on his lips – tongue, too. *Gross!* "I swear to you, once we get home, I will do everything in my power to fix this. For now, though..." She shook her head. "Any incantation I could try would simply take too long. This isn't like battle magic. It's a lot more complex."

"Can't blame a guy for asking."

"What? Don't like being carried around?" I asked.

"I just don't want to slow you down, pumpkin."

"Here's an idea." I pulled the iron rod from my back and handed it to him. "You smack anything that gets near us and let me worry about how fast we're moving."

"Who runs Barter Town?"

"What?" I glanced up over my shoulder at Dad, riding piggyback once again.

"I swear, Tam Tam, once we get back, you and I are spending the entire day watching movies."

"Uh huh. We'll see about that."

We finally stepped out of the cell, mission accomplished and ready to give hell to anyone who stood in our way.

Much as when we'd freed my dad, the landing outside of Mom's cell was now clear of the body that had been there when we stepped inside. The floor was still stained with blood, but it was no longer slippery. Cabbage and his people had been hard at work. They were like the elves in that story about the old shoemaker, except they apparently cleaned up bodies instead of making boots.

Again, I was forced to consider how absolutely fucking creepy this was. Pity, that it wasn't like I had much choice for bedfellows during this mission.

Cabbage, Arugula, and some of their soldiers were waiting for us as we emerged. Upon seeing my mother, they all dropped to one knee.

"All hail Lissa the Benevolent, Queen of the Monarchs!"

Lissa the Benevolent? I'd have to remember that the next time I got in trouble for sneaking vodka out of the liquor cabinet.

"Thank you so much, my friends," Mom told them. "I will never forget all you've done for me and my family."

"Not all us," Cabbage replied, pointing at me. "The princess led the charge, she did."

Mom looked at me with one eyebrow raised, causing me to grin. "What can I say? I'm both a princess *and* a badass. I will be wanting a tiara, though."

Cabbage stepped toward me. "No crowns do we have, but perhaps suffice this will in the hours ahead." He held out what appeared to be a fancy silver bracelet, ornately carved with images of leaves and trees. It was pretty, although probably didn't quite go with my sweater, or what was left of it.

After a couple of moments, Arugula stepped in, once again smacking Cabbage upside the head. "Found it upon the dead Queenshield we did. More than a bauble it is. Try it and see."

"Really? I'm surprised Grunge didn't pocket it first."

She glanced past me, toward where the little pixie stood, throwing him a sour glare. "Try, he did. Convince him otherwise, I was forced to."

Oh, okay. That made more sense. From the dead guard, eh? That probably meant it was more than a mere fashion accessory. I plucked it from Cabbage's grasp and clamped it onto my left wrist, staring at it for a second or two. "Is that it?"

Arugula shook her head then made a gesture as if karate chopping something. Kung fu gnomes. Definitely a movie my brother would watch.

Not really grasping what that might mean, I imitated her move ... first with my right, then, after she rolled her eyes, with my left.

Whoa!

In the space of a millisecond, a tower shield appeared strapped to my arm, expanding in the time it took me to blink. Think one of those collapsible police batons, except a lot cooler.

"That's handy," Dad commented from my back.

"Yeah. Also means they weren't pulling that stuff out of their asses after all."

"What?"

"Um, never mind. Just wool gathering."

I gave my wrist another flick and the shield collapsed in on itself, once again becoming a bracelet. "Okay. This is seriously cool."

"More than cool," Arugula said. "Down we must go. Alas, our scouts have told us as empty as it was, now it is not. Necessity it is."

Ah, I saw how it was. Resistance was mounting below, and I'd pulled the unenviable job of meat shield. At least with this thing, I had a small chance of making it down without becoming a pin cushion.

Speaking of which, though...

"All right, Tamara," Mom said. "Let me take the lead. The sidhe and the Draíodóir have always held mutual respect..."

"No," I replied, waving her off. "We're long past that. Trust me. Here's how it's going to play out. Dad and me in the front. Dad, keep your head down until we're close enough to bust theirs. Mom, you're behind us. Provide cover fire if the castle will let you. If not, keep yourself and the others safe. Don't worry about us."

"I always worry about you."

That was sweet, but also a very mom thing to say. Too bad platitudes weren't going to help much if we got absolutely peppered from below.

"Riva, you stay with my mom. Mom, can you..."

"Of course, dear. This isn't my first rodeo, you know."

"Thanks, Mrs. Bentley."

"I'll bring up the rear," Grunge *heroically* volunteered. "Make sure, um, nobody sneaks down after us."

Still, weasely coward and thief that he was, his information had proven solid. We'd gotten my mother back because of him. It wasn't something I'd easily forget.

"Okay," I replied. "Keep yourself safe and stay against the wall on the way down. Don't let anyone get a free pot shot at you."

"Didn't plan to."

"Cabbage, have your people stay back until we get close enough to charge. Then ... I don't know. Maybe bite their fucking ankles off."

29

We were more than halfway down, our progress so far uninhibited, when I saw the first of the Queenshield. Don't get me wrong, I could hear things happening below. There was little doubt the queen's soldiers were waiting for us, quite a few from what I could tell.

What I almost missed, though, was them sending an assassin up to try and flank us.

It was luck more than anything, catching the barest glimpse of a black-gloved finger peeking out from beneath ... *something* as it held onto the very edge of the stairs below us.

If my father hadn't done his little climbing trick earlier, I wouldn't have even thought to look.

But as I locked my eyes on where the rest of the hand should be, seeing nothing but empty space, I caught sight of a slight shimmer in the air.

Had I been a betting girl, I'd have said the sidhe were using some kind of magic to cloak themselves. Not quite invisibility so much as bending light around them, like in that one alien movie Chris liked, I forget the name. Either way, I guess they figured they'd send up a scout or two to try and ambush us.

Clever.

Not clever enough, though.

Making sure to not stare too obviously, I whispered, "Be ready," in a voice low enough that hopefully only my father would hear.

I felt him tense up, then, with a flick of my wrist, I activated the shield. It expanded to roughly four feet high in less than a second. In the next moment, I brought the edge down into the space where the finger was peeking out.

The result was instantaneous. The stair beneath me was stained by that strange colored fairy blood, as there came a scream of pain to my immediate left ... a scream which rapidly got further and further away as its owner took the express route back down.

"Tam Tam, in front of you!"

I was prepared for it, though, having heard a faint sound as something else scrabbled up onto the steps immediately in front of us. I spun, bringing the shield up, just as a second Queenshield threw aside his ... um ... enchanted cloak I guess, and struck out at me with his double-sided spear. The spearhead collided with the shield, making a screech as metal met metal. But then there came the far less pleasant sound of iron impacting with bone as my father swung the rod I'd given him, nearly decapitating the sidhe with it.

Before the soldier's body could even hit the floor, I heaved it to the side, sending the dead guard falling after the first.

"Nice try, assholes!" I called down after them.

"Subtle as always, Tamara," Mom said from behind us.

"Be nice, Lis," Dad chided before saying to me, "We make a pretty good team, pumpkin."

"Yep, minus maybe the cutesy nicknames."

"Oh, I don't know. I think that makes it even better."

"We're going to have to agree to disagree on that one."

"Well, perhaps one thing we can all agree on," Mom said, "is that the response going forward is likely to be a lot less friendly."

Sadly, I had a feeling she was right.

"Okay, everyone, playtime's over," I called out in a loud whisper. "From here on in we move fast. Everyone stay a few steps behind me, let us take the brunt of the assault, but keep pace and stay alert. We don't want to risk being flanked, but we can't give them time to regroup and fortify either."

Holy shit. I almost sounded like I knew what I was doing.

In response, the weight upon my back suddenly felt like it doubled.

"Dad?" I glanced over my shoulder to find him in that strange halfway form again, even though I knew it was uncomfortable for him to hold for long. "You sure you want to do that?"

"*Better this way,*" he snarled. "*I can see more of the spectrum. Easier to spot if they send more assassins.*"

Well, damn. I knew werewolves had good vision but hadn't realized it was that good. Sadly, that was a gift I hadn't inherited. Figures. They could probably do cool things like track body heat, while I was stuck tripping over my own two feet in the dark. Oh well, at least I didn't ever feel the urge to sniff anyone's butt. Tradeoffs and all.

"*Are you okay with the extra weight?*" Dad asked.

"Right as rain. Gives me more momentum to use if we need it. Let's..."

"Hold on a second, Tamara," Mom interrupted.

"What for?"

"This." She stepped to the edge of the stone steps,

overlooking the drop down – exactly where I'd said not to go. Before I could say something, though, she screamed out, "*Sèididhteine!*"

A ball of fire launched forth from her hands straight downward. I barely had time to utter a quick, "holy shit," before there came the dull sound of an explosion from below, followed by a rush of hot air ascending past us.

Okay, that was ... interesting.

"That was for you, Curtis," Mom said, stepping back in line.

"*Love you, too, babe.*"

"Get a room, you two."

"Earth daoine!" a gravelly voice called out, interrupting our banter. It seemed to come from everywhere at once. "I see you are not as dead as my men thought."

"Captain Urinal?" I asked the empty air around us.

"It's Uriel!" came the terse response, met by a few chuckles from Riva. "But that doesn't matter. What does is that I wish to commend you on getting as far as you have. Not only have you managed to quell many of the lowguard, but you've sent several of my soldiers to the next life as well. Not my finest, mind you. Don't flatter yourself. But enough to have gained my attention."

"There's a lesson to be learned here," I called back, realizing this guy was probably using some kind of magic to converse. "Don't leave losers in charge of my parents."

"Enough, Tamara," Mom hissed, apparently not a fan of my snarky banter. Jeez, some people always had to be critics. "Esteemed Captain Uriel of the Queenshield," she called out. "You and your men are formidable, the most honored in the Garden. But know that my dearest kin are not to be trifled with, and we will happily die defending one another."

I was tempted to add, "We will?" but figured that

might put a slight damper on whatever point she was trying to get across.

"Know that you may stop us, but not before many more of your men are laid low. It need not be this way, though. I am a servant of your queen as much as you. Perhaps we can come to an agreement that will..."

"I wasn't talking to you, Draíodóir traitor, or the filth you have lain with."

Well, that was just plain rude.

"But, perhaps you have a point," Uriel continued. "Your defeat at the hands of the Queenshield elite is inevitable, but I acknowledge it could potentially be a costly victory ... and at a time when our beloved queen can ill afford interruption."

And that right there was our ace in the hole. He'd practically admitted that now was a piss poor time for them. Cabbage had been right. With the queen hosting a godly gala, it would be the height of embarrassment to admit that her fortress had been breached by an Earth chick and a handful of gnomes. Sure, it was likely that every single guest of hers could vaporize us as soon as draw breath, but there was one other important matter to consider: the Draíodóir loved their pomp and ceremony, meaning Brigid likely did too. Messing with that could cause a loss of face on her part, something almost certainly intolerable to an arrogant as fuck fairy queen.

I glanced back at my family and friends. They'd all proven themselves today. Hell, even Grunge had done his part, sleazy dirtbag that he was. And I had no doubt we could still give the Queenshield plenty of hell. But Uriel was right. With them aware of our presence, it was only a matter of time. We were deep in enemy territory with our only route of escape blocked by god knows how many angry fairies.

But, though Uriel's words were dripping with enough

arrogance to make a CrossFit bro blush, he'd let slip enough for me to understand there might still be an out for us.

"What did you have in mind?" I asked the open air around me.

"Be careful, Tamara," Mom warned. "The sidhe speak true but are known to twist their words to their own advantage."

Hah! Wouldn't that be a hoot? To end up being lawyered to death after everything we'd done.

If Uriel was fond of word games, though, he played it close to the vest. In typical tough guy speak, he simply said, "My terms are this: surrender and you'll be taken alive. Refuse, and we shall cut you down like mewling glincurs."

"Would you mind rewording that a bit since I have no fucking idea what a glincur is?"

"They're the fae equivalent of rats," Mom offered.

"Thanks, I really didn't want to know." Then, a bit louder, for the sake of our audience, I called out, "I have a counter proposal. Let us go and we won't embarrass you by leaving a trail of your dead asses in our wake."

Dad let out a sigh from his place on my back.

"What? Their offer sucked, so mine did, too. This is how you negotiate."

"I see there's a reason you're majoring in environmental science and not business," Mom replied.

Bunch of negative Nancys, all of them.

"You test my patience, daoine," Uriel finally called back.

Mom made to open her mouth, but I held up a hand. I had this.

"I don't care one bit about *your* patience, Uriel. But I'm willing to bet that your queen's patience might be tested if you don't wrap this up quickly. Yes, I acknowledge you'll probably win in the end, but we both know it'll be costly. And let's face facts, at the end of the day, there'll be one person left holding the buck to answer for that ... and it won't be..."

There came a *thunk* sound, followed by a whistle noise from below.

What the hell? Had Uriel metaphysically hung up on me? Or, maybe rather than deal with all the baggage I represented, he'd decided to kill himself instead. That would be awfully convenient.

"Look out!" Cabbage cried from above us.

Too convenient as a matter of fact.

My eyes opened wide as I caught sight of something – no, make that two somethings – rapidly rising up through the tower shaft toward where we stood.

Two gleaming balls of silver, the size of bowling balls.

No, scratch that.

Cannonballs!

Shit!

I was barely cognizant enough to raise my shield, turning and hoping it was wide enough to protect both my parents, despite knowing I was a hair too slow.

In all fairness, though, who expected them to attack in the middle of negotiating? It was a prick move, plain and simple.

But, fortunately, where I sucked, Mom was on the ball.

She screamed out "*Sgiath creideimh!*" in the split second before the metal spheres exploded.

A prismatic, semi-translucent wall of pure energy rose up in the same moment shrapnel came flying at us from every direction.

Pain lanced through my thigh even as I was still taking in the shock of what had happened. More cries met my ears, these coming from above my position on the stairs.

But thankfully Mom had managed to divert the worst of it. Though I'd been near certain we were about to be cut to ribbons, it seemed only a handful of the razor-sharp shards managed to get through before her spell had taken hold. The rest hit the barrier and clattered off to fall down below, where I really hoped a few of the Queenshield were still waiting.

Where the spell hadn't reached, it looked like the stonework had been peppered with small arms fire. Shards of metal, like needle points, stuck out from nearly every surface.

I looked down and saw that included me. A sliver of metal had sliced my hip, a few drops of blood already starting to stain the side of my jeans. Painful but minor. And hey, it could've been worse. The fuckers could've shot me in the ass.

I was the least of my worries, though.

"Mom, Dad..."

"I'm okay, Tam Tam," he said.

"Close," Mom replied, eying a few shards which had hit the wall next to her, "but close doesn't count."

Thank goodness.

"Hold the protection spell if you can," I told her, before turning my attention to the rest of our group. "Riva!"

"I'm ... okay, Bent," she replied. "Just took one in the arm. Stings like a bitch, but I'm fine."

"Grunge?"

"He hid behind me," she added.

Not hard to believe.

I pressed a hand to my leg, preparing to let Uriel know that on Earth cheap shots got you a thorough ass kicking, when I spied the gnomes gathering in a circle a few steps above Mom.

I couldn't really see what was going on from this angle, but their heads were all lowered ... as if staring at something lying on the ground.

Oh no!

"Hold the line, Dad," I said, putting him down. "I need to go check on something."

Mom joined me, power continuing to radiate out of her, as we moved to check on our diminutive but stalwart allies. Three steps down, but still leaving me high enough to see, I made out the tiny needle-ridden body lying in the center of the gnome circle, her mate by her side.

"Arugula!"

Had Mom not cast her spell when she had, we likely would've all been cut to pieces. As it was, though, a few pinpricks were little more than a painful annoyance to anyone my size. But to a gnome, it was like being struck by a barrage of arrowheads.

"Pushed me out of the way she did," Cabbage said, his ruddy face completely distraught. "Took the brunt of the attack."

Arugula was still alive, if barely. She turned weakly toward him. "Our ... our people need their king. Need their ... freedom."

I turned to my mother. "Can you..."

She stifled the rest of my question with a single word. "Silver."

All at once I understood. Iron didn't seem to affect the gnomes, but they were likely susceptible to silver the same as me and my parents. Taking into account the size of the gnomes, those blasted needles had done catastrophic damage.

Arugula turned her head toward us. "Monarch Queen. It was ... an ... honor to be your friend."

"The honor is all mine," Mom replied. "And I swear, so long as I draw breath, your people will have a home in mine."

Arugula coughed up a mouthful of bluish blood, then nodded before glancing my way. "Princess. My people need..."

"Their freedom," I finished for her. "You helped me when you had no reason to. I won't forget that or your people."

She smiled weakly before addressing Cabbage again. "The wall, quickly. Take ... me ... there."

"Here?" Cabbage replied, his eyes damp and blood-shot. "But this place..."

"A reminder always to Brigid I will be," Arugula replied with a blood-stained grin. "Even if ... hunts us all down ... never again will she be free of us."

I had no idea what she meant, but Cabbage nodded to his men. Three of them stepped forward and lifted Arugula's body, carrying her to the tower wall. There, they helped her stand, propped up against the stones.

Arugula spread her hands and began to glow faintly. As she did, a strange thing happened. Her body began to meld into the stone of the wall, sinking into it as if it were something other than solid rock.

Before she could be fully submerged in the masonry, however, her body stiffened and turned to stone.

When the process was done, it was nearly impossible to tell where the wall ended and Arugula began. It was as if her effigy had been carved into the rock from the very beginning.

It also explained the smile on her face when she'd told Cabbage what to do. This was the gnome version of a final *fuck you* to the queen of the fairies, ensuring Arugula's essence – as part of a race Brigid loathed – was forever-more a part of this castle.

As far as endings went, hers was heart-rending. I didn't even try to stop the tears which spilled from my eyes at her passing. Yet, it was also epic, both in terms of her heroism and sheer ball-busting spite. Saddened and angered as I was by her passing, it was hard to deny this was an epitaph that would be remembered for ages to come.

But right then I wasn't worried about future generations. No. I had the here and now to worry about.

Clamping down on the sadness, I embraced the rage slowly forming in the pit of my stomach as I turned back toward the front of our group.

If Uriel wanted a war, he was going to get one.

30

With a renewed sense of purpose, we eventually resumed our original marching order, ready to take the fight to the enemy.

Uriel, however, wasn't done with the talking.

"Are you still there, daoine?" came his voice at last, echoing as if the very stone around us were conveying it.

"Whatever you were hoping to do, asshole, it failed," I called back, envisioning twisting his well-coifed head off. "Unless you were trying to piss me off, because congratulations. You have my full attention now. You may wish you didn't."

"I must ... apologize for that unprovoked attack."

Wait, what?

"Two of my men took it upon themselves to act without permission. They have sullied both their own personal honor, as well as my own, and have been removed from their posts to await punishment."

The hell? "You killed one of my friends. So you can take your punishment and shove it up your ass."

"Tamara..." Dad whispered in my ear.

"Don't start with me," I hissed back.

"I understand your pain," Uriel replied, sounding genuinely remorseful.

Fuck this guy. I didn't want his pity or condolences.

"And I believe I may have a compromise that will satisfy our mutual needs."

"Needs? Let me guess. You're still trying to keep your queen's teatime from being interrupted? Well..."

"As you are still seeking freedom, despite having breached our innermost sanctum," he replied.

"So we're back to square one."

"Here is my offer," he said, all arrogance suddenly gone from his voice, "and I suggest you consider it seriously, as another one like it shall not be made."

I held my tongue, waiting to see what foolishness came next. Maybe he was hoping we'd all agree to commit ritual suicide in return for the occasional flower put on our graves. If so...

"You have proven yourself a worthy foe," he continued. "Indeed, you have made it farther than any invader in my time of service. Your temerity sullies my honor, yet is worthy of respect. As such, I offer this boon. Face me in unarmed combat: warrior to warrior. I will order my men to stand down, if you do the same. Should I win, all your brethren shall surrender peacefully and accept their fate."

"And if you lose?"

"My men shall stand aside, allow your people to leave the way they came, giving you enough time to return to whatever hole your allies dragged you from."

"And what about after?"

"There is no *after*," he replied with a humorless chuckle, "Your world is beyond my grasp. But those who remain in the Garden shall have to rely on their own wits if they wish to evade capture again, although I can assure you they will know what it means to have angered the Queenshield."

"Oh gleef," came a squeak from above, Grunge no doubt realizing his days of flying under the radar were over.

I held up a hand to hopefully stifle further commentary. The last thing I needed was my parents explaining that I shouldn't act rashly. No duh.

Uriel was offering us a way out, but it was a shitty one. But was it really any shittier than our other options?

If we raced down there, guns metaphorically blazing, there were only a few outcomes as far as I could see.

The likeliest was we'd be killed. That kind of solved all our problems right there, albeit not in any way we really wanted. It was also possible we'd be overrun and captured. If so, what they did to my dad might be small potatoes compared to what happened to the rest of us, especially now that we'd almost certainly pissed Brigid off. A lifetime of imprisonment, torture, and mutilation at the hands of a tyrant who wasn't likely to get bored with it anytime soon didn't sound appealing in the least.

Mind you, that was being pessimistic.

It was also possible we might be able to break through Uriel's line and make a run for it ... while being hounded by probably every soldier in the land, assuming the big B herself didn't decide to intercede.

Even if we somehow made it back home, that wouldn't help the gnomes or Grunge. And what guarantee was there that being back on Earth would make us safe if Brigid was hellbent on revenge?

Considering the things I'd already fought in the relatively short time since learning about my heritage, who was to say what other *devotees* Brigid might have? And that wasn't even considering the Draíodóir. They worshipped the fairy queen, drew their power from her. Family or not, I had a feeling we'd have all of Crescentwood out for our blood.

And if that happened, it would rile up the Morganberg pack. Best case was we'd be pariahs. Worst case was another invasion of High Moon, perhaps even worse than the one my uncle had led.

That right there settled it for me.

I loved my family more than anything in the world. Riva was part of it, and Cass was rapidly reaching that level. However, despite everything, I also felt a responsibility to High Moon. Maybe it was because I embodied both supernatural races bordering it, yet was a part of neither – forever stuck in the middle. Or maybe I just didn't like seeing innocent people wiped out whenever the forces around them got bugs up their asses.

Either way, I didn't want my decision here today to be one that spiraled out of control, leaving my home and the people within it a lifeless wasteland.

Uriel's compromise wasn't ideal. He'd made it more than clear that, even if I won, his troops would be plastering our faces on wanted posters across the land. But, at the same time, his offer was tied to his own honor in the face of his queen, and I was beginning to see that was a powerful force in this world. If I spit upon that honor, I'd do nothing but make things worse. But, if I did something that let him save face, then perhaps we'd merely be wanted men and women, nothing more, with no personal stake in it.

The gnomes were already hidden from Brigid's gaze. Perhaps I could convince them to let Grunge join their fold, preferably without eating him. If so, that could work to keep them safe.

There was still the issue of Possessed Riva and whatever had happened after she'd zapped me here, but at that point we could deal with it as a family.

"I've made up my mind."

"Honey..."

"I have to do this, Dad." I turned to my mother, seeing the expectant look on her face. "Don't try to talk me out of it."

"I wasn't going to," she replied.

"You weren't?"

"Tamara, you've always been a stubborn child. I'd have a better chance trying to convince ice to stop being cold. I was merely going to offer you some advice."

"Oh." Damn. I really hated when she cut me off at the neck before I could throw some sass back. I'd even rehearsed it in my head. "Okay, so what advice do you have?"

"The sidhe are faster, stronger, and more agile than humans. Not as strong as you, but they're very long lived. I know for a fact that Uriel has centuries of experience beneath his belt. He's ... practically a legend among my people. In fact, he actually is a legend."

"You're making surrender sound better by the moment."

"Don't be a snot. I'm simply telling you what to expect. Even unarmed, you're dealing with a master warrior here. You can't underestimate him."

"Is there anything in my favor?"

"Of course. He's likely never faced anyone like you before, which means he's almost certainly going to under-estimate you. Let him. The sidhe are formidable warriors but they share their queen's pride."

"Followers of Brigid arrogant? You don't say."

Mom narrowed her eyes at me. "Wait for an opening. You're stronger than he is and can absorb more damage. Use that to your advantage. And when you finally see a chance to strike, be merciless. Do not, under any circumstances, let up until the battle is decisively won."

Her suggestions essentially boiled down to letting him beat me up until he got tired and made a mistake. Can't say I'd ever had a coach offer me that same bit of wisdom, and with good reason. It was pretty much awful advice.

Of course, I'd already nearly gotten my ass handed to me by one of these sidhe today, and according to Uriel that guy had been nothing but a chump. So perhaps her cautionary words were best not dismissed out of hand.

Either way, I was in for a fight.

Jailbreaks from impenetrable fairy fortresses couldn't be easy, could they?

And that wasn't even counting the fact that somehow I still had to fit my promise to Arugula into all of this.

Needless to say, I had a feeling my day was still young ... assuming I lived past the next five minutes.

"Captain Uriel," I called out before I could think better of it. "I accept your terms. Prepare to defend yourself."

The rules were simple enough. I'd meet Uriel down on the ground floor. There, the space was wide and flat enough to allow for a proper battle ground. Both of our respective parties would remain on the stairs: mine above and his below, within sight of the battle but not allowed to interfere. In the event of his victory, Mom would instruct our side to drop their weapons and surrender. If I won, though, Uriel's men would back off, allowing us a clear path to the sewers.

Oh yeah, we were definitely getting the raw end of this deal.

Still, I could worry about wading through pink fairy shit later.

I helped dad down off my back just before we reached the ground floor. He already had my iron rod of doom, so all that was left to hand him was my wrist shield. I gave it to him and turned away but then hesitated, remembering I had one other item on me. The pendent Mom had given me was made of that same brighdril material as her tether. The last thing I needed was an unbreakable length of chain around my neck for Uriel to strangle me with.

I unclasped it and handed it to her.

"I'll keep it safe," she said.

"You'd better. I want that back."

I gave both my parents a hug, followed by one from Riva, before I turned and headed down.

"Give him hell, Bent!" Riva called after me.

Good to know I had a cheering section.

"Smash his gleefing tolph sack, Girl!"

Okay, maybe a larger cheering section than I thought.

Uriel was already there, facing the opposite wall as if in thought or prayer, his long white hair falling to the middle of his back. Say what you will about the guy, but he must've had access to some killer conditioner. Not a split end in sight.

Color me jealous.

The sidhe captain turned to face me and a different kind of color raced to my cheeks. He was shirtless, his muscled abdomen so flawless that Michelangelo would've likely rejected it as being too unrealistic to carve. I mean seriously, this guy's abs had abs. You could've bounced quarters off his stomach all day long, followed by body shots until your tongue wore out.

No offense to my cutie of a beta wolf, but this guy was a Porsche to his budget hatchback. Too bad his challenge hadn't entailed seeing which of us could fuck the other to death first. At least that would've been a fight I wouldn't have minded losing.

Still, the dead serious look upon his granite chin suggested he was there to battle not bone, so it was best to pick my jaw up off the floor and get with the game.

Speaking of which, I had a feeling it was best to follow his lead, so as to be as limber as possible for this. I peeled off my already ripped sweater, tossed it to the side, and started to stretch, thanking the heavens I'd worn one of my better sports bras today.

A frown creased Uriel's face as I did so.

"What?" I asked, suddenly self-conscious. "Do I have a zit or something?"

"If we are being frank, the sight of your flesh so immodestly bared sickens me."

"The name's Tamara, not Frank, and don't knock it until you try it."

Oh god. I did not just say that in earshot of my parents.

Desperately pretending that I didn't hear a pained sigh coming from my mother's direction, I cracked my knuckles. Fuck it. Maybe Uriel's prudish attitude was another weakness I could take advantage of.

"So, are we going to fight or stand here undressing each other with our eyes?"

The look of revulsion that crossed Uriel's face was, I won't lie, ever so slightly insulting, but it told me I was right. Hell, if I was smart, I'd simply unsnap my ... screw it. It's not like I hadn't already done the same thing in front of a werewolf pack.

"Hold on a second," I said, removing my boots.

Uriel's eyes opened wide. "What are you doing?"

"Getting ready for our tussle." I winked at him, putting a little extra flirt into it as I unbuckled my jeans next.

"Tamara," Mom snapped in her best parent voice, as if I were a toddler who'd ripped off her diaper and raced out onto the front lawn.

I merely held up a hand, once I'd finished folding my jeans anyway. "No comments from the peanut gallery."

"Go, Bent!" Riva cried in response. "You sexy thing you!"

At least one person in the audience had taste.

I tried to focus on battle tactics, because otherwise it would be too easy to get caught up in the fact that I was in front of my parents – wearing nothing but my underwear, and about to tangle with a half-naked supermodel.

Oh, yeah. This was definitely one to remember for future therapy sessions.

A dark purplish flush appeared on Uriel's face. Strange, since I hadn't popped him one yet. But then I realized that was probably the way fairies like him blushed. Aw, the poor guy was embarrassed.

However, embarrassed or not, he still stepped forward and faced me, his expression a thing of stone itself.

"Prepare yourself, daoine. Pray to whatever gods you have that they have mercy upon you. For I shall have none."

31

Uriel's words might have chilled me to the bone under other circumstances. After all, a seasoned nigh-immortal soldier telling you he's about to get biblical on your ass is typically not good for a long healthy outlook on life.

As for me, well, I couldn't think of any gods that I cared to give the time of day to, much less the one somewhere beyond the sealed off doorway to my left. No. She'd be lucky if I gave her the courtesy of explaining how far up her ass I was planning to plant my boot.

Of course, I wasn't wearing boots at that moment. I wasn't wearing much at all. And, truth be told, Garden or not, the stone beneath my bare feet was a bit chilly. Oh, well, at least I wouldn't die all sweaty and gross.

"Let's get ready to rumble," I whispered, and then the talking was done.

It was rare for me to be afraid before a wrestling match. Hell, even during the state finals a few years back, knowing that the press would be watching, I was still pretty frosty.

But right then, as we stepped forward to grapple, I felt

the barest sliver of fear worm its way up my spine. It was Uriel's eyes or, more precisely, the way they moved. In the space of a couple footsteps I could see him sizing up my arms, my legs, my stance, all of it — and not in a salacious way either. Mind reading wasn't among the gifts I'd inherited from my parents, probably a good thing, yet I could instinctively tell he'd analyzed my steps in those few moments and likely devised about a dozen countermoves.

Not good. One of the key lessons my coaches had tried to drill into me over the years was to never ever let your opponent win the psychological battle. Why? Because the moment you lost in your mind, you'd almost certainly handed victory to your opponent in real life. And there I was doing exactly that.

I needed to get my head in the game. Needed to push my emotions to the side. Needed to hope for an opening so I could...

And sometimes providence was there to hand you a freebie on a silver platter.

Uriel stepped in, faster than I was expecting. He grabbed hold of my arm with one hand and then ... my boob with the other?

Okay, he probably hadn't meant to. I'd instinctively jerked away, obviously not enough to escape his attack, but enough to shift my body so that his hand went to second base instead of wherever he'd intended.

The result was almost comical. He pulled away as if he'd stuck his hand in a box of scorpions instead, his face awash with something akin to horror.

Again, color me somewhat insulted. I can't say I'd let a ton of guys fondle my breasts in my time, but those who'd gotten there had been far more appreciative than this clown.

More importantly, it broke the spell of his invulnerability that had begun to cloud my thoughts. His guard was down for only an instant, no more, as he gazed down at his soiled hand like he was tempted to gnaw it off at the wrist.

Too bad you needed a working jaw to do that.

I lashed out with a right, catching the prudish asshole in his perfect prissy mouth. Teeth went flying and so did he, across the floor to land in a heap about ten feet away.

"Way to go, flesh rat!" Grunge called back from the stairs.

Flesh rat? Someone remind me to kick his ass when this was done.

But it wasn't over, not yet. The blow would've likely been enough to kill a normal person or leave them crippled for life. But Mom had already warned me the sidhe were tough.

She wasn't wrong.

Before I could cross more than half the distance to where Uriel lay, he kipped up to his feet as if I'd done little more than push him to the ground.

In the next second, he raced forward to meet me head-on. I threw another swing but telegraphed it hard. He blocked it effortlessly then stepped inside my defenses.

Whoa. Personal space.

What the hell? One punch to the kisser and this guy was suddenly going all Christian Grey on me? That was ... unexpected.

What was even more unexpected, though, was him spitting a wad of blood into my face.

A tiny bit got into my eyes, stinging like heavily over-chlorinated pool water and leaving me momentarily blinded.

The next few moments were a dark symphony of pain as I was struck at least half a dozen times, all of them strategically placed: an open hand shot to my windpipe, a chop to my solar plexus, then a kidney punch right before I was tossed over his shoulder like a rag doll.

Blinded, unable to breathe, and with the wind knocked out of me, the best I could do was greet the floor with the back of my head.

My ears picked up the shuffle of feet and then pain exploded in my face as Uriel drove a fist down into my nose. Just my luck, too, as my healing had finally compensated for it being smashed earlier.

Good thing my throat was still protesting from his other blow, otherwise I might've had to add choking on my own blood to my list of grievances.

"Did you really think I've never been tempted by a harlot before? That it would be so easy to gain the upper hand?" Uriel mocked from above me, his voice loud and clear in my ears – about the only place he hadn't managed to nail me. "I am the captain of the Queenshield. There is no contingency I haven't trained for, including the call of flesh, not that yours could ever hope to tempt one of my superior blood."

And we were back to body shaming again. I swear, this guy would be a hit over on Twitter. Social media wasn't so much my concern as was survival, though. And that was looking less likely by the second in a fight that had just barely started.

There was no way I was going to beat this guy with nothing but snark and a pair of breasts – perky though they might be. He was right. I was stupid to hedge my bets on such a strategy. And now here I was, about to die in my underwear like this was rough sex gone bad.

"Come on, Bent!" Riva cried.

"You can do it, Tam Tam."

Again with the Tam Tam. I really needed to make an alpha decree against that nickname, assuming I survived.

More shouts of encouragement came, not all of them

for me. Some were screaming for Uriel to finish me off, something I had a feeling would happen sooner rather than later. I couldn't see who was making the taunts, but I could hear them all with crystal clarity, enough to tell me where each stood in relation to where I now...

Wait! My ears.

Goddamn, I could be so fucking stupid sometimes.

I couldn't see Uriel for shit, at least not until I got a chance to wipe this crud out of my eyes. *Gah!* I swear, it was like he had freaking vinegar for blood. The thing was, he was probably counting on that. After all, a blinded foe was likely a beaten foe.

I needed to regroup, use the weapons at my disposal, and stop playing this guy's game.

But first I needed to choke in a quick breath, something made less easy by the contemptuous slap he gave me across the face.

"Pathetic, as expected," Uriel said from above where I lay. "There's no point in prolonging this."

Fuck it. Breathing could wait, as I desperately tried to tune out all sounds except those immediately around me.

An intake of breath by him, held, then the slightest huff of air being displaced – so low even I could barely make it out, as if someone were moving – or perhaps delivering a killing blow.

There was no time to do anything save roll to the side as quickly as I could.

Less than an instant later there came a meaty *thud* from where my head had been, followed by a hiss of pain from my foe.

No time to lose.

My short tenure as a supernatural hybrid had been punctuated by several fist fights. Not to toot my own horn, but I'd done pretty well for myself. A good deal of that had been through a combination of my own physical might as well as the fact that my opponents had mostly been werewolves – fast as two rabbits fucking, but still large and ponderous, using their bodies like giant meat hammers. Comparatively, Uriel and his Queenshield were like a surgeon's scalpel in their moves. My normal tactics, basically hitting and being hit back until one of us fell, were useless against them.

And that made sense. I was strong but, truth of the matter was, despite Chief Johnson's nickname, I was no ninja. Take my strength away and a mixed martial artist would likely have me for lunch ... in a normal brawl.

Grappling, though, was a whole different ball of wax. Hell, I didn't even need to be able to see so long as I maintained contact.

All of that went through my mind at the speed of thought, even as Uriel was still letting out a pained grunt – the only heed he gave to the fact that he'd likely pulped his fist against the unforgiving stone floor.

Before he could pull away, I shot my hand out and grabbed hold of his wrist. That was only to keep him from escaping, though. Next, I rolled my legs back over my body, hooking them around his arm.

Normally, such a move would work the opposite of how I had planned, allowing an opponent to pin the shit out of me. But there were no referees in this match. Also, where I was giving away the advantage in leverage – even if momentarily – I still had the upper hand in strength.

Already overbalanced as he was, it didn't take a lot to

send him tumbling over me and onto the floor. It wasn't a hard throw, nothing that would finish a warrior like him. But it hadn't been designed to. The move had been meant to do nothing more than put us on equal footing, flat on our backs – the advantage now mine as I still had a hold of his wrist.

It was time to make a fairy omelet, but first I had to crack this egg.

Positioning my foot against his rock-hard body, I both pushed and twisted at the same time, putting my own unsportsmanlike spin on the classic arm bar until...

Crack!

"Argh!"

His arm broke at the elbow, but I wasn't finished yet. An image of my father flashed before my closed eyes, him as he'd been, and as he was now – after what this fucker had done to him.

Though I wasn't in the hollows and there was no outside force affecting my emotions, I saw red nevertheless.

"Make a wish, asshole!"

I didn't admit this often, but the truth was my own power frightened me. I knew I had a temper. Most of the time it was easy enough to keep in check. But when I lost it, I tended to really lose it.

Both my aunt and uncle had learned that lesson first-hand. Now it was Uriel's turn.

Holding his wrist with an iron grip, while my legs did the bulk of the work, I twisted and pulled, ignoring his screams as well as the gasps that came from both sides.

Hot blood spurted across my legs and midsection as Uriel's flesh tore asunder – the feeling akin to being squirted with caustic drain cleaner.

Nevertheless, my minor discomfort was nothing compared to his.

With a grunt of effort and the sound of rending meat, the lower half of Uriel's arm pulled free, albeit I doubted as cleanly as that Doppelganger's had.

I gave one more kick, shoving his writhing form away from me, then scrambled back, dropping his arm and finally getting a chance to wipe away the acrid blood obscuring my vision.

Gah! It stung like a motherfucker. I blinked several times, certain my eyes were as red as a weasel's, as fresh tears streamed out of them.

It wasn't great, like trying to look through a wad of cotton, but at least I could mostly see again.

I guess it could've been worse. Fairy blood was definitely a lot higher in pH than a human's, but it was a far cry from movies such as Alien. If that had been the case, I had a feeling I'd be trying to rub clean the two holes burnt straight through my skull.

Yeah, it definitely could be worse but, looking across the battlefield to where Uriel was inexplicably getting back to his feet, I realized it could be a fuck-ton better, too.

He should've been down for the count. Between shock and blood loss, he should've been getting ready for his new job pushing up her majesty's royal daisies. Instead he was actually upright, even if the look on his face wasn't exactly pleasant.

Of far greater importance to me, though, was the stump of his arm, bloody and ragged, yet not nearly as gory as I expected. Blood should've been pouring out by the bucketful, being that I must've severed at least a few major veins and arteries in my hasty amputation.

Instead, it was barely dripping. And the end of the wound itself was – there was no doubting my ears – *sizzling*. Sure enough, within moments, even the dripping had stopped.

Holy shit. Self-cauterizing blood. Talk about a handy

feature to have. Wish someone had told me about it ahead of time.

"As I said, daoine," he wheezed. "I have prepared for every eventuality."

Then, as if to prove himself correct, he actually charged at me.

Jesus fucking Christ, what was it with this guy? Dude had some kind of crazy Napoleon complex, despite being over six feet. Either that or he was afraid of getting smack talk from his buddies for losing to a girl.

No matter the case, he leapt mid-stride, spinning, and lashing out with some kind of crazy fae capoeira kick.

And where there was one, there was a dozen more. Kicks, more kicks, and the occasional punch were thrown my way as Uriel somehow became an inhuman whirlwind instead of a corpse.

With my eyes semi-clear and my other senses likewise at full, I was able to block some of it. Sadly, that left plenty to get through my defenses, peppering my ribs and sternum with rapidly accumulating damage. Worse, he was so relentless that I wasn't able to mount much offense of my own.

Instead, the one-armed fairy dynamo began to drive me back, forcing me to retreat, to seek a reprieve from his seemingly tireless attacks.

It was only a matter of time before I ran out of room. Then what?

"Um, Tamara, honey..."

"Not now, Dad!"

"Bent, I know you're kind of busy..." Riva called out to me.

No shit.

"...But it's about to get real drafty down south."

What?!

I looked down at the exact wrong moment, catching a

kick to the chest that sent me staggering back. However, hard as the blow had been, my mind was suddenly preoccupied with other things ... such as the fact that Uriel's caustic blood had seemingly eaten through the hem of my panties, which were now hanging onto me by a few strands of thread at most.

And just like that my life had become a cheap porno. All at once, my strategy for distracting Uriel seemed a lot less wise, especially now that I was seconds away from giving every fairy in the room – not to mention my parents – a free show.

Not exactly how I envisioned my last stand.

Though the smart thing would've been to keep on fighting and ignore my lady bits, what can I say? I had just enough modesty to make this a major issue. Go figure. Guess there wouldn't be any nude beaches in my future.

Despite a part of me screaming that all I was doing was leaving myself open to getting clocked, I dropped my right hand to my thigh in the hopes of holding things together for a moment or two more.

It was a move that would've made every last one of my coaches scream their heads off. At the same time, I can't say I ever had a unitard disintegrate mid-match, so fuck those guys.

But maybe it was the right move after all. Despite Mr. Planned for Everything's boasts about having prepared for naked distractions – seriously, what the fuck kind of training regimen did they have here – he hesitated mid-spin as his eyes fell to my crotch.

"Take a picture, it lasts longer."

Um ... on second thought, don't.

I didn't know if fairies had access to Snapchat or not, but the last thing I needed was postmortem revenge porn to cap off my day.

There was no way I could adequately defend myself

naked while my parents were watching, so I stepped in and shoulder checked Uriel, catching him with enough of a glancing blow to knock him away and give me some breathing room.

Rather than follow up, I made a mad dive roll to where I'd dropped my pants, feeling the last strands of cotton snap just as I snatched them up and...

Before I could hop back into my jeans, a rough hand grabbed me by the shoulder and spun me around.

"It matters not how much flesh you bare, strumpet! Your death is all that ... mmmphrh!"

I didn't think, I simply acted.

With his remaining hand holding onto me, leaving him with no other to defend himself, I pulled the opening of my jeans down over his head, looped one hand around them to close them tight, then stepped in and kneed the fucker in the crotch, hoping sidhe warriors had at least one thing in common with human males.

Based on the pained gasp that came from the seat of my pants, I assumed the answer was yes, but I wasn't finished yet.

Realizing there was no way I was going to beat this guy in a fair fight, I grabbed the back of his neck before he could recover, dragged him with me toward the nearest wall, then slammed him face-first into the stone facade with everything I had left.

Masonry cracked from the impact, but so did bone. There came a satisfying crunch, muffled only slightly by the denim, and then Uriel fell limp in my grasp.

I let him fall, yanking my pants off his ruined head as he hit the ground.

It was stupid of me, but I prioritized covering my ass over making sure he was finished this time.

Doubly stupid as I slipped my jeans on without bothering to check first if the insides were covered with fairy brains ... which, fuck me, they were.

Oh god, it's all slimy!

Dancing back and forth, like I had to pee badly, I dared a glance down.

Amazingly enough, Uriel was still there – dead as a doornail.

"You actually did it. You won!"

If I wasn't so skeeved out by the squishiness around my lady bits, I might've taken insult with my mother's tone. As it was, though, she was right.

That last blow, totally instinctive on my part, had pretty much turned his skull to pulp.

I had a feeling his magic fairy blood wasn't going to help him much with this one. Even so, I was tempted to stomp on him a few times, just to be safe. Nothing worse than thinking a fight is over, only to have the bad guy pull a Michael Myers on you.

Before I could turn the rest of him into paste, though, Mom marched down the stairs to where I stood.

She handed me back my pendant and smiled ... a moment before ruining the bonding moment by going into parent-mode.

"Put your clothes on, Tamara. This isn't a peep show."

"Yes, Mom."

As I slipped my boots and the remains of my sweater back on – all while desperately wishing for a shower – Mom stepped past, just as the rest of our contingent joined me on the ground floor.

"Well done, Princess," Cabbage replied solemnly.

"That was quite the show, Girl," Grunge added. "No offense, but I hope to never see anything like that again."

Riva, thankfully, was there to smack him upside his turban. "Don't listen to him, Bent. You were smoking hot out there, in more ways than one."

I nodded my gratitude to her just as my mother said, "On the honor of your captain, I demand you disperse and let us be on our way."

"I think not, Draíodóir," one of the Queenshield replied in a throaty growl. "Twas Uriel's honor that was at stake, not ours, so he did swear. And he is no more to say otherwise. Our honor lives or dies by the queen alone, and it is her will that all interlopers be brought to justice."

32

"I thought the sidhe were known for keeping their word."

"There's a lot of nuance to be had," Mom replied, raising her hands in a defensive gesture that told me spells were likely incoming.

Not good. I'd nearly exhausted myself fighting just one of these fucks. Now we had to deal with a whole regiment of them?

"Tamara!"

I turned at the sound of my father's voice, to see him tossing something my way. It was my shield bracelet. The moment it left his hands, he changed, more than doubling in size to that of a monster wolf – his lack of legs leaving him no less menacing.

Catching the bracelet, I snapped it onto my wrist. It would help, but I still didn't like our odds, especially since the sidhe blockading the downward stairs were all armed with the same and more.

This was a losing battle, no two ways about it. My parents were dangerous as all hell, but my father wasn't at full capacity and mom … well, her magic stemmed from this place. Though I hadn't seen any of the Queenshield utilize magic themselves, I wasn't stupid enough to think they hadn't dealt with the Draíodóir before. That left Cabbage's people and their sacks of tacks. Call me cynical, but in a battle of warrior elves against tiny gnomes, I wasn't quite ready to bet my life savings on the latter.

There had to be another way.

My eyes fell upon the bricked-up doorway leading out of this tower, the outline clearly visible and the thrum of that unearthly music still audible beyond it.

Up was futile. Down was a battle we couldn't win. Through that door, however, was the unknown. And in the unknown perhaps lay a chance. It was likely infinitesimally slim, considering I doubted gods liked having their cocktail hour interrupted. But maybe we could cause enough chaos to make a run for it.

And if not, dying at the hands of omnipotent beings in a grand ballroom was at least cooler than being killed by a bunch of backstabbing minions in a dungeon.

Besides, Arugula had wanted me to plead her case before the queen. Who knows? Maybe I'd even get a word or two in before being vaporized.

"I know you can hear me, Dad," I whispered, my voice extra low so as to not tip off the Queenshield. "And I can hear you, too. I need you to tell the others to follow my lead. No questions asked. Got it?"

There came the brief sound of shifting flesh from behind me.

"*You can hear me?*" Dad whispered back, just as low.

"Loud and clear."

"*When did that happen?*"

"A couple months ago. I was saving it for a surprise ... um, surprise! Now enough with the questions. Are we good?"

"*Ready when you are, Tam Tam.*"

Hearing him whisper my nickname in his half-wolf voice was a bit weird, but whatever. I had a whole bucketful of weird on my plate right now. That was the least of my worries.

Now to only hope the barrier ahead of me wasn't the thickness of a bank vault.

Only one way to find out.

"Now!" I cried, taking off with everything my legs had to offer.

I've noticed that during moments of stress, time seems to slow down. Even more so when I happened to be putting my all into moving fast. It's strange. Maybe it was my brain's way of marking the moment, knowing it could be my last, one final memory should it need to flash my life before my eyes. Either way you looked at it, my senses picked up a lot in the split second it took for me to reach where Uriel's body lay.

There came the ripple of flesh as my father resumed his mega-wolf form, my mother's questioning intake of air as she likely prepared to ask what the hell I was doing, as well as several surprised grunts from the rest of our party.

Perhaps most satisfying, though, were the cries of shock that came from the Queenshield blockading the downward stairs, as I grabbed hold of their commander's battered body and flung it their way.

My plan was to distract them for a moment, not add insult to injury, although I can't say that last part bothered me much. Call it icing on the cake.

No matter the case, I didn't have time to stand there and gloat, or even see if my aim had been true. Instead, I turned both my focus and speed toward the stone façade that had once led from this tower to the main floor of a goddess's castle.

It was time to test who would be the victor in the battle between hybrid and solid rock, as I raced forward, lowered my head, and rammed my shoulder into the wall.

There came a roar of sound, extra loud to my sensitive ears, as the mortar practically exploded from the force of the impact. My arms weren't happy with me, but I was pretty sure the wall was a lot less pleased.

Heavy sections of stone gave way, clouding the air with dust, but then I was through.

Amazed that had actually worked, I skidded to a halt, almost tripping over the stones I'd dislodged. Wouldn't that have been embarrassing?

I kept my footing, though, spinning back and crying, "Come on!"

I coughed some dust out of my lungs then turned to see if I could spot a way out ... only to realize I couldn't see much of anything.

For a moment, I thought it might be a combination of the dust and my eyes still stinging from Uriel's blood. But I blinked a few times and realized that wasn't the case.

It was pitch black all around me, the only light being whatever spilled out of the tower opening.

The fuck?

Was the party over already? Had Brigid sent her fellow gods home and turned off the lights on her way to bed?

Maybe so, for it was only then that I realized it was eerily quiet. The unearthly music we'd been hearing from this place had fallen silent ... seemingly in the same instant I'd made my grand entrance.

Guess they don't like party crashers here.

Beneath my feet, I beheld immaculate stonework, finer looking than any marble I'd ever laid eyes upon. This was definitely the place. But where the hell was everyone?

Regardless, all of this was a minor issue. Dad had freaking night vision and Mom had her magic. Turning the lights off and hoping we were too spooked to make a run for it wasn't going to work.

Sounds followed me into this new space: the fall of multiple feet, murmured voices, and then my mother's surprised cry of, "What are you doing, Curtis? Put me down!"

Guess Dad figured she might need a bit more persuasion to give up and run.

Sure enough, I turned back to see Riva, Grunge, and the gnomes stepping through the opening. Hot on their tail was Dad. Tucked beneath one of his massive arms was my mother, looking none too pleased.

I stepped toward them, looking to fend off any arguments.

"Don't start," I told my mother as Dad put her down.

"How dare you take that tone with..."

I'd expected as much, so I talked right over her. "Make with a light spell or something. We need to move." Then, turning to my father, I added, "Head up to the front and scope out our vanguard. I'll see if I can dissuade the Queenshield from following."

Fortunately, Dad seemed to realize this was the time for action not questions. He pulled himself forward with his massive forelimbs, moving like some kind of oversized gorilla – the silvered stumps of his legs making a clacking noise where they touched the marble floor.

Behind us, some of the Queenshield had stepped up off the stairs, but not nearly as many as I'd expected.

The one in charge now, the guy who'd given us the too bad, so sad answer to whether or not they'd honor Uriel's deal, actually smiled at me.

Why did I have a feeling that didn't bode well?

"You may very well wish you had died by our hands,

daoine," he said, continuing to stand his ground. "Now your fate is in *hers*."

Behind me, the clack-clack of Dad's legs became more rapid fire, as well as more distant.

"Don't get too far ahead of us," I called after him.

But the clacking only grew more insistent as it moved further away.

"Bent, I don't think he's listening," Riva said.

What's he doing?

"The work of the queen, this is," Cabbage cried, sounding far more frightened than I'd ever heard him. Poor little guy was likely losing it now that his mate was gone.

"Mom?" I prodded, keeping my eye on the Queenshield continuing to just stand there.

A moment later, she cried out, "*Solais!*"

And yet the darkness remained.

"Was ... something supposed to happen?" I asked, glancing over to find her looking confused.

She raised her hands in a casting gesture, but as she did the length of brighdril still coiled around her arm began to unravel. The anchor spike shot off into the darkness as if pulled by a giant electromagnet. It quickly reached the limit of its length, pulling my mother off her feet by the anklet still around her leg, and dragging her off into the gloom – so pitch black that she was gone from sight in less than a second.

"Mom!"

Much as I wanted to race after her, I had no idea where she'd been carried off to. Worse, there came no answering cry to mine. And then, much to my horror, I realized there was no scent to guide me either. It was as if she'd been completely swallowed up by the darkness.

I turned back toward the Queenshield soldier, who now looked smugger than ever.

He smirked at me. "I did try to warn you."

"Quick!" I shouted. "Everyone back inside. We need to…"

But this place, whatever it was, was ready for that. Before my eyes, the damage I'd done to the wall began to repair itself. Stones lifted from the ground of their own accord, flying back to where they'd been displaced. The mortar which had held it in place regenerated around them.

The last thing I saw before we were all plunged fully into darkness was the insufferably conceited grin of the sidhe guard, and then the final stone repositioned itself and all became blacker than the blackest night.

"Everyone gather around me. Follow my voice," I said, making a mental oath to invest in one of those keychain flashlights when this was over.

If this ever was over.

Much as I wanted to tell that voice of doubt to shut its pie-hole, I couldn't.

"I said get over here!"

All around me I could sense movement. For a second, the heebie-jeebies took hold, kind of like they did whenever I was in the hollows, and I was tempted to start swinging blindly.

Fortunately, I held myself in check.

"What's happening?" Riva asked from right next to me.

"Oh, the usual. We're being fucked but not in the good way."

"Story of my life lately."

"Everyone else here?"

"W-we stand tall and proud, princess," Cabbage replied from down around knee level.

"Keep doing just that," I said, trying to sound reassuring. "We'll get out of this. Grunge? Sound off."

There came no reply.

"Grunge?"

"He was right next to me," Riva said.

"All right, calm down. He probably just ... ran off to loot the bathroom or something."

"What are we going to do?"

"For starters, I'm going to turn the lights back on. Stay put and don't move."

As the wall had rebuilt itself, I'd made it a point to note its location relative to where I stood. I'd knocked it down once. I could do so again.

And if I had to bust a couple of Queenshield heads in the process, so be it. Worst case, we could run back up the stairs and figure it out from there. Who knows, maybe we'd get lucky and a couple of giant eagles would fly by and offer us a ride.

First things first, though.

I lowered my head and bolted forward, preparing for impact in three...two...

My countdown ran out and I hit nothing. In fact, I was at least five steps past where the wall should've been when I put on the brakes and began to inch my way forward, trying to figure out how I could've been so off in my guesstimate.

Impossible.

There was no way in hell I'd been this wrong. The damned opening had been maybe ten feet away when it had closed back up again.

Okay, calm down. There's more than one way to gauge distance.

My lack of night vision sucked, but it wasn't the end of

the world. If anything, it had forced me to get creative with my other supercharged senses. For example, sound bounced. A normal human could train themselves to tell how far something was by the echo it produced, not unlike a dolphin in the ocean. My hearing, however, was several times greater, allowing for all sorts of nuance a regular person couldn't hope for.

"Hey!" I shouted, my ears listening for the echo that would tell me roughly how far away from the tower wall I was.

But there came no echo. It was as if I were standing in an infinite field of nothing. It wasn't possible. I'd...

Except we were standing in the grand ballroom of a freaking goddess. Who was to say what was and what wasn't possible in a land where she could track you down anywhere just by saying her fucking name out loud?

Time for plan B.

Also, time to figure out what plan B was.

I made a one-eighty toward where I'd left my friends. "Don't move. I'm heading back."

Nothing except barren silence greeted my entreaty.

"Um, guys? Riva? Cabbage? Anyone?"

No response came back and then, a few seconds later, I realized it was far worse than I assumed. Their scents – all of them – were gone, too.

Refusing to believe my own senses, I headed back the way I came – passing where they should have been and continuing on for a good twenty feet before coming to a halt.

I cried out for them again, to no avail.

And then, with no idea what else to do save panic, I picked a direction and ran.

Running in total darkness wasn't the brightest plan in the world, a move borne of nothing but complete hysteria. Doing so in the woods was a good way to end up tripping on a root and eating shit as you slammed into the ground face first.

A cavernous chamber such as this held equal danger, as there existed the possibility both of tripping and running into something solid.

The thing was, I was pretty certain that wasn't going to happen. My footsteps, dull against the smooth floor, still provided some sound, as did my own voice. And yet those sounds told me the same thing over and over. No matter how far I ran, there appeared to be no sign that I was nearing a wall, or any other obstacle for that matter.

After what had to be at least a mile of nonstop running, I finally slowed and stopped.

So was this it, then?

Was this Brigid's wrath? No battle, no fury, no anything? Simply leaving me to either starve or go mad in an endless void.

I had to admit, as far as fates went, that was a particularly gruesome one.

And, against someone like me, a person who stupidly believed she could punch her way out of any situation, it was extra terrifying.

I was alone, more alone than any person should ever hope to be. I had no family, no friends, not even a TV to pass away the hours. All I had was the damnable floor beneath my feet, the only thing solid in this place beside myself.

Fuck it.

Tempting as it was to sit down and cry, I realized I had one last avenue to attempt. If that didn't work, then despair was definitely back on the table.

If I couldn't find my way back to the tunnels beneath

this place, then maybe I could dig my way there. And yes, it sounded batshit crazy to me, too. But faced with the alternatives of wandering forever or losing my mind, it seemed like the least onerous of paths.

The choice made, I dropped to one knee and drove a fist into the marble flooring.

Fuck!

Go figure. Even for a super strong hybrid, hitting solid rock wasn't exactly a vacation. And they made it look so easy in the movies.

Nevertheless, there came a *crack* from beneath me and, when I touched the floor, sure enough, there was a divot missing.

Remembering a retro game Chris had on one of his many consoles, I said, "Time for some real life Dig Dug."

"MY, YOU ARE A PERSISTENT ONE."

The voice seemed to come from everywhere at once, even the fucking floor, like I was standing inside a giant amplifier.

Guess I've finally gotten management's attention. "I'm good that way. Too stupid to know when to quit."

"YOU ARE NOT INCORRECT, CHILD. FOR I CONTROL EVERY LAST MOLECULE OF THESE LANDS, DOWN TO THE LOWLIEST GRAIN OF SAND. IF I SO WILL IT, YOU WILL DO NO MORE THAN BEAT YOUR OWN HANDS BLOODY."

The voice – female, with an accent of indeterminate origin, and containing enough raw arrogance to make my mother sound positively humble by comparison – wasn't lying either. As if to prove her point, I felt the divot beneath my fingertips begin to fill in until it was as if I'd never touched the floor.

"DO YOU UNDERSTAND THE FUTILITY OF YOUR ACTIONS?"

"Never heard of the word, lady. And whatever you undo, I can simply do again."

Yeah, it was boasting, nothing more, but to prove my point I pounded the floor once again, sending shards of marble flying.

"I can do this all day." Okay, that was a lie. I could maybe do it a few more times before pummeling my hand into a useless slab of meat, but she didn't need to know that.

"*FOOLISH CHILD OF EARTH. DO YOU, EVEN NOW, NOT UNDERSTAND TO WHOM YOU SPEAK?*"

"I know full well who you are," I replied, standing up straight, a smile crossing my lips. "And I have only one thing to say to you."

"*OH?*"

Screw it. If you've gotta go, go big.

"Eat a bag of dicks, Brigid!"

33

I'll admit, I expected to be struck down with lightning, boils, or maybe even a plague of locusts. Truth be told, I probably deserved it, too. After all, I'd not only broken into Brigid's home while she had company over, but had then taken the verbal equivalent of a big steaming dump right on her coffee table.

People had been shot over far less.

On the flipside, I'd love to hear how the minstrels spun this one when they wrote the next epic poem to her greatness. *And verily the intruder doth bade our fair queen to sup on a sack of penises, for they were indeed mightier than the sword.*

The silence stretched out for a second, then two, making me wonder if she was going back to her original plan of leaving me to rot in the dark.

Then a beam of blinding light shone down from above, seemingly from the heavens themselves – not that I could see anything up there. It illuminated a spot maybe thirty feet away, a single point of visibility in the unending darkness, but bright enough to light up the area around it for perhaps double that distance, revealing the vast nothingness of this space.

But what sat in that circle of light was more than enough to make up for the emptiness of the cavernous room.

I beheld an enormous crystal throne made up of strange and contradicting angles, like something the makers of Game of Thrones might design while high as balls. It was both beautiful and terrible to behold, seeming to suck in the light that poured down upon it – the insides of its translucent surface smoky, ominous, and full of ... um ... movement, like it doubled as some sort of crazy ass aquarium.

However, that all paled in comparison to the woman who sat upon it. Her gown was simple yet magnificent – a sundress similar in design to what Riva had worn upon her arrival here, but seemingly made of intertwining leaves of varying green. Upon the woman's shapely form, though, it seemed more opulent than even the finest gowns worn at the Academy Awards.

As for the woman – *goddess* – herself, she was, in a word, perfect. Not a flaw could be seen upon her complexion. She possessed light brown skin, amber eyes, and hair that was such a ridiculously wonderful shade of chestnut as to make actual chestnuts look like bad knockoffs in comparison.

She wore no makeup, but didn't need any, somehow looking as if she simultaneously belonged on the covers of Playboy, Cosmo, and Sports Illustrated.

In short, a part of me instantly hated her for looking so good, yet – all the same – if she'd beckoned me over to play tongue hockey, I probably would've had a hard time thinking of reasons to say no.

The only thing sitting upon her brow was a simple

circlet of flowers, yet there was no mistaking her for anything but the apex of royalty ... or divinity.

In truth, despite my outburst, I felt compelled to drop to one knee before her.

She was a woman who inspired, nay commanded, worship.

But she was also the woman who'd ordered my father's legs lopped off. So, it was a fair bet to say she could kiss my ass if she was expecting me to prostrate myself and tell her how fucking pretty she was.

Rather than either fury or indignation, she was staring at me with barely concealed bemusement etched upon her face. Somehow that made it even worse.

I so hated throwing out a good zinger, only to get snark in return. Regardless, she was a goddess, probably infinite years old. If anyone knew how to throw shade, it was bound to be her.

Her expression likewise said she'd be happy to wait until I rotted to dust before speaking first. Fuck it. Losing a Mexican standoff sucked, but it was the person left standing in the end that counted.

"Brigid, I presume." I didn't bother with that whole choosing my words wisely cliché. If I wasn't already fucked by now, I doubted a social faux pas would sink me.

"*Queen Brigid,*" she replied. Grrr, even her voice was perfect, as if she might break out into a Whitney Houston song at any moment and make it sound fabulous. "Or Your Majesty, if you prefer."

"You're not my queen."

"In that you are mistaken, foolish child of multiple worlds."

"Yeah, well, Valdemar can munch on that same bag I offered you a minute ago."

Her response was to raise one corner of her mouth in a

smirk. Guess I scored a point with that one, even if it wasn't really my intention.

The short, action hero answers were rapidly going to grate on my nerves, so I decided to cut to the chase. "You kidnapped my parents – imprisoned my mother and crippled my father."

"Kidnapped?" she replied, as if that were a new word she was tasting for the first time. "I think not, child. They were offered up as spoils of war. Should I have turned away the entreaties of a devout follower simply for the sake of not causing hurt feelings?"

Oh yeah, she was definitely mocking me now. "You know what happened to your devout follower, right?"

"Indeed. It is why your parents still draw breath. The covenant for the Window of Worlds was left unfulfilled. As such, the offered sacrifice was thusly rejected. I believe your species understands the sanctity of contracts, do you not?"

Goddamn my aunt and the machinations she'd put into play. At the time, I'd been interested in nothing more than making her pay for her betrayal on Christmas, but it seemed that in stopping her I'd inadvertently saved my parents' lives, too. It was dumb luck on my part, nothing more, but I'd take it.

Sadly, Brigid seemed to have no interest in allowing me even that small victory.

"Alas, in making their lives worthless to me, your short-sighted stupidity only served to make things infinitely worse."

"Why? Because I pissed you off?"

In an instant, Brigid went from bemused to ticked. Darkness gathered in her eyes, making them appear like infinite pools of blackness. "*Because you released things which were never meant to be released!*"

Much as I like to think I'm brave in the face of danger,

I'll admit I shrank back a step. Sue me. It's not like I'd faced off against any gods before.

The façade of tolerance toward my snark was apparently at an end now, because an aura of flame ignited around her, burning white hot, enough to make me take another step back or risk my eyebrows being singed. She rested one perfectly manicured hand upon the armrest of her throne and began to drum with her fingernails, each tap sounding like thunder.

No doubt about it. I was way out of my league, but I still had a bit of fight left in me. If she was hoping I'd curl up into a fetal ball and cower ... well, she was still a few vulgar displays of power away from making that happen. "You're just mad because you didn't get your way."

"Insolent pup. Soon enough, none of us shall *get our way*. And the fault falls entirely upon your shoulders."

My thoughts immediately raced back to Possessed Riva and the other things I'd seen with her that night in the glade. Brigid might've had a point, but I wasn't about to admit it. "What can I say, I spoil movies on Facebook, too. Sue me."

"I will do far better than that, child." *Oh boy.* "You may not realize this, but I have debated long and hard what to do with you. It would be simplicity itself to erase you from existence, making your last second of life an eternity of torture as I plucked you apart piece by piece." *Double oh boy.* "But I realized there's a far more appropriate fate. In your ignorance, you have set events in motion that the cosmos itself might be unwilling to forgive. So ... it is only right that *you* correct this."

"Correct this?"

So that was her game? I was going to be given some half-assed quest to ... do what? Sign over the deed to the hollows? Needless to say, I was a bit underwhelmed. As far as godly wrath went, I'd seen better in B movies.

Brigid made the barest of gestures with her fingers and a strange odor caught my nostrils, alien yet familiar. *What the?* A few moments later, I spied movement in the darkness. Something was headed our way.

As it entered the fringes of the light cast out from the throne, I realized it was ... a body – floating horizontally toward the light, held aloft no doubt by her power.

A lump formed in my throat, thinking it was one of my parents – my mother judging by the size. But then it got closer and I saw both clothing and features far more familiar than I would've liked.

You've gotta be fucking kidding me.

It was me, or shall I say a near perfect impression of me, one wearing the clothes I'd worn a few days prior.

The doppelganger was still missing its arm, but in its place had been grafted some kind of silver harpoon, looking way too sharp for my personal edification.

Call me crazy, but I had a feeling it wasn't there for ceremonial purposes only.

"Arise, my new champion," Brigid said, no doubt relishing the look of confusion upon my face.

It was as if she hit a switch. One moment, the doppelganger was lying there in mid-air – neat trick by the way – looking as dead as when the gnomes had paraded it out. The next, it sat up and pushed itself off the non-existent *table*.

It looked around, wild-eyed, before settling first on me and then on Brigid next. The creature glanced between us before backing up a step.

"Now now, my new pet. There's no need to fear. If anything, I have an offer that, as the humans are fond of saying, you can't refuse."

"Really?" Other Me replied, sounding somewhat less than convinced. It squinted its eyes and ... um, adopted an expression that made it look like it was trying to take a crap right there on the floor.

The fuck?

Or at least it did until Brigid held up a hand. "I'm afraid I can't allow that. This offer is contingent on you remaining in that form. Call it ... karmic justice, another human colloquialism if you will."

"I'm familiar with it," the doppelganger said. "So you mean I'm stuck like this?"

"What's wrong with looking like that?" I asked, feeling a bit put out. I swear, it had been nothing but nonstop insults since I got here. Good thing I had a healthy self-image, otherwise I'd probably develop a complex.

The doppelganger held up its harpoon arm and glared back. "Let's just say, I have a bone to pick with you."

"Good comeback. Your mom write that one?"

"No, but your mother might eat my..."

"Speaking of mothers," Brigid said, interrupting our trash talk, "here is my offer. I wish for you to pledge the lives of this daoine's parents to me. Offer them up as a blood sacrifice to be made upon your victory."

"Okay ... and?" Other Me replied.

"And in return, you shall be rewarded." Brigid glanced sidelong at me. "It would please me greatly to see that face serving loyally in my Queenshield. And if such is not to your liking, I can return you to Earth with treasure enough to make you a queen in your own right ... or a king, whichever suits your fancy."

The doppelganger raised an eyebrow. "And all I have to do is kill this bitch?"

I turned to Brigid. "Leave my parents out of this. Do with me what you want, but let them go."

"You get that line from a movie or something?" Other Me asked, no doubt enjoying my discomfort.

"Yeah, the same movie that ends with me killing both your asses." Okay, perhaps that was my mouth writing a check my body had no hope of cashing. I needed to dial back the threats, especially to the fairy queen. "My parents aren't a part of this. It isn't right to use them as pawns on some chess board. My mother worships you for Christ's sake."

Brigid raised an eyebrow. "Word of advice, child. Never mix deities when you're speaking to one. But that minor faux pas aside, your mother calls me her patron yet still consorted with a low beast ... beneath a blood moon no less. Are you saying I should overlook such an insult?"

"A merciful goddess would."

That was apparently the exact *wrong* thing to say as the entire room rumbled, hard enough to crack even the marble beneath our feet. Even the doppelganger, who was ostensibly far more in Brigid's favor than me, looked ready to shit a brick.

"*Merciful?* Do you have any inkling as to my power? Here I am absolute. If I command the trees to speak, they will. If I decide the dead should walk, they do. If it is my desire that a wandering spirit be made flesh so as to guide the lost, so shall it be..."

"What does that..."

"*If* I was so inclined, I could have your parents flayed alive so that I might bathe in their blood, only to make them whole so as to do it again and again, night after night. So do not speak to me of mercy or I will show you what it truly means to have *none*."

"I ... retract the statement."

Goddamnit, I really needed to watch my tongue here. Power and sanity apparently didn't go hand in hand where Brigid was concerned, something I would be wise to remember. Much as I enjoyed throwing shade at assholes, this was one of those situations where a bit of honey would catch more flies.

My fear seemed to mollify her a bit, as the marble beneath us instantly repaired itself. I could only imagine how much life must suck for her subjects on days when she woke up on the wrong side of the bed.

"Better," Brigid replied. "Perhaps you are not as hopeless a sow as I anticipated." My left eye twitched but I said nothing. "Though I need not prove myself to one as low as you, I will show you some of the mercy you think me incapable of. I offer you this boon. Your parents will be witness to what transpires here this day. Your unfortunate friend, too."

Brigid inclined her head ever so slightly, then shapes began to emerge from the darkness behind her. They were no more than silhouettes, encased nearly entirely in shadow, but I could see just enough of their forms to make out my parents and Riva. They hung in midair, suspended above the ground, unmoving. Yet, at the same time, it was hard to say how, but I sensed that they could see me.

I took a step toward them before I was even aware my feet were moving, but Brigid was quick to raise a single finger, enough authority in that simple gesture to halt me in my tracks.

"Now now. There shall be none of that. Believe me when I say, you will never reach them unless I will it to happen."

She didn't elaborate on whether that meant she'd kill them or simply make it so that I was running for eternity on a giant hamster wheel, but she really didn't need to. By now, I was firmly convinced she could've done either had she a mind to.

So, I did the only thing that seemed remotely sensible. I stopped moving and nodded.

"Excellent." Brigid turned back toward the doppelganger. "And you? What say you of my offer?"

Other Me threw a glance my way and grinned, telling

me everything I needed to know. "A big cash prize and this bitch's head? What can I say, Your Majesty? You're talking my language."

"Very well then," Brigid replied, seemingly pleased with how things were turning out. "You may now have the honor of battling to the death for my entertainment."

34

I had to give the fairy queen credit. She was direct in what she wanted. If anything, High Moon could use a few more girls with attitudes like hers – albeit perhaps with a bit less murderous insanity.

That would have to wait, though, because the doppelganger had taken Brigid's words literally. It crossed to where I stood in the blink of an eye, throwing punches and kicks with such speed that I was barely able to keep up.

But keep up I did, until I realized its attacks were nothing but a feint, a way to keep me busy until such time as it saw an opening. Too bad I was a moment late in figuring that out.

The doppelganger lashed out with its new harpoon attachment, slicing a wicked gash along my shoulder.

The wound burned like someone had poured battery acid into it, causing me to cry out as I backed up, doing my best to defend myself while trying to staunch the blood now freely flowing down my arm.

It hurt *a lot*, albeit I wasn't sure if that was because of the silver or the fact that the blade was jagged as fuck, no doubt meant to cause maximum damage with minimal effort.

Probably a bit from both columns.

"Not bad," Other Me said, lifting the blade to its lips and licking it ... then immediately spitting it out. "Eww. Whatever the fuck you are, you taste terrible."

"Funny. My last boyfriend never complained." Oh god. I did not just say that.

Other Me snorted laughter. "Doesn't mean shit, honey. Human boys will tolerate anything for a lay."

"I guess you would know considering how bad you stink."

In return I got nothing more than a shrug. "Hence why your race invented body spray. Hell, a few spritzes and maybe I'll see if any of your lycanthrope boy toys would be up for a spin. How much fun would that be? They get to fuck you and I get to slit their doggie throats the moment they squirt their little red rockets."

This thing was no doubt trying to get under my skin, and doing a fair job of it, but I'd been taunted with worse over the years. Any woman who's ever stepped out of her proscribed *place*, especially in this age of internet tough guys, knew that much. I remembered checking out some online forums in the weeks before the state finals and, well, let's just say they were an ugly place to be if you didn't have both a penis and an inferiority complex.

Comparatively speaking, this freak was lobbing softballs. Mind you, that didn't mean I wasn't going to enjoy ripping its fucking head off any less.

First I had to catch it, though, which was easier said than done.

Seemingly content with the latest round of smack talk, it raced back in, making Uriel look like a slowpoke in comparison. It lashed out with a kick, almost faster than I could track with my eyes, catching me in the stomach. It wasn't a haymaker, nothing that would come close to finishing me off, but it was enough to double me over for a moment, causing me to lean forward and expose my face as a tempting target.

The glint of silver caught in my periphery and I leapt back as quickly as I could, landing off balance and sending me careening onto my ass.

Not good.

I'd just barely beaten this thing the last time we tussled and that was when I was fresh. I'd been on the go for hours at this point, fighting one battle after another. To say the idiot light on my tank was flashing wasn't an understatement.

Worse, fighting in the forest had been to my advantage, forcing this thing to slow down so as to navigate the terrain. Here, it was nothing but a wide-open space, meaning I had to figure out a way to... *Oh shit!*

In the time it took to blink, the creature was upon me, the business end of that harpoon flying my way with terrifying speed, intent on impaling me like a bug.

I barely had time to lift my arms to...

Clang.

"What the fuck?"

I had to silently echo my double's statement, but then I realized what happened and almost had to laugh.

So intent had I been on fighting this thing hand to hand, that I'd forgotten I was still wearing the shield bracelet. Moving my arms frantically had activated it at the last second, providing me with both cover and a chance.

I gave a shove and the doppelganger, still trying to ineffectually stab me through the shield, went flying.

Sadly, it was a nimble little fuck, able to tuck and tumble midair then land on its feet —moves I'd expect more from my cousin Mindy than from myself.

"You didn't say she had one of those," Other Me snarled at Brigid.

I fully expected the goddess to snap her fingers, causing the one bit of protection I had to vanish. However, she merely rolled her eyes. "I didn't say anything of the sort either way."

Oh well. I guess it was good to know her highness was an equal opportunity bitch.

The doppelganger was likely thinking the same thing based on the glare it shot her before turning to face me again. "Fine. Doesn't matter anyway. How long do you think you can hide your slow ass behind that thing before I get through it?"

"Long enough for me to rearrange your otherwise super cute face."

"Aww, that's so sweet," Other Me replied. "You mean like this?" It raised its harpoon hand and then did something I wasn't expecting. It stuck the blade in its mouth.

Holy fuck!

It jerked its arm twice, slicing through both cheeks and giving its face – *my face* – a gruesome Glasgow smile. The creature's thick mud-colored blood dripped to the floor and it grinned at me, teeth plainly visible through the ragged wounds.

"Like that, do you? I didn't think to bring a mirror with me, so maybe I'll check it out on the real thing before I finish you off. What do you think of that? Finally make you as ugly on the outside as you are inside."

"Sticks and stones may break my bones, but I'm going to shatter the fuck out of yours."

"Bet you'd love to believe that."

Once again, it launched itself forward in a flurry of blows and kicks, no doubt looking for an opportunity to shank me good and proper.

I had a big-ass tower shield now, though, its weight no

more than a box of Kleenex to me. As a result, it made for an effective deterrent between me and Ms. Stabby Arm there.

Unfortunately, hiding wasn't going to win this battle and I had a feeling it was right. It was only a matter of time before it either found an opening or Brigid got tired and decided to zap my shield away at the wrong moment.

I needed to go on the offensive. More importantly, I had to time it right so as to find an opening of my own. Sadly, this thing was like a capoeira fighter on meth. So quick and nimble was it, that it was able to throw the next attack almost immediately after the last, fast enough that I was barely able to compensate as it was.

All the while, I could sense it prodding and probing, looking for an opportunity to nail me with something other than a glancing blow.

Call me pessimistic, but I had a feeling it would find an opening in my defenses long before I found one in its. So that meant I needed to create one by doing something it didn't expect – something I'd have to be crazy stupid to try.

Fuck it. Fortune favors the bold.

I watched its movements as best I could while still maintaining a defense, waiting for ... not a perfect moment, but a good enough one.

Now!

With a flick of my wrist I collapsed the shield, freeing up my arm to rocket forward into the space previously occupied by the screen of solid metal, now a wide-open path to the doppelganger's stupid face.

ARRGGGHH!!! OH GOD!

I caught it solidly in the jaw, snapping its head back and causing its eyes to roll into its head. But I'd been wrong about fortune favoring the bold. No, if anything, it had laughed at my stupidity.

Through nothing more than ill-timed coincidence, the Doppelganger and I had lashed out simultaneously: me high, it low.

It wasn't a fair trade in the least – a solid jab versus a harpoon in the side, almost in the exact spot where I'd been impaled by the Queenshield during our first meeting.

The pain was enough to stop me in my tracks, as if someone had set a blender loose upon my insides. And it was only going to get worse.

The blade was serrated, meaning it was meant to do more damage on the way out than in. And the Doppelganger, stunned as it was, was on the verge of toppling backward.

If it did that and pulled its pig sticker along with it, I'd likely be torn apart, unable to do much more than bleed to death on the ground.

Fighting the urge to double over, I focused the entirety of my will toward forcing my arms to move, grasping hold of the metal shaft where it stuck out from my body.

"Yes," Brigid whispered from her throne, the glee obvious in her voice.

Oh, this is going to really hurt...

Too bad I had no choice but to do it now and quickly, like ripping a bandage off. Anything else would likely cause me to die of either blood loss, shock, or both.

Gritting my teeth, so as to not bite through my tongue, I held the shaft steady with one hand, then brought the other down on it with as much force as I could muster.

JESUS MOTHERFUCKING CHRIST!

The weapon's handle snapped in half, freeing me. Sadly, as much as I'd tried to brace the part still stuck in me, the reverberations from the blow were pure agony to my insides.

I gave the Doppelganger a shove, sending it tumbling away dazed. It wouldn't stay that way for long, though, as surely as I couldn't finish this fight harpooned like a dying fish.

The only factor in my favor was that the blade still inside me was razor sharp.

This is so gonna suck.

"Do it," Brigid said. "Do it and I shall grant thee a boon."

"Boon this," I spat, choking on the taste of copper in the back of my mouth, amazed I still had enough blood to cough up.

Oh well, that likely wouldn't be the case in about three seconds.

Two...

One...

Fuck me!

I grabbed hold of the shaft sticking out the front of my body and shoved, nearly falling over from the pain as the weapon sliced through muscle, skin, and probably other parts I didn't care to think about.

Good thing you only need one kidney to live.

Realizing I was about to drop, regardless of whether or not I wanted to, I reached behind my body, grasped the harpoon end – cutting my fingers in the process because why not – and pulled it all the way through.

Absolutely spent, I flung the weapon away into the darkness and collapsed, feeling my life's blood spilling out of me and staining the opulent floor.

"A boon was offered, thus a boon shall be granted."

"I ... don't ... want ... anything ... from ... FUCK BURGERS!"

The reality was fuck burgers hadn't made the offer, Brigid had. That last part was more a result of the flames which erupted from the matching pair of wounds in my side. It was like she'd decided to barbecue me from the inside out, going for well done.

On the upside, it was a hell of a wake-up call.

I sat bolt upright, unable to even scream, and looked down at myself. The wounds, both in and out, had been cauterized. The fresh burns weren't exactly a vacation in paradise, but at least I wasn't bleeding out anymore.

"One is often expected to thank their patron for a boon."

In response, I threw double middle fingers Brigid's way. "H-here's my thanks. Pick one and spin on it."

The bleeding had stopped, but that didn't mean I wasn't hurting like a motherfucker. Sadly, my rest break was almost over. Across the way, the doppelganger was beginning to stir, brushing off my punch much easier than I was going to recover from its attack.

Against my better judgement, I clambered to my feet, fell, then got up again. I tore my sweater off, once more leaving my top covered in nothing but a sports bra – one that had seen better days if we're being completely honest.

"That strategy didn't work against my brave captain," Brigid replied lazily. "What makes you think it will have any effect against your foe now?"

"S-shut up."

This wasn't for my opponent so much as for me. I ripped the fabric, ensuring I wouldn't be wearing this ensemble again, then tied it around my middle, making it as tight as I could. As far as bandages went, it sucked, probably full of fairy germs, but it was the best I could do with what I had.

The doppelganger sat up, shook its head, and spat out

a tooth. – a permanent smile still etched onto its face. "Not bad, but not good enough."

"Bring it," I replied in a voice that hopefully sounded more confident than I felt. Flicking my wrist, I once again activated the shield. I had no delusions about winning this fight defensively, but for the moment I was happy to have something to put between us.

Too bad some moments weren't meant to last.

"Let's make this more interesting, shall we?"

I no sooner glanced Brigid's way than the shield disintegrated to dust along with the bracelet, leaving me defenseless.

She threw me a grin that practically had *fuck you* tattooed across it. "You didn't appreciate my boon. Perhaps you'll like a bane more."

At that point, I didn't care if it was a death sentence. All I wanted to do was race over there and wring her perfect neck.

Unfortunately, my opponent was on the move again, my punch to its face having barely slowed it at all. And, while it was now missing the harpoon blade, the broken silver shaft grafted to the stump of its arm still looked sharp enough to do plenty of damage.

It charged me head on, no doubt sensing that I wasn't in much condition to evade it.

"Aww, you look sad," it said, the gruesome *smile* upon its mug still dripping blood. "What say I cheer you up?"

It jabbed the weaponized prosthetic at my face and I just barely caught it in time. We began to grapple, both of us trying to overpower the other.

Under other circumstances, this wouldn't have been a contest. But I was running on fumes at this point – literally, as I was pretty sure Brigid had thoroughly cooked my goose with her so-called boon.

The best I was able to do was hold off its attack ... barely.

"You know," it said, slowly starting to force me back. "You never did tell me what you are? Other than a cunt, of course."

"I... *really* don't like that word."

"Too bad!"

It lashed out with a kick to my midsection, rekindling the fire in my gut and almost causing me to double over puking, but I managed to hold my defense – stopping the pointy end of the shaft about an inch from my face.

"Come on, spill. I promise I won't tell a living soul."

Evil bitch Tamara kicked out again, this time nailing me in the shin and knocking my leg out from beneath me, dropping me to one knee.

Oh yeah, today kept getting better and better.

"Tell me what you are, and I promise to make it quick." It grinned, fully aware that leverage was on its side as it pushed ever closer to carving my face like a turkey. "Well, maybe not *that* quick."

"W-why do you want to know?" I asked, hoping to buy a moment or two.

"I keep a kill journal. Just want to make sure I jot you down correctly after it's over."

"Kiss my ass."

"Fuck it," it hissed. "I'll just put you down as another dumb twat and call it a day."

The creature doubled its efforts and my defenses faltered. I couldn't keep it from stabbing me. All I could do was redirect it...

No!

I'd been hoping to push the jagged metal of its arm off course enough to miss me, but all I did was nudge it a bit lower.

Realizing I'd done nothing more than give it an easy

kill shot, I could only watch in horror as the metal shaft plunged toward my heart ... and instead struck the butterfly pendant still hanging from my neck, causing it to flare up and envelope us both in a cascade of light.

My mother had given me the pendent as a Christmas gift, heavily hinting there was more to it than meets the eye. According to her, it was meant to potentially help me at college – more so against the weird things I'd ended up fighting there than with my studies.

Unfortunately, there hadn't been time for her to tell me either what it did or how to activate it. That hadn't stopped it from meaning the world to me, though, hence why I'd worn it to the negotiations.

Now, struck by my foe, it flared to life, nearly blinding both of us in the process.

The doppelganger raised a hand to its eyes and backed away, as the flare of light was replaced by a tingle where the pendant touched my skin.

Whatever this thing did, it was about to activate.

Come on, disintegration ray!

"Now, this is interesting," Brigid remarked from her throne, bitch that she was.

A moment later, fire erupted from the floor directly in front of where I knelt, causing me to instinctively shrink back until I realized it wasn't giving off any heat.

What the?

And then, before my eyes, my mother appeared. No, not my mother, an image of her – ever so slightly translucent. It was her as she appeared when she was angry, her hair a wreath of living flame and her body almost godlike in the power it was radiating.

Okay, now blast this thing already!

"*Hear me,*" the image said, it's voice echoing. "*I am Lissa McGillis – Queen of the Monarchs and high priestess of the Draíodóir...*"

Come on. Make with the death magic.

"*You have attacked my only daughter, dared to spill the blood of my blood. Know that there is no place you may hide where I cannot find you. Flee now or suffer my wrath.*"

And with that, the image vanished – no lightning storm, no force punch, no magic, nothing.

I turned to where my mother continued to float in midair at the edge of the light. "Seriously? That's it?!"

Talk about fucking lame. It was like the witch equivalent of an angry parent yelling at a schoolyard bully.

I should've known it would be something arrogantly useless like that.

Great. One more thing to add to the list of regrets before I died, not getting a chance to properly bitch her out for this.

I fully expected the doppelganger to rush back in and resume where we'd left off. Embarrassed as I was, I was tempted to just let it shank me and be done with it.

However, it stood its ground, eyes wide.

"You're a Draíodóir?"

"What about it?" I replied, pushing myself back to my feet, unsteady as they were. No point in making its job easier than it should be.

"That makes no fucking sense."

I raised my fists, not quite ready to call it quits yet. "Welcome to my world. Nothing in it makes much sense."

"But Draíodóir aren't strong."

"What can I say? Some of us are. So how about it? Are we going to do this or keep jawing all day?"

The doppelganger eyed me cautiously, glancing down at my hands. "What are you playing at?"

That's when I realized it wasn't mocking me. It was

actually being careful. This thing had likely had a run-in with the Draíodóir in the past, knew how dangerous they could be. And now, having listened to my mother, it had concluded that's what I was.

Maybe I could use that to my advantage.

But how?

I readjusted my stance, causing it to flinch to the side a bit.

What the?

And that's when it hit me. It was expecting me to cast a spell, waiting for it, no doubt planning to dodge and then race in to finish me off.

"Draíodóir aren't strong," it repeated, continuing to glance down at my hands. After a moment, a smile crossed its ruined mouth. "Unless ... that bitch was lying."

"Don't call my mother a bitch."

"She isn't really your mother, is she?" it asked, grinning. "What are you then? Some kind of Jon Snow bastard? Maybe a failed science project?"

"I'm warning you."

"Save it. I don't know what you are, but you aren't a witch."

Its voice was confident, but I could've sworn I saw the slightest bit of unease in its eyes. That was it. I needed to throw it off its game for a split second, just enough to leave me an opening. If so, maybe I could finish this.

I wracked my brain as our standoff played out, trying to remember a spell – something I could preferably pronounce in a way that sounded like I knew what I was doing. *No, not that one. Nope, no way could I say that without shredding my vocal cords. Probably not that either...*

"Fuck it. You're mine."

The doppelganger bolted toward me.

Got it! I held out my hands before me and screamed, "*Sèididhteine!*"

I expected the creature to flinch as I tossed my bluff out, just enough to hopefully let me step in and break its neck.

What I didn't expect was the concentrated bolt of blue flame that shot forth from my palms, blasting my opponent with a deluge of power.

Da fuq?

35

In the space of an instant, the fight was over. As I stood there, staring over my still-smoking palms, the doppelganger fell to the ground without any further comment. Most of its abdomen had been burnt clean through by whatever had just happened. The rest quickly caught fire and began to burn.

Though it was kind of strange to watch my own body being consumed by flames, I was a lot more weirded out that I was somehow the cause.

"Well done, Tamara."

That thing is well done all right.

So stunned was I, that I barely registered Brigid's tone was suddenly a lot less smug.

The spell was a bluff, nothing more. I couldn't do magic. I *couldn't... Ugh!* What I could do, though, was double over in pain, both from exhaustion and the grievous wounds I'd suffered.

"I know what you're thinking," Brigid continued. "It's written all over your face."

As far as I could tell, the only thing written on my face

was agony. But then, a moment later, the pain wracking my body disappeared. *What the?*

I looked down and noticed a faint glow around me. Glancing toward Brigid, I saw she had her hand raised, a similar glow enveloping it. I felt tingly all over, but the worst of the hurt was gone. I can't say I was in great shape, but I was able to push myself to my feet without instantly toppling over.

"Better. Now, as I was saying..."

"I'm not a witch," I said meekly, forgetting for the moment that I wanted to rearrange her face. "I can't do magic."

"Have you ever tried?"

I opened my mouth, only to close it just as quickly. Truth of the matter was, I hadn't. Incredulously enough, it had never even crossed my mind to try. I don't know why. I guess I simply assumed I had full stock of my gifts ... even if my senses had developed after the rest. Was that what was happening? Was my body continuing to evolve after twenty years of being repressed by those damned pills?

And that spell. I'd seen others cast it before. My cousin had practically turned me into a french fry with it barely a week ago. But it hadn't looked like that. "The fire spell..."

"Even I must admit that was an impressive casting, novice or not," Brigid replied, sounding less the evil bitch and more as if she were actually pleased by the outcome of the fight. "Although, perhaps that has more to do with your proximity to your patron."

"My patron?"

"Me, of course."

The fuck was she talking about? "But you're not my patron."

"Quite the contrary, child. I am the patron of all Draíodóir, of which you are one." She held up a hand. "I know what you're going to say, but your human theology has nothing to do with it. Believe in what you choose, reject or embrace me, it matters little. All of that is meaningless compared to one's lineage. You are descended from those whom I first graced with my favor, hence you are of my blood. So it is with all beings touched by the divine ... or the infernal. The spark of power is always traced back to the source. You may pray to whomever you wish, but you will always be one of my children."

I was sorely tempted to invite her to eat another bag of dicks, one covered with STD frosting, but – much as I hated to admit it – what she was saying made sense. Pissed off as I'd been at my parents when I first learned what they'd done to repress my powers, even I couldn't deny I was still their daughter. There was the old saying about blood being thicker than water, after all. But what if that held true for the things that made us different as well, the divine spark for lack of a better term?

If so, Brigid was right. But she was also wrong, too.

I took a step toward her. "Except, if that's the case, you're not my only patron. Are you?"

I half expected the question to enrage her, or at the very least send her into another one of her snits again. Let's face facts, I was still neck deep in shit with no chance of a life preserver.

Rather than blow her shapely top, Brigid instead smiled. This time, however, it wasn't predatory. If anything, she seemed genuinely pleased.

"And so you finally begin to understand." She rose from her chair. "You are correct. I am not your only patron. In that, you are quite unique." She turned upon her dais to glance around the dark room. "Wouldn't you agree, my dear guests?"

It was as if someone flipped on a light switch – which, for all I knew, they did. Except it was a freaky light switch. Because, in the space of me blinking my eyes against the sudden brightness, everything about the room changed.

Gone was the barren wasteland of darkness. In its place was more what I'd envisioned earlier, an opulent ballroom fit for royalty.

No, not royalty ... divinity.

The marble beneath me, now fully illuminated from above, was so finely polished as to be reflective, making me glad I hadn't worn a skirt today. But that was the least of the wonders on display.

Brigid's throne had moved and now sat up against a wall, one adorned with gold, silver, and other metals I couldn't begin to identify – all of them different colors and gleaming as if they'd been freshly polished. Above us appeared the illusion of a perfect sunny day. I say illusion because elaborate chandeliers hung from it, suspended by either magic or invisible chains. That and I felt no warmth from the sun hanging high in the sky.

Mind you, what did I know about reality in a place controlled by a goddess?

Gone was the doppelganger's smoldering corpse, as if it had never been there to begin with. So too, was there no longer any sign of my parents or Riva. However, try as I might to panic, it was a little hard to focus as I was currently a bit overwhelmed by all the other ... um ... beings that had appeared.

Several fairies stood in attendance, including members of the Queenshield – their faces stoic and unreadable as they stood at attention. However, they might as well have been the unwashed rabble compared to the rest.

All around me, sitting upon thrones of different design than Brigid's but no less opulent, were other ... entities.

It was hard to explain, but I could sense their divinity.

If anything, they were hard to look at, my eyes watering whenever I would try to take in their details directly. No doubt about it, Cabbage hadn't been wrong. I was in the presence of not one, but multiple gods.

Some appeared human, but the ideal form of human – kinda like Chris Evans as Captain America, but more so, if that was even possible. Others were the type that would get a few more stares walking down the street. There was a four armed elephant-like creature with tusks made of pure obsidian, a demonic looking muscled brute with horns that shimmered in a multitude of colors, a being that looked like someone had lopped off a man's head and replaced it with an eagle's ... and many more.

All of them were seated in a wide circle, somehow with me – wearing nothing more than a ratty sports bra over my top half – in the middle. Oh, yeah. This was grand.

As amazing as they all were, only one other than Brigid seemed to draw my gaze toward it. In this case it was like opposite day. She was the beauty, no doubt about it. I didn't consider myself a slouch by any means, but next to her I might as well have frump tattooed on my forehead. This other ... thing, though, was definitely a beast. Seated as it was, it was still gigantic. I made a guesstimate that it would likely stand fifteen feet high if an inch. In form, it looked like some kind of bizarre science experiment gone wrong, as if someone had bred a gorilla with a bulldog, then thrown in some lion genes for shits and giggles.

The creature must've noticed me staring because it smiled, revealing – of course – a row of shark-like teeth in its mouth.

It wore thick plated armor, dull, grey, and pitted, as if it had survived countless battles. In short, everything about it screamed alpha predator, save for the fact that it was seated with a goblet in its hand. Even so, it seemed to radiate an aura of barely contained violence ... one that felt vaguely familiar.

No way.

But somehow I knew it was true.

"Valdemar?"

The beast nodded its heavy head once toward me, causing all those around it to gasp in surprise. Guess the big guy wasn't known for moving around much.

"My esteemed guest pays you the highest honor," Brigid explained. "Not many of mortal blood are able to garner his attention."

"Oh." I turned back to him and waved. "Thanks!"

There was no doubt about it. Summary disintegration was almost certainly still on the table. But, if I was going to die, I might as well go out asking a few questions first.

"I thought you and he were ... um ... not cool with each other."

Brigid actually laughed, as did several of the others present. Valdemar merely took a sip from his goblet, spilling some of the drink down his massive chin. I guess it was safe to say at least one of the two gods I was related to wasn't housebroken yet.

Brigid leaned forward ever so slightly. "Our so-called conflict is a mortal conceit, nothing more. The whims of tiny beings looking for any excuse to slaughter one another."

Valdemar grunted in response, sounding like something had exploded in his small intestine.

"Yes, yes," Brigid replied to him. "I was getting to that. There does, of course, exist rivalries among the divine, but their causes and reasoning are beyond the mortal ken to understand."

I sincerely doubted that, but it was her house. Let her have her dog and pony show.

"So, he's my other patron?" I asked. "And that makes me unique?"

Again, laughter erupted at something I'd said. Either they thought I was an idiot, or I had a future as Fairy World's foremost comedian.

"No, child," another of the gods replied, a thing that looked like some kind of bipedal hyena with the face and breasts of a woman. "There exist myriad races other than your own. As such, there exist other hybrids, those who draw their strength from dual wellsprings."

"Indeed, dear Sekmahset," Brigid said before turning back toward me. "However, there are no others in existence who draw their strength from three."

"Three?"

"In fact, since the dawn of time as you know it, there has been only one other who could lay claim to such a heritage."

"Yeah, you kind of have me stuck at the three part," I said. "I mean, I know basic biology and all, and maybe a bit of mythology as well, but usually we're talking two..."

Brigid silenced me with a wave of her hand. "You are aware of the circumstances around your conception, yes?"

Unfortunately, I was. I'd grown up with some bullshit story about my parents meeting at college – about as milquetoast of a romance as there was. But the reality was more some supernatural sex fantasy, like something ripped from the pages of a bad romance novel in which the protagonists meet, fight, and then fuck each other's brains out ... all beneath a blood moon.

"Kinda wish I wasn't, but yes, I'm familiar."

"Then you are aware your parents weren't the only ones present."

Kinky. Never took my folks for the threesome type. And now there was an image I was never ever scrubbing from my brain again. Wonderful. "Um, you mean the blood moon?"

"I mean those who exist between worlds."

"Those who..."

"We have no name for them. They are timeless, formless, homeless ... existing in the spaces between worlds, the endless void in which nothing should be able to survive, yet does."

A sinking feeling was beginning to form in my gut. I'd assumed that whatever Possessed Riva was, she was maybe a rival faction – another god or race that was simply jealous because Brigid and Valdemar got all the love around High Moon. All at once, though, I realized it was potentially much worse than that, especially because of the undertone in Brigid's voice ... something I didn't expect to hear coming from an all-powerful goddess: fear.

"Yes, child," she continued, "you do perceive correctly. This is no mere banquet or celebration. My fellow divine and I have met to discuss the threat this represents to the multiverse. Believe me. It is no accident that you are here this day."

I raised an eyebrow, skeptical of the convenience of what she was saying. Before my better judgment could warn me against mouthing off, I said, "No. It isn't an accident. I'm here because my asshole aunt offered up my parents as a sacrifice to..."

Brigid held up a hand again. "They're safe. I merely wished to put forth the threat to see if you would rise to your challenge." Challenge?! What the fuck was she yammering about now? She wasn't finished, though. "I must admit, until recently, I thought nothing of it. You are correct in your assumption of how and why your parents came to be here. But hindsight can be insightful, even to the divine."

"I have no idea what any of that means."

"*The multiverse is a sentient thing,*" a booming bass voice said, causing me to almost jump out of my skin. It was so deep that the very floor beneath me rumbled for several seconds after it had finished. I turned, wondering who'd said that, only to find Valdemar leaning forward in his seat, his fingers tented. "*And like all sentient beings, it seeks to preserve itself.*"

"Um, okay?" It was all I could muster. Brigid and he might be on equal footing, but Valdemar definitely won when it came to raw intimidation.

"*In order to protect itself, the multiverse will set events in motion. Some call this fate, but it is little more than self-preservation, as enacted by a being as high above us as we are above you.*"

Oh yeah, that wasn't arrogant at all. "So, you're saying the multiverse actually kidnapped my parents?"

"What we are saying, child," Brigid continued, "is that it set these events in motion, events which led to you being here at this time. You may not believe it, but that matters little. This confluence of events – your parents' capture, the release of these creatures, and your appearance here now, including your unrelenting pursuit of your goal to the point of daring to challenge the divine itself. None of these are mere coincidence. But the will of the multiverse can be a fickle thing. As such, it wasn't until after you arrived in my Garden that I and my fellow divine realized this."

"But Possessed Riva ... err, this nameless thing, whatever it is, is the one who sent me here. How does that fit into this?"

"These beings I speak of exist outside of creation, and thus are not susceptible to its influence. However, the same cannot be said of your friend, whose soul was still present in her body up until that point. Though none of us here can know for certain, perhaps the multiverse was able to act through her, using her spirit as a conduit to plant the suggestion within the outsider's head."

Okay, this was getting way too trippy for me. I was a college student studying environmental science. It was difficult enough for me to grasp the things being done to our planet as industrialization marched ever forward. And now this chick was asking me to figure out the politics of multiple universes? Not happening.

"Let's back up a bit here," I said. "Forget omnipotent beings and stuff like that. What does this have to do with me, challenges, blood moons, any of that?"

"*Those who exist outside can only be released by one who has been touched by them, an infinitesimally small possibility even in the vastness of the multiverse,*" Valdemar replied, his words far more eloquent than his brutish form might suggest. "*But thousands of years ago such a thing occurred nevertheless.*"

"A hybrid, a being of two gods and three lineages, was born to walk upon the world you call Earth," Brigid explained.

Translation, two other star-crossed lovers decided to fuck each other's brains out in a sacred glade during a blood moon, although I figured it might be best for my sanity to not ask for a play by play.

"This hybrid alone possessed the power to shatter the Window of Worlds, allowing the chaos of the void to bleed forth into your reality, in turn affecting all others."

"*But,*" Valdemar continued. Jeez, you'd have almost thought these guys had rehearsed this shit. "*The hybrid, unbeknownst to those who had influenced its siring, also possessed the power to right those wrongs, to drive the chaos back and reseal the fracture within the multiverse.*"

"It did so at great personal cost, but in the end redeemed itself," Brigid added, picking up the baton flawlessly. It was tempting to tell these two to get a room.

"And so the wounds between worlds healed and existence continued ... until the present day."

"When I came along?"

Brigid nodded. "Your predecessor was the first of its kind, and in truth meant to be the last."

"*Indeed, we sought to ensure such a thing would not happen again, fostering rivalries among our followers and instituting taboos. But eternity is a long time even for a god, and the whims of chance are powerful.*"

Rivalries? Taboos?! If I was hearing this asshole right, the whole cold war between Crescentwood and Morganberg – hell, the fact that both sides had actively tried to kill me – all of it was for nothing more than to keep someone like me from happening again. Son of a bitch.

"And despite all of that, I somehow still managed to be born and release these things anyway," I replied, seeing where this was going.

Brigid simply raised a finger to the tip of her nose. Snarky bitch. "Alas, yes. But where history repeats itself in one instance, so too may it in another. As such, we decided to test your mettle. To see if you were indeed worthy to redeem yourself as your predecessor did so many millennia ago."

"Test my mettle?"

"Of course. Every battle you have fought, every obstacle you have encountered since arriving here – all of it was to test your strength, your ingenuity, your will to survive."

"All of it?"

Brigid shrugged. "In truth, my dear captain was to be your final test, but providence deemed otherwise, providing one more hurdle to throw in your path. And what better obstacle to overcome than one's own self, metaphorically speaking anyway? You'll forgive us, but it seemed too perfect an opportunity to ignore."

Son of a... "That *opportunity* almost gutted me."

She inclined her head and grinned, the meaning clear – almost only counted in horseshoes and hand grenades, of which that fucking doppelganger had been neither. What a bunch of assholes! Not that it would be wise to say so ... directly anyway.

"I get it. I'm too stupid to quit. But why me? I mean, not to sell myself short, but you're freaking gods. Any single one of you could smite me like a bug beneath your boot and be done with it. So, you'll excuse me for not buying that chosen one crap. And yes, I set those things free. I understand that, but it was an accident. I wasn't trying to end the world or whatever they want to do. So, instead of playing games, why don't you guys shove them back into their bottle and, I dunno, maybe give me community service? You know, tell me to pick up trash on the side of the Garden for the next hundred years or so."

There came several gasps of surprise, not to mention a few angry crashes of thunder from the assembled god squad. Guess these guys weren't used to being mouthed off to. Once again, I was reminded that I was by far the low woman on the totem pole here. If I was forced to fight my way out due to causing insult, I put my odds somewhere between laughable and no fucking way.

Much to my surprise, though, it was the big ugly master huntsman himself, Valdemar, who attempted to smooth things over. "*Be at peace, Tamara Bentley,*" he rumbled. "*These are trying times for both mortal and divine.*" He glanced toward Brigid, as if checking whether he should go on. She gave him the smallest of nods. "*Know this. If we could set things right, we would. But, though our influence outside our own realms carries far, we ourselves are tethered to our homes, our life forces bound to that which we have become one with.*"

"But ... you're all here now."

"Are they?" Brigid stood and actually approached me. "Or have you failed to notice yet?"

She gestured at the godly beings seated all around us, beckoning me to ... what? I mean, yeah, most of them were freaky-deaky. What of it?

Brigid began to circle me, her eyes locked onto my being as if daring me to solve whatever insane riddle she hadn't spoken. All the while, the others sat, as if waiting for a game of hot potato to begin and...

Wait! That was it. All of them, save Brigid, were seated. However, none of the rest had even tried to move. Unless, that is, gods were simply lazy fucks.

"I see you begin to understand," Brigid said approvingly, stepping back toward her own throne. "What you see here are their avatars, tiny bits of their life force imbued into host bodies, that they might speak through them. Mighty as that life force may be to one such as yourself, it is but an illusion ... as is all that you see here."

"Hold on. What do you mean by that?"

However, Brigid decided to ignore me, because why wouldn't she? "And therein lay the true threat. For what can easily be done today, shall be difficult tomorrow and, soon enough, impossible the day after."

Why couldn't these chuckle-fucks just hand me an instruction manual instead of all the goddamned metaphors? "Losing me again."

Once more, Valdemar seemed to be the one destined to cut through the word jumble. "*The Window of Worlds has been shattered, but it is only one among many. There are others, many more. But soon, those too will be destroyed, one by one ... each severed string reverberating from world to world. As each tether to the multiverse is severed, so too will our abilities wane. Those who revere us shall grow weaker — as shall we, cut off from their worship. When the last window is closed, sealing off Earth from the multiverse, so too shall the ties between other worlds begin to unravel ... until all realities are left adrift and alone, easy prey for the entropic chaos that will follow."*

Okay, maybe I was a little hasty in thinking his word vomit would clear anything up, but I think I got the gist of it. Basically, if Possessed Riva kept doing whatever she did in the hollows, it would be bad. But the other stuff he mentioned wasn't exactly promising either. "What do you mean those who worship you will grow weaker?"

"Draíodóir, lycanthrope, all races touched by the divine," Brigid said, continuing their annoying back and forth. "Their powers shall wane, cut off from our influence, even as those from the void grow stronger. In turn, the divine, too, shall be made less than we are, as those voices who nourish us with their supplication fall silent."

That didn't sound good. "Pardon my French, but how the fuck am I supposed to help if that happens?"

"Because you are a child of three worlds, drawing strength from each. You will continue to stand tall even as those around you falter."

"I still don't see how..."

She tapped her fingernails against her armrest again, once more causing booming thunder to erupt. "Tell me, child. What did you see upon first awakening in my Garden?"

"Huh? I mean, Riva and Grunge I guess, although I didn't know what he was and I almost ended up decking her."

"No. I mean upon *immediately* awakening."

The memory of that had thankfully faded, no doubt to spare my sanity, but if I tried – not that I wanted to – I could still faintly remember the tentacled nightmare hellscape.

"Remember when I said all of this was but an illusion?"

I nodded, not sure how to answer otherwise.

"This realm, my Garden – it is my wish that it appear to all as their idyllic version of what such a place might be. That is how all who come to these lands perceive it. Except you. Do you have any idea how rare a gift it is to see past the magic woven into the very essence of reality, even if only for a moment?"

I shook my head, having no real clue. Hopefully it was a rhetorical question.

"And you saw what you were able to do during the fight with your doppelganger, yes?" In this case, she didn't wait for me to answer since it was pretty obvious anyway. I mean, I'd cast a freaking spell and a badass one at that. "Your heritage and lineage are unique, having only existed once before. You have potential you have only begun to tap."

"And yet Possessed Riva ... err, the void thing, kicked my ass anyway."

"No. It simply sent you here. And why is that? Did it actually care whether you saved your parents? Or did it send you away because it wasn't certain of its ability to kill you?"

I opened my mouth, but no words came out. Holy shit, was I actually buying this load of crap from this crazy bitch? I mean, I'd watched Possessed Riva kill Dr. Byrne like it was nothing. There'd been no doubt in my mind she could've done the same to me. If anything, the only reason she hadn't was because the real Riva had still been in there somewhere.

Unless that wasn't the case, merely my perception of it.

"*I sense you begin to believe,*" Valdemar said. "*That is the first step. The next is accepting your task, embracing your fate as our champion ... as the multiverse's champion.*"

I glanced among them, considering all that had been said. Normally, this was the part of the movie where the hero would reject everything they'd heard, tell everyone they weren't the chosen one, then run off and have some adventures that finally convinced them otherwise.

Screw all that. I had a healthy enough sense of self-esteem to not bother with that bullshit. Not to mention, I'd already accepted that life going forward was in no way going to be normal for me. What was an extra helping of insanity on a plate already piled high with crazy? I mean, dying at the hands of a doppelganger was really not much different than being killed by a being from outside time and space. Either way sucked, but it's not like one made you any deader.

Yeah. Once you started to accept the weird, it wasn't too hard to go with the flow once things got even weirder.

Still...

"What say you, Tamara Bentley?" Brigid asked, after allowing me what she no doubt considered ample time to consider things. "Will you be our champion?"

I looked her in the eye and smiled.

"That's an easy one. No fucking way."

36

Thunder boomed, lightning crashed, and there came a litany of echoing voices expressing pure disbelief at my answer. I let that play out for several moments, trying my damnedest not to flinch.

When one held all the cards, it was best to sweeten the pot rather than call.

Finally, I held up a hand, mimicking Brigid's favorite gesture. Wasn't sure if that would work or simply get me atomized, but – amazingly enough – the assembled god squad stopped their blabbering and quieted down.

"That is, no way ... unless there are a few concessions made."

Brigid's eyes flashed with power and she stood up, instantly enlarging to twice her original size. "You would demand terms even knowing what is at stake?"

If she was trying to intimidate me, she was doing a hell of a job. But I intended to hold my poker face to the very end. "Yes. For starters, I want you to bring my companions here to this place. My parents, my friends ... *all* of them."

It wasn't a lot to ask, and it seemed Brigid realized

that. She grinned, as if finding my terms quaint, then inclined her head.

A regiment of the Queenshield standing nearby turned my way. For a moment, I thought she might give the order to arrest my brazen ass, but instead they stepped aside, revealing my companions as if they'd been there all along.

Mind you, the confused and terrified looks on their faces said otherwise.

"Oh, gleef," Grunge mumbled, glancing every which way. No doubt it was partially due to being surrounded by so many beings of power, but likely also because his pockets were stuffed with stolen swag.

"Bent!" Riva cried, running my way.

I caught her in a big hug.

"Who are these guys?" she whispered in my ear.

"Just the various gods of the multiverse," I said, letting her go.

She glanced at me sidelong. "You ... haven't been talking back to them, have you?"

Ah, she knew me so well. "Of course not."

"We are so fucked."

Both my parents and the gnomes approached at a more modest pace. My father was in his mega-wolf form, making his progress easier, with my mother by his side. Cabbage and his gnomes were behind them, all looking decisively nervous.

As they stepped into the circle of the gods, my parents broke off from each other. Mom turned toward Brigid and dropped to one knee before her. Dad meanwhile had no doubt noticed Valdemar. Kind of weird to see a terrifying wolf monster with a wide-eyed, open-mouthed stare. But there you had it.

After a moment, he composed himself, letting out a snarl toward his patron god. I guess that was a good thing, as Valdemar merely inclined his head, causing Dad to turn and make his way to my side.

"Rise, my child," Brigid said to my mother. "I offer no forgiveness for your transgressions nor apology for any actions taken here. But know I also offer no ire."

I half-expected Mom to lose her cool at that, maybe break out into some arrogant pontification like her people tended to do. But she merely nodded and rose to her feet, an unreadable expression upon her face as she too joined us.

When, at last, all of them were gathered around me, Grunge included, I stepped forward.

"Thank you. Now here's the rest of my conditions..."

Thunder rumbled from on high again, but fuck these guys. They were over a barrel and we both knew it.

"I am to be returned home, along with those I came with and those I came here seeking. In addition, I would ask that this sylph's ... err ... record be wiped clean."

Grunge threw me a quick look of gratitude, before finding something interesting on the floor to stare at. Oh yeah, my hero.

As for Brigid, she remained tight lipped but so far hadn't lost her shit at what I'd asked. Okay, time for the bonus round.

This one's for you, Arugula. "The gnomes shall be offered asylum. I want them given equal status to the rest of fairykind, or whatever you call yourselves."

"Absolutely not!"

"Then feel free to save the multiverse by yourself, because I'm officially on vacation."

"Multiverse, Tam Tam?"

I turned to my father. Guess they'd been allowed to watch the fight but not the after party. "Long story. I'll explain later."

Good timing on my part, too, because it seemed

Brigid was ready for the hissy fit I'd been expecting. "You do realize I hold the lives of your loved ones in my hand. All I need do is clench my fist and..."

"I've seen that movie about a dozen times, thanks," I interrupted. "The plot gets old after a while. I will point out that you're dealing with someone who is... What did you call me that one time, Mom? Oh yeah, a pigheaded snot. Do *anything* to my parents and you'll find me one-hundred percent focused on coming back here time and time again, irregardless of whether reality is unraveling at the seams."

"That isn't a word, Tamara."

I stuck my tongue out at Mom then turned back to Brigid. "Here's the deal. I don't work for free. I expect to be doing enough of that once I graduate. But I'm not unreasonable either. I'm not asking to be made lord of the flame pits or anything like that. All I want is to go home and for you to take my friends here off your hit list. I don't think that's too much to ask in exchange for the tasks laid out before me."

There came murmurs from all around us as the various gods leaned in and whispered among themselves. Though a few shot me glares, as if disgusted that I – a mere mortal – would dare stand up for myself, most of the shade seemed to be thrown Brigid's way. And why wouldn't it be?

If history was to be believed, one of the hallmarks of immortality was being petty as can be. If anything, it was probably seen as a virtue among their kind. But, if the doomsday scenario they'd laid out was one tenth as dire as they made it out to be – and to be fair, I wasn't entirely convinced – then now was not the time for Brigid to stamp her feet and act petulant.

After a tense moment, the fairy queen's eyes once again flashed with power, but then she took a long breath ...

which was kind of odd, since that wasn't something I figured gods would do.

When she looked at me again, I got the sense I was definitely off her Christmas Card list. Regardless, she said, "Very well. I hereby grant asylum to the Nibelung. They may reside in the Garden and will be afforded the same status granted to my children the sylphs. Does that satisfy your needs?"

Somehow, I got the feeling that fell into the back-handed compliment pile. I mean, after all, Grunge lived in a dirt burrow and scavenged potato chip bags for clothes. Of course, he could've just been a dirtbag. Everything I knew about the little skeeve seemed to point to that. So, rather than ask him, I glanced toward Cabbage.

He made a back and forth motion with his hand, which I took to indicate that Brigid's offer wasn't the best in the world but could definitely be worse. Finally, he nodded.

I turned back to face the goddess. "Deal."

"So be it." She glanced at where Grunge and the gnomes stood, her expression unreadable. "You are free to go ... in peace."

Cabbage stepped forward and bowed to Brigid. Then he turned to my mother and did the same. Finally, he faced me. "In your debt we are, Princess."

"I'd say we're square, but you're welcome anyway."

"When home you get, forever watch over you and yours we shall."

"Um ... thanks?" Oh yeah, because that's what I needed to ensure I never slept again.

Cabbage smiled at us all, then gestured for his gnomes to follow as he led them into the crowd – fairies of all shapes and sizes stepping aside to let them pass.

Grunge was a little slower to leave. He took a few tentative steps away then stopped.

Maybe he wanted to say goodbye, too, but didn't know how.

But then he took a few more steps, and a few more, and finally let out a whoop of joy.

"My eyes! They're still in my head. Gleefing honor is satisfied. Yes!" He looked over his shoulder to where I stood. "Goodbye, Girl. With any gleefing luck, our paths won't cross again."

And with that, the little shit walked off whistling, quickly disappearing into the crowd, his pockets still bulging with ill-gotten gains.

Oh well. Long goodbyes really weren't my thing anyway.

"As for you, Tamara Bentley," Brigid continued, "you may return home with your parents so that you may work to fix the problems you have caused."

Definitely a bit of shade there. No doubt about it. If I somehow managed to be successful in doing ... whatever I was supposed to do, I'd have to make sure the Garden stayed off my list of potential vacation spots.

That was a concern for tomorrow, though. First things first was getting out of here. "Come on, Riva. Get over here with us."

"You misunderstand me," Brigid said. "I am only sending you and your parents back to Earth. She must stay."

"Hold on, what?"

"Your friend cannot return with you."

"Then no deal."

Brigid sighed, looking very human for a moment. "Tamara Bentley, you must understand that she..."

"I *do* understand. Riva's my best friend. And everything I did here for my parents, I would do for her. She's part of my family."

"But..."

"Non-negotiable. Take it, leave it, or blast me to atoms. But I will not leave my friend behind."

"Um, Bent," Riva said in a small voice. "It's okay. I mean, if it comes down to me or the universe..."

"Multiverse," I corrected. "And don't think for one second I wouldn't choose you." I realized my eyes were getting all damp as I spoke, so I added a bit of levity. No point in getting all weepy in front of primordial beings. "Besides, do you really want to stay here with all these prudes?"

"At least they're cute prudes."

Before she could say anything further, I turned back toward Brigid – who was looking more irritated by the moment. "Send us back. *All* of us."

"Your insolence grows tiresome," the queen of the fairies stated flatly. Call me crazy, but I had a feeling she was one bit of snark away from not giving a shit if reality survived or not. "Begone from my home ... *all* of you. And may fate be so kind that you never come to regret obtaining that which you asked for."

Huh. Just a wee bit ominous sounding.

I opened my mouth to reply, but suddenly realized we were no longer standing in Brigid's throne room. Instead, I was back in that nightmare landscape of insane angles, strange perception, and tentacles ... so many tentacles.

It was only for a second, but it was more than enough to sear nightmare fuel into my brain for years to come.

And then it all vanished, leaving nothing but the void.

37

Go figure, being kicked out of a plane of reality wasn't any more pleasant when done by a goddess than by a rogue monster from the space between worlds.

Well, if what I saw, or thought I saw, while in the middle of being transported was any indication, I'm not sure I could blame those things for wanting out. It was a whole lot of nothing, pretty much a boring as fuck place to spend eternity.

A moment later, my feet touched down on solid ground, or flooring anyway. And then they immediately buckled, causing me to grab hold of a nearby bookshelf to keep from falling on my ass. I'd almost forgotten while stuck in negotiations with a goddess that I was beaten to all hell. Guess whatever Brigid had done to take the pain away was only temporary because damn, all of a sudden I hurt again ... a lot.

"Are you okay, Tam Tam?" Dad called out.

I forced myself back up, trusting that my werewolf healing would keep me on my feet for a little longer. "Yeah. Just ... a bit winded."

"Where are we?"

I looked around to find my parents a few feet away in the familiar looking space. Both appeared how they had in the Garden ... meaning my father was still missing his legs.

Goddamn that bitch! "I'm so sorry, Dad. I should have asked her to..."

He waved me off with a smile. "It's fine, pumpkin. I doubt she would've granted it anyway, heretic that I am."

"But Valdemar..."

To that, he actually laughed. "Valdemar is a god of battle, of the hunt. He values strength above all else."

"But..."

"But he also celebrates those who have suffered in his service. There is great honor to be had in displaying one's scars proudly."

"The pack..."

"Is yours now. We've already been over this."

"Don't underestimate your father, Tamara," Mom said, leaning down and giving him a kiss. "He is a man of extraordinary strength and grace ... except perhaps when it comes to dancing. No offense, dear, but you've always had two left feet."

"Not anymore," he replied with a chuckle.

I was glad he could joke about it, but it still pissed me off, made me want to punch something really hard. Something like...

That snapped me back to the here and now.

We were in the Crendel place, where this insane adventure had begun. Except it was ... clean. There was no sign of the battle that had taken place here. No body, no blood. Hell, even the buffet spread had been cleaned up.

More importantly, there was no sign that anyone was still here. No scent of wolves, or witches, and no sign of Chris either.

Dad had told me that time in the Garden passed

differently than here in our world. But this, it was almost like we'd been brought back to a point before...

I took a deep breath through my nostrils. No. That wasn't the case. I could still smell the residual odors of both Draíodóir and werewolf alike. But they were hidden beneath other scents, like fake pine, the type you'd find in, say, floor cleaner.

"What happened here?" I asked myself.

"Where is here?" Mom repeated from earlier.

I took a moment to explain why this place had been chosen as a neutral meeting site for the peace talks. At least until Possessed Riva had...

Shit, Riva! "Um, guys. Where's Riva?" Sure enough, we seemed to be the only three who'd appeared in this room. "You don't think..."

"Queen Brigid gave her word in front of an assembly of the gods," Mom replied. "She wouldn't risk losing face by going back on it."

Call me crazy, but I didn't put much faith in some asshole goddess's honor, especially considering how my father had been returned home. "Riva!" I called out. "Where are you?"

"I'm in here, Bent," came the reply a few moments later, coming from the direction of the back parlor.

"Thank goodness," I said, heading that way. That was a load off my conscience.

"Honey?" Dad asked from behind me.

"Back in a sec," I replied over my shoulder. "Then we can head home."

The word sunk in like a weight upon my chest. *Home.* We were all finally back in High Moon. We could be a family again. Tears sprang to my eyes as I limped from the living room to the kitchen.

We still needed to make sure Chris was okay. That was going to be top priority. But I refused to think he was otherwise, not now, not after everything we'd gone through. He had to be okay ... *had to.*

First, though, I was nearly dead on my feet. Being that I had to pass through the kitchen anyway, I took a chance and popped open the fridge.

"I love you, Chief!"

Sure enough, a couple cans of soda had been stuffed back inside by whoever had cleaned up this place. I grabbed a Mountain Dew, cracked it open, and took a swig – relishing the feel of sugar and caffeine hitting my empty stomach.

"Soda's in the fridge if you want any," I cried back toward my parents. I had no idea what they'd been fed while in fairy hell, but there was nothing quite like a little taste of home.

That done, I stepped into the back room.

Riva stood at the window, looking out at the Crendels' backyard. She was still wearing the Amazonian outfit the sidhe had provided her with. It was a good look on her. Considering how I was dressed ... or not dressed, I kind of wished I'd thought to grab an ensemble like that before we'd left.

"I was here, wasn't I?" she asked, glancing my way. "I mean, right before we were sent to the Garden."

"You remember that?"

She nodded, then turned to once again face the yard. "It's like I told you, like living in a waking dream."

"A waking dream that's over now."

She continued staring out the window. "I know that, but... You ever get the feeling you're missing something?"

"All the time."

"No, I mean *really* missing something. Like right now."

"Not following."

"There's ... something out there."

"Yeah, an empty field."

"No. There's more."

"Oh, yeah. There's the Crendels' bomb shelter. You remember that place, right? You told me Bobby Crendel kept putting the moves on you while you guys were waiting out the werewolf apoc..."

"Tamara?" Mom called from behind me. "Who are you talking to?"

"Just bs-ing with Riva." I stepped aside to let her into the back parlor. "Guess she appeared in a different room than us."

"Riva?"

"Yeah."

"Hey, Mrs. Bentley," Riva said idly, her attention still focused out back. "I think ... we should go out there and check it out."

"Why?"

"Why what, Tamara?" Mom asked.

"It's calling to me." Riva looked my way. "It's hard to explain, but ... it is."

"Okay. We can come back later if you want. But right now we need to check on Chris."

"I agree," Mom said. "But why would I want to come back here later?"

"Not you. Me and Riva."

"Okay, but first we have to find her."

"She's right here."

"There's no one there, Tamara."

That finally was enough to drag Riva's attention away from the window, not to mention my own.

"Don't joke, Mom. It's been too long of a day."

"I'm right here, Mrs. Bentley."

Mom looked confused, an expression I didn't see all that often on her face. There was one other problem, too.

My mother wasn't known to be a practical joker. She was too ... well, practical.

All at once, I didn't feel so good, and it had nothing to do with my injuries. "She's standing here right next to me, Mom."

I put a hand on Riva's shoulder or tried to, watching in horror as it passed straight through her body.

———◆———

Brigid's warning about Riva immediately came back to haunt me. I'd thought she wanted her to stay behind as some sort of hostage, but the truth was far worse, hitting me only now. Riva didn't have a body to return home to. That void thing had cast her spirit out. With Possessed Riva nowhere to be seen, my friend was nothing more than a ghost – yet one I somehow could both see and hear.

Fortunately, when one's mother was a witch queen, you didn't have to do a lot to convince them that something weird was afoot. Ever the pragmatic one, Mom accepted my word on the matter rather than suggest I perhaps consider therapy. But as for how to fix this, she had no immediate answer.

"It could be your mixed bloodlines," Mom suggested, when asked why I could see Riva and she couldn't. "Or..."

"Or?"

"Let's be honest, Tamara. You pushed your luck with the queen of the summer fae, even more so than was warranted. This could be a curse. Something to cause you to think you're seeing..."

"I'm right here," Riva stated, sounding both angry and terrified in the same breath.

"She says she's not a hallucination."

"Which, in all fairness, is something a hallucination would probably say. But, another possible answer is the bond between you. You've shared so much over the years, maybe Brigid sensed this and decided that, for now anyway, Riva's soul could share your body, too."

"I like that theory a lot better than the other."

"You're not the only one," Riva replied, her eyes once again turned toward the window.

"But this still doesn't make any sense. I mean, you were ... real in the Garden."

"Thanks, I think."

"You know what I mean. You were there. We could see and touch each other." I turned to my mother. "You and Dad both saw her. So how does that make any sense?"

Before Mom could answer, though, a recent memory flashed through my mind, something Brigid had said when questioned about mercy.

If it is my desire that a wandering spirit be made flesh so as to guide the lost, so shall it be.

I'd glossed over it at the time, figuring it to be nothing more than the arrogant pontifications of an egomaniacal goddess. But the reality was Brigid had been merciful after all. She'd willed Riva to have a body from the moment of our arrival, perhaps knowing I'd need a friend to help guide me back onto the path whenever I strayed.

"Brigid..."

My mother nodded. "It wasn't wrath that compelled her to insist Riva stay behind..."

"It was mercy," I replied, finally understanding what she'd meant. "Mercy which I then threw back in her face."

Riva turned toward me, understanding in her eyes despite me being undeserving of it. "It's not your fault, Bent."

"How do you figure that?"

"You stood up for me," she said. "Told that bitch you weren't leaving me behind no matter what. As for her, let's face facts. She could have just come out and said what she meant rather than playing games."

"I guess so."

"You guess so what?" Mom asked.

"Oh, that was Riva. She was saying that even though Brigid was trying to be merciful, she was still an asshole about it."

"Not really what I said."

"I'm paraphrasing here." I shook my head. "Listen. It doesn't matter how or why. What matters is that we'll figure this out. I promise."

"I know we will." Riva turned away again, almost as if, despite what had happened to her, the backyard was somehow the important thing here. "But before we do, I really need to go out there."

"Why? It's nothing but an empty field."

"I realize that, but I also can't help but feel there's something out there I need to see."

"Listen..."

"I'm sorry, Bent. But I have to go." With those words, she took a tentative step forward, closing her eyes in the moment she should have collided with the plate glass window ... and then she stepped right through it. A moment later, she popped her head back in. "Just for the record, that was really fucking weird."

"That's one word for it," I replied as she ducked back out. "Hold up. I'm coming with you."

"Tamara..."

"Just ... wait here with Dad. I'll be back in a few minutes. I dunno. Maybe check to see if the phone works. Call us an Uber or something."

Alas, Riva's method of egress wasn't one I could follow, not unless I wanted a mouthful of broken glass. So I stepped to the backdoor instead and opened it.

Brrrrr!

And of course forgot that it was the dead of winter here in High Moon, a bit of a shock since it was close to bikini weather in the Garden. Still, it was nothing I couldn't handle ... at full power anyway, which I wasn't close to.

I wrapped my arms around myself and followed after Riva, who was already halfway to the doors which led down into the Earth and to the shelter beyond.

Ghost she might be, but she wasn't any faster than usual, so I caught up easily enough. "Hold on. Let's do this together."

Riva flashed me a smile of gratitude, but beneath it lay raw naked fear. "It's getting worse the closer I get."

"What is?"

"I don't know, except to say it's ... the most godawful feeling I've ever had."

I couldn't say I felt anything but the cold, but I was there for her. "Like I said, we'll do it together."

I had no idea how long we'd been gone. Could've been days, weeks, or years – although hopefully not that last one. Either way, it appeared to be around late afternoon.

The wooden barn doors were loosely shut, no latch or lock holding them closed. Though Riva could have simply stepped through them, she seemed hesitant now that we were actually there. I pulled them open, letting the fading light of the day down below.

"Ready?" I asked.

"Not really."

"Then I'll lead the way."

The wooden steps creaked beneath my feet, but no other sound followed. Why would it? I was the only one there, physically anyway.

Down below, the packed dirt walls quickly gave way to poured cement, a testament to the Crendels' commitment to the prepper cause. But it was what lay beyond that caused my heart to catch in my throat.

I expected the heavy vault door.

However, I'd assumed it would be intact. Instead, what lay before me – *us* – was a twisted mangle of metal covered with deep gouges. I wasn't a forensics expert by any means, but it had obviously been attacked by something powerful.

"What the hell?"

"I don't know," I replied. But I fully intended to find out.

Despite the stillness of the air, telling me there was nothing down here except me and my spectral friend, I walked forward slowly. The way ahead, through the shelter's entrance, was dark, the light from above not strong enough to penetrate any further.

I took a deep breath, letting the smells of this place fill my nostrils. I mostly caught the scent of dust and neglect. Nobody had been down here for a long time. But beneath that there was more ... something unpleasant, an odor that told me to turn around and never come back.

But still we crept forward.

"T-there should be a light switch just to the right of the door, if I remember correctly," Riva said, sounding positively terrified, a feeling I was beginning to internalize. "Mr. Crendel told us that it's connected to a solar array further down in the field."

"Yay for him," I replied quietly, unwilling to raise my voice as I reached the doorway.

Pushing the destroyed hatch to the side with a squeal of tortured metal, I reached in and, after several moments, found the switch Riva had told me about.

Hesitating, somehow sensing that we were about to see something we didn't want to see, I turned it on.

For a moment, nothing happened, making me think the system was dead and thus we'd be spared the sight of whatever was causing my nose to practically scream in protest.

Then there came a hum of power, followed by a string of LED bulbs lighting up and illuminating the cramped bunker and everything within it.

It was the space of an instant to know how terribly right I'd been. Inside was a sight I could never hope to unsee ever again.

Dark stains covered the walls, my nostrils identifying it as the dried remains of blood and viscera. Skeletons, mangled and in pieces, lay all around. Though it was hard to tell amidst the carnage, I counted five skulls in all.

A rusted handgun lay in the grip of one of the bodies. Though it was possible, probable even, that it wasn't the same, I'd seen a similar weapon used against a pair of were-wolves early on during the siege of High Moon.

It had been ineffective against the beasts then, as I could only imagine it had been once more in this place – a shelter which had somehow become a crypt.

It was impossible. This wasn't the way things had played out that night.

Yet, some voice in the back of my head was screaming that what I saw before me was real.

I'd been told the Crendels – Edgar, his wife, and son – had fled High Moon in the days following the attack by the Morganberg pack. Yet every single instinct I had was telling me that was a lie, that I was looking at their remains now. But if that were the case, if they'd somehow never left this place alive, that meant the truth about the two bodies alongside theirs was far worse than anything I could imagine.

Please God, don't let these be Riva's parents.

Sadly, despite being a child of multiple gods, I was certain that none had heard my plea.

38

"Bent? What is this?"

"I – I don't know."

"Who are they? Why are they here?"

"I don't know!"

That was a lie, though. Whatever was going on here, it shouldn't have been possible. Yet, somehow it was.

"This is some kind of sick joke, isn't it?" Riva asked, stepping past, and partially through me to get to the cramped space beyond – an odd sensation, like having a breeze blow right through your body.

But that was the least of anything on my mind at that moment.

None of this was right. I'd seen her parents after the siege. I...

Except that wasn't true. I hadn't actually seen them after the attack. The reality was I went back to school just a few days after, while the cleanup was still going on. I'd only returned once classes ended for the holidays. And yes, while I'd seen Riva and their house...

Her home. I remembered how it looked right before Christmas. I'd picked her up for a sleepover and all had been well. But then, after what had gone down with my aunt, there had been nothing but silence from Riva – until I'd gone looking for her and found her house utterly trashed, the damage from that night months ago still evident as if it had never been fixed.

Or ... as if something no longer felt the need to maintain an illusion of normalcy.

But if that was the case then...

I dropped to my knees, all the strength gone from my legs as the implication hit home. This was supposed to have been a safe place, where Riva and her family could ride out the storm while I went and took care of business.

But the awful truth was I hadn't gone back and checked on them at all that night, so preoccupied was I with fighting my uncle and his werewolves. It had been utter chaos. They'd been all over the town like cockroaches, running rampant like a pack of monsters unchecked.

The thing was, my uncle had also put a hit out on Riva, sending two werewolves directly to her home, where I'd taken them out of the equation.

But what if that hadn't been it? What if he'd had others searching for her, too – tracking her scent, or mine for that matter?

"Tell me this isn't real, Bent," Riva cried. "Tell me!"

"I ... I ... can't."

"They can't be my parents. They can't be! Because look! I'm not here. I'm still... oh god!"

"What is it?" I asked, fearing whatever she might say next.

"I *was* here. I remember it. But where am I then? Where is my..." Riva sank silently down next to me. Horror was etched upon her face, but no tears flowed from her eyes. How could they? She had no body.

And because of that, I couldn't take hold of her and offer what little comfort I could.

"I remember," she said at last, her voice haunted and distant. "That night. I remember what happened."

"You already told me. You said..."

"It was a lie. I didn't even realize it at the time. But it was that thing speaking through me, creating a narrative that even I believed ... because I wanted to believe it."

That *thing*? I remembered back to what she'd told me, right after we'd found my father — that the story of how she'd escaped being mindwiped that night wasn't true. I hadn't given it much thought at the time, but now her words played back in my head, and I realized maybe I didn't want to know the truth. I'd assumed that thing from the void, whatever the hell it was, had taken possession of her mere days ago. But what if I'd been doing nothing more than fooling myself this whole time?

"You don't have to..."

"You're wrong, Bent. I do. They deserve it." She pointed toward two of the bodies, their limbs entwined with one another. "My parents. Someone needs to know. Someone who's still alive."

"You *are* alive."

"Am I really?"

Sadly, I had no easy answer to that.

"It was fine at first. That part about Bobby Crendel hitting on me, that actually happened." Her voice was robotic, almost as if the memory were playing back of its own accord, as if she couldn't stop it even if she wanted to. "But then there came a knock on the shelter door. Mr. Crendel wanted us to ignore it, but his wife convinced him otherwise. I don't think she quite bought that things were as bad as we said they were. Either that, or she figured one of the neighbors might need a place to hunker down for the night."

She got up and walked to the door, as if reenacting what happened.

"I tried to tell them, tried to warn them, but Mr. Crendel ignored me, said I was acting crazy and that if I didn't stop I could find somewhere else to spend the night. And the werewolves were smart. Mr. Crendel didn't just open the door. He had an intercom and all. But the wolf was someone he knew. Called him by name and all, like they were best friends."

She backed away, continuing until she reached the far end of the shelter, plastering herself against the wall.

"It happened fast after that. He opened the door, screamed, and then tried to pull it closed again, but it was too late. The werewolves, a pair of them, were too strong. They tore through the door and gutted Mr. Crendel where he stood. All the while, my parents screamed for me and Bobby to get back."

By now the tears were flowing freely down my face. Some for me, but an equal amount for my friend who could no longer cry.

"Mrs. Crendel was next. They took her head off before she could even grab a gun. M-my father, he was so brave. He stood there, took aim, and emptied his handgun, acting as if each bullet might be the one to do the job. But they ... they..."

"You don't have to," I said. "I knew what they were capable of. I should have come back. Should have checked on you. Hell, I should have never left you..."

"Don't you dare say that!" Riva cried. "Don't. This isn't your fault, Bent. Without you, there wouldn't even be a fucking High Moon right now. So please ... this isn't on you."

"But..."

"Please."

I nodded. What else could I do?

Riva's eyes lost focus as she once more backed up against the wall, as if the memory was once again taking hold.

"After it was … over, the wolves came for me and Bobby. Oh god, you should have heard him beg." She lowered her voice an octave. "Take her. Do what you want with her. I won't tell anyone."

"What an asshole."

"Tell me about it," she said bitterly. "Didn't matter, though. Guess they either didn't like his whining or wanted to save me for last. Either way, his pleading didn't last long. And then…"

I didn't want to hear what happened next, but at the same time I needed to know.

"Then it was as if time stopped, except it didn't. It's hard to explain, but something began to speak to me, from inside of my head. I thought I was going crazy, like my life was flashing before my eyes. But the voice, it said it could save me and…"

"And what?"

She let out a laugh, although there was no humor behind it. "It told me a story. Said my best friend had done it a great service. That it wished to offer you its thanks, a boon it called it. Saving me was part of it. And all I had to do was accept its offer."

I didn't need to ask what her answer was. Nor would I judge her for it.

"You know what the funny thing is, though?"

"What?" I replied after a long moment of silence.

"My parents were lying dead in front of me. I was standing there, covered in Bobby Crendel's blood, dripping with it … and yet I didn't think about them at all. All I could think about was not wanting to die, that I would do anything to keep living."

"That's nothing to be ashamed of. You're still here with

me. And I wouldn't give anything in the world to change it."

"Not even if it meant saving reality?"

"Fuck reality. It's overrated."

"Funny you should say that, because right after I said yes, things got trippy. It's like that's the point when the dream began. I can still see flashes of it all, like I was there, but it's hard to tell what's real and what's not. Almost like blacking out drunk and remembering bits and pieces from the night before. Like I'm fairly sure I, or it anyway, vaporized those two werewolves. I mean for real. There wasn't even ash left. Then the next thing I knew I was standing there looking up at you, except this big black wolf had you in a chokehold. I wanted to help, but all I could do was stand there and watch."

I felt a chill run down my spine. So it hadn't been a hallucination after all. I mean, I'd sorta already come to that conclusion, but in a way Riva had actually been there for me ... even when I couldn't be there for her.

"Who's down there?!"

What the?

There came the sound of heavy footsteps descending the outside stairs. So distraught had I been at this horrific reality laid bare at my feet, that I hadn't heard anyone coming our way.

Now, here Riva was, once again with her back against the wall.

The only difference was, this time she was with me.

Except maybe that didn't matter. The voice called out again as I stood and turned, but then I realized I recognized its owner.

"Chief?"

A flashlight beam was shined into my face from the space outside the shelter, momentarily blinding me, but I saw enough of his big burly frame to know who was there.

"Ninja girl?" he asked, stepping forward. "What in tarnation are you doing down here dressed like that?" His eyes opened wide as he took in the sight behind me. "And what in the name of the seven hells happened here?"

I didn't really have an answer to that, numb as I was, with tears still streaming down my face.

Perhaps sensing my despair, he said, "All right, we'll figure this all out later. For now, I need you to skedaddle yourself out of there. Don't touch nothing." He then looked past me. "Same with you. You're that Kale girl, ain't ya? Riva wasn't it?"

I was in the middle of wiping my eyes when that bombshell hit. "Wait. You can see her?"

"Mostly," he replied. "She's a bit dim, more a shade than anything. But yeah, I can see her just fine ... as well as the tether connecting you two. Huh. If that don't beat all."

"W-what tether?" Riva asked, her attention thankfully diverted from the remains of her family.

"Now, don't go flapping your gums at me, girl. Just because I can see you don't mean I can hear you. My ears are good, but they ain't blessed like my eyes."

I repeated her question for both our benefit.

"You and she," he explained. "You're astrally connected. Don't go asking me how. I don't know the whys of any of this. Just that I can see it. And before you go wondering out loud, just know there's very little that escapes my attention here in High Moon, and leave it at that. I ain't got eyes in the back of my head, but these peepers of mine don't miss much."

He waited for us to exit the shelter then stepped in and surveyed things.

"This ain't right," he said after a few moments.

"I know. What happened here ... it's..."

"You ain't listening, Ninja Girl. I mean it ain't *right*. This isn't the way it was." I wasn't entirely sure what he meant, so I figured I'd keep my mouth shut until he explained. It wasn't hard to do. Both Riva and I were mostly at a loss for words at the horror before us. "I was here, right in this spot, not long after the Crendels bugged out – doing a routine check of the place to make sure there was nothing for vandals to grab."

I was almost afraid to ask, but I did anyway. "What did you see?"

"Nothing! At least nothing like this. Everything was fine. Door was locked and I didn't have a key, but there was no way anyone was getting in there without a truckload of dynamite, so I left it be. And it wasn't just then either. I checked out the entire property before you and the Draíodóir showed up today. And I mean the *entire* property. None of this was here. The door was closed and locked and..."

"I saw the same thing at Riva's house. I tried to tell you..."

"I know." When I raised an eyebrow at him, he continued. "One of the neighbors phoned it in this morning. Sent one of my boys to check it out. Damnedest thing. He thought it was a break-in or something, but told me all the damage looked old. Figured he might've been drinking on the job. Ain't unheard of. I was just about to pop on over there myself when word reached me that all hell had broken loose here. Speaking of which, I see you brought Curtis and Lissa back. Don't look at me that way. Of course I checked the house first. Now, care to explain how you managed that?"

"You wouldn't believe me if I told you." He simply glared at me overtop his sunglasses. "Okay, maybe you would believe me. The short version is I got zapped to the

Garden where a bunch of gnomes decreed me a princess and had me lead an invasion force against Brigid's castle."

"An invasion... You do realize I was only here cleaning up the mess a couple of hours ago, right?"

Guess that explained how long we were gone. "Time passes differently over there," I replied with a shrug.

"Seriously, you invaded Dùn nan Dé?" At my nod, he laughed. "Damn, girl. You got some brass balls on you."

I wasn't in the mood for quips, though. Instead I turned and gestured back toward the entrance of the shelter. "You said you don't miss a lot here in High Moon. I mean, you can even see Riva. So how did you miss *this*?"

The good humor left Chief Johnson's voice. "That's what worries me. You may not see it in the day to day, but there's enchantments up the wazoo all over this town, old ones. The original founders who first set up High Moon, they put them in place and each subsequent generation has added to them. Yet whatever is happening here cut through it all like a hot knife through butter. And then there's what happened earlier."

"What?" I asked, unable to take my eyes off the shelter but also realizing I needed to know.

"Some of the ... let's call them precautions I set up for your little meeting. They started going off like crazy. Needless to say, I hauled ass to get over here, figured I might need to bust a few skulls to get folks to simmer down. But there wasn't anything to simmer. Both sides were gone, in a hurry from the look of things. All that was left was a mess, as if there'd been a hell of a scuffle, not to mention all the blood. But no sign of lycanthrope, Draíodóir, or you."

"What did you do?" Riva asked, which I repeated, giving voice to her.

"Cleaned up best I could and reset the wards. Wasn't much else I could do, not with an entire town to keep watch| over. That's why I'm out here now. You and your folks must've set them off when you ... came back."

A part of me wanted nothing more than for this day to be over, to be spared from anything further. But I had to know. "The ... thing that did all of this. It's old and powerful. I need to know if anyone else..."

Johnson, however, held up a hand. "I can answer that easy enough. All's been quiet otherwise. Same with the squawk box. Don't get me wrong, neither the Draíodóir nor the pack tend to broadcast their business over the air, but usually when either side gets their knickers in a twist there's some spillover. But, aside from earlier, it's been what most might consider a slow day, save for a couple of fender benders over near Crossed Pine. Fools out driving with hangovers."

No doubt noticing that Riva and I were continuing to stare at the carnage, he stepped in front of the door blocking our view. "Now, I believe you. No need to worry about that. Can see the evidence with my own two eyes. If you say something old is out there, I won't argue. But whatever it is, it caused its chaos and moved on. Don't know why. Don't care why. I just know that right now it's quiet and you both look like you should be taking advantage of that."

"But..."

"Go home. I got a t-shirt in my trunk you can borrow and your car's still out front. I have no doubt your mom can start it if'n you lost your keys in the Garden. Take your parents and get yourselves back where you belong. And before you ask, that ain't a suggestion."

"But Riva's parents..."

Johnson stepped forward and put a meaty hand on my shoulder. "Let me take care of this."

"Take care of it?"

"Word of this can't get out. Folks wouldn't understand.

So I apologize in advance that there won't be a proper funeral. But you have my word, they will be put to rest with the utmost respect. And when it's done, you'll be able to mourn proper."

"I..."

"It's okay, Bent," Riva said. "I trust him."

"I ... it's ... but it's not right."

"No, it isn't," she replied. "And I'm not sure there's any way to make it right. But for now, I need to leave this place. I think we both do."

She was right. They both were.

We needed to get out of there, take time to figure things out – to mourn and heal. And maybe in time we'd also come to remember there were things to rejoice as well. After all, we'd stormed the castle of a goddess and saved my family.

But we also needed to plan ... to figure out how to find the thing wearing my friend's skin and, more importantly, how we were going to send it back to the hell from whence it came.

EPILOGUE

Chief Johnson was right. Jump starting a car was no problem for my mother. Handy skill to have. And one I might, one day, be able to duplicate if what I'd done in the Garden hadn't been a fluke.

But new powers weren't my priority as we drove home in silence.

It was weird. Though months had passed for my parents, I hadn't actually been gone all that long. Yet, as we navigated the mostly empty streets of High Moon, it felt like ages since the moment I'd left home.

Yes, I'd been successful in my quest, but at what cost? The truth, as it turned out, was more awful than I could have ever guessed.

Because of this, when we finally pulled into our driveway – Riva's shade sitting behind me, visible through the rearview mirror – it was hard to feel the joy I should have.

I hoisted my father onto my back, the plan being to hustle ourselves inside as quickly as possible. After all, we had neighbors. With his injuries, he should've been in the hospital undergoing months of physical therapy. Hell, I should've been in a bed alongside him.

But the normal physical limitations of others didn't apply to us. Pity the same couldn't be said of our emotions.

The plan was to move fast, but I hesitated anyway as we passed the small army of garden gnomes still standing guard in the front yard. I nodded respectfully to them, but then bowed my head even deeper as I spied one with a yellow hat – Arugula – a crack now running down the center of her form, the only indication that something was wrong.

With tears threatening to fall again, I hustled up the porch, only for the door to open before I could reach it.

"You're alive!" Mindy cried from the threshold before realizing I wasn't alone. "Oh my goddess, Tamara. You did it! Holy shit!" She turned away from us. "Guys! They're back!"

Guys?

We had barely set foot in the foyer when Cass stepped into view from the kitchen. "Who's there?" The question fell off her tongue, a huge grin replacing it upon her face, but then she saw my father. "Curtis? Oh no. What did they...?"

She was cut off, however, by the teenaged boy hot on her tail. "Who's back? Is it...?"

"You're okay!" I cried upon seeing my brother.

Whatever words Chris may have had for me, though, were lost the moment he laid eyes on our parents. "MOM! DAD!"

He blindly threw himself into Mom's arms as she stepped forward to meet him, grabbing him tight like a drowning man might a life preserver. It wasn't often I saw my mother tear up, but right then she was crying hard and not caring who saw her – and I loved her all the more for it.

Chris pulled away and came for Dad next, stopping short when he saw that I was the one holding him up. "Dad?"

"Help me over to the couch, Tam Tam," he said.

Everyone followed as I set him down.

"How about a hug for your old man, champ?"

Chris stepped in and grabbed hold of him, and gladly, but eventually he stepped back. "Oh my god, Dad. What did those bastards do to you?"

It said a lot about the mood that my mother didn't immediately scold him.

Dad, however, maintained his veneer of good cheer, although it was hard to tell if it was real or simply a brave face. "I'm okay, champ. Had a rough time, but I survived. And don't you worry. I'll be back on ... maybe not my feet, but I'll be fine in no time."

Mom sat down and put an arm around him. "I'll make sure of it."

After a few teary minutes, Chris turned to face me, both of us blubbery messes. "You did it."

"Told you I would."

He gave me a lopsided grin back. "I guess maybe you don't suck after all ... too much anyway."

After everyone had gotten in their proper hugs, greetings, and no small amount of crying, I stepped away to let Chris get some quality time with our parents – most of which seemed to involve him riddling them with questions about all the cool stuff they saw on the other side.

Cass and Mindy both joined me in the kitchen, where I'd gone to see what was in the fridge. By this point, my healing had begun to compensate for the worst of my injuries, but I was practically starving as a result.

"Just between us," Mindy said, "I hope your mom doesn't blank him, not after all this."

I grabbed a package of cold cuts and tore it open. "I'll talk to her, but a lot depends on whether he can keep his big mouth shut."

"Blanked it is then," she replied with a chuckle, as I popped a hunk of sliced turkey into my mouth. "Hey, take human bites."

"Save it for the humans," I replied after swallowing. "So ... not to bring the mood down, but what happened? After I left, I mean."

"Left?" Cass asked. "We all thought you got blasted into nothing. Or at least I did. Freaked the crap out of me, until Mindy explained you'd likely been teleported somewhere instead."

My cousin nodded. "Was just a guess on my part, based on what I saw happen. Not that it helped much. For all I knew, you'd been sent to the middle of an active volcano."

I grabbed a bottle of orange juice from the fridge and took a swig from the container. "A volcano would've been more fun. So what happened next?"

Cass stepped next to Mindy. "Let's just say your cousin here is pretty awesome ... for a witch anyway. She got us out of there."

"Don't sell yourself short," Mindy said. "You did your part."

I gestured for them to continue. "Okay, so tell me who did what parts."

"After you *left*, panic kinda broke out. That thing, your friend..."

"That wasn't Riva."

Cass nodded. "Sorry. The thing that looked like Riva.

After you left, it seemed to lose interest in the rest of us. Or at least I think it did. Was hard to tell with everybody losing their shit."

"Everybody but you," Mindy said, before turning to me. "You should have seen her. While everyone else was preoccupied with saving their own butts, she ran upstairs to grab your brother."

I flashed Cass a smile of gratitude, but she held up a hand.

"It wasn't just me. Mindy came up to get us. I was about to jump out the window with Chris, but she grabbed both of us and then poof. Next thing I knew we were standing in your backyard."

"Smart thinking," I said.

"Desperate thinking," Mindy countered. "I got lucky. That place was warded, but whatever that thing was, it must've fizzled them out."

"Well, I'm grateful to you both. Don't tell Chris I said this, but thanks for saving him, both of you."

"Anytime, cuz."

"Same here," Cass added.

"What about the others?" I asked after I'd polished off the lunch meat, starting to feel better with a bit of food in my stomach.

"We've been on the horn ever since. David, your aunt, Earl and the rest, they all made it out."

"All except Uncle Clay," Mindy replied, shaking her head.

Cass put a hand on her shoulder, offering her comfort for the loss.

It made my heart glad to see it. Two mortal enemies, yet I could tell they were slowly forging a bond of friendship. Maybe the peace meeting had, in some fucked up way, actually caused some good to happen after all. Only time would tell.

But that could wait for now.

"Come on," Mindy said. "We should get back before they smother Chris with hugs."

"I'll be there in a second," I replied. "Still filling the tank."

Cass raised an eyebrow, but I nodded to let her know she should go ahead.

I watched as they both stepped through Riva, who'd been standing in the doorway looking out at the living room. After a moment, I approached her.

"They look so happy," she said, still facing away from me. "It's nice to see that some good came out of this."

"Yeah. I just wish..."

"Don't say it. Please. Just don't."

I started to back away, to give her the space she needed, but she wasn't finished yet.

"It's weird, Bent. I mean, it feels so raw, like someone just ripped my heart out of my chest. But, now that the memories are coming back, it also feels old." She turned to face me. "Is that strange?"

"I'm not sure I understand."

"It's like at some level a part of me has been mourning them for months. I'm just now realizing it, though. So, while this all feels new, it also doesn't. I ... don't know what to think or feel." She seemed to consider this for a moment and, when next she spoke, there was an edge to her voice that hadn't been there before, "No, that's not right. I know at least one thing I should be feeling."

"Anger." I lowered my gaze from hers. "You should be furious ... at me."

Riva shook her head. "You may tick me off from time to time, Bent, don't get me wrong, but this isn't your fault."

"It feels like it is."

"This is all on your uncle and the werewolves he sent

after me." She let out a sigh and some of the fury seemed to drain from her. "But they all died a long time ago and I simply can't bring myself to hate them all, even though a part of me wants to. I know they're people inside and people do stupid, horrible things. But people are also good. I mean, there's your Dad and Cass and, even at my most cynical, I can't believe they're alone." She let out a sigh. "I guess my parents raised me right after all."

"I never had a doubt."

"Me neither." The ghost of a smile appeared on her face, one that was sad but proud all the same. "And I intend to honor that."

"Good, because..."

"But first I need to find that bitch running around in my body. After that, I can figure out the rest." Riva paused for a moment, then looked me in the eye. "But you have to know, none of this is your fault. It never has been and never will be." She placed a spectral hand on my shoulder. "I love you, and nothing will ever change that."

"I love you, too."

She turned around again, back to where my parents continued to dote on Chris in the living room. "I'm glad we were able to bring your family back home. And I think I'd like to focus on that ... for now."

"They're not just mine," I said, to which she glanced over her shoulder. "You've always been a part of this family, Riva. Now you're a part of it more than ever."

She smiled again, but there was a bitterness behind it, one that I think we both realized might never be fully gone. "Maybe. But they can't even see me."

"Then I'll be their eyes and ears. Let me be your window to this world."

I held out my hand and, after a moment, she put hers in mine. I couldn't physically feel her as we entwined our fingers, but I could sense her there, nevertheless.

"I guess we're in this together now."

"I wouldn't have it any other way," I replied as we turned back toward the living room, where our family was waiting for us.

"I really don't think this is a good idea."

"We appreciate your opinion, dear, but so long as your father and I are footing at least part of the bill, we don't need to particularly care about it."

"You might not, but Dad does. I'm his alpha."

"Over in Morganberg, pumpkin, but here I'm still your father."

Somehow, I knew he was going to pull that card. I was running out of arguments. I couldn't even use the aborted peace conference as ammunition, as both sides had quickly agreed, in the days following our return, to postpone negotiations for the time being. Twice now, plans for talks had gone awry. With Possessed Riva still on the loose, the elders on both sides had cautioned that this new threat took precedence.

As alpha, I could've ordered the wolves back to the table, but that wouldn't mean dick if the Draíodóir didn't bother to show. Besides, as my parents pointed out, the existing treaty was still in effect.

In short, it was the same shit as before, just now on a different day. Still, I wasn't going down without a fight.

"I need to stay here in High Moon."

"Then I suggest you get a job and start paying rent." Mom smiled, knowing she had me over a barrel. "Or you could return to school and finish your degree. You've only missed a week or so. You can catch up easily enough ... provided you don't screw around."

"Your mother has a point, Tam Tam," Dad said from

up on the porch, a mug of coffee in one hand and a cane in the other. He took a couple steps toward us, raised an eyebrow, then looked down. "Is it me, or am I taller?"

Mom moved to his side, entwining her arm with his. "I may have added an extra inch. Makes you look even sexier."

"Gross!"

My protests aside, I couldn't help but be amazed. It had been two weeks since we'd returned and Dad was already walking with only limited assistance. Another few days and he'd likely be able to ditch the cane. What would have been months of physical therapy for anyone else was nothing for someone with a werewolf constitution.

In all fairness, Mom's ministrations didn't hurt either. Once the thrill of the reunion was out of the way, she'd set to work immediately. Dad wasn't wearing normal prosthetics below the knees, but something she'd returned with after a trip to Crescentwood. She called them constructs, which I took to mean they were almost certainly magically enhanced – probably with regards to helping Dad get used to them because, quite frankly, he took to them like a fish to water.

They weren't perfect. They didn't change when he did, meaning his days as the alpha of Morganberg truly were over. Had he wanted, though, he likely could've secured the spot as my beta. Missing legs or not, he was still a mega-wolf, the only one in the pack – now and likely for the foreseeable future.

Turns out there was a reason David had only changed into a normal werewolf when facing off against Possessed Riva. Things had been too crazy for her to tell me at the time, but Cass had since filled me in. The ritual they'd used on him in the sacred glade, the same one Grandma Nelly had tried to use on me before being assassinated, had failed. The glade – once the so-called Window of

Worlds – was now nothing more than a simple clearing in the woods.

Brigid had been right. In bringing these creatures fully into our world, they'd destroyed whatever made the glade special, ensuring it couldn't be used to send them back.

The thing was, all had been quiet since. There'd been no sign of either Possessed Riva or any similar such beings. Both of my parents had sent feelers out to other packs and covens across the country, but all such entreaties had come back negative. So far as they could tell, with the exception of what had happened in High Moon and its sister town, all seemed normal.

It was as if these void things had simply disappeared.

I wasn't so easily convinced, though. I had a feeling it was only a matter of time before we – *I* – would have to deal with the threat they represented. But for now, all we could do was wait.

Problem was, it hadn't taken my parents long to suggest that I could just as easily wait back at school.

It didn't matter if I was the alpha of Morganberg or not. With both of them ganging up on me, it didn't take long before they wore down my defenses.

Now here I was standing outside, Mom's car packed to the gills with my stuff and me holding the keys. I might've been a hybrid of both races, but it was hard to win against parents who held black belts in brow beating.

Despite the inevitable defeat looming over me, though, I still felt the need to push back. "The pack..."

"Will be fine," Dad said. "David and Cass can manage things until spring break, with me there to advise them. Trust me. I know a thing or two about this stuff."

He didn't need to rub it in. Truth was, he'd probably forgotten more about werewolf politics than I'd ever learn.

"And those void creatures?"

"We really need to come up with a better name for

them," Dad replied. "But either way, if we hear even the slightest peep we'll let you know. Believe me, pumpkin. I like this reality. I don't want to see it unravel any more than you do."

"You promise?"

"I give you my word, my alpha."

Mom poked him in the side with her elbow. "Don't indulge her, dear. She'll get a swelled head."

"Me? A swelled head?" I replied with a grin. "You'd think I was my mother's daughter or something."

"Never forget that you are."

"Oh, I won't. Princess of Monarchs is starting to grow on me."

I hated to leave but, at the end of the day, I had to begrudgingly admit my parents were right. What if these things were playing a waiting game? It could be days before they reared their heads again, or it could be years. If so, what was I to do in the meantime? Sit around keeping watch, all while life passed me by?

"This feels so weird," I said, passing the sign telling us we'd left High Moon and to please visit again.

"You're telling me," Riva replied from the passenger seat. "But hey, it's not all bad."

"So long as you're with me, it never will be."

She smiled at that. "Thanks. But I meant practically. Think about it. I can feed you the answers during tests, eavesdrop on conversations to let you know who's talking smack about you, not to mention sneak into any locker room I choose."

"Mom's going to flip if she hears about any of that."

"Are you going to tell her?"

"Nope."

"Me neither. And even if I wanted to, it's not like she'd hear me."

"Good point. Still, it's strange. I mean, school feels so … unimportant right now."

"You might not think that if you end up bagging groceries for a living."

"I meant in the short term. Yeah, waiting is a waste of time, but I almost feel like we should be out there actively searching for … well, your body."

"Can't say I wouldn't mind getting it back. I'm starting to miss touching *things*. But, even if we tried, you heard what your mom said."

"I know."

Actively hunting these things had been one of my first suggestions after a few days spent recuperating. The thing was, that was easier said than done. The Morgan-berg window of worlds – in actuality a spot where the walls between realities were thin – wasn't alone. Not by a long shot. Supposedly there were thin spots all over the globe.

The problem was finding them.

Though there wasn't a lot to go on, Mom had surmised that Possessed Riva and her buddies would probably be drawn to these thin spots like sharks to chum. Good for them, but not so easy for the rest of us, as you basically had to stumble across one to know they existed.

And once found, they were jealously guarded.

"Goddamned paranoid bastards," I said. "Even after my parents explained how dire the situation was, the other groups they reached out to all denied having any knowledge of these thin spots. If you ask me, they were playing dumb."

"Can you blame them?" Riva replied. "I mean, if you discovered a diamond mine in your backyard, would you be advertising it on Facebook?"

"True. But a diamond mine isn't going to potentially end the world."

"Fair point."

"It sucks. If we could find these spots, these other windows, we could maybe head those things off at the pass. But instead we're fucked. So it's back to class for me."

Riva nodded. "There isn't much we can do about it. I mean, it's not like we know there's one in Ohio, about a hundred miles south of the Michigan border. Or the one in western Kentucky, hidden in an old civil war graveyard. Oh, and then there's the one a few miles from your school, in that abandoned farmhouse the locals think is haunted."

I laughed. "Oh god. If it were only that easy."

However, a moment later I realized I was alone in finding this humorous.

"Um, Bent?" Riva asked, putting a hand on my arm, causing it to tingle.

"Yeah?"

"Is it me, or were those examples I just said kinda oddly specific?"

"Were they? I thought you were making that shit up." I glanced at her and realized she was staring ahead wide-eyed. "You were making it up, right?"

"I ... don't know."

"Are you okay?"

"I'm not sure. I feel kind of weird."

"You need me to pull over so you can throw up?"

"Not ghost puke kind of weird. More like the someone walking over my grave type."

I glanced her way again, my eyes narrowed. "You don't think that thing in your body is doing something..."

She waved me off. "No. Nothing like that. This is going to sound strange, but those places didn't just pop into my head. I mean, I was joking around at first, but then I realized it was like reading from a map in my mind. Oh wow."

"What is it?"

"The more I think about it, the more I can see ... up here anyway." She pointed to her head. "Like, there's one in Lake Michigan about 20 miles from the eastern shore-line, and..."

"Are you shitting me?"

She shook her head. More importantly, I knew her. I knew when Riva was kidding around, but there was nothing in either her tone or expression to suggest she was.

"Bent ... I think I somehow know where these thin spots are."

"How?"

"Beats the shit out of me. I just do."

"Are you sure?"

"No," she said. "But at the same time, yes. It's hard to tell, but the more I focus on it, the more certain I become."

It made no sense, except that maybe it did. I didn't begin to understand what had happened to my friend, except that her body was no longer hers, leaving her as some kind of disembodied spirit. But maybe that was part of the answer. What if there was still a connection to her body, however tenuous, and somehow she was able to share in the ... I dunno ... senses or knowledge of the entity currently in the driver's seat?

It seemed a long shot. But then again, hadn't we just successfully stormed a fairy queen's castle? Long shots were apparently our new normal.

"You said there's one in Ohio ... as in the state we need to drive through anyway?"

"What are you thinking, Bent?"

"Oh nothing. Just wondering if you're up for a little detour."

"We don't know if this is real."

"We don't know that it isn't," I replied with a smirk. "And what if it is just your imagination? Oh well, we waste a few hours sightseeing. But if it is real, maybe we can actually do something about this mess."

"You realize how crazy that sounds, right?"

"Yep. Welcome to my world."

"Think we can actually do it?"

I reached over to the GPS, adjusting the route to take us further north. "I think together we can do anything."

"Does that include saving the world?"

I smiled as I turned my attention back to the road ahead of us.

"There's only one way to find out."

THE END

Tamara Bentley will return in
BENT, NOT BROKEN
The Hybrid of High Moon - 4

BONUS CHAPTER
BENT, NOT BROKEN

THE HYBRID OF HIGH MOON - 4

"Time check."

"How the hell am I supposed to know? Do you see a watch on my wrist ... or any way to put one there, for that matter?"

"Nobody likes a negative Nelly," I replied.

"Well, we had at least two and a half hours when we left, but somebody had to go and get lost on the way, even though it's only a couple miles."

"Sorry. I didn't realize the roads out here were such rat mazes."

"You should have brought your phone, like I said."

"Can't. Mom might be tracking me."

"Seriously, Bent?" Riva replied, as we continued to sneak across what had once been a field but was now overrun with dead brush. "You really think she's checking on you twenty-four seven?"

"Maybe."

Okay, fine, she probably had a point. Even so, last time I'd talked to Mom she'd read me the riot act. Our little detour to Providence County, Ohio had not gone unnoticed. The sorcerer in charge of the coven there had been somewhat less than receptive upon our arrival, much less so when I requested to be shown their holy glen, as they called it – a spot where the walls between worlds were thinner than normal.

Doing a bit of name dropping and identifying myself as the Princess of Monarchs had only resulted in them calling my mother to complain, especially once I'd threatened to pop him and his buddies in the jaw if they didn't let us investigate their land for voiders – my own personal pet name for the creatures trying to destroy such thinspots.

Needless to say, my mother had been very *persuasive* in cutting our road trip short and curtailing our plans to proactively hunt down these creatures.

Once I'd arrived back at school, Mom hadn't let me off the hook – warning me that I had better not even think of turning off location services on my phone, or salting it against scrying, for that matter – not that I had any idea how to do that without totally fucking it up.

Fortunately, Riva's newly discovered sixth sense had already detected another of these thin spots not too far from campus. The upside was it was easily drivable from school. Downside, though, it was supposedly haunted.

Less than a year ago, that would've been easily laughed off as ridiculous. But now I knew better. The monsters in the closet weren't always imaginary. Hell, I'd fought more than my fair share of strange beasts since discovering my true heritage, a few of them while at school.

I'd thought that might simply be a case of having my eyes opened to the weird underworld that existed around us, full of all sorts of nasty things most people assumed existed only in myth and legend.

But now I had to wonder. Knowing there was a thin

spot close to Bailey University, a so-called Window of Worlds, changed the game. If the sacred glade close to my hometown was any indication, these thin spots seemed to act as a lure to things extranormal.

It kind of reminded me of an old show my father use to watch, *Buffy the Vampire Slayer*. The gist being that her town sat upon something called a hellmouth which, in turn, attracted all sorts of nasty beasts to it.

As Riva and I crossed the unused field, I had to wonder whether I should maybe pick up a few seasons on Blu-ray for some pointers.

However, that would have to wait. I had less than two hours before my evening class ended, having blown it off so I could have plausible deniability for leaving my phone behind in my room while we drove out here – hopefully leaving Mom no reason to be suspicious when I didn't answer.

Sadly, while my spectral friend could somehow sense these thin spots, she wasn't able to give precise turn-by-turn directions for how to get to them, resulting in us running behind schedule.

Chances were this was a snipe hunt anyway. We had no way of knowing when or where these voiders might strike. Riva could sense their targets but seemed unable to draw a bead on the creatures themselves. The problem was, sitting around and waiting for them to strike was maddening, not to mention seemed counterintuitive to actually stopping them. Besides, at the end of the day, I wasn't renowned for my patience.

So here we were.

Sadly, we'd come in blind. With my parents' directive against anymore road trips, and me being coy about Riva's ability to sense these things, I couldn't exactly call and casually ask what – if anything – we could expect to find out here.

Left unsaid was what we'd do if we found the spot we were looking for and nothing else? I mean, it's not like we could keep round the clock surveillance on this place. I had school to worry about and Riva was incorporeal. Even if I'd been able to leave her out here to do nothing more than watch the place, it's not like she could call me if something happened.

In the rapidly fading light of day, the derelict farmhouse waiting at the end of the field certainly looked like it could be haunted, nestled as it was on a neglected patch of land with several threadbare trees growing around it. I had no idea why this place was empty – whether it was death, bank foreclosure, or something else – but the house and land looked like it hadn't been occupied for at least a decade, if not longer.

"What do you think?" I asked as we crouched behind some bushes, not that Riva really needed to hide since nobody but me could see her.

"I think maybe for once I'm glad I don't have a body, because if Illinois cannibals are a thing, this is definitely where they're living."

"Remind me not to ask you for any pep talks in the future."

"If you don't want to know, you shouldn't ask. How about you? Sense anything?"

If there was anyone, cannibalistic or not, staring out at us, they were invisible to me in the gloom beyond the windows. As for the rest, I closed my eyes and took a deep breath, smelling dirt, decay, rotting wood, mold, and even old cow manure.

That was only on the surface, though. Having near-werewolf level senses could be a mixed bag at times, but even I had to admit it was seriously cool what a super-charged nose could do. Scents weren't merely good or bad now, they were a whole tapestry of layers to explore, driving home how little of their environment humans actually perceived in their day to day lives.

There was definitely more here, the faint scent of living creatures. That was another marvel of enhanced senses. Once you identified something by its smell, your brain became sort of like a Wikipedia of odors, returning a hit for a familiar scent. That was how it was now, mundane as it might be. There were mice and rats around, a few cats, too. There'd also been some larger animals in the area recently, like...

"Um, Bent? I think we're being..."

"Shh, focusing here."

"Yeah, you might want to hurry it up. This is weirding me out a bit."

As Riva tried to get my attention, the faint sound of dried grass being trampled registered in my ears, a sound that was rapidly getting louder.

"Oh, shit, I think something's coming!"

I opened my eyes. "What?"

Riva pointed toward the far edge of the field, where a wide stand of trees stood. At first, I didn't see anything, the growing shadows doing little to improve my view. My ears were definitely picking up something, though, a lot of somethings.

Then I saw them, dark shapes against the trees, just barely visible, but definitely headed our way.

I stood up tall and turned to face whatever was coming toward us, as it was painfully obvious we'd been spotted, or I had anyway.

"Get behind..." I trailed off as my nose identified the intruders. "Never mind. False alarm."

"What is it?"

"Just a herd of deer."

"Oh," Riva replied, sounding relieved as the creatures drew closer, their antlers now visible enough to identify them. "Um, I thought deer usually ran away from people."

She kinda had a point there. "Maybe they grow them stupid out here."

It was a herd all right, and they were definitely heading this way ... quickly. As they approached, their hoofbeats became louder, more frantic, and I picked up their exhalations as they breathed.

Maybe something had spooked them.

If so, they needed to know this direction wasn't any safer.

"HEY!" I shouted, waving my arms, hoping to scare them off.

"Way to get their attention."

"They're deer," I replied, "not psycho rednecks with banjos."

It's not like I'd never seen deer before. Hell, you couldn't drive around my home state after dark without at least a fifty percent chance of one running out in front of your car, and that wasn't even counting hunting season.

That said, usually they had a healthy respect for people. These, however, were either seriously scared or hadn't been near any major highways lately, as they continued our way undeterred.

"What do we do?" Riva asked.

I was still debating that myself. Being trampled wasn't high on my list.

However, just as they were about to converge upon my personal space, the herd broke off – half of them going left and the rest going right.

That was kind of odd. Even odder was when they all suddenly skidded to a halt, encircling where we stood.

Yep. Definitely starting to get creepy.

"Bent?"

"I've got this," I said, before facing the ... um ... deer

continuing to stand there staring at us. "Listen up, you stupid forest rats. I don't know whether deer get rabies or not, but I can assure you I am one blade of grass that punches back."

Probably not the best speech I'd ever given, and almost certainly pointless against a herd of brainless...

The sound of rippling flesh caught my ears a moment before the transformations began.

Or maybe not so brainless.

In the space of seconds, antlers retracted, fur receded, and hooves became hands. When it was finished, I found myself surrounded by a group of naked strangers, all of them staring at me none too kindly.

"Weredeer. That's new," I muttered.

"Not really," Riva replied, standing next to me but apparently unseen by our guests. "Native American folklore is full of them."

"Maybe I should start reading more." Then, a bit louder, I said, "So ... how are you guys doing?"

Silence and more glares met my greeting.

Guess it's going to be the hard way then. "All right. Listen up. I don't want any trouble."

"You've got wolf stink on you," one of them said, breaking their freaky silence, a middle-aged woman with greying brown hair. "That and ... something else."

The glares from the rest continued, but if these yahoos were hoping to intimidate me, they were staring into the wrong headlights.

"Yeah, well wolf beats deer any day of the week. So how about you all back off a bit before I take this personally."

"Great, Bent," Riva said. "Piss them off why don't you?"

I was about to ask if she had any better suggestions when there came the sound of footsteps approaching from the direction the herd had appeared. It was a single set this time, and they sounded human.

Sure enough, a moment later, the deer Johns at the northern end of this circle jerk stepped aside, revealing a busty, raven haired woman with tawny skin.

She met my gaze for a few seconds, then turned her head and spat on the ground. A moment later, she held her arms out to the side and once again there came the disturbing sound of flesh rippling and bones crackling. A pair of antlers sprouted from the sides of her head, different from the ones that had adorned her friends — continuing to grow ever longer and wider until they spanned at least seven feet.

Whoa.

The woman's body followed suit, growing taller and bulkier by the moment, until she towered over me and the others around us.

"Um, Bent?"

"Yeah?"

"I'm gonna go out on a limb here and assume we'll be a bit late getting back."

"Ya think?"

———————— ❧ ————————

To be continued in
Bent, Not Broken
The Hybrid of High Moon – 4
Coming soon!

AUTHOR'S NOTE

Despite this story ending on a somewhat dark note – and if you're the type to read Author Notes first, I won't be a dick and spoil it – I'm writing this with a big smile on my face.

Why? Because there is something ridiculously fun about writing the third book in just about any series, but especially horror and fantasy.

The first book serves as your origin story. That's the place where you get to meet the main character who'll you'll likely be spending a good deal of time with – assuming some asshole author doesn't kill them off. The second book is all about expanding upon that character's world. We already know who's showing up to the party, but this is where you learn about all those nooks and crannies the author was hiding – or didn't know about – in the first story.

But the third book ... that's where things can really get fucked up. Oh, you think you know these characters and what's going on? YOINKS! There goes the carpet from beneath your feet. Too bad, so sad, but shit just got real.

For me, stuff like that is simply an absolute joy to

write, allowing my imagination to take the story to places it would be difficult to do while still establishing the so-called rules of a particular world.

While I can't say for certain we'll meet Grunge, Cabbage, or Brigid again, I had a lot of fun breathing life into them and their alien world. As for Bent, well, the road is only going to get tougher for her from here on out. But, with any luck, it'll continue to be an entertaining ride.

I hope you will join me again on this journey to whatever adventures next await her and her friends.

Rick G.

ABOUT THE AUTHOR

Rick Gualtieri lives alone in central New Jersey with only his wife, three kids, and countless pets to both keep him company and constantly plot against him. When he's not busy monkey-clicking words, he can typically be found jealously guarding his collection of vintage Transformers from all who would seek to defile them.

Defilers beware!

Also by Rick Gualtieri
THE HYBRID OF HIGH MOON
Get Bent!
Hell Bent
Bent Outta Shape
Bent On Destruction
Bent, Not Broken

TALES OF THE CRYPTO-HUNTER
Bigfoot Hunters
Devil Hunters
Kraken Hunters

THE TOME OF BILL UNIVERSE
THE TOME OF BILL
Bill the Vampire
Scary Dead Things
The Mourning Woods

Holier Than Thou
Sunset Strip
Goddamned Freaky Monsters
Half A Prayer
The Wicked Dead
Shining Fury
The Last Coven

BILL OF THE DEAD
Strange Days
Everyday Horrors
Carnage A Trois

Made in the USA
Monee, IL
03 January 2023

24262361R00249